Madcap Masquerade

PERSEPHONE ROTH

Dreamspinner Press

Published by
Dreamspinner Press
4760 Preston Road
Suite 244-149
Frisco, TX 75034
http://www.dreamspinnerpress.com/

Madcap Masquerade
Copyright © 2009 by Persephone Roth

Cover Art by Anne Cain   annecain.art@gmail.com
Cover Design by Mara McKennen

ISBN: 978-1-61581-239-4

Printed in the United States of America
First Edition
December 2009

eBook edition available
eBook ISBN: 978-1-61581-240-0

Dedicated with respect and affection
to some talented ladies who
had a big impact on my life.
No need to name them here…
they know who they are.

CHAPTER 1

LOEL WOODBINE, DUKE OF MARCHE, woke at his accustomed time on the day he learned of his engagement. His valet arrived as usual, setting down his burdens to pull back a judicious number of curtains, allowing in just the right amount of light after a late night at Mrs. Dahlram's Tearoom. The sun shone from its accustomed seat in the firmament, several degrees past its zenith. As Marche sat up against the pillows, the manservant placed the breakfast tray and daily newspaper over his lap.

"Good morning, Negus," Marche said. "I trust that it *is* a good morning."

"Aye, that it is. Every day in your employ is a good one, sir."

Marche looked at the man over the top of the *Morning Post*. "Oh dear, have you been unlucky at cards again? If you need a loan, you have but to ask."

"Nay, sir. The cards always do well by me. It is the blasted nags as have a mind of their own."

"Ah, I see. Let me rephrase my question. Have you made some ill-considered wagers?"

"Ill-considered." Negus repeated the term as though savoring a mouthful of ale. "Your Grace always has the precise word."

Marche frowned, golden brows drawing together over eyes of dark amber. "You called me 'Your Grace.' Just how much money do you need?"

"Well, sir, I had information from a rascal what I thought was reliable, bein' me own baby sister's husband and all, and I put down a month's wages." Negus shook his head. "And then I made another bet so as to win back my losses like. As I am known to serve a gentleman of the highest quality, I was given leave to mark down an amount and sign my name, which you yourself taught me to do, thankee."

"I may live to regret it. Since you don't mention the amount right away, may I assume it's more than a month's wages?"

"I owe more than fifty guineas, sir!" Negus burst out.

"The devil you say!" Silver rattled against china. "I am afraid that stretches my purse a bit at the moment. Fifty guineas! What were you thinking, man?"

"It were a powerful good tip, sir."

"Apparently, it was not all that powerful, or we wouldn't be having this conversation. How soon must you make good on your note?"

"Soon, sir."

"Well, I don't see how I can manage it before the week's end. I will be attending Lady Bolbracken on Saturday, but until she hands over my allowance, I'm on the rocks myself. High rank does not, alas, guarantee ready wealth."

Negus kept his expression carefully neutral at the mention of the duke's great-aunt. Thrice married, thrice widowed, turning a tidy profit each time, Willamina, Lady Bolbracken, held the strings of a very deep purse, and she could be quite generous. However, she considered that subsidizing the lifestyle of her great-nephew conferred the right to a say in how that lifestyle was conducted. After all, Lord Marche represented her when he went about in society, and she would not tolerate behavior that reflected badly on their decimated but lofty family. As the only heir to her fortune, he was expected to attend certain social functions and to be well groomed while doing so. Negus knew that his master chafed at being a performing bear, as he put it, but Marche accepted that he was a prisoner of his birth, and, when he wasn't on display, he was left to his own devices. As the valet thought about the forms those devices sometimes took, his impassive mask slipped a trifle.

"What the deuce are you grinning at?" Marche raised his voice.

"Sorry, m'lord. I believe my troubles have given me a nervous twitch."

"You'll be fortunate if that's all they give you."

"That's the gospel truth, sir. The betting parlor is under new management, and the bookkeeper has got a new fellow works for him, as in doin' the collectin' like. A large fellow he is, nearly as large as your lordship and you six and a half feet in your stockings."

"Do I take it that you've been threatened with dire consequences?"

"Dire consequences! Didn't I just say that your worship always has the precise word as what is needed? That's the mark of a first-rate intelligence and no mistake."

"Oh, do stop fawning. It doesn't suit you. I plucked you from the gutters because I saw something in you. You're common as horse dung in the streets, but you give me no more respect than I've earned. That is why I tolerate your comic theater manner of speaking and your damnable gambling, not to mention that face of yours, which could do double duty as a saddle bag."

"I've a hangdog look; it is true, sir. Me own mother told me so."

The duke sighed. "Well, I can't let you be thrashed by a bookkeeper's hired man, even if you are ginger-haired. It just won't do to have you sporting bruises while on duty, and, if by chance, this large fellow breaks one of your limbs, how will you serve me at all? While you can still draw breath, why don't you lay out my clothes? I will have my tea and think on your predicament."

"Aye, sir." To the rustling sound of newspaper pages being turned, Negus proceeded across the room to a large armoire. The valet chose a bottle-green jacket with short tails and a black silk waistcoat liberally embroidered with vines of gold to go over the duke's customary buff-colored breeches. He was touching up the shine on a pair of black calf-length boots when Marche swore under his breath and crumpled the paper in his big fist. The valet hurried to take away the breakfast tray as his master rose. "What is it, sir?"

"Damme, Negus, I am engaged to be married."

"Are you, sir?"

"It is printed here in the Society section of the *Morning Post.* Therefore, it must be true."

"As you say, m'lord." Negus paused. "Who are you tyin' the knot with then?"

"Just a moment." Marche retrieved the balled-up pages and spread them open on the bed. "I was so shocked that I confess I didn't catch the young lady's name. This is bound to be my great aunt's doing, you know. She threatened me not two weeks ago over luncheon, claiming that an unwed man above thirty is a scandal."

"The old dragon's got a lot of company in that opinion."

"You've become a bit too familiar, don't you think?"

"It's a regrettable failing of mine, sir. I'll do better; I swear."

"You do swear; that's true enough, and I am in no fit shape to flog you this morning."

Negus smiled at the timeworn joke. "Have you not found the hussy's name yet, sir?"

"Yes, I was simply recovering from the second shock inside of ten minutes. I may need a drop of restorative in my tea. My dear aunt has outdone herself this time. I am to marry the Honorable Miss Valeria Randwick, daughter of Julius, Earl of Blythestone."

"Never heard of her."

"No one has, but when I was a lad, I knew someone who knew her father. The Blythestone lands bordered ours before Sir Julius lost Lamberglyn Park and all the rest of it. He had unfortunate political connections, an obstacle that he might have overcome had he not fallen gravely ill. He was still quite a young man when he exiled himself from England, taking his pregnant wife to Brittany to live in what I heard were greatly reduced circumstances. It was never proved whether the threat of violence was a real one or the imaginings of a mind unhinged by disastrous turns of fortune. Whatever the truth may have been, he chose to flee, unwisely, as it happened. He trusted an agent to sell off his holdings, and the blackguard sent him only a pittance of the profits, absconding with the rest of the money." Marche frowned. "I haven't thought of that sad story in nearly twenty years. Now the hapless earl has passed out of this world as well as out of mind, and I am to marry the child he spirited out of England in the womb." The duke sighed heavily. "She'll probably be the type that's prone to the vapors."

"It all sounds powerful romantic to me, sir." Negus held up Marche's snowy white shirt, adopting a casual tone when he spoke again. "I suppose you've a reason now to attend on Lady Bolbracken before Saturday."

"I suppose I have." Lord Marche slipped his arms into the sleeves of the tailored garment. "How very convenient for you."

Negus cocked his head as he navigated the complexities of Marche's cravat. "That's the first time you've not had the precise word, Your Grace. This ain't convenient for neither of us, I wouldn't say."

"If you insist on being factual, I'll finish dressing by myself."

"Pardon me, your lordship." Negus waited for Marche to shrug into his jacket before he pulled the man's tawny shoulder-length hair back and tied it with a simple black ribbon. "I'll do me best to pretend this marriage is a good idea."

"And so will I." Lord Marche sighed. *Poor Miss Randwick, I hope for your sake that you are not a naïve young girl who yearns for true love and a houseful of children.*

"VALERIA!" Anne Kermartin, the Randwick's housekeeper—who also cooked and had been a nanny in her time—heard no reply. "Where is the girl?" she muttered as she ended her search where she'd begun it. There was no one in the kitchen except for the marmalade tabby licking a paw by the hearth. Seeing she'd be getting no help, Anne tied an apron around her plump middle and set about getting dinner started. She'd got as far as chopping cabbage to add to the pot over the fire when she heard voices outside. A moment later, Valeria came through the side door that let onto the herb garden.

"Where have you been, miss?" the housekeeper asked, ignoring Valeria's attire. She had already expressed her opinion on the wearing of trousers by females, and she was not a woman to waste her breath in futile exercise.

"Dear Anne." Valeria bent to kiss the woman's furrowed forehead. "I've been helping you with dinner as I promised."

"I'll not lie to your mother for you."

"Since when?" Valeria replied pertly.

"What a vulgar turn of phrase! You're a lady in name, but lately you've been acting the hoyden, cutting didoes as if you've no shame at all. I don't think you know how bold you've become, living as we do. You've no one to set an example for you."

"What about my mother?"

"The countess barely has time to eat and sleep after the work is done."

"I take your meaning. Perhaps if I were to contribute more to the running of the household, Mama would have time for other things, such as teaching me deportment."

"I would not presume to tell you your duty, miss."

"Since when?"

Anne changed the subject. "What have you got behind your back?"

Valeria laid a brace of dressed rabbits on the cutting board. "I told you I was helping you with dinner. What do you say to a nice bit of meat in the stew?"

"Bless you, girl. I am tired to the bone of fish and fowl."

"I am tired to the bone of everything." The tall young woman sat and put her chin in her hands, her morning glory eyes going vague as she stared into the middle distance.

"Everything?" Anne went back to chopping. "Did I not hear my nephew's voice just now?"

"Randall was returning from the village when I came out of the forest. Naturally, we walked together."

"I hope he did his job well."

"He got the cow serviced by Mayor Loic's bull," Valeria answered matter-of-factly. The doings of the barnyard and stable were no mystery to her, and she saw nothing shameful in them. Animals simply did as Nature intended and were humans not of animal nature as well? "That's why we had to walk so slowly. For poor Blossom's sake."

"Valeria!" Lady Amandine, Countess of Blythestone stood poised in the doorway, a hand clutched at her bosom.

"Mama!" Valeria hurried to offer support, towering over her dainty mother as she settled her in a chair and offered a cup of tea. "Good heavens! Are you all right? You gave me such a turn. You looked as though you were going to faint."

"What would you expect when I hear my only daughter speaking like a plowman? If your father were alive, he would die of shame."

"Mama—" Valeria began.

"No! I won't hear it. I have let you run wild long enough. How I wish we could have provided for you as we did for your brother. In a convent, the nuns would have seen to your training in dignified deportment." Amandine sighed. "However, I could not bear to be parted from both my children. My selfishness is to blame for your circumstance."

"Mama, no! I am glad you didn't send me away. I wish Valentine could have stayed as well."

"You know that was not possible, my dear. We could not take the chance that our enemies would harm him."

Valeria held her peace, though she chafed at it. When she was small, she'd looked for lurkers in every shadow, but as she grew, she came to see that her father's fears were of his own invention. Not for the world would she have suggested aloud that he was a bit soft in the head, but she knew it to be true. She did as her mother did and indulged the gentle, deluded man until his sudden death. Valeria banished the memory of her father's face when his body was pulled from the river.

"And we are not speaking of your brother," Amandine was saying. "Your father and I hoped that one day you would marry well and know the bliss of wedded life, even though we were doomed to exile here."

Valeria snorted, tossing the thick braid of dark auburn hair over her shoulder. "Long and plain as I am?"

"You're a handsome lass, miss," Anne was goaded into saying.

Amandine gave the housekeeper a sharp glance before she spoke. "Listen to me, daughter. It is true that we are reduced to living hand-to-mouth on foreign soil, but we are still of the highest quality. It does not matter that I have turned our home into a laundry so we may supplement what our garden provides. Nor does it matter that I am chief laundress of a staff of three. I am still Lady Blythestone, daughter of the Earl of Danswell, and shall be until I die. No one may take that from me, even if fate has taken all that goes with those proud names."

"You have been working too hard, dear Mother," Valeria said quickly, anxious to head off one of her mother's bouts of black depression. "Anne and I are preparing rabbit stew. Won't you put your feet up until it is ready?"

"I have not yet told you the news."

"What news?"

"There was a letter in the packet that Randall delivered from town. It is there on the floor where I dropped it. Do be an angel and fetch it for me."

Valeria strode across the kitchen, her long legs making little of the large open space. As she bent to pick up the sheets of creamy vellum, she noted the crest at the top. She didn't recognize the blazon, but she was certain of the lofty quality of the letterhead.

"You will never guess the contents of that blessed letter," Lady Amandine said. "The answer to all our prayers is in there."

"Good heavens," Valeria said, exchanging a doubtful glance with Anne. "I cannot imagine."

"It is the best news possible. You are to be married, my girl! Six weeks ago, your hand was asked for and I sent a reply accepting for you. Today the official answer arrived. In three months time, Loel Everett Woodbine, the Duke of Marche, only heir to the Brackenmourse, Falkertin, and Marche fortunes, will make you his bride!"

"I have never even met the man!"

"My mother met my father on their wedding day, and they had a happy life together."

"Grand'Mere was French and betrothed in the cradle. We live in more modern times."

"I am shocked by your reaction," Amandine said. "I thought you would be happy to hear that such a man had offered for you. Why, his endowment is the largest in all of England!"

"I am sure Miss Valeria is merely stunned," Anne said. "When the news has a chance to sink in, I know that a clever girl will see the advantages of such a marriage."

Valeria's expression clearly revealed her shock at this betrayal. "Anne, how could you say that when you know…." The girl's words trailed off.

"What does Anne know?" Amandine demanded.

"I- I was considering entering a convent," Valeria stammered with swift invention.

"Perish the thought! One *religieuse* in the family is quite enough. How can you speak of locking yourself away, as well? Am I never to see my family as one again?"

"I am sorry, Mother, but I would rather take vows than marry a stranger."

"And I would rather be in our estate at Lamberglyn Park with your father still alive and both my children at my side, but sometimes we have no choice and we do as we must. I know my Julius would say the same if he were here." Amandine rose and went to the door. "I am going to lie down for a bit. By the time dinner is ready, I expect you will have resigned yourself to this marriage, and I hope you realize that I only want what is best for you."

"Yes, Mama." Valeria curtsied as the lady left the kitchen. "How eager she is to marry me off to this no-doubt ancient Englishman with a name for each of his fortunes. I was born in Brittany; I have lived here all my life, and I've no wish to leave. I cannot even imagine what life as a grand lady would be like, but I doubt I will like it."

"I noticed how red and chafed my lady's hands are," Anne said softly. "When I came to work for your family, your mother had the smoothest, whitest hands I'd ever seen, like porcelain they were. To see them now, so rough and work-worn, near breaks my heart. She was never raised for a life such as we live, but she does the best she can."

Miss Valeria Randwick closed her mouth on whatever she would have said next and thought about Anne's words. Valeria had been conceived here, in the region the French called Bretagne, and had never known another life. She loved the old farmhouse and the ancient orchard, loved hunting game and tending the garden, loved wearing men's clothing when no one was around, but most of all, she loved Randall Cleary. How could she marry a stranger when her heart was already given away?

Valeria picked up a knife and began chopping turnips as she considered her dilemma. A clever girl should be able to solve this problem.

CHAPTER 2

"YOU had not heard? My dear, where have you been? It's the *only* gossip." Darby St. Denis, Baronet of Strand, smoothed the front of his russet coat, drawing attention to the rich gold brocade of his vest as his eyes roved the large elegant room.

"Strand, you know you always have the best gossip first," said Neville Stokes, Viscount Tarmegent, Darby's best friend and fellow Dandy.

"Hear, hear, Tarmy," agreed Crispin Ludstall, Baron Snowhurst, as he arrived nibbling a breakfast cake. "Please tell us, Strand."

"Draw near, infants, and you shall hear the sordid secrets behind the most glorious fête of the season."

"The Marche wedding?" Crispin blurted out.

Darby's pale blue eyes narrowed as he winced. "Of what else would I be speaking? It is, in fact, the party we are attending at this very moment. Watch your bloody drink, Snow!"

Crispin reeled back and narrowly avoided spilling mulled brandy on Darby. "Sorry, old man, a bit in my cups."

"What did you hear, Strand?" Neville got back to business, ignoring Crispin's drunkenness at ten in the morning.

"Do you recall the gossip a few months ago concerning the Behemoth's sudden betrothal?"

Crispin and Neville nodded. It had been the talk of their set for almost twenty-four hours: the famously unmarried Duke of Marche engaged to a mystery maiden! The cream of the nobility had received invitations to the wedding ceremony and a week of revels at the Woodbine family seat of Wandeleigh. Then the prince regent had raised fresh rumors when he announced that he would attend.

"A weeklong party," Crispin mused aloud. "Marche must be spending a fortune."

"Several," Darby said. "Lady Bolbracken is footing the bills, of course. In fact, I hear the entire affair was her idea from beginning to end."

"Is that your gossip?" Crispin asked. "Because I have already heard it. Everyone knows the Behemoth dances to the tune she pipes. I'd do the same if I stood to gain several fortunes when she finally passed on. You must do better than that, Strand."

"Did you also know that the bride has not arrived yet?" Darby had the satisfaction of seeing his friends' eyes widen in surprise. "Had you heard that this marriage is being forced on the lady?"

"I heard what we all heard," Neville said. "The girl's family is in reduced circumstances in Brittany, which might as well be France, God save them. I understand that they were glad to sell her off to the highest bidder."

"The highest, indeed." Another man joined the conversation, his voice as rich and sweet as melting marzipan. "Lord Marche will be one of the richest men in England when his aunt finally leaves this world."

"Murdmont," Darby said without any particular greeting in his tone. "We were just observing that Marche will someday have a fortune to match his stature."

"Several… if the lady ever dies," answered Malcolm Jonas, Lord Murdmont. "She is above seventy and still meddling in the affairs of others."

"As you are Lady Bolbracken's man of business—as well as an expert on the subject of sticking your nose where it is not invited—I will take your word regarding her activities. However, as she is, by extension, my hostess, I will not speak ill of her and so shame my class and those that had the raising of me," Darby answered.

He felt no particular loyalty to Marche or Marche's great-aunt, but he was a guest at their home, and besides, he didn't like Sir Malcolm. Though Murdmont dressed in expensive clothing, he had no eye for style, and this was a sin young Lord Strand could not wink at. Therefore, it was with some pleasure that he fired the opening shot, fully aware that an exchange of volleys might spark a feud that could conceivably involve his descendants.

Murdmont's posture stiffened, his shoulders drawing up in his black coat like the wings of a raven. "Are you saying I am impolite, sir?"

"I am saying that you intrude, sir."

Sir Malcolm looked at the three impeccably clad young men, a sneer curling his long upper lip when he spoke. "You poncey fops should be grateful that a man of my intelligence would deign to speak with such empty-headed sops. If you were of my getting, I would cane those fancy clothes to bloody rags on your backs."

Darby drew back in surprise at the viciousness of Murdmont's salvo, and it took a moment for him to react. "How dare you," he choked out, but the other man was stalking away like a heron through the reeds. "How dare you threaten me," Darby finished lamely.

"Murdmont's handsome enough, but he's got no character whatsoever," was Crispin's opinion.

"My thanks, Snow; I hadn't noticed," Darby said, his gaze following Murdmont as the lawyer left the room.

"Well, he can't talk to you that way," Neville said. "Your father would have him hanged."

"I wouldn't bother Pater with something so minor… nor has he resumed communication with me. Fetch me a platter, would you, Tarmy? It will be some time before the wedding feast—if there is to be one at all—and I feel the need of a restorative."

HER GRACE, Lady Bolbracken née Willamina Frances Alberta Woodbine, Dowager Duchess of Brackenmourse and Dowager Countess of Falkertin, looked about the recently refurbished suite with a satisfied glint in her eyes. "The girl will adore it," she predicted.

Lord Marche turned from the window, haloed by the milky morning light. "How pleasant for her," he answered without inflection.

"I wish you wouldn't do that, Loel," Willamina complained. "You stand there like the very golden ideal of a man, the very image of the archangel Michael—without the flaming sword, of course—and then you open your mouth and destroy the illusion."

"I make no claim to perfection." Marche ran a finger along the ornately carved and gilded frame of a large mirror. "Do you really think my betrothed will like these rooms?"

"Why would she not? Everything is rose and cream, velvet and satin, edged in lace and gold."

"I am not sure I'd have much in common with the creature that could be happy in such a cage."

"What an unpleasant thing to say! I will have your promise again that you will not hurt this girl intentionally. If you wish to be angry at someone, turn your temper on me."

Marche bowed low. "I know when I am outmatched," he said. "And I do understand why you wish me to wed. I would rather not, but I know my duty. Let's have no more talk of cruelty to new brides. Let me pour a toast to my fiancée, whom I hope to meet soon."

"You are my only heir," Willamina said over the rim of her goblet. "The world has taken all my family but we two. Three sons and two daughters I gave; the least you can do is provide one small infant to carry on the bloodline."

"You're being a bit dramatic, are you not?"

"I am seventy-two and thrice widowed; I'll be as dramatic as I like." She glanced at the window. "God's Whiskers, where is the girl?"

"They travel by boat," Marche said reasonably. "Even a small storm could have delayed them for days. As long as the sideboards are covered with food and the drink does not run out, our guests will wait."

"Even the prince regent? Does nothing ever shake that maddening level-headedness of yours? Or is it simply that you do not care enough to become emotional?"

"Ask those who reared me."

"You go too far now."

Marche bowed again, his forelock shadowing his brow. "I beg your forgiveness, ma'am. What shall we talk of then?"

"Your new life as a husband will do. I do not expect that you will give up your clubs, your house in Town, or your... intimate friends, but I would like you to spend at least one weekend a month with your wife. Moreover, I hope that you will apply yourself to the getting of an heir. I cannot force you, God forfend, but it would mean so very much to me. And any child of your loins would immediately become heir to all my holdings. There, I cannot be plainer than that."

"I prefer it to the usual cat and mouse games. Since I never cared to wed, I am happy to let you choose a bride, and I'll do what I can to give her children, if that is what she wants."

Lady Bolbracken held out her hand and her great-nephew shook on the bargain. "I doubt I could ever disinherit you, you know. Like all women that stray into your orbit, I am a little infatuated with you... for all the good it does any of us. Is it not ironic that this Valeria—reared in isolation—can have no clue as to the catch she has landed?"

"I am sure I've no idea what you're talking about, and we've left our guests alone long enough. These chambers are beautiful, and I thank you for preparing them for my lady."

"There, now that was charming. This is the face you must show to your wife."

"As you wish, aunt. Soon I shall have so many faces that I will be in danger of becoming confused as to who I am."

"Don't talk nonsense, Loel," she said as she took his arm. "And send some men to look for the men you sent to look for the wedding party."

Marche nodded and escorted his great-aunt downstairs to break their fast with the horde of guests. Beyond the sunroom windows, he saw that the late snowfall was coming down a bit thicker than when he'd watched it from the bridal suite. The second search party had gone out by sleigh rather than carriage, and it looked as though they were in for a proper storm. Marche sighed heavily at the thought of being trapped indoors for days with his fellow aristocrats. They'd be underfoot the entire time, and there would be precious few chances for the sort of intrigue that diverted Marche. He spared a fond thought for the alluring and accommodating Ganymedes of Mrs. Dahlram's Tearoom as he turned from the view, but he must now set his mind to lulling a woman into a kindly regard for him.

It would probably behoove him to prepare some sort of speech to acquaint the young lady with his habits. Better that she knew what to expect and had no reason to question his lengthy absences. He would do as he pleased in any case, but he reckoned that his wife deserved the courtesy of knowing his schedule. But perhaps she wouldn't be the inquisitive type at all. She might be the sort of girl who was happy with a title, a garden, and a lapdog. He wondered idly if she'd take a lover and decided that he would not let on if he found out. The idea that his wife might take another to her bed roused nothing in him but mild curiosity. The most intriguing thing about her thus far was her continued absence: one delay after another until Marche was half-convinced that the girl didn't want to wed at all.

"My lord," Lady Bolbracken's second chamberlain approached and bowed. "It is time."

"Has my lady arrived?"

"That is beyond my knowledge, sir. *My* lady bids me conduct you to the hall."

"I can find my way. I am sure you have more important duties."

"Not today, sir." The second chamberlain allowed himself a respectful smile. "Today it is my honor to escort you to your wedding."

Marche squared his shoulders. "Wish me good luck," he said as he walked through the door the servant held for him.

"SHE'S here without proper escort or even one maid, my lady! What's to be done?"

"Calm yourself," Willamina told the chambermaid. "Take me to her at once."

From the serving girl's panicked demeanor, Lady Bolbracken expected to find a draggled, frightened survivor of the storm waiting for her. When she entered the little-used antechamber off the *porte-cochère*, she stopped in her tracks to gape. A very tall young woman in a deep-hooded cloak of white fur stood there like the very Queen of Winter come for a visit. Her regal bearing revealed her nobility, and she had the classic features of a statue of Athena. As Willamina stared, the goddess came to life, sinking into a deep curtsy with a soft susurration of crumpling brocade.

"Miss Valeria Randwick?" Willamina said in hope.

The visitor looked up and spoke in a voice that was low but exceedingly pleasant, with a hint of an accent. "I am Valeria Caroline Juliana, daughter of Amandine and Julius Randwick, Earl of Blythestone. And I have the honor to be affianced to your heir, my lady."

"My dear, you are utterly charming," Willamina exclaimed. "Rise and allow me to embrace you as one of my family."

The bride had to stoop to kiss the old lady on either cheek, but her carriage made her every gesture elegant. She moved with a languid grace that suited her height, showing a tendency to remain in repose unless speech or action was required of her. Willamina didn't know if this was due to laziness or docility, but she could deal with either or both given the bride's other attributes. The girl had handsome features and long limbs to pass on to her offspring, along with a calm nature. Satisfied that she'd chosen well, Willamina took Valeria's hand.

"Is there anything I may send for? As you know, the ceremony should have started some time ago. I wonder if you feel you might collect yourself soon. I don't wish to hurry you, but if I could make an announcement to the guests, I know it will ease many minds."

"My mother was regrettably taken ill, but I am quite ready," the bride said with an admirable economy of words.

Positively glowing with contentment, Lady Bolbracken sent a footman scurrying ahead while she led Valeria down the hall. At the arched doorway of the chapel, the young woman unfastened the brooch at the neck of her cloak, letting the garment fall. The usher at the entrance jumped to catch the cloak and folded it carefully over his arm. The bride paused to nod her thanks before turning her gaze forward again. As the notes of a stately air were played, she fixed her eyes on the pulpit and paced forward in time to the music. For all the notice she took of them, the illustrious spectators might have been painted on canvas.

Marche forgot to breathe as the beautiful vision floated toward the altar in a pristine confection of white satin that covered her from her chin to the floor. She wore a short veil of snowflake lace and the coils of her dark auburn hair were crowned with a chaplet of tiny rosebuds. Her sculpted face shone with the purity and resolve of a Joan of Arc. She was by far the tallest woman he'd ever met and the most beautiful. It wasn't until she met his eyes that he perceived how anxious she was. He assumed the journey had been a harrowing one and mentally berated his aunt for bullying the girl into going forward before she recovered. The poor child was probably on the verge of fainting.

"Father," Marche murmured as he leaned toward the bishop. "I'd be forever indebted if you might shorten the solemnities somewhat."

"I understand, my son." The prelate glanced at the lovely young bride. "I will hasten your happiness all I may."

The bride stopped before the altar, and Lady Hapwood, the matron of honor chosen by Lady Bolbracken, handed her a bouquet. The bishop took the ring from the best man, also chosen by the duchess, and the ceremony began. In half the usual time, Loel and Valeria were bound in holy matrimony in the presence of their peers. As was traditional, Lord Marche turned to kiss his new wife. He lifted the gossamer veil and gazed into pellucid eyes the color of a summer's twilight. Inexplicably drawn, he leaned to touch his mouth to his new wife's with gentle pressure. A moment after their lips met, the bride collapsed like a string-cut puppet. The guests gasped and cried out as Lord Marche caught the lady in his arms. Before anyone could move, he had carried her out of the chapel, beyond the view of curious eyes.

"Are you all right, girl?" Marche asked, ignoring the knocking at the vestry door behind him. "Is it just a case of the vapors or something more serious?"

When the bride didn't respond, Marche called on skills learned from acquaintances in the theater and loosened the bodice of the wedding gown. He reached down the back of the delicate garment and unfastened the top stays of the corset. As the laces parted, Marche had a view down the shadowy front of the dress, and he sat back suddenly. "Go away," he said automatically when the pounding at the door started up again.

"Open the door, Marche," Willamina said.

"It is at my lady's request that I locked it, and until she gives me leave, it shall remain so. Will you not leave us in peace now?" Marche stared at the door until the sounds of footsteps receded. When he turned back, the bride's eyes were open. "Well now," he drawled. "Who are you and what's your game, my lad?"

"You have every right to be angry, sir." The young man scrambled up to sit stiffly on the bench. "But I hope you will hear my explanation before you judge me."

"I believe I just asked for an explanation."

"I- I am—" The young paused, and then continued in a firmer voice. "My name is Valentine Edward Albion Randwick; I am the Earl of Blythestone, and Valeria is my sister."

"Is she now? And how do you come to be in her dress?"

"She loves another and has no wish to marry you."

"I see, but why this elaborate ruse? Why not simply refuse me?"

"It is not so simple. She has not reached her majority and could not marry without our mother's consent. I agreed to pose as her while she elopes to Gretna Green with Mr. Cleary." Valentine squirmed a little. "And frankly, my mother was so happy that your wealth would restore our family that Valeria could not bear to disappoint her."

"And where is your mother?"

"She gets terribly seasick, sir. She had to take to bed at an inn where we first came ashore. She refused to get back on the ship for the trip up the river."

March shook his head. "You must have known that you would be found out eventually."

"Of course, but Valeria knew how the crossing would affect our mother, and she calculated that you would not risk the humiliation of revealing my gender until you could find a way out of the marriage, thus saving her the trouble."

"Clever girl. Does she look at all like you?"

"We were often mistaken for twins when we were together."

"Then what a prize I lost." Marche fell quiet with a thoughtful frown. "Or so it seems."

Valentine held his peace while he waited for his heart to stop pounding. It hadn't been difficult to speak the lines he'd rehearsed, and, after three months' practice, he was used to moving about in female attire—the skirts weren't so terribly different from the monk's cassock he'd been used to. Despite the preparations, he'd been terribly nervous, but all had gone well... until Marche kissed him. When the big man's lips had touched his, he'd felt such a stirring in his lower belly that he had been afraid he would lose its contents. A wave of dizziness had addled his thoughts, and his limbs had not obeyed his commands. As he'd fainted, he had felt the most remarkable pulse of pleasure, and his staff had become hard as it sometimes did in certain dreams. Mere proximity to this duke weakened him and caused a sensation in his middle that unnerved him. It was the oddest reaction, and he wondered if it might not be caused by the instrument of torture called a corset.

"Blythestone," Marche broke his silence. "I would like you to hear a proposal."

"As I have deceived you so deliberately, I feel honor-bound to make some sort of reparation."

"I thought you were doing this because you are determined to spare your sister the horror of marriage to me."

Valentine blushed. "You are not as we imagined, sir," he admitted. "And I am not proud of the methods we had to use, but I could not refuse, even if it compromised my morality."

Marche raised his eyebrows. "Satisfy my curiosity. I had no idea my fiancée had a brother."

"I have been in hiding at my father's command," Valentine said, his tone making it clear that he had no more to say on the subject.

"I see. Perhaps one day you'll trust me enough to elaborate, but for now, all I wish is your cooperation."

"And you shall have it, sir."

Marche looked into the young man's earnest gaze and hesitated, but only for a moment. "I am but a man of straw at present, but I stand to inherit a staggering lot of money and land... if I play my great-aunt's game. She wishes me to be married. As it happens, I have no interest in women, carnally speaking, but I agreed to take a wife and do my best to continue the bloodline." The duke paused. "You look a bit pale, Blythestone."

"You are very… frank, sir. The boldness with which you admit your… lack of interest in the fair sex has taken the wind out of me."

"If you cannot swallow that, then the game is up before it begins."

"I think it is wickedness, but it is your wickedness. I am not so easily put off, but I do wonder at your callousness toward your aunt."

"Do not mistake me; I love the old trout. However, I cannot be something I am not, and she is not in the good health she pretends. Do you think it might be possible to continue the masquerade for a bit longer?"

"Have you any idea how much longer? You see, my mother thinks that I escorted Valeria to her wedding. As soon as she is well enough to travel, she will come here straightaway, and you cannot expect me to fool her."

Marche smiled. "No, I suppose I cannot, but neither will I predict my aunt's death."

"I certainly did not mean to say that I wish her end to be hastened!"

"Despite her torment of me, neither would I. We need only deceive her until we leave on our wedding tour."

"Very well. And what of my mother?"

"What think you of this? I shall send an army of servants to the seashore—laden with all the comforts and delicacies they can carry—to tend to your mother until she recovers."

"With that sort of coddling, she might never be well enough to travel." Valentine paused. "Oh, I see. Very cunning, sir, but it will not delay her forever."

"We shall leave on our bridal trip at the end of the week. Your mother will be ensconced here at the manor with the entire staff at her service to await our return. She and my aunt can deal with each other. That should keep their noses out of our affairs."

"You have a talent for this."

"You sound as though you disapprove."

"Deception and blandishments are the Devil's tools."

"Perhaps Old Nick won't mind if I borrow them for a bit."

Valentine gasped at the man's irreverence. In the months since Valeria had fetched him from the monastery, he'd seen and heard many shocking things, but this man was breathtakingly cavalier. "Have you no fear for your mortal soul, sir?"

"Prove to me that I have one and I will take more care. Now, will you help me or not?"

"I hope to, sir," Valentine said firmly. "For, by my faith, you need it."

"Capital! We shall need a great deal of luck to maintain this charade, but if we brazen it out, I think few will question it."

"Very well, I shall play my part, but do not expect any heirs from me."

"You have a fair ration of pluck." Marche smiled again. "Come then and let's meet our guests as man and wife. Straighten your garments a bit; it won't matter if they're in slight disarray, all the more convincing, really."

"Might I have a few more moments?"

"Certainly, but remember that the prince regent himself is here to wish us joy. Do you really want to keep him waiting?"

Valentine swallowed his heart back down to his chest as he walked to the mirror by the door. With cold fingers, he smoothed his pinned-up hair, straightened the chaplet of rosebuds, and requested Marche's help in doing up his corset. "My mouth is dry," he observed absently.

"Then come and whatever drink you desire will be brought to you, Lady Marche. I promise you that the receiving line will be over with quickly and you may retire to prepare for a night of wedded bliss."

Valentine put his hand on the other man's arm and lifted his chin bravely. "If I feel overwhelmed, I suppose can simply pretend to swoon again."

"And I shall be there to catch you," Marche said with a mocking half-bow.

CHAPTER 3

"AH, HERE they are!" Darby St. Denis noticed the stir by the ballroom doors. "The happy pair."

Neville Stokes tugged on the tails of his burgundy watered silk jacket, running his fingers along the velvet lapels. "Do you see the prince regent?"

"How can you miss him?" Crispin Ludstall slurred. "Prince George is the big round one with—"

"You're extremely drunk, Snowhurst," Darby interrupted. "Prince George is resplendent in a spanking blue military-cut jacket and exquisitely tailored buckskin trousers worn Beau Brummel fashion. Not a wrinkle to be seen. Isn't he magnificent, Tarmy?"

"Incomparable," Lord Tarmegent agreed. "I hear his waistcoat is gold thread all the way 'round."

"That's a powerful lot of thread." Lord Snowhurst giggled.

"Snow." Darby took his friend's arm, digging his fingers into muscle. "If you speak again, I will not recognize you the next time I see you. Do you understand?"

Dimly through the haze of alcohol, Crispin realized that Darby was threatening to snub him. If Lord Strand cut him publicly, he might as well be dead as far as the fashionable set was concerned. He took a breath to apologize but thought better of it. Darby had told him not to speak again, so he would remain silent until further notice.

"There's a good fellow." Strand patted Snowhurst's rosy cheek. "Let's get in the receiving line. I want a closer look at this long lass who so enflames the Behemoth that he repairs with her to the nearest closet the moment they are wed."

"That gown she's wearing is a dream," Neville said. "It looks as if it's made of spun sugar and dewdrops."

Perhaps she'll let you borrow it, Crispin thought. Darby gave Crispin a sharp look as they stepped into the line and the smirk evaporated from Snowhurst's face.

"Great fishes, she's not lacking in inches!" Darby said. "A lesser man than Marche would have to scale her like a mountain."

"A fine healthy filly," Neville agreed. "She should make an excellent brood mare."

Crispin sulked but held his tongue as his companions passed remarks on the bride.

"If you are wondering, my dear Snowhurst," Darby said with his uncanny ability to know what Crispin was thinking. "Making judgments on all and sundry is not only acceptable; it is expected of a rake. However, it is never acceptable to belittle His Highness. He is our sovereign lord while his father is unable to rule, and we owe him the respect of his position. Do you understand?"

"Yes," Crispin said. "The prince is not fair game."

"And you drink to excess too often, but that is your affair. I only ask that you learn to curb your tongue when you are in your cups."

"My dears," Neville said. "Marche has unbuttoned his jacket. Look at his watch fob! It is the size of a pumpkin!"

Crispin joined his friend in marveling over the accessory; however, Darby was staring transfixed at the bride's face as she looked up at Marche. Strand had not marked it from a distance, but the new duchess had the face of a Shakespearean heroine, a Rosalind or Hippolyta, Queen of the Amazons. She called to mind Lord Byron's stanzas, for she walked in beauty like the night, all the best of dark and bright, her loveliness too dramatic for everyday wear. Glossy dark hair with a warm tinge of copper contrasted vividly with smooth pale skin and eyes the color of hyacinths at dusk. Every line of her coltish frame was elongated slightly like one of old Mr. Gainsborough's paintings, and she moved at a measured cadence that soothed the eye. She was not the current ideal of beauty, but she was so striking that the other women in the room looked like milkmaids beside her. Darby found it difficult to take his eyes from her face.

"Oh dear, they are leaving," Neville said.

Lord Strand shook himself from his trance as the Duchess of Marche took her husband's arm and began moving away. "Blast it! I was so close."

"It's not as if you won't have another opportunity to congratulate the bride and groom," Murdmont said from several places ahead of Darby. "You will be here for the entire week, I trust? Or at least as long as the food and drink are free, I'll wager."

Lord Strand gave no sign he heard the insult. He was smitten and the object of his fascination had been removed from his sight. Devastated, he leaned upon Lord Tarmegent's shoulder and directed him to find brandy. A poem was beating at the inside of his skull like a dove in a cage, and his fingers itched to transcribe deathless words in tribute to a love that could never be.

"YOU did well, by my reckoning," Marche said softly as he left the crowd of well-wishers with his bride on his arm.

The new duchess didn't answer until they were alone in the bridal suite with the doors closed and locked behind them. "Truly, I am beginning to wonder if most people are not somewhat... unobservant," Valentine said. "It is difficult to credit that I could fool so many into believing me a female."

"People see what they wish to see, in my opinion." Marche went to a sideboard that held a collection of spirits in crystal decanters. "I find most are generally absorbed in themselves, and the few who do notice details about others are usually plotting against them. Would you care for something to drink?"

"The water I had at the reception quenched my thirst quite well."

"There are other reasons than thirst to imbibe. For instance, some drink wine for the pleasure of the taste. I see by your expression that you doubt me. Here." Marche held out a crystal goblet. "Take a sip of this Bordeaux. Most will not have French wines in their Town houses for fear of being thought unpatriotic, but my aunt has kept the country cellars well-stocked."

Valentine took the glass, inhaling cautiously as he brought it to his lips. The perfume of cherries, vanilla, and other elusive scents wafted up from the deep burgundy liquid. Tilting the goblet, he took a small drink. Having tasted only the vinegary watered table wine of the abbey where he'd been raised, the rich silkiness of the Bordeaux was a revelation.

"Good?" Marche inquired.

"I have never tasted anything like it."

Marche smiled at the innocent delight on the young man's face. "Aren't you eager to get out of that rig? Or do you enjoy dressing as a woman?"

Valentine's cheeks grew warm. "I was not sure if it was safe."

"Once I close a door, the staff knows better than to disturb me. Unless you fear someone can see into a third-story window, you may do as you please."

Lord Blythestone set his glass down and immediately unfastened the jeweled clips that kept most of his hair piled on top of his head. The shining tresses came sliding down like skeins of dark silk as he shook free the last few pins.

"So it is not a wig," Marche murmured, pouring another measure of wine.

Valentine froze in the act of reaching for the laces of his gown. "Are you yet here, sir?"

"As I am your wedded husband, I saw no cause to leave."

"I would prefer to change in private."

"I am afraid that would look a bit too odd. Overcome your shyness, lad. We are both men, and I promise I shall not tease you."

"I have just thought: what am I to put on once I remove this gown?"

"If this were an ordinary wedding, you'd not need clothing at this point, but I see that a bed gown has been laid out for you."

Valentine picked up a garment nearly as frothy as the one he wore. With a sigh, he let it drift back down to the velvet bedcover. "I shall need help," he said.

"I beg your pardon?"

"I cannot get in and out of this costume on my own without a knife."

Marche chuckled as he came to stand behind the young man. "Your sister's plan seems to have more than a few difficulties. Wait, do not pull; some of your hair is caught."

Valentine stood quietly as Lord Marche carefully freed a strand from one of the gown's myriad tiny hooks. He sucked in a big breath as the other man began working to open the back of the garment. It had taken Valeria and Anne three-quarters of an hour to imprison him in the welter of whalebone, flounces, and cords that defined a shape nature had never intended. Warm fingers brushed the skin of Valentine's back and a quick little shiver went through him, setting off another flurry of feathers in his belly.

"Are you cold?" Marche asked. "I could build the fire up a bit more."

"Not on my account, sir. Pray continue with your task, the sooner to be done with it."

"If that is your pleasure, it is my command."

"Sir." Valentine spun to face the tall duke, the half-open gown swirling and slipping down to settle in heavy folds around his waist. "I have noted a deplorable tendency of yours to speak mockingly as though I were your wife in truth, and I find it most disconcerting."

"I am only practicing for our public performance."

"Oh." Valentine's guileless face underwent a rapid change. "Do forgive me, sir, for my unseemly outburst. I assumed the worst of you with no good reason."

Marche blinked. The lad's gullibility was beyond belief. He no longer wondered how Miss Valeria Randwick had convinced her brother to go along with her nursery room scheme, but he did wonder how a young man above eighteen could remain so innocent. "I was teasing you a little," Marche confessed. "Forgive me if I presumed upon our proximity."

"No, you are quite right, sir." Valentine turned his back as he let the gown slide to the floor and divested himself of the layers of undergarments. "It is a most practical idea to rehearse in private." The young man's voice was muffled as he pulled the diaphanous nightgown over his head. "I was given a brief tutelage in feminine manners, but I think it would be wise if I were to appear as a retiring sort, unused to high society."

"You are from Brittany, as I hear it told. No one I know is from Brittany, so no one will be likely to question any oddity of manner so long as you explain that—"

"We spoke thus in Bretagne," Valentine interrupted in a soft Frankish accent. "How provincial you must think me."

"Very good," Marche approved. "You have a talent for this, Sir Valentine."

"For playacting?"

"Yes, for playacting." Marche tossed back the contents of his goblet. It was barely half past the hour of nine, when his evening would normally commence, but he was expected to retire early and get a good start on reproducing. Idly, he wondered if there might not be a deck of cards in one of the drawers when Valentine cast a look over one shoulder as swift and lethal as a bolt from a crossbow. Marche reached out without thought and palmed the young man's smooth cheek. Waves of silken hair glided over the back of his hand as he rubbed his thumb over a soft earlobe. Valentine turned away, biting his lip to stifle a gasp as the duke embraced him from behind. Paralyzed by conflicting impulses, the young man didn't resist as Marche pulled him closer. He felt something hard slot neatly into the crease between his buttocks and everything south of his navel melted in a delicious rush of heat. As Valentine sagged against the other man's solid bulk, Marche got a better grip on him. "Lord Blythestone," Marche said daringly, his lips moving against the young man's nape. "Have you ever bedded a man?"

Valentine shook his spinning head, giddy with the sensations bombarding his nervous system as Marche's big hands squeezed and stroked. "I've not bedded anyone."

The small caresses ceased for a moment. "No one at all?"

"I do not think I ought to be doing… *this*."

"There's nothing immoral in it, Blythestone. We *are* married, after all."

"Lord Marche, I have told you that I do not find such mockery amusing."

"Is my touch so repulsive?"

"No!" Valentine inhaled sharply as Marche nipped at the side of his neck.

"How does it make you feel when I do this?" Marche licked the spot reddened by his teeth.

"I have no words for it. It reminds me of descriptions of exaltation, when saints are beatified."

"Surely that's a good thing."

"I cannot say. Is it right that a man's touch should set such a fire in my blood?"

"I do not ask such questions. I simply enjoy the light and the warmth."

"Do you not wish for more?" Valentine said breathlessly as Marche's hand spread across his lower belly.

"Indeed, I do," Marche's breath was warm on Valentine's cheek as he leaned forward. Capturing the young man's lips in an awkward kiss, he let his hand slide down to stroke Valentine's stiffening shaft through the layers of silk and satin.

Valentine moaned into Marche's mouth as a strong wave of pleasure tightened his groin almost painfully. Nothing he had ever read or been told had prepared him for the overwhelming tide that swept all else before it. "Wait!" he gasped, breaking away from Marche's embrace. "You do not even know me; why do you wish to… have carnal relations with me?"

"You are an attractive young man and I like attractive young men."

"So this is nothing more than physical pleasure for you? But indeed, how could there be more to it when we have barely been introduced."

"You rate physical pleasure too meanly. What you just felt was only the smallest taste."

"Then may I take it you have warmed yourself at many fires?"

"None as bright as yours."

"I cannot credit your audacity, sir! Love is a sacred gift, and it offends me to hear you make sport of it."

"Our first quarrel." Marche grinned.

"Do you take nothing seriously, sir?"

"My inheritance. I take that very seriously indeed."

Valentine was silent for a few moments. "Perhaps you can burn all that money to keep you warm," he said at last.

"That was a riposte worthy of any salon in London," Marche said. "I begin to believe that this masquerade will be a most wonderful diversion."

"I shall pray that it will prove so." Valentine knelt beside the bed and folded his hands. After several silent minutes, he rose and said goodnight to the other man. Climbing beneath the goose down coverlet, Valentine lay down and closed his eyes. The long journey, the stresses of the day, and the draught of wine conspired lull him into sleep as soon as he was recumbent.

Marche poured more Bordeaux and watched the flames, trying to disregard the presence of a comely, enticing young man in his bed. He was unpracticed at denying himself pleasure and accustomed to readily available and accommodating partners. Despite Blythestone's favorable physical reactions to his caresses, it could not even be determined if the lad were inclined toward his own sex or merely extraordinarily inexperienced. Marche reached down to relieve his reaction to the brief encounter, squeezing the surge under the layers of buckskin and linen. His gaze slid slowly sidewise until it rested on the sleeper. Between the wealth of tumbled hair and a fold of the comforter, all that was visible were the fire-gilded contours of nose and cheek, and a curved line of dark lashes, yet they moved Marche more than any blatant display of naked flesh ever had. Valentine shifted slightly, the sweet curves of his upper lip coming into view and Marche's breath caught at the strong hot pulse that shot through him. The duke gripped his shaft tightly, clenching his jaw to hold in a small cry as he spilled in his breeches.

Bemused by the swiftness with which he'd achieved release, he sat unmoving until he heard a soft snore. Flinging the rest of the wine into the fire, he doffed his soiled clothing and got into bed. Edging closer until he could put an arm around the other man, he cautiously spooned against his back. With his face buried in thick fragrant hair, Marche truly relaxed for the first time in months.

CHAPTER 4

VALENTINE dreamed that he slept with his back to a roaring fire, and when he woke, he missed its pleasant warmth. A discreet knock at the door banished the remnants of the phantom hearth, and he sat up quickly. After a moment, he heard Marche on the other side.

"May I enter?"

Valentine took a deep breath, and he remembered to use the upper registers of his voice when he called out permission. The door opened, and Marche stooped to retrieve the tray he'd set down. Carrying his burden into the bedchamber, he deposited it on a side table, knocking one or two small items to the carpet. Valentine remained where he was, the coverlet clutched to his chest.

"What a fetching sight you are with your hair tumbled on your shoulders and your eyes heavy with sleep. I assumed you would not be ready to face your guests so early, and I have brought you something to break your fast. No one will think it strange, although the cook gave me a few odd looks when I presented myself in the kitchen to act as your servant."

"I shouldn't wonder," Valentine said, sliding his legs over the side of the bed. "You are a duke after all."

Marche paused to admire the young man's long, shapely limbs as the bed gown slid up to mid-thigh. Never had he seen such an attractive youth, and the irony of his situation did not escape him. Again, he vowed that he would sip Valentine's yet-untasted sweetness before this charade ended. The seduction of the beautiful, unworldly young man would at least keep him entertained. "Will you come and take a morsel?" he coaxed.

"I would rather have a pair of breeches, but I suppose that is not to be. The baggage with my trousseau was in the carriage yesterday, but I can't imagine where it may have gotten to."

"I think that if you open your wardrobe, you will find everything you need to play the part of a duchess."

Valentine left off eyeing the honey cakes to look at the bow-front mahogany armoire. Curious, he was drawn across the room to open one of the marquetry doors. Within the shadowy recesses of the huge wardrobe were half a dozen gowns, a morning dress, and a riding habit along with several pairs of shoes and boots. "How is this possible? I brought only two gowns with me for day and evening."

"You reckon without the will of my sweet aunt. She had three seamstresses and Lord knows how many maids up all night sewing, using one of your gowns as a pattern."

"And the shoes?"

"A footman rode all night to London and back. He brought these as well." Marche opened a drawer full of gloves. "You look a bit vaporish. Why don't you come and sit down?"

"I don't wish anyone to go to such trouble on my behalf."

"You married a duke, if it had escaped your notice. You are *Lady* Valeria now, Your Grace. A lift of one of your lovely eyebrows will bring an army of servants on the skip."

"I feel a bit queasy," Valentine said as he sank onto a dainty chair covered in pale rose brocade.

"Have some tea and a scone. This currant jam is very good and the honey cakes are still warm. If nothing tempts you, I can send for whatever you fancy. I've heard that in Brittany, breakfast is still taken in the old style with sausage and porridge washed down with ale."

"I think one of those small cakes might help to settle my stomach," Valentine said. "And a cup of tea would be nice as well."

"Allow me." Marche busied himself placing three of the honey cakes and a large dollop of sweetened cream on a small plate. "Do you take anything in your tea?"

"Sugar, please, just a little."

The duke set the eggshell-thin cup on a saucer and carried it with the cakes to where Valentine sat. "There you are. You can't say no to that."

As Valentine picked up one of the tiny cakes, his eyes traced the lines of the crest on the bone china. Taking small bites, he let his gaze wander about the room as he ate. He had known, in an abstract way, that Marche's family was wealthy, but here in Wandeleigh's manor house, everywhere he looked, he was confronted with the evidence. It was not an ostentatious display; however, even the most mundane items were crafted of the most expensive materials. The handle of his butter knife was solid gold, deeply incised with the Woodbine coat of arms. Abruptly, the crumb of sweet cake in his throat felt like a piece of gravel. "I am not sure—" he began before he had to swallow again. "I am not sure I can maintain this masquerade. It seems certain that someone will see through the disguise."

"I shall be at your elbow to guide you, and as we've discussed, you've your country upbringing to blame for any... irregularities of speech and manner."

"To be sure," Valentine said, somewhat stiffly. "But I am a *man*, not a woman, and someone is bound to notice, sooner or later."

"Then let it be later. Do you ride?"

Valentine nodded. "I am not in practice, but I fancy that I can manage not to part company with a well-trained horse."

"Then I propose a gallop after breakfast. A few of the guests may join us, but I will make sure our horses are the swifter. I am afraid you're required to make an appearance at dinner, but most of the guests' attention will be on their plates. Afterward, we might take a stroll for our digestion, and you can see a bit of the grounds. With forethought, we should be able to stay on the move until it is time for bed again."

"You have given the matter some consideration, I see. As I am a stranger in this land, I shall be guided by you until I have learned enough to make informed decisions on my own. In the meanwhile, this illusion was only intended to last until Valeria was safely wed. How may I help to foster it further?"

"Your onerous duty it will be to appear at my side in an ever-changing array of fashionable gowns, more of which, I understand, are being sewn or purchased at this very moment."

"You are overlooking something."

Unused to having his pronouncements questioned, Marche raised his eyebrows in surprise. "Pray tell me what that might be."

"A dresser, sir. As you are quick to point out, I did not plan to be in female regalia for an extended period. If this charade is to go on indefinitely, I shall require the aid of someone who knows the intricacies of clothing who can also dress hair and apply paint."

"You looked absolutely perfect when you arrived yesterday."

"That was the handiwork of my sister and Mistress Kermartin, whose services, you will understand, are not presently available to us."

"You *really* did not look beyond your nose when you agreed to come here, did you?" Marche folded his arms. "Well, I can do nothing about this difficulty immediately, but surely your hair need not be dressed to go riding."

"I cannot deny that our plan has many short-sighted deficiencies. If you will kindly refrain from mentioning this fact more than once in each conversation, I will do my best to remember how Valeria pinned up my hair, and I daresay I can dab on a spot of color."

"Brave lad," Marche said, relenting in his stern treatment. It was hardly Valentine's fault that Marche was frustrated, and browbeating the young man would only make him anxious and prone to mistakes, or so the duke told himself. "I'll leave you to finish dressing while I have a word with the staff. No one will disturb you."

"Thank you, sir." Valentine's voice stopped Marche at the door. "It is very kind of you to make this situation easier for me."

"It benefits me as well," Marche replied brusquely as he left the room. Leaning his back against the closed door, he tarried in the antechamber before going out into the hall. Young Blythestone had a definite effect on Marche, and they would be spending a lot of time in one another's company. His Grace was not put out by the idea; he simply hoped the lad would share his considerable charms before an alternate outlet became necessary. Mrs. Dahlram's Tearoom—with its compliant Adonises—was miles away in London, and while a servant might be dispatched to fetch a half dozen pairs of shoes, Marche didn't think the delivery of a fancy-boy would be countenanced or condoned.

"There you are, Loel!"

Marche hastily rearranged his features as he turned to face Lady Bolbracken. "Good morning," he said brightly, leaning to kiss her fingers. "I trust you slept well?"

"Well enough. We old folk pass the night like babies, you know: awake every few hours and fretting about nothing. Isn't it curious that the end of life is much like the beginning? And you? How did you sleep?"

"I can honestly say that I've not passed such a pleasant night in years."

Willamina searched her great-nephew's eyes. "You are telling the truth," she said in surprise. "Do you mean to say that you like the girl?"

"Very much. She is unlike any female of my acquaintance." Marche paused. "Though she does remind me somewhat of you in your sweeter moods."

"I found her charming, as well, though our meeting was brief. Is she not receiving this morning? I will quite understand if she wishes for privacy on this of all days."

"My lady is somewhat... overcome by her first night as a wife. I hope to coax her into a ride before the midday meal. If that does not suit, she shall name her diversion, and I will cheerfully indulge her, be it a rubber of whist or a boar hunt."

"You please me greatly, Loel. I was going to wait until tomorrow to tell you, but I cannot keep it to myself a moment longer. I wish you to know that Wandeleigh is yours, a home for you and your wife, where you may raise your children. "

"That is a most generous gift." Marche bowed deeply.

"It would have come to you eventually, along with all the rest." Willamina shrugged, making light of the moment as she started back down the stairs.

Marche hurried to catch up with her and took her arm as they descended. "I meant what I said about my bride. You could not have made a better choice for me."

The lady's seamed face brightened. "Then I am doubly happy. I have already ordered a full wardrobe for the girl, and if she doesn't care for any of it, she may burn the garments and choose for herself. I wish to spoil her, Loel; I warn you."

"I feel the same impulse, ma'am. Valeria is somewhat shy. She has told me that she feels rough and backward when she compares her manners with those of her new family, and, on that account, she is nervous about appearing in public."

"Pish!" Willamina sniffed. "She will soon become used to us, and anyone that dares jeer at her comportment will rue his lack of tact."

"I daresay, but until then, perhaps she might be granted some latitude?"

"My dear boy, Valeria is young, healthy, and appears to inspire some affection in you. I would not care if she ate from a trough and wore breeches to the Winter Ball. I count myself blessed that she is a modest and exceptionally well-mannered young lady."

Marche smiled. "I'll leave you here," he said as they reached the ground floor. "I must have a quick word with Negus about my business affairs in town."

"Why do you keep that scoundrel about you? He's no fit servant for a gentleman, you know."

"He is useful to me in many ways; very cunning with a cravat and frankly, I like his sauce."

Willamina shook her head, fluttering the fine vanes of the egret plumes tucked into the curls of her wig. "You should not trust him, my dear. I have known actors in my time. Fiction is their craft, and you can never be sure who they are from day to day. Mark my words. He will play you false one day."

Marche bent over her hand again, brushing his lips across her knuckles before he straightened up. "I am sure you are right, because you are always right. Now, if that's settled, I have much to do and little time in which to accomplish it. It is my hope that Valeria and I will see you at dinner. Until then, will you continue to honor me by acting as my hostess?"

Having made his aunt happy for once, Marche strode away from the public areas of the vast mansion and exited the building at the back of the east wing. His step didn't slow on the cobblestone courtyard as he automatically avoided the toe-stubbing humps that helped the draught-horses keep their footing on icy days. This had been his favorite playground until he went away to school, and he knew every inch of it blindfolded.

As he expected, he found Negus in the tack barn. "Your Grace!" The valet looked up from his cards. "You should have sent for me instead of walking all the way out here. Angus was just sayin' that we've seen our last snow of the year, but it's still nippish."

"I needed a breath of air," Marche said, looking around the circle of card players. "Good morning all."

"Good morning, Your Grace," the head groom said, rising and tipping his hat as the other two hostlers followed suit.

"I am not here to spoil your fun. I just need a moment of Negus's time."

"Not to worry, my lord," the groom said. "It is high time we were puttin' tack on a few horses."

"My thanks," Marche said as Negus joined him in the square of sunlight that fell through the open doors.

"How may I be of service, m' lord?"

"My great aunt has recently put me in mind that you were once an actor."

"As you know, sir, but briefly."

"I would imagine so. When I found you in the theater district, holding horses for ha'pennies, I was but fourteen, and so you could not have been more than sixteen."

"As your lordship always has a point when he speaks, I shall wait as patiently as Balaam's ass until he reveals it."

"My point, clown, is that there are only a few roles in the theater for adolescent boys. What parts did you play?"

"Why does your lordship ask?" Negus's gaze narrowed in suspicion.

"May I not show an interest in you as a person?"

"Am I to swallow that you come all the way to the stables because you were taken curious of a sudden, sir?"

"Damn your hide, Negus, just answer the question!"

Negus drew himself up to his full five feet and a half. "I was a most affectin' Juliet, accordin' to some."

"Were you indeed? Now, you see, that is very interesting. Come with me, please."

"Of course, sir." Negus picked up his winnings and followed his master. "May I offer my congratulations on your wedding?"

"You may and thank you. I'll not insult you by asking if I can trust you. You know my secrets and you've never divulged a single one to my knowledge."

"Your secrets are my secrets, sir."

Marche tousled his valet's bright red hair with casual affection. "I am about to entrust you with one more confidence, and let me say in advance that your new duties will be accompanied by a rise in your wages. My aunt has just given me Wandeleigh and all its revenues, by the way. I shall soon be a duke in more than name."

"Has she indeed, sir? Congratulations!"

"The trouble is she reckons I owe her a baby," Marche said as they entered the private wing that housed the family quarters.

"Then gird up your loins and get your lady wife with child."

"That might prove difficult."

"Your Grace." Negus lowered his voice. "I know females aren't your choice of game, but surely you can close your eyes and think of all that money."

"That is not the problem," Marche said over his shoulder as he opened the door of the bridal suite. He gestured Negus into the drawing room and knocked on the door in the opposite wall.

"Come in," Valentine answered.

"Give me a moment," Marche told his valet as he went into the bedchamber.

Valentine put aside the book he'd found on the night table and rose to greet Marche. The military cut of the royal blue riding habit suited his coltish frame and disguised the breadth of his shoulders. He'd managed to get his boots on by himself, but the hat had defeated him and lay crushed upon the carpet amid the debris of bent pins.

"You looking charmingly dishabille," Marche said, reaching out to stir the curls escaping Valentine's loose braid. "It needs but one thing to complete the picture of a happy bride."

Marche swept Valentine up with an arm around his lower back. Taking young man's jaw in his other hand, the duke ducked his head and fastened his lips to the pulse that beat in the white throat. Sucking gently, Marche flicked his tongue against the sensitive skin. Valentine swayed, leaning against the other man's chest as bolts of knee-weakening pleasure lanced through him at each stroke of Marche's tongue. He staggered a bit when the duke released him and held him at arm's length for inspection.

"Perfect." Marche touched a fingertip to the reddened patch of skin on Valentine's neck. "A love mark to mark my love."

"Thank you, I suppose," Valentine said after he caught his breath.

"It is the small details that bolster a really big deception, and I would like you to meet someone who has been my confidante for many years. Negus is my valet, and I trust him with my reputation. I hope you will as well for we need an accomplice in this."

"You are certain we may trust him?"

"He has never betrayed me."

"Does he know a discreet lady's maid?"

"Just a moment and we will ask him," Marche said, calling out to Negus.

The valet came in and made a deep bow to Valentine. "Your servant, my lady," he said, his eyes on the hem of the riding habit.

"Negus, I'd like you to meet Sir Valentine Randwick, Valeria's brother."

"Sir?"

"Take a good, long look. Does my bride not strike you as somewhat more handsome than pretty? More dashing than dainty?"

"If you say so, sir."

"Negus, this is no time to start behaving. Take a hard look at my wife and be honest."

The valet met Valentine's eyes in silent apology and traveled on, roving the property with the permission of the owner. "I'll take your word, sir, but I still see a woman, tall and handsome, but a woman to be sure."

Valentine spun toward Marche. "You have rehearsed this beforehand to humiliate me!" he accused.

Negus's eyes widened. "By the Blessed Brigit! You *are* a man!"

"Perhaps you could announce it once more," Marche said. "I do not think they heard the news in Town."

"Beg pardon, sir. I am quite recovered now and it shan't happen again. Would Your Grace care to tell me what you're perpetratin'?"

"That's a very good word, Negus," Lord Marche said before he explained the situation to his valet.

"I see," the elfin redhead said, taking another speculative look at Valentine. "May I say that you're both as mad as bees in a bottle?"

"You may not. Will you be so good as to help with all the female foofaraw?"

Negus rubbed his chin. "I'll be gettin' a large rise in me wages, did you say?"

"Colossal."

"Very well, my lord." Negus clapped his hands together softly. "Let us see what I remember from my misspent days on the boards. It is lucky the fashion these days is all for the natural look and that yon lad has wind-roses in his cheeks and the longest lashes I never saw."

A quarter of an hour later, the valet had coiled Valentine's braid into a bun that fit neatly under the nautical-looking hat. Teasing several tendrils loose to hang in long curls against the young man's brow, cheeks, and neck, Negus tweaked the gold netting of the useless little veil and stood back. "That should do for now, sir," he said. "When you return from your ride, I'll be here to make sure you are decked out proper for dinner. You've hardly any whiskers to speak of, but I've a sharp razor that will make short work of any sprouts."

"I thank you," Valentine said. "But this ruse will not hold for long."

"Not so long as we are in residence," Lord Marche said. "Once we set out on our bridal trip, we will be among strangers and can drop the charade."

"Perhaps you can contrive to lose me somewhere along the journey."

Marche frowned. "I suppose a tumble from the rotting tower of some old castle or other would be a simple means out of our predicament. You could vanish, and I could play the grief-stricken widower, but let's hold that in reserve, shall we?"

"You are older and presumably wiser," Valentine capitulated.

Negus made a noise suspiciously like a man stifling a laugh. "Shall I go and bring the horses round, sir?"

"What a spanking good idea," Marche said. "If we are to have company, please inform them that my bride and I will be down directly."

"Aye, sir."

"And Negus?"

"Sir?"

"Doesn't Her Grace look lovely?"

"She lives up to the title, sir." The valet smiled as he turned away.

"You do look lovely," Marche said to Valentine.

"And I am growing used to your humor, husband," the young man answered.

"Good lad. A bit of humor will go a long way to seeing you through the next few hours."

Valentine took Marche's offered arm. "I am not used to making light of serious subjects," he said as they swept into the hall. "But I shall make an effort."

CHAPTER 5

"SAINTS save me, Snow, there she is!" Darby St. Denis elbowed Lord Snowhurst aside for a better view as the Duke and Duchess Marche walked into the courtyard.

Crispin Ludstall staggered sideways and jostled a sorrel gelding. The horse stamped a hoof, narrowly missing his toes. "Damn your eyes, Strand!"

Neville Stokes, Lord Tarmegent, grinned at Crispin's outrage. He did not intend to climb aboard one of the large, unpredictable beasts, but he wouldn't have missed this show for a dukedom. Darby was madly in love again, which meant everyone else in their set soon would be. Life was so much more pleasant when they had something to focus on to fill their time.

"Did you see that, Tarmy?" Crispin asked as he brushed nonexistent dirt from his clothing. "Strand pushed me right under that animal's hooves."

"Haven't you heard, old boy? Love is blind… and maladroit, seemingly."

Crispin took a pull at his flask and offered it to his friend. "Even so, Strand might have a care for my new suit."

"Oh, I agree, my dear. It would be a sin to sully that fabric."

"Do you really like it?" Crispin preened.

"Desperately. I wish I had the flair to wear a peacock waistcoat with a plum jacket."

"Well, I have always been ahead of my time. I must say I adore your jonquil satin."

"Then you don't think my waistcoat makes me look like a gargantuan canary?"

"What? Heavens, no! I would never utter such words about you, dear."

"No, it's not really your style, is it? I *will* find the blackguard that *did* say it though."

"Let me know when you do and I shall avenge your honor."

Neville raised an eyebrow as Crispin swigged more brandy. "Much obliged. What do you propose as a just punishment?"

"I shall most likely vomit on his shoes."

"Be quiet, you witless wag-tongues!" Darby hissed. "My goddess approaches."

As Marche escorted Valentine to the horses, Darby stepped forth from the small crowd and began to declaim. "A shiver of reverence runs through my frame when in my hearing someone speaks your name. When the sound of your step draws near, my heart beats so loud, I scarcely can hear. My pulse thunders and my blood becomes as flame. Without you, the world is cold and drear." Lord Strand finished with a sweeping bow in front of the newly wedded couple.

Valentine looked up at Lord Marche for direction, gloved fingers tightening on the muscles of the man's forearm.

"What a charming wedding gift," Marche said. "Strand, you have outdone yourself. I am no fit judge of poetry, but I am moved, sir. As is Lady Marche."

"I must agree," the prince regent said as he arrived with his small retinue. "Just delightful, Strand. And your bride, Marche. Delightful. Very winning creature. Just delightful."

Valentine lowered his eyes in embarrassment and succeeded in appearing demure.

"Thank you, Your Highness," Marche said.

"She seems quite biddable as well," Murdmont said from behind the prince. "Very refreshing to see such ladylike behavior in such a robust young woman."

"How kind of you to say," Marche replied coolly before addressing the prince regent again. "Do you join us, Your Highness?"

"Me? Good heavens, no! I've an urgent game of faro awaiting me. However, if I had a nymph like your bride to pursue, I would, Apollo-like, make the effort. Damme, so I would!"

"How like a nymph of the fountain," Darby said loudly. "Her fame shall ring from every mountain. She shall never fade so long as I have breath to sing her praises and…." The poet's words trailed off. "I've not finished writing it yet."

"It's a lovely beginning, sir," Valentine ventured to remark.

"My Lady!" Lord Strand bowed profoundly. "You honor me. Allow me to serve you as your knight and champion. Give me but one token of your favor."

"No, she bloody well won't," Marche said, drawing Valentine away from the besotted young nobleman. "Come, my dear. Here is your horse."

Negus stood ready to offer a leg up. Valentine looked at the sidesaddle in confusion for just a moment before putting himself in the hands of Marche's valet. With a minimum of fuss, Negus got the young man aboard the horse with a knee hooked around the saddle horn.

"I had not thought of this," Marche said, looking up at his bride. "We will keep to a slow pace until you feel comfortable in that saddle." The new master of Wandeleigh and his lady rode off side by side. The guests who joined them for the ride followed a few lengths behind, chattering merrily as they traversed the well-maintained fields and parklands.

"It's beautiful," Valentine said when they drew rein at the crest of a gentle slope. On the leeward side, a layer of snow remained, covering the dry grasses like a lace shawl carelessly dropped on an autumn stroll.

"Yes, I daresay you're right," Marche mused. "But all I can think of is what perfect snowballs it would make."

"How so?" Valentine asked.

"It's melting a bit, you see, and so holds together better than fresh snow. Every boy knows this."

"I have never made a snowball."

Lord Marche's expression changed with comic rapidity. "That will never do!" he declared, sliding down from the saddle and holding up a hand to Valentine.

Because it was expected, Valentine allowed the man to help him to the ground. Large hands went around his waist, and he was lifted down with an ease that testified to Marche's great strength. The now-familiar roiling sensation churned in Valentine's lower regions, and he was bedeviled by a most extraordinary conundrum. He was absolutely certain that he didn't want the other man's hands on him, and yet he craved that touch with all his being. It was terribly trying, not to mention distracting at a time when he needed to focus on his task. Glad that the cold required gloves, Valentine gave Marche his hand and walked to a patch of snow.

"You simply scoop up a goodly handful and pat it into the shape of a ball, thus." Lord Marche held out the lumpy sphere he'd fashioned.

Valentine took the snowball and brought it close to his face. He loved the way snow looked as it floated down from a slate dark sky, and he loved the ephemeral chill of it on his tongue, but at the monastery, it was classed as a nuisance and assiduously swept away as soon as it landed.

"It's not for eating." Marche chuckled. "It's for throwing."

Valentine's smooth brow puckered in consternation. "Why would I throw it?"

"It's a game, you see. Two opposing sides choose their ground and hurl snowballs at one another until a victor emerges. I hear the king of the French is very keen on it."

"I see. That sounds much more sensible than hurling cannonballs at each other."

"That is a most unpatriotic observation, you know. As it happens, I agree with you, but it wouldn't do to repeat such sentiments in casual conversation."

"I am only a woman," Valentine replied. "Surely my opinion would not be taken seriously."

"That sounded very like sarcasm. You are learning quickly, my blushing bride."

"I may be ignorant of the world in practical experience, but I have read many books, sir."

"Indeed? And how did your education prepare you for this situation?" Marche smirked. The smug smile was wiped from his face by the snowball that struck him from close range.

"I absorb and employ new information very swiftly," Valentine said, bending down for more ammunition as laughter rose from the onlookers.

"What are you doing?" Marche asked.

"I am patting a goodly amount of snow into the shape of a ball."

"Minx!" the duke exclaimed as he ducked and dashed toward the shelter of his horse.

Valentine pursued, snowball in hand, smiling at the sight of the big man in retreat. Halfway up the slope, Marche's boot slipped on ice and he tumbled backward. He crashed into Valentine's knees, catching the young man in his arms as they went to the ground. They came to a stop, and Marche rolled once more so that he was topmost. Valentine's hat had come off and loose tendrils of hair were spread upon the snow. His lips burned red as berries, and Marche longed to taste their sweetness again. Raptly, he gazed upon the soft curves parted in a gasp for air, white teeth peeking out of the warm, wet rose petal folds.

"Damme, we're married," Marche whispered fiercely. "Why shouldn't I kiss you?"

The lords and ladies cooed and tittered, winking and nodding knowingly as the duke stole a kiss from his hoydenish bride. It was the verdict of this jury that the Behemoth had found a mate to match him, and the couple was unexpectedly captivating. Who could predict what gauche but thoroughly entertaining thing they would do next?

Valentine put his hands on Marche's chest as the other man claimed his lips in a kiss that clearly conveyed a deep hunger for more. And Valentine's traitor flesh wanted to give him more, wanted to surrender to this glorious force, but the power Marche wielded over him was frightening in its intensity, and he could not allow himself to give in. Though he burned with a heat that should have melted the snow under him, he pushed the duke away.

"Forgive me," Marche said. "I could not resist."

"Your apology might smack of more sincerity if you would get off me."

A slow smile spread over Marche's handsome face. "I cannot say it is my pleasure to comply, but I will do as you ask." He stood and offered his hand to Valentine. "I really couldn't resist," he said softly. "And it enhances the illusion of newlywed bliss."

"I understand, but must you be so demonstrative in public? Simply holding my hand or giving me a tender look would accomplish the goal as well as your methods and would not require the exertion of flinging me to the ground and putting your tongue in my mouth."

"Your way doesn't sound like much fun at all." Marche bowed slightly as Valentine passed him, headed for the horses.

"Your way is scandalous."

"Val." Marche caught hold of the young man's elbow. "If we keep our audience focused on our scandalous inability to keep our hands from one another, they won't even think to question your... female-ness."

Valentine thought a moment before he answered. "You are right," he said at last. "Be patient with me, sir. I thought you were merely indulging your carnal urges. I do not know why I am so ready to believe the worst of you, but I will endeavor to mend this fault in myself."

Marche closed his eyes briefly and when he opened them, Valentine was already in the saddle. He realized what he'd felt was a pang of shame for letting young Blythestone deceive himself. The duke didn't care for the feeling at all and concentrated his attention on the curve of Valentine's calf in the knee-high riding boot. *All is fair in love and war, and to the victor goes the spoils.* These were the principles with which Marche was raised. His physical needs had been so well taken care of that he'd never felt any lack or been conscious that there was anything missing in his life. The Duke of Marche had never known true want... until he met Valentine Randwick. He wanted this beautiful, intelligent but naïve young man, and he would have him.

CHAPTER 6

"HONORED guests," Marche began as he rose from his chair. "I cannot tell you what a pleasure it is to have you here to share in my newfound joy. My duchess and I are overwhelmed by the generosity of the wedding gifts and the warm wishes extended to us. I hope you will stay for the remainder of the week and enjoy the hospitality of Wandeleigh Hall, but alas, my bride and I must leave your pleasant company for the happiest of reasons. On the morrow, we set out on our first journey together as man and wife."

There was a polite round of applause and a few calls wishing the couple bon voyage. When the room was quiet again, Marche remarked that he hoped they would all attend the ball that evening. Bowing to his guests, he took Valentine's arm and escorted him from the room.

"Thank you," Valentine gasped as soon as they were out of earshot in the hall. "It is a marvel to me that women wear corsets all the day long. I can scarcely breathe. It was all I could do to eat some soup and a few scallops. I do hope your cook is not offended."

"You are expected to be too excited to have an appetite. Shall we go? You have barely two hours in which to get dressed for—" Marche stopped speaking abruptly and put an arm around Valentine's back. "Steady there," he said soothingly, as though cajoling a fractious mount. "You look a bit paler than usual."

"I am quite all right now. You may unhand me. It is just this damnable corset."

Marche's lips curved up at the sound of a curse word on Valentine's lips. "It seems I am corrupting you by the hour. Within a week, I will find you with a flask of brandy in one hand, cards in the other, and brace of pistols on the table in front of you."

"I have never tasted brandy." Valentine chose the least objectionable topic as they continued down the hall. "The abbot railed against it at least once a month. He said that ale and wine are gifts from the Almighty, but brandy, you see, is not brewed, but *distilled*. The name comes from the Dutch words for burnt wine and—"

Marche picked one word out of Valentine's conversation. "Abbot?"

"I assume you know the term," Valentine said briskly, quickening his steps as well as his speech.

"Of course." Marche lengthened his stride to keep pace. "But one typically speaks of one's *priest* railing against vice in the Sunday sermon, not an abbot."

Valentine opened the door of their suite and hurried inside. "My lessons were taken at a monastery," he temporized as he crossed to the bedchamber door. "I do hope that satisfies your curiosity."

"It's fascinating, but why would you seek to hide it from me?"

"For fear you would find it fascinating." Valentine took off his dainty pale blue gloves and placed them carefully on the vanity table.

A knock forestalled whatever Lord Marche would have said in reply. "Negus is here, sir," the valet called out.

"Excellent, come in," Marche said as he opened the door. "If you will be so good as to help my lady prepare for the ball, I will go and attend on my aunt. If she doesn't get a bit of personal attention, she'll come looking for us. We cannot put her off forever, but I will do what I may."

"As you wish, my lord," Negus inclined his head as his master brushed past him. "And now, my *lady*, why don't we make sure you shine down every chit at the ball, as is only proper, you bein' the bride and all. Are you game, young sir?"

"I shall do my best."

"That's the spirit, sir. Have you clapped eyes to the gown Lady B had run up for you?" Negus moved a tapestry screen aside.

"Oh dear," Valentine said, focusing on the low-cut bodice of the high-waisted gown.

"Not to worry, bonny lad." Negus produced a length of embroidered silk from the bag over his shoulder. "A shawl and a strategic fichu of lace, and you'll pass muster. Why don't you have a rummage in that chest and see if the lady loaned you a brooch that will do for this gown."

Valentine did as Negus asked, sorting through the glittering array of necklaces, bracelets, earrings, and tiaras. He found a large brooch of enamel fashioned in the likeness of an iris flower that met with Negus's approval.

"That's just the thing," the valet said. "Now let's get you out of that rig and into this one."

"MY DEAR boy." The dowager duchess offered her cheek to be kissed as Marche entered her withdrawing room. "You've neglected me shamefully, but I understand completely."

"Do you?" Marche murmured for her ears alone.

"I have been married three times, sir," she replied archly before dismissing her retinue of intimates. "We should speak seriously before you depart," she said once the room had cleared. "What if something should befall me whilst you are gallivanting about the Continent with that enchanting creature?"

"You find my duchess enchanting?"

"Yes, I do, and don't try to divert me. We are going to have a serious discussion, and then you may take yourself off to get dressed while I do the same. So you see? Our talk will be brief."

"I am at your command, ma'am."

"I hope you noted the presence of Murdmont at the festivities?"

"My sense of smell is in good working order."

"Don't be impertinent. Sir Malcolm has overseen our accounting houses for decades and has taken over as my private attorney, as well you know. Some might find him unsavory, and I know that many look down on his origins as a tradesman, but he has an eye for opportunity that is unblinking. Do you imagine it is easy for a man of low birth to rise to the level where he may purchase a title? I will not always be here to steer the family fortunes, and I would go to my final rest in peace if I knew there was a sharp fellow looking out for your affairs."

"If it eases your mind, I'll not oppose it," Marche said.

"It does ease my mind. Pray forgive my bluntness and the raising of such vulgar matters as finance, but sometimes things must be said aloud. I have revised my will to reflect your new status as a man with a wife, and I hope you will not mind that I set aside a goodly amount in Valeria's name. Murdmont arranged for me to buy Lamberglyn and rest of the old Danswell lands that border Wandeleigh to the west. This will be my gift to Valeria."

"And so Julius Randwick's estate returns to his daughter," Marche said. "Very neatly done."

"I thought it had a nice symmetry to it, and this way, the dear girl will always have her own money. There is not much that is more galling for a woman than having to depend on a man for income." Willamina sighed. "Now let us speak of more pleasant matters. I do hope that you enjoy each moment of your honeymoon. This time is given to you to be free of care while you become acquainted with one another. Once you return home, your social demands will fill most of your days."

"Do not, dear aunt, remind me again; I implore you."

Willamina reached up to touch his cheek. "You have always been a dutiful boy, Loel, but I never felt that your heart was in it. You have a pleasant smile, but you don't laugh often, and I have only seen you cry once. Tell me; I must know. Was I too distant, too stern? I knew I was too old to be a mother to you when your parents died, but I tried to give you some guidance."

"I have always thought of you as a mother," Marche said, kissing her hand. He knew that if he were a better man, he would admit this masquerade to her. However, he'd been pretending to be something he was not for most of his life, and it had become a habit that was hard to break.

Touched, it was a moment before Willamina trusted her voice. "I hope you will know happiness," she said at last. "As much as may be granted a man of your station."

"If you insist on being maudlin, you will make dull company."

Willamina smiled as her great-nephew rose to his feet. "Bon voyage, my dear," she said. "And you cannot hide Valeria away for much longer, you know. I can see you are infatuated, but you must share her with the world eventually."

"Infatuated?" Marche repeated.

"Be as coy as you like. I know your mind better than anyone save that mountebank you are pleased to call a valet. I have seen your eyes when you gaze on her. I am satisfied of your fondness and of your future happiness."

"I'll not dispute you for I haven't the time. I am sure Negus is waiting most impatiently to help me dress. Will you promise me a dance this evening?"

"Rogue." Lady Bolbracken's eyes sparkled as she struck him with her fan. "Go to your bride. Dance with her and take her off to bed. Show her you love her and sleep well before your journey. Tell Valeria not to worry about her mother and that she may choose a lady's maid from the Town house staff before you sail. Did I remember to tell you about the carriage? The barouche is at your disposal for as long as you require."

"You may have mentioned it, but not above a dozen times. Now, if you have no more instruction for me, I must dress."

"Go then, dear boy. We'll likely not exchange more than three words this evening, and I shall sleep late, so again I will say bon voyage and mean it with all my heart."

Marche bowed and took his leave. He was glad that his aunt was finally prepared to treat him like an adult and that the affection between them could be expressed, at least in words. However, it increased his feelings of shame in deceiving her. Irritably, he shook off the pangs of conscience like a man plagued by wasps. In due time, the real Valeria would reach her majority, and the charade would no longer be necessary. For some reason, the relief that Marche expected to feel did not attend the thought. *It's only that I haven't bedded the lad*, he reasoned. Indeed, he was enduring his longest stretch without a bed partner since he'd begun his sexual career shortly after puberty. Having identified the source of his uncharacteristic weakness, he resolved to remedy it as soon as possible.

NEGUS stood back and assessed his handiwork. "I am a-feared there's no hope for it. You make a most uncommon ravishin' female."

Valentine raised an eyebrow. "Why is the term ravishing considered a compliment? Have you any idea what it implies?"

The valet's freckled cheeks spread in a grin. "You and His Grace must have the most lively conversations," he said.

Valentine turned to regard his reflection in the large mirror. The gown of lavender satin was gathered just under the bust line to fall in lavish pleats to the floor. The Grecian style left his arms and shoulders bare, but Negus had disguised his musculature with a fringed silk shawl embroidered in violet, ivory and moss green. Lady Bolbracken's magnificent brooch secured the wrap at the sternum, with the soft folds adding to the illusion of the modestly padded bosom. Around Valentine's neck was a magnificent choker of diamonds, amethysts, and pearls that came up to his chin and dangled pendant gems over his collarbones. His hair was swept up and pinned with jeweled clips before being allowed to cascade down his back in a fall of long dark curls. No fashionable woman appeared in public without cosmetics, but Negus had applied them sparingly. Valentine's vivid coloring—violet eyes with dark brows and lashes, ivory skin, and rosy cheeks and lips—didn't require much paint to emphasize it.

"You are quite right, though." Valentine sighed.

"Sir?"

"I do make a convincing woman, if one is prepared to accept the height."

"And the strength of your jaw, sir, among other things," Negus said. "It does take a deal of skullduggery to get you up as a female, never you doubt it."

"I know you're trying to reassure me, and I do appreciate it. I wish others were as considerate."

"*Others* meanin' His Grace?"

"Why does he take such delight in teasing me?" Valentine burst out. "Oh good heavens! Pray do forgive me. It is unseemly for me to discuss your master with you."

"The duke and me don't always stand on ceremony." Negus winked, holding out a pair of elbow-length gloves. "If I may be so bold as to speak plainly with you, as I would to a mate…."

Valentine nodded permission as he took the lavender gloves with the Woodbine crest picked out in tiny pearls.

"I been with the duke since we were green lads, and I seen 'im all manner of weather, if you take my meanin'." Negus rested a finger along the bridge of his nose and winked.

"I do, and I can see that you are much more to him than a servant."

"Fate made him a duke and me a guttersnipe," Negus said without rancor. "Neither of us had no choice in our birth, and society give us precious few after that. But Lord Marche chose to be me friend, and I have been his as far as I may."

"It is a pity you can only be equals in private."

"Careful, my lady," Negus joked. "You'll be taken for one of them bluestocking hussies."

"I do not know the term."

"Well, it seems there's a circle of high-born ladies what like to gather and natter on about books and such. They like a Greek poem as well as a pretty bit of needlework."

"And for that they are, of course, considered odd and a subject for contemptuous jibes, I take it. If I were a woman in truth, I would wish to have an education." Intent on his words, Valentine did not notice that the door had opened behind him. "Until recently, I was largely ignorant of the conventions of our society, and I have been constantly shocked at the willful idiocy of some of them. However, none is more baffling to me than the position to which women are relegated. How can men be so shortsighted as to make fools of those they will take as partners for life? I do understand that a fool is easier to control, but surely men do not truly wish for wives who are naught more than living dolls. How dull that would be."

"A man and his wife may be equals in private," Marche said from behind Valentine.

The young man pivoted on his elegant heel. "I would sooner take vows than live such a half-life. These few days of pretense have been a preview of Hell's antechamber. How could anyone bear to carry out so large a deception for years and years?"

"They go a little mad, I would suppose."

"I agree. To maintain a dual nature inevitably entails a great fear of discovery. No sane person could bear it for long."

"Do you truly believe that?"

"Your Grace," Negus spoke up. "Your clothes are laid out for you."

Irritated by the interruption, Marche answered curtly. "Have you finished with the lady?"

"No, sir, I had not, not quite. There were one or two things I meant to say, by way of askin' Lord Blythestone to be patient with you, pointing out a few of your better qualities, like. No matter; you're in a hurry to be rid of me, I see, so I'll scarper off to me cupboard."

"Negus, wait. I've not complimented you on Valentine's appearance. He will outshine every lady at the ball."

"Then thank the lad, sir. It is his fair face that shines and not those fripperies."

"I see. Well then, I suppose I had better do what I may to make myself presentable."

When His Grace was dressed, Negus stepped back and touched his brow as though tipping a hat. "'Til the morrow, m'lord. I'll have the carriage 'round front, ready to go when you've had your breakfast."

"That will do nicely. Good night to you, then."

"Thank you, Negus," Valentine called after the valet.

"It's a pleasure to serve you," Negus said with a bow.

"I would swear that you take a deplorable pleasure in being as disagreeable as possible," Valentine said.

"What has prompted this attack on your beloved husband?" Marche inquired.

"You spoke to Negus as though he were a forward servant."

"Negus *is* a forward servant."

"But not a gossip it would seem, else your proclivities would be well known."

"My… *proclivities*?" Marche smiled.

"You know what I speak of: your fondness for your own gender."

"It is more than a fondness, I assure you."

"You do not even have the decency to be ashamed of your aberration."

"Why should I?" Marche took two long strides to stand in front of Valentine. "Tell me why I should feel shame. For *if* I am as God made me, then it is He that causes this fire in my loins when I look at you. Tell me what shame there can be in that."

"There is a fallacy in your argument." Valentine frowned. "And I will find it."

"I fear you have no time just now for intellectual pursuits. Our guests are waiting for us to dance the first dance." Marche's scowl lightened. "Do not look so panicked; just follow my lead and you will do well enough."

"I am on tenterhooks. The thought of being exposed as a charlatan makes me queasy. I do not know if I could bear the staring eyes and pointing fingers."

"It will not happen as long as we are careful." Marche took the young man's hand. "Are you ready to take the stage once again?"

Valentine stared up at Marche in perplexity. "You are an odd and disconcerting blend of cold self-interest and sudden kindness."

"And you look quite adorable at this moment. I wish we were wed in truth, and I could take you to that bed and make all those fine nobles wait while I take my pleasure."

Valentine dropped his eyes. "I wish you would not say such things," he murmured.

"Because they disgust you or because they excite you?"

"Why would you suppose for a moment that your suit would be welcome?"

Marche chuckled warmly as he opened the doors to their quarters. "I have kissed you. Have you forgotten?"

"How would that be possible?" Valentine said stiffly as he swept into the hall.

"No matter what you may say, minx, your body does not lie. You crave my touch as I crave to touch you. Deny it and I will know you for a liar."

"Ah, here they are," the prince regent called loudly as he spotted the couple. "Pray do not deprive us any longer of the bewitching Duchess of Marche's company. Come, my dear; come and let me do homage to a goddess, and then you and your fortunate husband may commence to dance."

"You are young, beautiful, and a mystery," Marche whispered quickly in Valentine's ear. "They want to love you; let them."

Valentine lifted his chin and smiled sweetly at the rotund Prince of Wales. "Your Highness," he said in a soft voice brimming with respect. "It would be my honor... and my pleasure."

"Oh, would it? Would it indeed? Delightful," Prince George said. "Marche had better look sharp, my dear, or I might steal you from him. You are simply delightful."

Marche bowed. "As a loyal subject, all that I have is yours, Your Highness... except this one jewel. At the risk of being branded a traitor, I would never give her up, not even to you."

"The devil you say!" George struck a pugilist's pose. "Shall I thrash him?" he called out to the onlookers. "Oh, I say; I am feeling quite the thing today. What do you say, Marche? Will you fight me for the girl?"

"No! I beg you, sir. Please, do not hurt my husband!" Valentine cried out, taking hold of the prince's arm.

"There, there, my dear," George said. "I was only fooling about, and Marche knows it as well, don't you, Marche?"

Marche bowed. "Your highness is the soul of wit."

"There, you see?" the prince patted Valentine's hand. "I say, Marche, you *are* a lucky hound to have such a sweet defender."

"Indeed I am, sir, and with your permission, my lady and I will lead the first dance."

"That would be simply delightful."

Prince George bowed to Valentine and handed him off to Marche. Valentine curtsied and let Marche lead him to the center of the floor. All eyes were on the couple as Marche put a hand lightly on his tall bride's waist and took her hand. After a brief hesitation, Valentine remembered that his hand went on the other man's shoulder. They were poised to waltz when orchestra began to play a quadrille. Marche stepped quickly back, bowing to Valentine who sank into a deep curtsy. The dancing master called the figures, and Valentine kept his eyes on his partner, mirroring Marche's actions. After a few steps, other pairs joined them and the footwork became livelier. Finally, the music ended, and Valentine was greatly relieved until a country-dance was called for. Couples formed two lines, the men facing the women, and they skipped back and forth to a sprightly melody, changing partners on each pass. By the halfway point, Valentine was out of breath and a little giddy from being twirled around.

"My dear sir," he said faintly to his current partner. "I beg your pardon, but I feel somewhat light-headed."

Gilbert Traverton, the marquess of Hapwood and husband of the matron of honor, instantly spun Valentine out of the dance and offered his arm. "You look quite overcome, ma'am. Allow me to escort you to a quiet refuge where you may recover your vitality."

"Thank you." Valentine leaned on the young nobleman as his dizziness worsened.

Pulled into an impromptu reel by two vivacious belles, Marche did not notice as Gilbert walked Valentine to the door of the ballroom. Lord Hapwood opened the door of a withdrawing room and gestured to Valentine to precede him. With a quick glance up and down the hall, Gilbert closed the door. "Allow me to prepare you a restorative," Hapwood said as he went to the sideboard. Selecting a faceted decanter, he poured an inch of dark amber liquid into a tumbler. "Here you are, ma'am," he said, offering the drink. "Brandy will do you right."

Valentine didn't make a fuss about his ignorance of strong spirits. The fumes rising to his nose already made him feel more alert. Perhaps a few sips would strengthen him. Putting the glass to his lips, he swallowed half the contents. The brandy blazed a trail down his throat to set a fire in his belly that warmed him from the inside out. If only he could loosen the suffocating corset, he was sure he would make a full recovery. "Thank you," he whispered. "I feel better."

To Valentine's surprise, Gilbert went down on one knee and gazed ardently up at him. Taking the tumbler, Lord Hapwood set it on the floor and clasped Valentine's hand. "How I have longed for an opportunity to be alone with you, lady," he said. "You have stirred my senses and overthrown my caution. You look at me with the eyes of heaven, and I entreat you to take me there, my angel." Valentine was so taken aback that he could think of nothing to say in reply. Gilbert hurried to fill the gap of silence with more heated declarations. "Never have I seen a lady of such noble stature who yet looks as innocent as any milkmaid. There is a light of purity in your face that beckons me like a beacon to a ship lost at sea. If you will not look kindly on me, I swear I shall perish from the lack of your warm affection as flowers in the winter die for lack of the sun. Will you not show mercy?"

Valentine tried to pull his hand from Gilbert's and lost a glove for his trouble. "Sir—" he began before the persistent lord interrupted him.

"You have no match, and it is not fair that you should go to the Behemoth before better men were granted the honor of paying court. It is not fair, I say, and I must have you."

"My lord!" Valentine tried to rise but was hemmed in by the nobleman now pressed against his knees, gripping his hand like a lifeline.

"Nay, do not flee." Gilbert put a hand on the arm of Valentine's chair and leaned closer. "Give me but a kiss, one sweet kiss, and I will be content for now."

"A kiss?" Valentine repeated, trapped as much by his clothing as by the other man. It was true that he was woefully ignorant of the customs of courtship, but he could not believe that it was acceptable to kiss another man's wife.

Hapwood smiled in anticipation of another conquest as he pulled Valentine closer. The smug expression was knocked from his face when Valentine's fist struck his jaw in an awkward uppercut. Gilbert toppled backward, knocking over the glass and measuring his length on the carpet as Valentine leapt to his feet. The door opened and Hapwood's wife minced into the room as he sat up in a puddle of brandy. The marchioness took in the scene, and her face curdled as though she'd caught wind of a very unpleasant odor.

"The least you could do is stand when a lady enters, Gilbert," she said. Her gaze dropped to his crotch, and she amended her statement. "Never mind, I see you have."

"Georgiana!" Hapwood scrambled to his feet. "You misapprehend. I was coming to the duchess's aid when I lost my footing on this cursed thick carpet."

"I marvel that you make the effort to lie," Georgiana sniffed as she turned her gaze from her husband to Valentine. "Ah, the blushing bride, an honor to have attended you. Lady Bolbracken would have us believe that you are a simple girl, convent raised and pure as dew, but I am not so easily cozened. Lord knows you look as pristine as fresh fallen snow, but that is just your art. I see the adventuress under your disguise." Lady Hapwood laughed. "Don't look so devastated, my dear. I won't give you away; I admire you."

"You admire me?"

"Of course. Your pose of artlessness is the best I have ever seen. When you enter London society, be sure that you may call on me as a friend."

Stunned by the lady's indifference to her husband's philandering, Valentine fell back on his natural politeness. "That is very kind of you."

"No, it isn't," Gilbert said. "It would be quite a coup for Georgiana to be the first to receive you in London."

"Pray do not speak when you know nothing of the subject under discussion," Georgiana replied. "We are not in public now, Gilbert, and if you want the rough side of my tongue, you may have it."

"Very well, my dear, but do not trifle with this one," Gilbert said, touching his jaw. "I feel as though I've been kicked by a horse."

"No more than you deserve," Georgiana said dismissively. "Come, we cannot linger here. There will be talk enough already if anyone besides me noticed your mutual absence. Let us return to the ball and give the duchess a chance to collect herself." With a small curtsy, she turned to take Gilbert's arm.

Valentine waited until the door had closed on them before he moved. His hand was beginning to throb with pain, but it was secondary to the shock of what had just occurred. If he were a woman in truth, he did not doubt that the encounter would have had a far different outcome. He glanced into the looking glass, but the reflection revealed little sign of the recent struggle. It was utterly absurd that a man had tried to make forceful love to him in this room and the only evidence was a damp patch of carpet. Pulling the silk shawl more closely around his shoulders, Valentine returned to the ball and Marche's side. As he arrived, Lord Strand stood forth and bowed.

"My lord and lady and noble friends, will you do me the honor of hearing some verses dedicated to the goddess bride?"

"Bloody nuisance," Marche said under his breath as the baronet made another flourishing bow. Leaning close to Valentine, he continued, "I missed you."

"I was… indisposed," Valentine whispered back as Darby St. Denis began to proclaim his adoration in language as florid as it was sincere.

When the ode finally ended, Valentine thanked the poet and declared he was quite overcome by the beauty of the offering. Taking the cue, Lord Marche announced that he and his bride would be retiring and that they hoped their guests would continue to make merry for as long as they wished. As they made their way to the entrance of the ballroom, Murdmont begged a moment of Marche's time. Out of respect for his aunt, Marche assented, and Valentine went on ahead, reaching the hallway to the private quarters with a sigh of relief. He nearly jumped out of his skin when someone spoke from the top of the stairs, but he recognized the voice and politely agreed to a talk in private. It didn't take long, and he was undressed and in bed when Marche arrived. Pretending sleep, Valentine listened to the other man move about the room until he fell asleep in truth.

CHAPTER 7

VALENTINE woke to the sound of loud voices. He saw Marche at the door, naked as the day he was born, shouting at someone in the antechamber. It was several long moments before Valentine made sense of the words. He was mesmerized by the sight of the duke's broad back, tapered waist, and long well-muscled legs. When he realized he was staring fixedly at the other man's firm-looking buttocks, he blushed scarlet and got up to put on a dressing gown.

"Now you've woken my wife, Murdmont," Marche said. "I shall have to consider whether the matter merits a challenge to a duel, but I tell you truthfully that if you do not leave my door this instant and have the good manners to save your business until after breakfast, then I shall be forced to thrash you in the hallway and be damned to who might see."

"Your Grace?" A newcomer joined the conversation.

"Negus? Damme, are you with the delegation from Bad Manners?"

"Sir, there is news, bad news that isn't suitable for caterwauling through shut doors."

"Why the deuce didn't Murdmont say that in the first place? We've been exercising our lungs to no productive good for half the morning. Let me be certain that my duchess is prepared to receive visitors, and you shall be given admittance."

Marche turned and Valentine's gaze dropped. It was as though his eyes were magnets and Marche's cock made of iron. Valentine simply could not look away. For some reason, a goodly few inches of flesh drew him like nothing he'd ever yearned for in his life. There bloomed within him a keen desire to touch it, to test the texture of skin that looked as soft as rose petals, to place a kiss on the very tip and feel it warm against his lips. A slow wave of heat caused his shaft to harden even as it liquefied his insides. Mortified, he gave his sash more attention than it needed. He was so flustered that he couldn't manage to tie a simple bow.

"Allow me," Marche said, taking the ends of the wide ribbon from Valentine's shaking hands. "Look at you; you're all a-tremble. Curse Murdmont for a clumsy villain! There." He finished tying the sash and looked into Valentine's eyes. "Are you ready, or would you like a few moments to gather yourself after being so rudely awakened?"

Valentine glanced at the windows. "It is not even dawn yet."

"Yea or nay?"

"I suppose we must let them in if we are to learn what all the bustle is about."

"Good lad," Marche said, patting Valentine's satin-covered shoulder. "I will deal with this, and we shall board our carriage and be away from this madhouse."

"And I may don male attire again."

"I cannot wait to see you in breeches."

"You had better find your own breeches, if you intend to entertain guests."

Marche looked down. "Ah yes. It is my habit to sleep *au natural*. I hope it does not trouble you."

"Of course not, why should it?"

"No reason at all." Marche smirked as he drew on a dressing gown of deep green.

"I have seen a cock before," Valentine said, speaking the word for the first time without referring to a male chicken. "I have one, too, you know."

"Indeed I do. I've had but the briefest touch, but I'll wager you've a handsome set of tackle."

Valentine held his breath as the other man moved behind him and slipped an arm around his waist. He didn't move as Marche's hand drifted downward and into the voluminous folds of his gown. Acutely aware that he was naked and aroused under all that satin, Valentine was frozen by conflicting desires. As Marche's fingertips brushed his bare belly, the knocking resumed.

"Hellfire! I had forgotten our unwanted guests." Marche yanked his hand from Valentine's robe and went to the door.

Valentine managed to walk to a chair and sit before Negus came in bearing a large tray. Behind the valet stalked Murdmont like a crow chasing a sparrow.

"Now, Sir Malcolm," Marche said. "What business is so urgent it requires you to be here before the day has fairly begun?"

"I regret that I must be the one to inform you, but the Duchess of Bolbracken has passed on."

Valentine looked up from the cup of hot chocolate that Negus was pouring. The young man's shock was patent on his guileless face before he lowered his head again, remembering that it was his husband's place to speak for them both.

Marche's eyes went to his valet. The small nod Negus gave him was all the confirmation Marche needed. "How? And how is it that you are the one to bring the news."

"Well, sir, I am the lady's barrister, after all." The candlelight gleamed on the dark wings of Murdmont's center-parted hair as he tilted his head to the side. "Her death hardly discharges me of my duties."

"Just so," Marche said stiffly as he turned to Valentine. "If you will excuse me?"

"Where are you going?" Murdmont inquired.

"To see my aunt, of course."

"In that case, we should all go."

Valentine got to his feet. "I agree," he said, going to take Marche's arm. "I should be with you at such a time."

Marche's gaze met the young man's briefly, and in Valentine's eyes, he saw compassion and the offer of support. "Thank you," he murmured as he let Murdmont lead the way to his aunt's rooms.

Willamina's personal physician was washing his hands when her heir entered. "I am so sorry, Your Grace," Dr. Sawyer said. "The dear lady has indeed passed over."

"She was hale as a carthorse at the ball," Marche said.

"She seemed in good health to me also, Dr. Sawyer," Murdmont added.

"The lady was not immune to the effects of time, but I did not foresee her death for several years to come," the doctor agreed. "There is no polite way to say this, so I will simply come out with it. I believe she was poisoned."

"The devil you say!" The way Marche loomed over the physician, it was not hard to see how he'd earned the sobriquet of Behemoth.

"I am afraid it would appear so, sir."

Marche went to the bed and stared down at the still figure decorously swathed to the chin with a rich coverlet embroidered with the Woodbine coat of arms. The old dragon looked terribly small in the big bed, and though the doctor had closed her eyes, her face bore the signs of agony. Abruptly, Marche knelt, took her limp hand between both of his, and bowed his head over it. "I shall miss you," he said.

Because it was the right thing to do, Valentine felt free to put a hand on the kneeling man's shoulder. "I am so sorry."

"Are you, ma'am?" Murdmont said, just loudly enough to be overheard.

Lord Marche's head came up. "Is it possible my hearing is affected by my grief, doctor?"

"If so, then we are both so afflicted," Dr. Sawyer answered. "What can you mean by your words, Sir Malcolm?"

"I'll not be coy for it is not in my nature," Murdmont said. "I have reasons, very good ones, to suspect the Duchess of Marche of having a hand in my client's death."

"You will explain yourself." Marche rose to his feet and started toward the attorney.

"Please, no violence in this room," the doctor said. "Out of respect for the deceased."

"You expect me to swallow this insult to my wife?"

"I believe he expects you to behave as a gentleman," Valentine said, disengaging his fingers from Marche's sleeve. He couldn't recall catching hold of the other man's arm, but he'd been dragged along as though he weighed nothing. "Allow Lord Murdmont to explain."

"Yes, this is quite a serious accusation, Sir Malcolm," the doctor said. "I should like to hear your reasoning in implicating this worthy young woman. However, I think we should first retire to the withdrawing room and leave milady in peace."

"Very well," Marche said, the muscles bunching along his clenched jaw. "Negus!" he called out. "Confound it, where is the man?"

"He did not accompany us from our quarters," Valentine said.

"Do you have some special need of him?" Murdmont asked as they moved into the next room. "For I think there are enough servants about to do your bidding."

"Yes, it is the comfort and the curse of great wealth to always have people about," Marche said. "I am still waiting for you to apologize to my wife or show just cause for your aspersion."

"It is a fact that yesterday Lady Willamina sent for me to alter her will to include this young woman."

"That is only natural," Doctor Sawyer said.

"My aunt only informed me of this last evening," Marche added. "My wife could have had no knowledge of it."

"Are you quite certain of that, Marche?" Murdmont turned his chilly gaze on Valentine. "Have you nothing to say, *lady*?"

Valentine did not have to think about his answer; he simply spoke the truth. "Lady Willamina stopped me on my way to my rooms last night. She requested a private talk and I went with her to… to this chamber. She told me she looked forward to knowing me better and that she had written me into her will." He looked up at Marche from his chair. "I had not time to tell you before now."

"So you see, she did know," the barrister said. "The gaining of riches is often a motive for murder, and I believe it will prove so in this case."

"There is no case," Marche said. "This is not a trial."

"Have it your way, sir. We can wait until we return to London and take this matter before a magistrate, or we can settle it here, with the prince regent presiding. I presume you will accept his authority as a judge."

"And who do you propose as jury?"

"Why, I assumed Prince George would be judge *and* jury."

Marche glanced from the dour attorney to Valentine. The young man sat on the edge of an elegant little chair in a welter of lace and rosebud satin, his glossy hair loose upon his shoulders, his earnest gaze fixed on Marche. "You must answer, my dear," Marche said as the silence stretched out.

"I have no objection to that arrangement," Valentine said. "I have nothing to fear for I have done nothing to cause the dear lady's death."

"Have your tribunal then," Marche told Murdmont. "And when it is over, I will insist on your apology or you will face me on the field of honor. Is that understood, sir?"

"I rely upon my wits rather than brute strength," Sir Malcolm replied.

"So you say. I have heard rumor that you rely upon the brute strength of others like the coward you are."

Murdmont gave Marche a sharp look, but before he could respond, Dr. Sawyer interrupted. "Gentlemen, please!" the doctor said. "I have sent the prince regent a short note acquainting him with the gist of the matter. I appreciate that our feelings are running at full flood just now, but we are Englishmen and we will not let our emotions rule us. Begging your pardon, ma'am," Sawyer bowed in Valentine's direction.

Valentine smiled faintly. "I am sure English*women* also were implied in your speech, sir."

"Indeed they were. Bravery on the battlefield is but one kind of courage. Now, my lords and lady, I will tell you what I wrote to the prince. I thought at first that the duchess might have contracted some terrible disease. She was wracked with vomiting and delirious when I arrived, and there was little I could do, other than make her last moments comfortable. It was only after her maids had attended to her that I saw the signs of realgar poisoning."

"Arsenic!" Valentine exclaimed without thinking. "It would have to have been quite a heavy dose to kill her so quickly, would it not?"

The doctor nodded. "You are very learned young woman it seems."

"I was schooled in a convent, sir. The nuns made use of realgar and orpiment in some of their medicines. Poor Lady Willamina, her end would not have been pleasant." Valentine paused. "Forgive me, Lord Marche."

"I do not care where you gained your expertise with poisons," Murdmont said. "It is enough for me that you have the crucial knowledge. I also find it interesting that you call your husband Lord Marche."

"It is no great mystery, sir," Valentine answered. "It is only that you are not part of my private life, and since I have no wish to bring you into it, I maintain a formal bearing in your presence."

"Rely upon your wits, man," Marche suggested when Murdmont did not immediately reply.

"You have taken a viper to your bosom, Marche. I do not blame you; the girl is ripe and you have a large carnal appetite, by all evidence. However, she is as cunning as she is comely, and I think you will cease to champion her when you have heard all the facts."

"You are wrong. I love my wife and there is nothing that can change that."

At these words, Valentine's heart fluttered within its cage of bone, beating wild wings, ready to fly. Clenching his hands into fists in the thick folds of his gown, he recalled that Marche was playing a part, and what did it matter to him anyway where the wretched rake's affections were bestowed? Why should his heart feel as though it wished to leave his chest when Marche spoke of love? Why did his traitor flesh rise at a mere glance from the man? Was he the same as Marche and the others that cleaved to their own sex? It seemed so to judge by the way he reacted whenever Marche touched him or simply stood too close. If he was scrupulously honest with himself, he would admit that he wanted to know what would happen if he let Marche have his way. "Thank you, husband," he said.

Marche moved to stand beside Valentine's chair, taking his hand so they faced Murdmont together. "My aunt engaged your services because she reckoned that you were a bit of a bulldog, Sir Malcolm," he said. "I can see she was right. As soon as your duties as executor of her estate are concluded, you may consider yourself let go."

"I assumed as much. Your indignation amuses me. Tell me; exactly how much do you know about your bride?"

"She is the answer to my prayers."

"Spoken like a smitten man." Murdmont barely refrained from sneering. "However, I guarantee you that she is not what she seems."

Valentine's gaze was stricken as he glanced up at Marche. *What were they to do now that Murdmont knew their secret?*

"Hold up there, Murdmont," the prince regent commanded as he came into the room behind a footman. "I would like to hear this as well, if you please."

Marche gestured and the servant set a chair in the middle of the room. The prince sat, carefully arranging the skirts of his magnificent blue velvet dressing gown. Graciously, he waved everyone back to his or her place. His favorite, Beau Brummell, stood artfully behind George's seat, adjusting the hang of his cape.

"Now then," the prince said, looking around the room. "Ah, Doctor Sawyer, I believe I am correct in saying that everyone would benefit from a dram of something heartening just now."

"A restorative is a very good idea, Your Highness. Allow me to pour a few glasses of claret."

"Terribly sorry to hear of the Duchess of Bolbracken's demise," the prince said to Marche. "I was quite fond of her. She was an original."

Marche bowed. "Thank you for saying so, Your Highness."

"Ma'am, I am sorry I must intrude on you under such sorrowful circumstances."

Valentine looked modestly down. "Your Highness is very kind and could never be counted as an intrusion."

George smiled fondly at Valentine before turning his attention to Lord Murdmont. "What's this I hear about you thinking this lady could have anything to do with murder?"

Murdmont bowed to the prince and repeated the information that the Duchess of Marche knew she stood to inherit a very great deal of wealth.

"So does Marche," the prince regent pointed out. "I don't see you accusing him of murder."

"He is a known quantity, my lord. Though he is brutish in appearance and has a violent temper, I do not think he could do murder in cold blood. This woman, however, is a stranger. Think you back to her arrival, days late without baggage or attendants. Who is to say that she is not an adventuress who has taken the place of the real Miss Randwick?"

"Preposterous," the doctor burst out. "Anyone may see for themselves that she is a noblewoman of exquisite breeding."

"I quite agree, sir," the prince nodded. "A delightful creature, but we must be fair and let Murdmont have his say."

"My point is this," Murdmont said. "Can this woman prove that she is Valeria Randwick?"

"Of a certainty!" Marche answered. "My aunt would not have let me wed a Gypsy, I assure you."

"No, I daresay she would not," the prince snorted.

Murdmont drew himself up stiffly. "This strumpet has hoodwinked you all with her demure demeanor, but none can deny the facts. She has knowledge of poisons. She has good motive for murder, and she was the last to see the deceased alive."

"You have not shown one shred of evidence that the lady has the nature to do such a thing."

"Allow me to continue, Your Highness. Earlier, the duke was surprised to find that his wife had visited his aunt. From this we may deduce that she keeps secrets from him."

"Swallop," Marche muttered.

"Nonsense, is it? Then I assume you would be surprised to find that your innocent bride has kept other clandestine assignations?" Murdmont said slyly.

"Assignations!" Marche repeated. "How dare you, sir!"

"How do suppose I came by this?" Sir Malcolm pulled an elbow-length glove from his pocket.

"That's—" Lord Marche paused and looked down at Valentine. "Is that your glove, my dear?"

Valentine stared at the violet velvet sewn with tiny pearls and his stomach rolled over. "I dropped it at the ball," he said.

"Would you care to tell us where?" Murdmont prompted.

"In a withdrawing room, the one with the chinoiserie drapes."

"And how did you come to be so careless?"

Valentine looked up at Marche. "I—" he began and faltered. No matter how he recounted the incident, it would sound unseemly.

Marche's brow furrowed. "Do not be afraid to speak," he encouraged Valentine. "I know you could never be guilty of impropriety."

"Your faith is touching, sir, but perhaps we should call upon the marquess of Hapwood and hear his account," Murdmont said.

"What is this cur yapping about?" Marche asked Valentine.

"It is difficult to explain. I have done nothing wrong, yet I will look extremely foolish or extremely guilty no matter what I say."

"You must speak the truth, my dear," Prince George said kindly.

Valentine laced his fingers together and spoke without looking at Marche. "I was dizzy from the reel, and Sir Gilbert offered to escort me to where I might sit out of the noise and bustle. He poured a glass of brandy for me and a few moments later his wife joined us. I cannot rightly say how I came to leave my glove behind."

"Is that the entire truth?" Murdmont pressed.

"Nothing else of any consequence happened."

"Hapwood's wife says differently. The marchioness claims that you attempted to seduce her husband and gave him the glove as a sort of trophy."

Valentine looked up in surprise at this lie. "That is not true, sir!"

"I fear we shall have to send for the Hapwoods," the prince said.

"It is true that Sir Gilbert held my hand and tried to kiss me, but I believe he meant to give me comfort." Valentine rose to his feet. "I do not like this talk of seduction."

"Are you unwell, my dear?" the prince asked. "I think we might take a few minutes and let the lady rest. Would you like to go to your boudoir, ma'am?"

"She must have a guard," Murdmont said quickly.

"I hardly think that will be necessary. Surely, you don't expect the girl to climb out of a third-story window. Go on, my dear. Someone will call on you before too long."

"Your Highness," Valentine said as he curtsied. The footman opened the door and Valentine walked through. He didn't wish to leave while others decided his fate, but, as a woman, what choice did he have? Now he faced an undetermined length of time in which to worry over what was being said and what Marche was thinking about his new wife's encounter with handsome Gilbert, Lord Hapwood. When a footman looked inquiringly at Valentine, the young man realized he was lingering. Picking up his heavy skirts, he hurried away.

CHAPTER 8

VALENTINE settled on the window seat and stared out through the small panes of leaded glass. The leafless trees and gray skies were a match for his present mood, and the blanket of white snow was a metaphor for his lack of ideas. How was he to explain that things were not as they seemed? The duke was not a trusting man to begin with, and now Valentine had seen his temper. How could he hope that Marche would even listen to him after hearing whatever lies the Hapwoods told? He supposed he would be lucky if he were given a ride to the gates of the estate in the clothes he'd arrived with. He'd be turned out in the cold without a penny to find his way as best he could.

However, it was not this bleak prospect that turned his heart to a lump of black ice in his chest. It was the thought of leaving Marche. Now that he faced it, it was clear to him what he would lose if he were banished. He had never known anyone like Loel Woodbine, and he was fascinated by him. He would miss the arrogant, brusque, stubborn man who had taken such shocking liberties with him but who had also taken him at face value, trusting him as an equal partner. Even though it was a terrible sin, he would regret never taking the opportunity to satisfy his curiosity about the way of a man with another man. Most of all, he would miss the camaraderie that had begun to grow between them. It made no sense, but it was true that he actually enjoyed the big man's teasing humor, the way he....

Valentine's reverie was interrupted when the outer door opened and closed again. Marche knocked at the bedroom door and called out. Before Valentine found his voice, the door opened and the duke strode into the room. Valentine rose, his unbound hair haloed by the winter sun as he silently waited for Marche to pronounce his doom.

"Fool," the duke said.

Valentine met Marche's eyes, as sharp and golden as a hawk's, and held that fierce gaze without flinching. "That is somewhat unclear. Do you mean that I am a fool, or that you are a fool?" he said, his nerves too frayed to censor his speech.

"I would say we are all fools below heaven, but in this particular instance, you are a fool for allowing yourself to be alone with a hound like Gilbert. I am a fool for believing for an instant that you would betray even a sham wedding vow. Murdmont is a fool to think he can make you take the blame for my aunt's murder. And Prince George is a fool for... well, dear George is not really the subject under discussion."

"Please be so good as to remind me of the subject. I've become lost in your list of fools."

"Don't be disagreeable. You are the one that went to a private room with a man who is not your husband. Married less than a week and already at the heart of two scandals."

"Cad!" Valentine exclaimed. "To think I was distressed at the prospect of leaving you."

"Leaving me?" Marche stepped forward and took hold of Valentine's wrists. "Where are you going?"

"Why must you be forever grabbing at me?"

"If I let go, I might lose you."

"Your jests are not welcome just now."

"I was joking about your scandalous nature. I am not joking about keeping you."

"It is not fair of you to toy with me. I have no experience in—"

Marche pulled Valentine against his chest and paused with his lips a breath away from the other man's face. "I am not playing," he said before his mouth touched Valentine's in a tender kiss. "I was so very angry with you," he murmured as a breathless Lord Blythestone gazed into his eyes. "When Hapwood boasted that he had tasted your sweetness… I have never known such rage. Had it not been for the presence of the prince's guards, I might have killed him with my bare hands."

"I did not betray you with the marquess," Valentine said. As soon as the words had tumbled from his lips, he realized he'd given himself away. By the look on the other Marche's face, he realized what Valentine's speech implied, and his next question confirmed it.

"Then you admit that there is something to betray?"

Valentine's gaze dropped to the level of Marche's collarbones. "Please do not be so cruel as to continue this game. Speak boldly, if you must, but speak honestly; I beg you."

"Like all men, I want to know my wager is sure before I place the bet, but I will show my cards first if you wish it."

"You risk nothing, sir," Valentine murmured, glancing upward. The look of fading anxiety in Marche's eyes told him he'd chosen the right words this time. Even though what he felt could condemn his soul, he would own up to it.

"Minx." Marche chuckled in relief. "I can scarcely believe I've been snared by a callow youth as careful of his virtue as nun, but damme if I haven't fallen into those big violet eyes, and I am like to drown there. Do you truly feel the same?"

Valentine plucked up his courage. He was not a child; he was a man, and he felt the same urges that all men felt. It was only that he'd been trained to deny his desires from a very early age, and it was not an easy habit to be shed of. However, if he could not tell this man what he wanted, he would lose this chance and be forever doomed to wonder might have been. "I—" Valentine swallowed, his throat gone abruptly dry. "I know you… want me," he began again.

"God's weskit!" Marche cursed. "Of course I want you. The moment I saw you standing in the doorway of the chapel and you were naught more than a broodmare foisted on me by my aunt, I wanted you. I could not understand how a woman could stir me so, for I have known since boyhood that I was not attracted to the fairer sex. When I discovered that you were a man, I wanted you with a lust hotter than hellfire. I knew it was unwise, but wisdom is no great bar to love."

"Love?"

"Now it is you who are cruel. It is not easy for me to bare my heart and—"

"May I speak?" Valentine interrupted.

"It would be a mercy."

"I know you want me," Valentine said again. "To my great wonder, I want you too." His breath was driven from his lungs when Marche tightened his hold, and it was a moment before he could go on. "I had resolved that the next time you importuned me that I would not resist, but I never thought I would hear words of love from you."

Marche leaned his forehead against Valentine's. "Had it not been for my aunt's death, I might have gone on deceiving myself about you. I might have seduced you and moved on to the next conquest, but the way you stood beside me was a revelation and seeing you threatened was a terrible shock. The depth of my fear frightened me."

"You were afraid?"

"Absolutely terrified." Marche smiled at Valentine's incredulous expression. "I was afraid that I was going to lose you just as I realized how much I had come to care for you."

"I confess myself overwhelmed."

"If you have naught more to say just now, perhaps I might kiss you again?"

"You are my husband," Valentine replied neutrally.

"And you are repaying me for every time I teased you."

"I am thinking of making it my new habit to replace the one of prudery."

"Why do I feel like a sausage that has fallen from the pan into the flames?"

"I would not even attempt to explain your feelings, sir."

"Are you certain? Then, if you'll not be needing your mouth, I'll have that kiss."

Marche leaned over Valentine, bending the young man over the arm around his waist, cupping the back of his head with the other hand. Valentine moaned softly as Marche's tongue traced the curves of his lips and darted between them. As naturally as ice melting in the spring, Valentine's lips drifted apart in a tacit invitation. When Marche's tongue waltzed in, Valentine joined the dance, thrilling to the feel of their wet flesh sliding together. He had a sudden vision of his shaft sliding against the other man's hardness in the same fashion and his knees went weak. Marche caught Valentine and bore him up without breaking the kiss. Indeed, he delved deeper yet, licking at every surface of the other man's mouth as his hand moved from the small of his back to the top curve of his buttocks. Valentine moaned again, clutching at Marche's broad shoulders as the tide of lust tugged at him. Blushing at his wantonness, he pressed his body against the duke's and was nearly swept away by the rush of heat from his center. Dimly, he was aware that the sash of his dressing gown had been loosened and that large hands were parting the edges to settle on his hips.

"Now I must cry mercy," Valentine gasped. "This is a vintage too potent. I must take small sips or lose my head entirely and make a fool of myself."

"I would not mind if you were a little foolish in the bedroom."

Valentine bit at his lower lip in sudden apprehension. "Are we going to… consummate the marriage now?"

"I would be a most prodigious liar if I said it was not my fondest wish. I long to bury myself in you and watch your pretty eyes as I fill your sheath for the first time, but I will not ask you to bend to my will in this. However, if *you* wish to make love, I am not the man to say you nay."

"It is very good of you to be so patient with foibles that must seem silly and childish to you. I feel a great desire to lie with you, but—"

"Shush," Lord Marche said, kissing the fragrant part in Valentine's hair. "Let me please you. You need do nothing but observe, and thus, when this mood comes upon you again, you will know what to do and you will not feel so…."

"Ignorant and backward?" Valentine suggested as the other man's voice trailed off.

Marche didn't answer. His tongue was busy with more pleasant occupations than speech. Starting at Valentine's hairline, he kissed his way back down to the young man's mouth. Gently, he kneaded the soft skin of Valentine's flanks, his fingers stealing around to cup the velvet hemispheres of Valentine's round backside. When Valentine flinched at the fingertips digging into his cleft, Marche gentled him with another rain of kisses and murmured reassurances. Leaving the tempting ass cheeks for now, Marche put his hands on Valentine's shoulders and slowly pushed the heavy brocade sleeves down, baring new avenues for the processional of kisses. Valentine clenched his fists, preventing the gown from falling all the way off, pulling it around to cover him from the waist down.

"You are so very beautiful," Lord Marche said, his lips moving against the young man's chest. "I cannot wait to see all of you, but I am content to unveil you in stages."

Valentine was grateful that Marche maintained a light tone. If he concentrated too hard on what they were doing, he was afraid he would become too embarrassed to continue, and he very much wanted to continue. Fortunately, his husband's caresses had the same effect on him that friction had on tinder. Willing the race of his thoughts to stop, Valentine gave himself over to pure sensation and refused to feel guilty about it. Maybe shame would find him later, but just now, he was kindling and he wanted to burn.

Marche moved behind Valentine, wrapping his arms around the young man's pliant waist and taking hold of his wrists in the folds of rich fabric. As he sucked and nipped his way down Valentine's nape and across his shoulders, he gently moved Valentine's hands around. The gown's satin lining slithered over young man's crotch in a very tantalizing manner. Not once, since he was a boy and Brother César had beaten him for his curiosity, had he ever touched himself in that area except to wash. The slow sensual sweep of the smooth material over his cock made him dizzy with the steady buildup of excitement. He felt Marche's warm breath on his ear and then the sharpness of Marche's teeth on the lobe, and the tiny pain sent a hot wire of pleasure lancing straight to his groin. His cock hardened from willow to oak as he leaned back against the other man. He opened his fingers and the dressing gown pooled at his feet in a subtle whisper of crumpling satin.

Marche pulled Valentine closer, spreading one big hand across the young man's taut lower belly and the other tenderly around base of his long neck. "By all I hold sacred, I swear I have never wanted another as I want you. This is another order of desire altogether, and I find that I am as uncertain as you are as to how I should proceed."

"Talk if you must, but touch me while you speak."

Marche's arousal pulsed with his reaction to these words. "Right gladly," he said. "As long as we are engaged in the physical half of our attraction, I am on steady ground, but I do not know how to love. The softer emotions are a foreign country which—"

Valentine gasped as Marche's fingers brushed the tips of his nipples, and he cried out as they returned to pinch lightly. "If I can learn to make love," he said breathlessly, "you can learn the rest of it. You are a clever man, after all, and you—" Valentine's words ended in deep groan as Marche rolled his nipples between thumbs and forefingers. He could not have imagined that anything could feel so good. Each of Marche's caresses was better than the last and steadily increased the magnitude of his pleasure.

"An even trade then," Marche murmured, drawing his tongue tip along the whorls of Valentine's ear. "You shall teach me how to love, and I shall teach you how to make it."

The tension in Valentine's groin tightened almost painfully as Marche's hand crept down, ruffling the hair between his legs and grazing the head of his hard cock. Abruptly, all he wanted with every fiber of his being was for Marche to touch his arousal again. The need was so big and so intense that Valentine thought he might faint from the force of it. Then Marche's large warm hand covered his shaft and wrapped around the column of flesh. When Marche squeezed firmly, Valentine melted against him, his head lolling back against Marche's shoulder. Marche craned his neck, taking Valentine's mouth in an ardent kiss as he moved his hand languidly up and down on Valentine's cock. The young man whimpered against his lover's lips as Marche fondled him. He could feel the ridge of the other man's arousal and instinctively rolled his hips, rubbing his buttocks against it. Marche thrust his tongue deeper into Valentine's mouth and shifted his stance, settling his hard cock in the crack of the young man's bare backside. Shuttling his hand on Valentine's shaft, the duke rocked his pelvis to the same sweet rhythm. Valentine's breath caught in his throat as the strongest sensation he'd ever felt gripped him in a velvet fist, lifting him up to glory and wringing from him a liquid strand of pearl.

Marche supported his lover as he went limp in the throes of rapture. Nuzzling at Valentine's nape, Marche held him close, caressing him through the aftermath. He pressed a tender kiss to Valentine's temple as he lifted the enervated body in his arms.

Valentine's eyelids fluttered as the duke put him down on the bed. A slow smile curved his rosy lips. "You are a miracle-worker, Sir Loel," he breathed.

"Am I now?" Marche sat on the side of the bed and smoothed a lock of Valentine's hair away from his face. "I thought my powers came from somewhere other than heaven."

"You have Satan's own charm, and I cannot resist you."

"Have I corrupted you thoroughly, then?" Marche laid his palm alongside Valentine's flushed cheek.

"Say rather that you have opened my eyes and shown me a larger world than the one I previously inhabited."

"And does this please you?"

"Mightily." Valentine yawned.

"Yes, I can see that you are beside yourself."

"I am sorry, but I cannot keep my eyes open any longer."

"Then sleep for a while. I will see to it that you are not disturbed again."

"But what about...." Valentine put a tentative hand on Marche's thigh.

"Ah yes." Marche smiled. "Do not worry. The swelling will go down on its own."

"But you have had no... satisfaction."

"Oh, but I have. To my infinite amazement, I feel fulfilled. To be sure, I would like to be lying sated beside you, but your joy is now mine. Is *that* not a wonder?"

"The greatest one of all in my estimation." Valentine covered his next yawn with his hand. "Do forgive me. I would like to continue your instruction in love, but you're doing quite well already, and I really must sleep."

Marche leaned in to kiss Valentine on each eyelid. Valentine put a hand on the back of Marche's neck and kept him there as he brought their lips together. Marche's heart expanded with an intense blend of emotions he'd not experienced since childhood, when each day held some new wonder to be discovered. He felt all of that innocent delight, the eagerness and the awe, but the feelings were enhanced and magnified by the connection he felt with Valentine. The more he gave, the more he received, and it baffled the cynical realist, making suspect all of his beliefs and assumptions about the world. It would take courage and vigilance not to fall back into his old comfortable ways, to give of himself without holding back. He must trust that this was real and would not disappear like the fog of breath from a winter windowpane.

Marche broke the kiss, touched his fingers lightly to Valentine's lips, and told him to go to sleep. Valentine would need to be rested for the ordeal that lay ahead. Marche had not told him of all that had passed after he had been excused. Murdmont had done his best to paint a portrait of the new duchess as a penniless adventuress, practiced in the arts of deception, with an overweening ambition to be wealthy and powerful. The attorney had called upon Lord and Lady Hapwood, among others, to give testimony. After an hour of this, Marche was incensed and Prince George was clearly ill at ease. The prince regent had summarily declared a recess in the proceedings until all concerned could collect themselves and see to a few creature comforts. Murdmont had not been pleased at the delay, but even his self-righteousness did not extend to gainsaying royalty. George announced his intention to interview the Duchess of Marche privately in the afternoon and left with his guards and his favorite trailing in his wake. After promising Murdmont a reckoning, Marche had spoken to Negus and come directly here.

Before he rose from the bed, Marche whispered a vow to his drowsing lover. "I will not let anyone or anything harm you." He wanted nothing more than to lie down beside Valentine, draw him close, and fall asleep to the sound of his gentle breathing, but that sublimity must wait for another time. He had work to do and very little time in which to do it.

Valentine was not a woman, but as long as he wore the seeming of a female in public, he would be treated as one with all a woman's supposed weaknesses. Marche was worried that Valentine might be held guilty on prejudice alone, and he could not allow that to happen. Regretfully, he rose, unable to forebear stroking the young man's glossy hair once more. Valentine stirred slightly, and Marche turned to go, determined to protect him and to find out who really caused Lady Willamina's death.

CHAPTER 9

"I AM utterly devastated." Darby St. Denis collapsed onto a chaise in the guest quarters. Pulling a square of lace from the sleeve of his aubergine dressing gown, he dabbed at the corners of his eyes before covering his face.

"What on earth has happened, Strand?" Neville Stokes asked as he sat down opposite his friend. "The day has scarcely passed the hour of eleven and you are awake and stirring? Snowhurst and I stopped by as a courtesy before going to seek sustenance. Never did we expect to find you up and about."

Hearing his title, Crispin Ludstall looked up from pouring himself a goblet of mulled port. "Eh? What's that, Tarmegent?"

"Nothing that need concern you, Snow. Why don't you sit down before you *fall* down?"

"Smashing idea," Crispin replied. "I do appreciate your concern and—"

"How could I sleep? Have you not heard?" Darby interrupted. "It is the most horrible news imaginable. Oh, woe and ruin!"

Neville and Crispin exchanged a glance, and then Tarmegent spoke again. "Do you think you could manage to tell us what has happened?"

"My goddess stands accused of foul murder!"

"Do you mean to say that Marche's duchess has done someone in?" Crispin exclaimed.

Darby leaped to his feet and dashed the goblet from Snowhurst's loose grip. The silver cup hit the wall and clattered to the floor, spraying the mint green carpet with garnet. "Do not dare to say such a thing, you sot!"

"Calm yourself, Strand," Neville said, taking hold of Darby's arm. "You have gotten yourself all wrought up, and your ill humors rule you just now. Sit and have a sip of this." Tarmegent took Crispin's drink and handed it to Darby.

"It is a calamity," Darby moaned, his head drooping. "How could any sane man believe that such a pure dove could commit such a black crime? She is locked in her chamber like a swan in a cage, and there is naught I may do to comfort her."

"Then perhaps you could tell us the particulars of the accusation," Neville said.

Darby took a deep snuffling breath. "I shall try. That plaguey serpent Murdmont discovered Lady Bolbracken's body late last night, and he is attempting to convince the prince regent that the Duchess of Marche is a murderess. By God, if his neck were between my hands—" Darby viciously twisted his lace handkerchief.

Neville glanced up for aid, but Crispin was pouring another drink. Reflecting that Crispin would be no help to him anyway, he concentrated on Darby's incipient hysteria. "Strand," he said in a careful tone. "If you do not calm yourself, I fear you will succumb to a fit of apoplexy. In light of your family history…."

On the verge of a tantrum, Darby paused as Neville's words penetrated the red haze of rage. His mother had been a tempestuous beauty given to flights of large emotion. One day, she had simply expired from excess of temper. At one moment, she was railing at her milliner for offering her a dowdy bonnet, and on the next, she was hitting the marble floor like a sack of coal. The lady was stone dead at twenty-three, which coincidentally was Darby's age on his next birthday. "Thank you, Tarmy," he said. "I am in your debt."

"Pish." Neville waved a hand as though clearing the air of a bad smell. "Do not mention it. The world would be a dull place without you to brighten it."

"I say, that's quite good." Darby looked toward the writing desk under the north-facing window. "Perhaps I should write it down."

"I vow I shall remember it for you. Now come, dear boy, I am fair famished, and Snow has almost finished your wine. Let us go and seek refreshment."

"I must dress and—" Darby caught sight of his face in one of the many mirrors. "Strike me! Look at me! I am blotchy as a poxy Frenchman. I shall have to paint for an hour before I am presentable."

"None will wonder or jeer if you show the effects of your concern for the duchess."

"That is very good of you to say, Tarmy, but we know better, do we not? Our *soi-disant* peers will laugh up their sleeves at me if I appear thus. After all, I do have a certain standard to maintain." Bravely, Darby rose and cleaned his teeth before applying a light coating of rice powder to his face. From small round tins and tiny tapered bottles, he stained his cheeks with liquid rose and dabbed a layer of carmine on his lips.

"Well done," Neville said. "You look as though you rose early for a brisk stroll about the grounds. Now come and take some sustenance. Snowhurst, we are leaving."

"Coming. Do you think Marche will show us the door now that Lady B has gone to her reward? I do hope not. If I return to London before the fifteenth, my monthly stipend will not have arrived and my creditors will hound me most unmercifully."

"You should buy a vineyard," Darby said as he donned a silver brocade waistcoat. "Then you would not have to rely on merchants."

"That is a capital idea, Strand," Crispin slurred. "It is getting to be a damnable nuisance, chasing after the grape. Care to loan me the funds?"

"We will speak of it when we return to Town," Darby said. "I feel certain that the cellars of Wandeleigh will be sufficient to your needs until then."

"I should lay in a few bottles in my room. Save me getting up in the night."

"Indeed," Neville said in the tone of voice that says the subject is closed. "Shall we join the other guests below stairs and see what they are saying about this shocking turn of events?"

Darby shuddered. "One can only imagine what that pack of vultures is saying about the dear lady. Yes, Tarmy, we must get down there and do what we may to save her name from a vile blackening. I may as well ask now; will you second me?"

"To be sure," Neville answered. "However, let us also do what we may to avoid violence."

"I will not suffer calumny to be heaped upon my goddess's noble head," Darby proclaimed as they walked into the hall. "Let slanderers beware!"

Tarmegent sighed. "Very well then, Strand. The lady is a diamond of the first water, and if you are set on championing her, I will stand with you, as always."

"And I as well." Crispin gestured dramatically, flinging the lees of his drink across the near wall.

"If only we might be allowed to choose goblets at twenty paces," Neville murmured as he started down the sweeping staircase.

VALENTINE rose from a seat by the fireplace when he heard the outer door open. In another moment, Marche knocked and entered, holding out his hands. Valentine crossed the room in a trice and was enfolded in an embrace intended to comfort that soon heated to another emotion altogether. Feeling like a shameless wanton, Valentine raised his face from the duke's velvet lapel and offered his mouth to be kissed. Marche was not slow to take the proffered lips, and a thrill ran the length of his spine as Valentine opened to him. A greater jolt rocked him when the young man responded in kind and their tongues slid sensuously together.

"You could make me forget all the world, aye, and the firmament, as well," Marche said as he broke the kiss. "However, we are not free to indulge ourselves just yet. By rights, we should be away on our bridal tour and enjoying our first month as man and wife, but—" He stopped at the expression on Valentine's face. "Why do you smile so broadly?"

"By rights?" Valentine's smile grew broader. "By what *rights* would two men be enjoying their honeymoon? I am sorry to find your speech amusing, but I confess that I do."

"I have called you minx, and though the word is not proper for a man, a minx you are in spirit, a very vixen, my oath on it. When you forget to guard your tongue, you show a quick and wicked wit. Would you were so more of the time."

"Nay, you are mistaken. I am the very soul of decorum at all times."

Marche squeezed his lover's resilient buttocks, and Valentine gasped. "When I part your cheeks thus, I'll wager your thoughts are less than chaste."

"Loel," Valentine said breathlessly, remembering the way Marche had fondled him with such tender self-assurance, bringing him swiftly to a climax that outstripped every physical sensation he'd ever experienced. "I pray you, do not tease me."

"You are temptation itself, but you are right; we must speak soberly for a few moments, but first you must eat a little. I have brought you chocolate and pastries. Though the prince has given leave for you to appear below stairs, I did not think you would wish to endure the attention of our guests."

"No, I would not. I thank you, my lord, for your gentle care of me."

"And I would thank you to forgo that formal tone when we are intimate."

Valentine took a sip of his hot chocolate. "I shall endeavor to be less formal if it pleases you," he said and knew from the warmth of his face that he was blushing.

"Have one of these pastries made in the Turkish style," Marche said. He was not practiced at speaking words of love, but he could show how he felt by doing his best to please Valentine.

Valentine bit into a crescent-shaped roll. The buttery layers filled with almond paste melted on his tongue. He finished in four more bites while eyeing the remaining trio. Marche watched with a fond expression as the young man took a second roll.

"If it will not disturb your digestion, I will talk while you eat." Marche waited for Valentine's nod before he continued. "Prince George will interview you privately in an hour's time. I am afraid that Murdmont will also be present, but he will not be allowed to question you. And if it will comfort you, the prince has succumbed to your charms along with half his court. You are the toast of fashionable society."

"Can you explain this phenomenon to me? I am unable to fathom why seemingly reasonable men profess to be smitten with me."

"You cannot seriously refer to young Strand as a reasonable man."

"Neither is he a Bedlamite, despite his unlikely infatuation with me, or rather, with Valeria. How foolish he will feel if he ever discovers the truth."

"It will not be a novel sensation for him, I promise you. If you would have my opinion on your conquests, I would say that you appear to them as a sweet but spirited young woman unlike any they have known. They are understandably mesmerized but also puzzled, I should imagine. What man can resist solving a mystery? Could you?"

"I find much merit in your theories."

"On the other hand," Marche said smoothly, "it is possible that they are all secretly practicing the Greek arts and are responding to your true nature."

"And now you have done it again. You have reverted from exemplary gentleman to mischievous child. Why are you compelled to destroy any good opinion another may form of you? It is becoming tiresome, Loel."

"Do I really do that?"

"With regularity, hence my use of the word tiresome to describe the habit."

Marche chuckled. "Perhaps if you did not react so passionately, I might not—"

"Do not dare to infer that your shortcoming is somehow my fault."

"Then I see no point in continuing this discussion. Did I mention that the prince is on your side? I think he would refuse to believe you guilty of adultery even if he were the man in bed with you."

"That is hardly what I would call justice."

"I do not care what it is called, so long as you are not harmed."

"I hope you do not mean that." Valentine paused. "I should have said that while I appreciate *your* wish to protect me, *I* would not wish to circumvent any laws."

"Let us speak briefly of your inquisitor, Murdmont. I have suspicions regarding him, but I must speak with Negus before I make accusations. Unfortunately, Negus seems to have chosen a most inopportune time to vanish."

"I've not seen him for some time, not since Lord Murdmont accused me of being an imposter."

"Nor have I, which is exceedingly odd. Say what you will of Negus, he has never failed me."

"You look weary, Loel," Valentine said tentatively.

Marche looked up from the floor. "Except for my aunt, no one has called me by my Christian name since my mother died."

"I am sorry; I shall not do it again."

"You misunderstand me. I find the sound of it sweet on your lips. Say it again, I pray you."

"Loel," Valentine whispered, "will you come and rest your head in my lap?"

Marche was on his feet almost before Valentine finished speaking. Kneeling beside the young man's chair, Marche rested his cheek against Valentine's thigh and closed his eyes. Valentine set down his cup and rested a hand lightly on top of the other man's head. Hesitantly at first, he stroked the tawny locks, loosening the ribbon that tied them back.

"This is most pleasant," Marche said as cool fingers massaged his brow and temples. "I wish it need never end."

"Give me ample stock of chocolate and crescents, and I will stay until the stars burn out."

"Minx."

"If you find my sauce too tart, I wonder what you shall make of the bona fide Valeria."

"Is she pert?"

"I have heard it said that she has a tongue like a buggy whip."

"Then I shall keep you and leave her to her fiancé."

"They will be wedded by now. It is strange; I thought I would be the one to give her away, but I was not even present."

Marche looked up and met Valentine's eyes. "If you wish it, we shall host a wedding for her so extravagant that it will set tongues wagging for months."

"That would please my mother immensely."

"And you?"

"It would please me as well." Valentine blushed again as Marche took his hands. "I wish to tell you something Lady Willamina said to me."

"I should very much like to hear it."

"I had been in her room but a few moments when she fixed me with a stare that I found difficult to endure."

"The Medusa Glare is what I called it as a schoolboy."

"A very apt description." Valentine said as Marche intertwined their fingers. "She regarded me thus for what seemed a long time, and then she told me what a clever lad I was."

"She saw through our little charade, did she?"

"She did, and I braced myself for her righteous scorn, but she did not reproach me with my deception. The lady was disappointed, but she told me that she had not seen you so happy since you were a small boy. She embraced me warmly and told me to love you well."

"You astound me."

"Imagine my astonishment."

"Why did you not tell me before?"

"There never seemed a time that was right for such a conversation. And I did not wish you to think that I might have a real motive for—"

"I could never believe such evil of you," Marche interrupted. "Even had my aunt threatened to expose you, I do not believe you would ever harm her."

"You have much faith in a stranger."

"You are no stranger to me now; you are a friend, and, dare I say, my lover?"

"I think the term would be correct, sir."

"I love it when the roses bloom in your face." Lord Marche rubbed the back of his hand against Valentine's cheek.

Valentine kissed Marche's fingertips and then rose to his feet. "If I am to receive royalty, I must bustle. Look at the state of me."

Lord Marche observed the disheveled young man from his vantage on the carpet. "Incomparable," he murmured.

Valentine made an impatient sound and went to the wardrobe. "How I wish Negus was here. I cannot use a razor with the same skill. I've not much beard, but any is too much."

Marche stood. "If you've no further need of me, I shall continue my search for the rascal."

"I will do what I may to make myself presentable. I only hope that bereavement and standing accused of murder will excuse any lapses in my deportment," the young man said as he ran his hand along the soft fabric of a morning dress.

"I like the dark pink one," Lord Marche said over his shoulder as he left the room.

Valentine held up the dressing gown of deep carnation and regarded it critically. He supposed it would do as well as any other and the bodice lined with swan's-down would be nice and warm over his linen shift. Pulling the raveled skeins of his dark hair into a tail, he tied it up with a ribbon and pulled it to hang down his chest for further camouflage. As he fussed with his tangled locks in the mirror, he wondered again how anyone was fooled. He was too awkward, his features too strong, and he was quite simply too large. A sudden bout of panic seized Valentine, and he clenched his fists until his nails dug into his palms.

He must be mad to believe that this masquerade could have any sort of pleasant conclusion. It would end in disaster. He would be exposed, and Marche would be made a laughing-stock. The ridicule would be instant and merciless; neither he nor Marche would be able to show their faces in society again. Or perhaps Marche would receive the sympathy of his fellow aristocrats and be forced to grit his teeth, smile, and pretend to be a pathetic dupe hoodwinked by a swindler bent on fleecing him. These and a score of other doubts assailed Valentine's thoughts until he could scarcely think at all. This was no state in which to face an interrogation. That horrible, sharp-nosed, sharp-eyed Murdmont fellow would see through him at once.

With an effort of will, Valentine took several deep, slow breaths and reminded himself what was at stake here. Raising his gaze to the glass again, he took careful stock of his appearance. Picking up a brush and a pot of carmine, he added a layer of scarlet that deepened the color of his lips. Carefully, he patted more of the paint to his cheeks to produce a ruddy glow. Unsure of what else he might do to improve his façade, he took up the kohl stick and attempted to line the edges of his eyes as Negus had done so deftly. He smudged the soft black and all efforts to repair it only made the mess worse. He gave it up as a bad undertaking and went to the jewelry box thinking that some sparkling gems might distract from his face. He was still trying to make a choice when Marche returned with the prince. "Enter," Valentine called out, holding the top of his gown closed at the neck.

"Pray forgive us, ma'am," Prince George called as the antechamber door opened. "I had the silly notion that you might be more comfortable in your own rooms."

"Not silly at all, Your Highness," Valentine said as he made an abbreviated curtsey. "I thank you for your great kindness."

"Do not mention it, ma'am; it is no more than any gentleman would do for a lady." Prince George took a chair and gestured the others to sit. "Now shall we dispense with this folly swiftly and return to celebrating the glad occasion?"

"That is my heart's fondest wish, Your Highness." Valentine raised his head and gave the prince a grateful smile.

George was enthralled by Valentine's eyes, by the deep blue-violet color vivid against the velvet black of cosmetics blurred from weeping. His heart went out to this handsome lass who had traveled so far from home to wed a man she'd never met and been dropped into the middle of an arcane murder plot. When the prince could tear his gaze away, he cast a dark glance at Murdmont. Sir Malcolm's eyes were also fixed on Valentine, but his regard was the beady stare of a rat intent on looting a bird's nest. Marche saw the look of murderous acquisitiveness and had difficulty controlling his temper.

Prince George caught the glower on Marche's face. "How you glare, sir," he remarked. "And with good cause. I would not wish to be in Sir Malcolm's boots should he meet you in some quiet and unpopulated corner."

Valentine was a bit shocked by the relish with which the prince uttered these words, but Murdmont's obvious discomfiture made his lips twitch in an incipient smile.

Murdmont took offense. "You find this amusing, hussy?"

"Lord Murdmont!" Prince George reprimanded. "I will ask the questions here."

Marche went to stand behind Valentine's chair in what Murdmont considered a most unseemly display, actually touching his wife's shoulder briefly before assuming a square stance that dared all comers.

"Now my dear," the prince said, leaning forward in his seat. "I apologize for the necessity of intruding into your private affairs, but I must inquire if— What the deuce?"

"Who's there?" Marche demanded, when the discreet knock sounded again.

"Forgive me, Your Grace," Negus called through the door. "But you did say as how you wished to see me the instant I returned."

"Pray forgive me, Your Highness," Marche said. "With your leave, I will speak with my servant for a moment."

"What is all this in aid of?" Murdmont exclaimed.

"Begging your pardon, but we shall not know until I speak with the man," Marche replied. He opened the door a crack, intending to slip through into the next room, but a sudden shove pushed him back.

Negus was thrown aside and a field of gingham eclipsed Marche's view.

"Oh, my poor lady," cried Anne Kermartin as she caught sight of Valentine. "Look at you, so pale and thin. What have these unnatural English been feeding you?" The Breton housekeeper scowled up at the towering nobleman who moved to block her.

Marche recovered his aplomb and made a short bow. "Welcome, mistress. As you can see, your lady has guests just now, but I am sure she will—" Marche saw Negus shaking his head as the plump woman interrupted.

"You may be sure of what you will, sir, but I shall see to my lamb."

"I have never!" Lord Murdmont sniffed. "Who is this... female person?"

"She is my family's valued servant, sir," Valentine said as he rose to his feet. "I will thank you to accord her the common courtesy of her age and sex, if you can find no other reason to remember your manners."

Marche's heart swelled as the young man defended the serving woman. Valentine's striking looks attracted Loel, and he had been lured in close by the youth's naiveté, but Valentine's pluck had captured his heart. When Blythestone forgot himself in his passion, he shone like the pure prismatic fire at the heart of a diamond. How could Marche resist him? "Your Highness," he said, forestalling Murdmont's reply. "May I beg your indulgence once more? Will you allow Lady Marche a few moments with her governess?"

"Governess!" Sir Malcolm's disbelief was patent in his tone. "This female is no fit companion for a young lady of quality."

"I was reared to be of a temperate disposition," Valentine said. "But if you continue in this tenor, sir, I shall become quite cross and begin to doubt your fitness to be a judge of quality."

"And what might that signify?" Murdmont sneered. "What will you do, you flibbertigibbet?"

"My lady need do nothing," Marche answered him. "I have already issued a challenge, but I will not stop at thrashing you in the hall to spare the ladies the sight of your blood."

"Marche!" the prince admonished. "If you please, sir, a bit more decorum." He sighed as he glanced around the room. "I confess I have little stomach for these proceedings. Lady Valeria, you may retire to your bedroom with your chaperone, if you wish. Marche, would you be so good as to send for Beau and direct him to bring my wide slippers? Oh, and Marche, some nourishment would not go awry. Lay in some provisions; there's a good fellow."

"At once, Your Highness." Lord Marche watched Valentine's exit from the corner of his eye as he spoke to Negus in an undertone. "Good work. You have put the cat among the pigeons, though I do not know how you managed it. Suffice it that you did." He clapped the elfin man on the shoulder.

Negus nodded. "I thought your young gentleman could use a bit of a woman's touch and someone to vouch for his history, and as I knew the inn where his lady mother was stoppin', I lit out for the river. I found what I sought, but I bid you be wary of that female. She fair took the hide off me with that tongue of hers. Scolded me cruel for anything and everything from the state of the weather to sort of carriage I drove."

"I shall be on guard. Is she truly the Randwicks' governess?"

"Housekeeper, she says."

"I see. Well done. Now, if you can manage one more task for me, pass by the kitchen and have something brought up for His Highness while you are having a plate. Send a footman for Mr. Brummell and return when you have restored yourself somewhat."

Negus nodded again and slipped into the hall. Marche turned back to the room, his gaze going automatically to the door behind which Valentine had disappeared. "What a quiz, eh?" he remarked. "Valeria's old nurse turning up like that?"

"It begs the question," Murdmont said sourly.

"And I shall ask it," Marche said. "Whatever shall we do to pass the time until the ladies return?"

CHAPTER 10

"ANNE, what on earth are you doing here?" Valentine asked as soon as the door was closed.

"That scrawny Englishman all but abducted me! But as soon as I heard that you were in trouble, I could not get here fast enough. Imagine someone doubting that you are you."

"But I am not me, or rather, I am not Valeria. This has become such a tangle." Valentine paused. "Will you sit?"

"I do not think sitting would be a comfort just now, thanks to the jouncing that knave gave me," Anne said. "But my stars, just look at you. Wouldn't that gown be lovely on your sister?"

"I daresay it would. Do you know where she is?"

"She and Randall have not returned from Scotland."

Valentine bit his lip. "And my mother?"

"I do not know if I should say."

"What does that mean?"

"It is a delicate matter, young master."

"Is she ill? You must tell me!"

"Nay, do not fret. She is well, as well as I have seen her look since your father passed away."

"I understood that she was still ill from the crossing."

"Ah yes, but Mr. Harston escorted her to Bath to take the waters, and she is much recovered."

"Mr. Harston?"

"Mr. Frederick Horace Harston, a gentleman of Lady Blythestone's acquaintance from the lovely inn Lord Marche arranged. Your lady mother is still his guest in Bath."

"I am… amazed."

"Aye." Anne nodded, reaching out to pat Valentine's hand. "It is a shock. My lady was always so reserved, and to see her on the shore with her bonnet flying off, laughing like a young girl at Mr. Harston chasing it… well, I cannot begrudge her this happiness. She has waited long enough for it."

"You think she is happy? Truly?"

"I do, young sir."

Valentine smiled. "Then I am happy as well and pray God that Mother's gentleman distracts her a while longer."

"I confess I expected more of a fuss from you after the way you behaved at our last meeting. A proper little monk you were and disapproving of all and sundry."

"I beg you not to judge me by that. It is mortifying enough that you aided in my transition from male to female, but to hold me to account for anything I may have said during that time is hardly fair."

Anne smiled, her cheeks dimpling as she gazed on the young man she'd helped bring into the world. "If only you might have been raised at home. They made a terrible prig of you at that monastery. Valeria has more manly swagger than you can muster. Nay, do not frown so at your Nan, bonny boy. I should have said it better. When Valeria coaxed you away from the abbot's side, you wouldn't have said boo to a goose, but today I saw fire in your eyes, and it put me in mind of your sire. I owe you thanks for that."

"No female owes thanks to the man who defends her honor."

"Spoken like your dear father. Now tell Annie, what's all the to-do?"

CRISPIN LUDSTALL spoke in an aside to Neville Stokes as they watched Darby St. Denis bandy words with Beau Brummell. "I do hope dinner is laid on soon, Tarmy. I could devour a boar with lashings of mint sauce."

Neville glanced at his friend's glass of port and judged the other man's mood by the level of the liquid. Unless he had lost count, Crispin was still well within amiable territory. "I confess to feeling a mite peckish as well. I think it is the weather that makes me want to eat like a bear."

"I must remember to speak with Marche's housekeeper about having an adequate supply of spirits brought up to my room. I was given quite a turn last night while seeking a drop."

"Oh?"

"Nearly turned my hair white. I was coming down the hall in my stockings when a most frightful apparition materialized before me."

"Was it Napoleon again?"

"Eh, what?" Snowhurst blinked bleary eyes at his companion. "Old Boney? Dash it, no! I bloody well wish he'd try invading my sleep. I'd give the little chap a hot welcome."

"I have no doubt." Neville raised his hand to cover a yawn.

"This is no Banbury tale, Tarmegent. Murder has been done in this house, and I saw an evil spirit rising from hell to hunt for souls."

"Really, and what form did this demon take?"

"He was tall and dark and dressed all in black. His eyes were black as the Pit and empty of mercy. I shook in my boots when he turned his gaze on me."

"I thought you said you were in your stockings."

"What?"

"No matter. Go on with your tale." After a few moments of silence, Neville glanced at Crispin again. "Are you quite all right?"

"Damme, it just struck me. The fiend was the spit of Sir Malcolm."

"Have you considered that it might have been Sir Malcolm?"

"No, it was a haunt; I am sure of it."

"Where did you say the hellish creature appeared?"

"At the door of the late duchess's quarters, where else?"

"And you are sure of the time? It was not later? In the morning, perhaps?" Neville gave his friend a long look.

"Of course I am sure. Why do you regard me so?" Snowhurst asked suspiciously.

"I am merely confounded. Do not trouble yourself with the cause." Neville turned to Darby. "Strand! May I have your ear for a moment?"

Darby looked annoyed at the interruption, but a footman approached Brummell at the same time. As the prince's favorite listened to the servant's message, Darby gave his attention to Neville. As Neville spoke quietly, Darby's jaw dropped. Immediately, he turned to Brummell. "Has the prince sent for you?" he asked.

"Yes, he has. Despite what others might say, his highness values my advice."

"I do not presume to imply otherwise. I wish to accompany you."

"Oh… well, I do not see why you may not walk with me. It will be up to Prinny whether or not he'll give you an audience."

"I do not need an audience, dear boy, if you will relay my message concerning the despicable accusations made against the Duchess of Marche."

Brummell's plucked brows rose toward his hairline in an uncharacteristic expression of genuine interest. "You have new information?"

"Information that points to another, more likely, suspect."

"Then let us not dally, sir," Brummell said as he started away.

PRINCE GEORGE'S features went slack as his favorite whispered in his ear. The prince regent's gaze went to Lord Murdmont, and he put down his spice cake as Brummell finished speaking. "That is most interesting news indeed," he said. "Please help yourself to a plate."

"Forgive my impatience, Your Highness," Sir Malcolm said. "Does the news touch on the current matter?"

"It does, sir, it does, but we will wait for the lady before I reveal it."

Murdmont pursed his lips in irritation, but did not press the issue. For a brief time, the only sound was the tapping of leafless branches against the glass and the clinking of silver on china. As Murdmont took out his watch for the third time, the boudoir door opened. All four men got to their feet as Anne Kermartin stood aside to let Valentine enter.

"Gentlemen," Valentine said softly, "please forgive me for keeping you waiting, but I had been too long in my dressing gown and it nigh afternoon."

"Not at all, my dear, not at all!" The prince regent came forward to take Valentine's hand and raise it to his lips. "Though I would not mind if you received in your bed gown, I do not begrudge you the time. I hope you will allow me to say that you are incomparable."

"I must agree with Your Highness," Marche said. "My darling, you make that ensemble look beautiful."

Valentine smoothed the skirts of fine willow green muslin embroidered in the Chinese manner. "It was one of Lady Bolbracken's gifts, a part of my trousseau. She showed me much kindness in a short time and from the first, welcomed me as a member of the family."

"And you could think of no better way to repay than her than to rob her of her life," Murdmont commented.

"I put it to you that you are no true gentleman, sir!" Brummell was moved to reply.

Prince George put a hand on his confidant's forearm. "Sir Malcolm is so affected by his client's death that he tends to forget himself. Shall we all sit and try once more to resolve this odious issue? Though, with all respect to me, this will still be a matter for the courts when we return to London."

"Indeed, Your Highness," Murdmont said. "However, we may establish certain facts that will greatly facilitate any inquiry the courts should convene."

"Just so," the prince said. "Here is a fact for you, sir. You were seen leaving Lady Willamina's rooms quite late last night. What do you say to that?"

"It was actually quite early in the morning. The lady had made an appointment with me the night before. Thus it was that I discovered the body and not her maid."

"A good effort, sir, but the witness puts the time somewhat earlier than dawn."

"I demand to see this witness!"

"And so you shall, sir, so you shall. I am no fool, Sir Malcolm. Did you think the whole of my investigation was to be spent in idle queries? Hardly. While we were sequestered here, my agents have conducted thorough searches. Thorough, sir. Some awfully damned interesting items turned up in your quarters."

Murdmont didn't flinch, but his face went blank and his words were measured as he spoke. "Pray, what do you mean by interesting?"

"I suppose incriminating might be a more precise word," the prince said.

"Absurd."

"Watch your tone, sir," Brummell said, careful of his patron's dignity.

"Am I to understand that Murdmont is now under suspicion?" Marche spoke up.

"If your duchess is suspect for visiting your great-aunt, then we must hold Sir Malcolm to the same standard, wouldn't you say?"

"Yes, I would, Your Highness," Marche answered, turning his gaze to Murdmont. "I promised you a thrashing, and you know I am a man of my word."

"Swagger while you may, brute." Murdmont's lips curled in a sneer. "You are called Behemoth not only for your size, but also because you belong in the world of Make-Believe. You lead a cosseted life padded with satin and swan's-down with a legion of servants to keep any unpleasantness at an arm's length. If you had the slightest inkling what was transpiring under your nose, you would cease bellowing and strutting and see that the broodmare your aunt purchased for you is a horse of another color entirely. You have spared the whip, sir, and—" Murdmont's tirade ended when Marche's fist shut his mouth for him.

"You have drawn his cork proper, sir," the prince commented as blood flowed freely from Murdmont's nose.

Marche winced as he uncurled his fingers. "Next time, I shall be sure to use another method. This one is damnably painful."

"You shall pay for this," Murdmont said, holding his sleeve to his face.

"At dawn," Marche replied tersely.

It did not show on Murdmont's face, but he was now twisting on a spit, and the fire was getting hotter. He had gone too far and no amount of verbal grease would allow him to wriggle free. If he did not answer Marche's challenge, he would lose all standing in the eyes of his peers. His presumed cowardice would bar him from the *ton*, and none in polite society would receive him. His only option was to accept, nodding curtly as he drew a handkerchief from his pocket to stem the bleeding.

"Do I have your word that you will not leave the grounds, sir?" the prince asked.

"Of course, Your Highness." Murdmont bowed and grew dizzy when he lifted his head. "If you will excuse me, I will seek out the physician."

Prince George gave his leave, and Murdmont stalked out of the chamber. Strand pushed away from the wall where he lounged, and Murdmont shot him a glance of pure poison. Darby shivered as he turned to peer through the open doorway. He caught sight of Valentine and instantly forgot all about Sir Malcolm. Drawn moth-like into the room, he made a sweeping bow to the group.

"Pray forgive this unforgivable intrusion," he said. "I heard raised voices and could not forbear to listen at the door. Marche, I beg you most desperately to allow me the honor of seconding you in the duel."

Marche raised an eyebrow. "Can you fence or shoot?"

"I would say that is a moot point since I fully expect that you shall punish Murdmont in a most satisfactory manner for his perfidy, thus robbing me of the pleasure. However, I assure you that I am capable with either weapon. It will not be my first step onto the field of honor."

"Very well, Strand. You shall stand with me when I defend my lady's good name."

"Thank you, Your Grace!" Darby made another flourishing bow. "I am forever in your debt."

"And you have my thanks, sir," Valentine said.

"My lady!" Darby went to one knee and gazed up at Valentine with his soul in his eyes. "If there is ever any service I may render you, you have but to raise your smallest finger and I will be at your beck. There is naught I would not do for one sweet word from the lips of such an angel."

"Yes, well, I think that will be quite enough of that sort of talk, Strand," Marche said. "You are embarrassing the lady."

Valentine's cheeks had indeed gone as pink as sunset, and he was fiddling with his pearl choker, the enormous diamond in his wedding ring casting shards of light on his gown.

"I beg your pardon," Darby said, rising to his feet. "You are such a sweet and gentle lady, and I have pawed at you like a mannerless hound. Please believe that my words are sincere, though they sound in your ears as the baying of a beast. It is only that I am thunderstruck by your beauty and your grace, and so I prate like a witless infant."

"You are far too hard on yourself, sir," Valentine said.

Marche cleared his throat. "If we are to duel at dawn, Strand, I would suggest that a good night's rest is in order."

"It has not even begun to grow dark yet!"

"Then perhaps you would care to visit the chapel and review your soul," Valentine suggested. "An hour or two spent in asking forgiveness would not go amiss before such an undertaking."

At last, Darby realized that they wanted him to leave. "Good advice, my lady." He bowed with all the grace of a dancing master. "Until dawn, then."

"He is very brave," Valentine said after Strand had gone.

"He is a hobbledehoy," Marche said and dismissed the subject of Darby St. Denis. "Your Highness, I should like to know what evidence you found in Murdmont's room."

"Eh?" George turned from Brummel to Marche. "What's that?"

"I was wondering what evidence your agents had found."

"Oh, pish, I was lying through my teeth, dear boy! Do you mean to say I fooled you as well? Delightful! Just delightful!"

"Very clever indeed, Your Highness." Marche bowed to his sovereign.

"I simply could not bear the man's treatment of this sweet lady." Prince George rose to bow in Valentine's direction. "However, one mustn't go around issuing royal commands. We had to appear to be taking the blackguard seriously... though what he hoped to accomplish, I cannot imagine. And now I shall leave you to your rest. Be sure I shall attend you at dawn."

"May I hope you will not bring your entire court, Your Highness?"

"You may hope, Marche." George giggled. "But I don't like your chances. Come, Beau. A spot of whist will be just the thing to put me back in good humor."

"Capital suggestion, Prinny. Might I suggest you change back into your pumps?"

The prince looked down at his embroidered footwear and chuckled. "Damme, yes. Imagine the scandal should I appear in my slippers." He put on his low-heeled pumps and went to the door that Brummell held open for him.

Marche bowed as the prince left and then turned to Valentine and Anne. "Well, ladies?" he said with a devilish tilt of his eyebrow.

"There is only one female in this room, your lordship," Anne made bold to say.

"You are quite right." Marche smiled.

"What is to happen now, Loel?" Valentine asked.

"There will still be an inquiry into my aunt's death, but at least you will be free of Murdmont's poisonous presence."

"And what of this duel?"

"It cannot wait."

"Loel!" Valentine exclaimed.

Anne looked from her young master to the imposing figure of Lord Marche and saw the lightning flash across the distance between them. Reminding herself that Valentine was neither a child nor subject to her authority, she cleared her throat. "Perhaps I should retire."

"Dear Anne," Valentine said, "you must be exhausted after your journey."

"I'll call for Negus," Marche said. "He can show your... governess to the servants' quarters."

"I would like to go as well and assure myself that Anne is well seen to."

"As you wish." Marche inclined his head to the young man and offered his arm.

Anne Kermartin shook her head as Valentine transformed before her eyes into a prim young beauty on her wealthy husband's arm. She was certain that no good could come of such a masquerade, but as she'd done from the beginning, she folded her lips and kept her own counsel. At least now, she was in a position to help if Valentine got into trouble, and, to judge by that rascal of a valet, trouble was a frequent guest of the duke's.

After Anne was comfortably settled, Marche led Valentine by a route that took them through the conservatory. "I spent much of my time at the monastery out of doors," the young man said as they entered the moist air of the large glass-roofed space.

"There is small difference indoors and outdoors in the monasteries I have seen." Marche watched the way Valentine trailed his fingertips lightly over leaves and blossoms as they passed. He found the gesture winsome and almost unbearably sensuous. "The unglazed windows and lack of heat—"

"What are we to do, Loel?" Valentine said as though Marche had not spoken.

Marche caught the young man's hand in his and pulled him behind the screen of pleached lime trees in wide wooden tubs. "What do you wish to do?" he asked, rubbing his thumb along the pulse point in Valentine's wrist.

"Events have occurred with such swiftness that I have scarce had time to think of the future, but when I do, it is no longer with any great anticipation."

"Give me a moment to puzzle that out."

Warmth spread through Valentine from the place where Marche's hand lay on his skin. "I only meant that I feel as though there is a dark cloud around me, and until it clears, I cannot see my way. I wish Valeria were here."

"Perhaps a message might be sent?"

"I do not know where she is precisely."

Gently, Marche tugged on Valentine's hand until the young man surrendered to the comfort of his embrace. "How can I ease your mind?"

"Return me to the moment before I agreed to Valeria's ridiculous scheme."

"I would not, even if I could. I could not take the chance that you and I would never meet."

"But we would meet," Valentine said softly, "for I would likely be your brother-in-law."

"I could not endure a lifetime of sitting across from you at the dinner table, fearing my wife would see the yearning in face, knowing I could never have you without betraying her."

"That would be a sad life, indeed."

Marche put a hand under Valentine's chin and raised his head. Seeking permission with his eyes, he covered the other man's mouth in a sweet kiss. "I will not let you be sad," he murmured.

"Marche," Valentine gasped as a large hand squeezed his backside. "We cannot... not here."

"Shush." Marche took Valentine's lips again as he caressed him. Moving farther into the shadows, the duke pinned the young man against a pillar, pressing close. Valentine's arms went around Marche's broad back, fingers digging into muscle as he responded to the kiss. Marche pushed a leg between Valentine's thighs, his hardness brushing the other man's through the layers of cloth. "Let me ease your mind for a few moments," he whispered. Valentine's lack of protest was all the encouragement Marche needed. Pulling back a trifle, he eagerly took hold of his lover's cock under the satin and squeezed firmly. Valentine moaned as Marche fondled him, banishing his worries for as long as pleasure held sway. Still timid, but wishing to confer the same grace upon Marche, Valentine let a hand slip down to rest on Marche's buttock. The big man reacted enthusiastically to the caress, stroking Valentine's rod to a faster rhythm. Valentine managed to work a hand between them to cup Marche's arousal and the duke instantly gave him room to play. Valentine squeezed rhythmically, testing the resilience of the hard flesh, thrilling to the way it curved warmly against his palm. Marche swallowed hard and a small, strangled sound escaped his throat as his cock pulsed and gave up its seed.

"Confound me!" Marche sighed, his warm breath stirring the hair near Valentine's ear.

"Forgive my clumsiness," Valentine choked out as his lover's hand brought him to climax.

Marche leaned his forehead on the cool marble of the column, his lips moving against Valentine's neck. "Your apology is most unnecessary."

"I hurt you," Valentine panted, sagging as his orgasm ebbed. "I heard you cry out."

Marche chuckled. "That was not pain."

Valentine's lids had begun to droop drowsily, but his eyes opened wide at Marche's words. "Do you mean to say that you... found release?"

"Can you doubt it?"

"I thought it might take more... effort to... Botheration! Why can I not say the words?"

For a few moments, the only sound in the atrium was the plangent splashing of the fountain, and then Marche spoke. "You thought it might take more coaxing to make me come?"

"You are so much more experienced. I imagined that you must be somewhat... jaded, and I am hardly skilled enough to...."

"To what?"

"To satisfy someone so sophisticated."

"But I am satisfied, Val, well-satisfied."

Valentine looked mystified. "It was so brief."

"I spent myself; I assure you." Marche kissed the side of Valentine's neck. "I was quick; I grant you, but my pleasure was great. I was merely overexcited by the fact that you were touching me so intimately. I will do better."

"I did not mean—"

"I know well what you meant," Marche interrupted. "You are possibly the best person I have ever known, and I hope the world does not spoil you too much."

"It is you that has been my ruination," Valentine replied as he was pulled into a fierce embrace. Wrapping his arms around Marche, he returned the hug before pushing the other man away. "We are very fortunate no one happened upon us; let us not tempt Fate any further." Taking the lead, he started briskly enough, but the lassitude that was the legacy carnal pleasure soon slowed his pace. By the time they reached their bedroom, he was asleep on his feet.

CHAPTER 11

VALENTINE woke and stretched languorously, scratching absently at an itch low on his belly. A small patch of dried matter flaked off at his touch, and the events of the night before rose in his memory like velvet wings enfolding him in sensual warmth. Feeling terribly wicked, he rolled onto his side to see if Marche was awake. His sleepy gaze widened on the empty half of the big bed, and he quickly calculated the hour by the quality of light in the room. It was not yet dawn. Valentine sighed with relief. Marche had not sneaked off to duel without him.

The sound of voices came faintly through the bedchamber door, and Valentine slid out of bed. Wrapping his nakedness in a quilted dressing gown, he pressed his ear to the door. He strove to hear what was being said, but the wood was too thick. "This is absurd," he whispered. Reminding himself that he was nominally mistress of the house, he turned the handle and entered the drawing room as though unaware he was not alone. "I beg your pardon," he said to the two men standing before the mantel.

"Forgive us for disturbing your rest, my dear," Marche said. "Hapwood was just taking his leave."

"There is the small matter of discharging my duty," Gilbert, Marquess of Hapwood said.

"What duty do you speak of, sir?" Valentine asked.

"I have the honor to act as second to Lord Murdmont, and as such, I—"

"He is here to inform me of the choice of weapons," Marche interrupted. "It will be pistols, as Murdmont has no skill with a blade."

"The duel is already set, sir," the marquess said. "There is no need for further insult."

"Perhaps there is no need, but there is great cause," Marche replied, "and such an abundance of fodder that I cannot abstain. If there were not a lady present, I would blister your ears with an accounting of Murdmont's defects. Indeed, if it were not for the fact that I am in mourning, I would acquaint you with my opinion of the sort of man that would stand behind a knave such as Malcolm Jonas."

Gilbert squared his shoulders. "I see you are determined to be unpleasant. May I suggest that the duchess retire?"

"You may suggest nothing concerning my wife, sir. Pray do not utter her name again lest you soil it."

"That still pricks, does it?" Hapwood smirked. "Were I not a gentleman, Behemoth, I would speak of the surpassing sweetness of yon lady's red— Unhand me, sir!"

Marche did nothing of the sort. Gripping the front of Gilbert's jacket in his fists, he lifted the other man several inches from the floor. The breath went out of Hapwood's lungs in a rush as his back slammed into the wall near the mantel. "Listen well," Marche said to the winded nobleman. "You are not to speak my wife's name nor touch so much as the floor that the hem of her gown has passed over. If I should catch you glancing in her direction, I will have your eyes for a watch fob." Feeling he had made his point, Marche let go, and the marquess moved away from him.

"You are mad," Hapwood choked out.

"Then you should fear me." Marche fixed Gilbert with his eagle stare.

"Your conduct is outrageous. This is a gentlemen's duel, not a boxing match."

"Perhaps you wish to dance with me again." Marche took a step toward Hapwood.

Gilbert recoiled, recovered, and feigned a nonchalant air. "You loom large now, Behemoth, but you may find yourself cut to size before long. I would bow to the lady as I take my leave, but I do not wish to provoke another bout of unseemliness."

"You have my leave to go."

Hapwood stiffened at the tone of command in Marche's voice. "I go, sir, but we will meet again and right soon. I hope your surgeon is skilled, for you will find that Sir Malcolm is passing familiar with a pistol."

"Please leave immediately, sir," Valentine said, surprising the other two.

Marche showed Hapwood to the door and closed it firmly behind him. "Young idiot," he said in an undertone.

"Was that for me or for Hapwood?"

"Hapwood, naturally," Marche said. "I am astounded that he called on me as Murdmont's second. He must owe a powerful lot of money." Valentine's brows quirked up in a perplexed expression, and the duke hastened to explain. "The marquess of Hapwood is quite out of Malcolm Jonas's orbit. Murdmont's title is bought, you see, while Travertons have been lords of Hapwood Chase since God said 'Let there be light.' Travertons also have an inbred horror of commerce or industry of any kind. I can only assume that Hapwood got into debt and borrowed funds from Murdmont, thereby obliging his support."

"Murdmont does that sort of thing?"

"His accounting house makes loans and investments, and he has sway over the fortunes of several peers. I have my late aunt's word that he is a clever man with a sovereign, or a penny, come to that. I am not certain of her regard for him, but she judged him a shrewd sort at mercenary matters and entrusted him with our business affairs."

Valentine glanced at the tall windows. There was a cold pewter glow in the east, but not one banner of sunlight on the horizon. It was not yet dawn. "I do not wish you to be hurt," he said to the falling snow.

Marche came to stand beside Valentine, putting an arm around his shoulder. "Nor do I wish to be hurt. However, I cannot slough off such an affront to honor. Perhaps my challenge was hasty, but to withdraw now is unthinkable."

"I wish I might defend my own honor."

"Do not say such things." Marche pulled Valentine into his arms. "I cannot bear the thought of you in danger."

"Do you suppose it is easier for me to bear the thought of harm coming to you?"

Marche held Valentine at arm's length and looked into his face. "That was a terribly short-sighted thing for me to say, eh?"

"Terribly, but I do not think it is a fatal flaw, sir." Valentine ducked his head. "I would very much like to kiss you now."

"Then why do you not?"

"I am trying my best to unbend, Loel."

Marche took the young man's face between his hands and tilted it up. "The monks must have been very stern."

"Stringent is not too strong a word, nor is rigorous. Some of the Brothers I would have to label intolerant, which I know is shocking in a religious personage."

The duke snorted. "We have had quite different experiences with religion. I would have said that intolerance is the hallmark of the English church."

"Not all of the monks were so narrow-minded. Our abbot was a follower of Saint Francis of Assisi. He believed that only in pardoning others may we be pardoned."

"Do you also subscribe to this faith?" Marche's lips brushed the corner of Valentine's mouth as he spoke. Valentine nodded. "How fortunate for me," Marche murmured as he took the other man's lips in a tender kiss.

Valentine returned the kiss, intensely aware that he was covered by the single layer of the dressing gown. "Will you come back to bed with me?" he said when the kiss ended.

"Of all the protestations of love you might have made, none could be sweeter than your invitation. You cannot know what it means to me to hear those words from you, but tell me truly; do you only say them because you fear my death? I see by your face that I have guessed correctly." Marche pulled Valentine close again. "I wish to lay with you and explore all the delights that may be savored by two; however, it would not please me if you felt compelled by circumstance. I wish you to welcome me with your body because your desire outstrips your finely developed sense of propriety."

"You do not believe that I desire you?"

"I believe that you believe that you desire me." Marche smiled into the fragrant waves of the young man's thick hair.

"I detect a note of condescension in your voice, sir."

"That is affection you are hearing. I am not surprised you do not recognize it as you are such a disagreeable and unattractive baggage."

Valentine smiled. "Then if I cannot dissuade you from this duel, what may I do to help you prepare for it?"

Taking Valentine's hand, Marche led him to a well-stuffed chair and drew him onto his lap. They sat thus with their arms around one another, Valentine's cheek resting atop Marche's head as they watched the flakes of snow drift to earth like thistledown. Neither spoke, content to be warm and alive and in close proximity, while the world beyond the windows shrouded itself in cerements of purest white. Not until the first rays tinted the pristine surface with rose did either man stir.

"Dawn," Marche said.

"No, it is a false dawn."

"The sun is over the horizon."

"So it is." Valentine got to his feet. "May I accompany you?"

"It is hardly customary for a lady to attend a duel."

"I am a Breton, or have you forgotten? For all you know, I attended duels every morning before breakfast."

"Minx! If you wish to observe, I daresay we may outface any who dare to— Enter!" the duke called out as he recognized his valet's knock

"Begging your pardon," Negus said as he opened the door. "That French female is in the anteroom and says she won't be kept out."

Marche got up and donned a dressing gown. "Let her in and be glad she is here. You may now be excused from helping Lord Blythestone with his fripperies and return to your usual duties. My cravats haven't been the same since I married."

To the music of Valentine's soft laugh, Marche retired to his dressing room with Negus. Anne and Valentine began the long process of making him presentable.

VALENTINE turned away from the small group of spectators so that his hat brim shaded his eyes from the early morning sun. His gaze returned to Marche, standing half a head taller than Lord Strand and the surgeon. The strapping nobleman had doffed his jacket and waistcoat, leaving him clad in his muslin shirt and smooth buckskin trousers. The first light of day gilded his profile and picked out in gold each short hair on his chin. The thought that Marche might never get to shave those whiskers sent a cold black wave of debilitating fear washing through Valentine. For a moment, the duke's image wavered like a mirage and Valentine's breath froze in his throat.

"You look unwell, my dear," the prince regent said. "May I offer the services of my physician?"

"I was merely taken a trifle vaporish, Your Highness."

"With cause, my dear, with cause. I cannot say I approve of your presence here, but I admire your pluck. You are a most delightful creature in every way."

"I feared I might cause a scandal by attending, but in Brittany a wife stands with her husband."

"Brava, my dear, brava!"

Beau Brummell patted his gloved hands together in discreet applause. "Brava, indeed, Prinny. I dare say there will be talk, but damme, one has to admire the flair of it, eh? Quite a grand gesture for a young lady. Original, if I dare say."

"You would dare say anything, Beau." Prince George giggled as he glanced about the glade that was much too artful to be natural. "Where the deuce is Murdmont?"

Hapwood was wondering the same thing, and his gaze strayed continuously to the gap in the hedge where the gate stood. Murdmont had roused the marquess well before dawn so that he might call upon Marche, but he'd not been seen since.

"Do you have the time, Beau?" the prince regent asked.

Brummell made a show of pulling a large gold watch from his pocket on a chain that glittered like light on water. "Thunderation! Looks as though the duffer has taken French leave."

Dr. Sawyer cleared his throat. "Your Highness, gentlemen, it appears as though Lord Murdmont is tardy and— ah, here are Lords Tarmegent and Snowhurst. What news?"

"A search of the house and stables has yielded certain facts," Neville Stokes said. Bowing in Marche's direction, he continued. "Your head groom tells me that Murdmont ordered him to harness your two fastest carriage horses to a curricle. When the man bade him wait until he spoke with you, Murdmont browbeat a stableboy into doing his bidding. Not wishing to disturb you before a duel, your groom returned to the stables to find a bruised stableboy and a missing carriage and pair. He begs to know if you wish him to send men after Murdmont. As Sir Malcolm is your guest, the groom is afraid he has overstepped his bounds."

"His rooms're cleaned out," Crispin slurred. "Murdmont's, not the groom's."

"I thank you for your industry, my lords," the physician said. "Gentlemen, it appears that we must continue without Lord Murdmont. Lord Hapwood, do you stand ready in his place?"

"I do," Gilbert said with less than complete conviction.

"Your Grace?"

Marche nodded. "I am ready."

The prince regent stepped forward and pointed to the box that Beau Brummell carried. "I wish to offer my dueling pistols," he said.

"I am obliged to Your Highness," Marche said as he eyed the brace of guns.

"As am I." Hapwood bowed. "There can be no question of the weapons being tampered with now, eh?"

The men chose weapons and the box was closed. Dr. Sawyer cleared his throat again. "I will ask you to stand back to back, sirs."

Delicate hand-sewn lace crumpled as Valentine clenched his fists in dread. The feeling that there was an invisible, unimaginably heavy object hovering overhead had grown stronger every moment since Murdmont had accepted Marche's challenge. The weight of anxiety had increased until Valentine could barely stand upright beneath it. He wasn't sure he could bear the sight of a pistol pointed at Marche's chest. Surely, Fate would not be so cruel as to snatch away his happiness just as he discovered it. The young man bowed his head briefly under the burden of his fears and said a prayer for Marche's safety.

Darby's heart swelled painfully as he gazed across the elegant little clearing at the young duchess. The line of her neck and shoulders was a sonnet, as graceful as the stalk of a beautiful flower bending before the breeze. Strand's soul ached for the means to express what he was feeling, and it was an effort to recall himself to the matter at hand. Poetry must wait until violence was done.

Hapwood and Marche held the curved butts of the pistols with the barrels pointed up. With a sleepwalker's tread, they strode twenty steps to the physician's count. To Valentine's eye, it proceeded at a dreamlike pace, and he wished for the power to slow time even further. He wished he were not impersonating a female and could stand with Marche without causing an uproar. To feel this terrible fear for a loved one's safety and be constrained from acting was a torment devised by Satan. His heart was beating so rapidly that he was amazed no one could hear it galloping as the duelists turned.

As the challenged, Hapwood had the courtesy of shooting first. He leveled his weapon at Marche and without much ado, pulled the trigger. Black powder caught fire and propelled the ball across the short distance that separated the men. It passed by Marche at shoulder height and was lost in the foliage behind him. Gilbert's face drained of color, but he stood his ground, putting one foot forward to present a slightly smaller silhouette.

"My quarrel is not with you, sir," Marche said as he raised his pistol above his head and fired into the air.

"Ah well, that could not have had a gladder conclusion, eh?" the prince inquired of all and sundry. "I trust honor is satisfied?"

"And I trust you have more ammunition," Hapwood said. "I believe it is my right to fire again."

"Indeed, sir," the physician said. "But surely… after the duke's gesture, you would not—"

"I see his gesture for what it is. He is all but shouting from the rooftops that I am not worthy of dueling with him over a matter of honor."

"Fool!" Valentine could not forbear to say. "Marche showed you mercy, and this is your thanks? You are no gentleman."

"Such unladylike speech from such sweet lips," Gilbert reproved. "I have vowed to sip their nectar again, but that must wait, my beauty, until I have slain your beast."

"How dare you, sir!" Several of those present spoke simultaneously, including Valentine.

Hapwood accepted a reloaded pistol. "I may be guilty of forwardness to a lady, but I am breaking no rules," he said. "Are you ready, Marche?"

"Loel, no!" Valentine cried out as Lord Marche took his stance.

Marche glanced once at his bride, his gaze conveying a complex emotion that gave Valentine an odd sense of peace. The young man drew himself up, his eyes shining with pride in his lover, putting aside his fear for now. Meeting Marche's gaze, Valentine smiled at him. Marche bowed deeply and when he straightened to face Hapwood, it was with a fond smile.

"What the devil are you grinning at?" Gilbert asked.

"Am I? Pray forgive me if it throws off your aim, sir."

Hapwood looked at his pistol. "Unlikely. I have had one shot to gauge the range, and this is a fine weapon. I'll not miss again."

"Nor will I. You had best make sure of me, sir."

Prince George offered the comfort of his arm to Valentine and absently patted his hand. "It will be over in a trice, my dear," he murmured.

Hapwood fired and Marche staggered back, going down on one knee as a red stain spread on the front of his shirt. The duke shook his head, his hair escaping its ribbon as he laboriously pulled himself back to his full height. One darting glance kept the physician at bay as Marche pointed his pistol at his opponent. The barrel wavered for a moment before it steadied, and the duke pulled the trigger. The ball struck Gilbert in the neck, and in moments, his life had pumped out of the large artery. Marche wavered and Valentine hurried to support him as he went to his knees. Darby was there to help lower Marche to the ground on his back. Dr. Sawyer left the unfortunate Hapwood's side to open Marche's shirt and examine the wound. Blood soaked into the wrap that Valentine used to stanch the scarlet flood as Dr. Sawyer judged the seriousness of the injury. "I shall have to do surgeon's duty here in the garden," he said at last. "Lord Strand, my bag, if you please."

"Will I live?" Marche gasped.

"I can see no indication that your lung was affected. You are a fortunate man. The ball has no doubt damaged some tissue, but no bones were struck. Once it is removed, infection will be your greatest worry." Dr. Sawyer smiled. "However, I can see that you will have a most devoted nurse."

THE candles were lit, the physician had been and gone, and Valentine could feel the big house settling for the night. He doffed his fine dressing gown and came to sit at the side of the bed. Marche regarded the young man with drugged serenity. After twice refusing laudanum, he had acquiesced when Dr. Sawyer insisted that he get a good night's sleep.

"You are the handsomest, most beautiful sight I have ever seen," he said slowly.

Valentine's smile was half-hidden in the shadow of a wave of hair. "I may take my pick of handsome or beautiful?"

"You are both, as well as comely, winsome, charming—"

"You are a veritable compendium, sir."

"Come into bed, Val."

"I shall as soon as I am certain you are asleep. The physician has ordered you to rest, and I will not be the cause of any strenuous undertaking."

"My little monk," Marche said fondly. "How I love you."

Valentine swallowed hard as salty moisture sprang to his eyes. "And I love you," he said in a small voice. "I have thanked God many times this day for sparing your life."

"Do you know I did not once believe that I would die this morning? Do you know why I was so certain? Because my place is with you, and if we were parted, the world would end."

"Strand's poetic bent has infected you."

"You inspire me to finer things."

"I am glad, sir, truly I am. When first I met you, I thought to tame you to a more decorous bearing, but it was you who changed me."

"Corrupted is the word you want."

"Not a bit of it. You corrected years of false teaching. Though I am hardly comfortable yet with my urges, I cannot believe there is evil in the joining of two people who love one another. God gave us this crude matter we call flesh so we may be one physically as well as in our souls. If this act were solely for the creation of offspring, it would not fill us with such joy of body, mind, and spirit. It is a celebration of love, or so I believe."

"That is a beautiful faith, my own."

Valentine blushed, a subtle wash of rose in the pearlescent candlelight. "Am I your own?"

Marche's voice dropped in pitch. "And none else's."

"Rest easy." Valentine leaned over the bed and put a hand on the sheet over Marche's chest. "Let us choose another topic of conversation, or better, let us be silent so you may sleep."

"How can I sleep? Laudanum is no match for the excitement of your nearness."

Involuntarily, Valentine glanced downward. A dune-shaped hump in the linen attested to the state of Marche's excitement. "So I see, but there is naught we may do about it just now."

"It would soothe me greatly if you would but stroke it gently."

A shiver skittered down Valentine's spine as he imagined suiting action to words. The torn silk rasp of Marche's drowsy baritone struck a sympathetic vibration in Valentine's groin in the aural equivalent of friction. A whirlwind of sparks swirled in his lower belly like fireflies in a jar. Ruthlessly, he extinguished them as he climbed onto the tall bed.

"You may embrace me," he said. "But nothing more."

Marche pulled Valentine to lie against the side opposite his wound and put his arm around the young man's shoulders. Valentine settled himself along Marche's great length, sliding his right hand beneath the covers.

"Upon my word, Blythestone!" Marche said as Valentine found his arousal.

"Do be quiet," Valentine ordered in a fierce whisper.

Marche complied, his breath stolen as cool fingers wrapped around his shaft and squeezed firmly. A deep moan broke free of Marche's throat, and Valentine's heart doubled its pace. Reveling in the feel of the warm flesh under his fingertips, Valentine let his hand wander at will from one delight to another. He savored the feel of the crisp hair curling around his knuckles, the heat and resilience of the hard column of flesh, the silkiness of the skin at the junction of thigh and torso, the weighty moleskin sack and the musky dampness of the cleft below. When the first rush of sensation lessened, he took hold of the shaft again, shuttling his fist up and down, over the tip and back to the root. Lifting his head, he traced the underside of Marche's stubbled jaw with a series of nipping kisses, his lips tingling with the burn of unshorn whiskers.

"Please," Marche gasped, his hand slipping down over Valentine's hip, seeking his center.

Valentine pumped faster, and the rod in his fist pulsed strongly, spurting a warm stream of thick fluid. The young man slowed his stroke, gently fondling the quivering shaft.

"That was a wondrous lullaby," Marche sighed.

"Are you well pleased?" Valentine stilled his hand.

"I am… enraptured."

"Then it should be easy for you to fall asleep."

"When I am ringing like a cathedral bell?"

"What a lovely thing to say." Valentine nestled closer. "I am happy you are not dead."

"I am happy to be alive." Marche kissed Valentine's forehead. "Good night, my own."

"Good night, husband," Valentine murmured sleepily.

As Marche closed his eyes, he fancied he heard his great aunt's gleeful laugh, the one she saved for occasions when a cocky buck got his comeuppance. "Rest you well," he said softly to her shade, and he drifted into sleep.

CHAPTER 12

"WHAT a quiz!" Crispin said as he lounged in a comfortable chair watching his friend Darby pack a trunk. "I was just in the card salon, and no one can talk of anything but Murdmont's decampment. He's ruined."

"To be sure." Darby folded away another pair of narrow buckskin breeches. "He will have to appoint a surrogate to deal with the peerage and the gentry if he wishes to continue doing business with them."

"Do you suppose he will have the gall?" Neville asked from across the room. Letting the curtain fall back into place, he joined the other two. "If I were him, I would retire, probably somewhere such as the Russian Empire."

"For his sake, I hope you are correct, Tarmy, but in truth, I do not care a fig for him, except to hate him with all my being," Darby answered. "He is a dastard, lower than the lowest worm that crawls in the ooze at the ocean's bottom. I vow he will not escape unscathed."

"You are not still bent on that mad scheme, surely," Crispin drawled.

"Do you not see me readying for a journey?" Darby turned with his sheathed saber in his hands. "And this will stay at my side until I find Murdmont and use it on him."

"I say, isn't that Marche's province?"

Darby fixed Crispin with a gimlet stare. "It is entirely your decision, Snow: either you can keep your cork-brained thoughts to yourself or you can leave my company."

"I meant nothing by it," Crispin said as he gazed into his half-empty cup.

"Then if you will excuse me, I will go and make my farewells to our host."

"I will come with you, Strand," Neville said. "To Marche's quarters and to London."

"Thank you, Tarmy. Knew I could rely on you."

"I am coming as well," Crispin said, shambling to his feet.

"Are you certain you would rather not remain here for another day or so?" Neville said. "I do not think the taverns are closer than five miles apart on the road."

"And let the pair of you have all the sport? I should say not. Tallyho!"

Neville met Darby's eyes behind Crispin's back, and they exchanged a glance of perfect rapport. With matching smiles, they caught up with their comrade, flanking him so that he was in no danger of falling as they traversed the great hall. At the antechamber of Marche's private quarters, they were met by the duke's valet. "Good morning, sirs," Negus said, touching his forehead. "How may I serve you gentlemen this fine day?"

"Is your master receiving?" Darby inquired.

Negus produced a silver salver from somewhere about his diminutive person. Darby, Neville and Crispin got out their cards and dropped them onto the platter. With another respectful nod, Negus disappeared through the opposite door. The young men had time to grow restless before he returned.

"The Duke and Duchess of Marche will see you now," Negus said as he stood aside.

The three young noblemen strutted into the bedchamber and bowed as one to the supine duke. "Gentlemen," Marche said, his voice tight with pain, "what is your pleasure?"

"I am taking horse for London with my companions, Your Grace," Darby said. "There we will seek out the cur called Murdmont and take his hide."

"What!" Marche sat up straighter and winced.

Valentine came in from the boudoir and went directly to the bed. "Please let Dr. Sawyer administer a bit more laudanum," he said. "And you," he turned on the visitors. "If you insist on stirring my husband to rashness, you will be asked to leave."

"We are going, most beauteous of ladies," Darby bowed low, presenting a well-shaped calf. "Murdmont will not escape justice."

"What are you speaking of, gentlemen?" Valentine's gaze went to Marche.

"These young fools want to go chasing off after Murdmont."

"Splendid," Valentine said and saw Marche's expression change. "Is it not?"

"I would prefer to trounce the cad myself, my dear."

"You will not be fit for some time," Darby pointed out. "And I *do* have the honor to be your second."

"Would it be any use for me to forbid you?" None of the trio would meet Marche's eyes. "If you will not be dissuaded, then you will at least wait for me to be ready to travel."

"That might be days or even weeks," Darby protested.

"How do hours suit you, sir?"

Valentine opened his mouth and shut it again without speaking. There was nothing to be gained in arguing with Marche. Instead of wasting his time in futile discussion, he would use it to pack those things that would make the journey more comfortable. Pulling the bell handle, he sent a footman after the physician. Dr. Sawyer provided Valentine with supplies, persuaded Marche to take a draught of painkiller with some brandy, expressed his opinion that they were all mad, and left them. Negus went to ready the coach and returned with men to carry the luggage downstairs. Seeing that preparations were well in hand, Valentine excused himself to change into a traveling gown. When he returned in a bottle green riding habit, he saw Strand and his friends helping Marche to dress. Anne arrived to report that the duchess's trousseau was safely aboard and that His Grace's saucy man bade her say that the coach was ready.

Marche got to his feet, swayed for a moment, and then Valentine's arm was under his hand. Leaning discreetly, the duke smiled. "Shall we, my lady?"

"I MUST say, I am a bit peeved," Valentine said as they settled into the coach. "I had hoped to be clad in male attire by now."

Lord Marche was forestalled from replying by the advent of Mistress Anne Kermartin, who was encountering difficulty in navigating her generous contours through the door of the high-sprung carriage. The duke moved as though to help but was sharply reprimanded.

"Do not dare to exert yourself," Valentine told his husband as he took Anne by the arm.

Negus noticed the delay and came around to the side of the coach to lend his strength. Anne gave a loud squeak as she popped through the opening propelled by a tug from Valentine and Negus's shoulder against her backside. The housekeeper collapsed onto the bench seat opposite Marche and Valentine, gasping for breath and looking mightily affronted. Negus folded the steps, shut the door, and gave the occupants of the coach a salute before going to sit with the driver. In the usual run of things, he would not do a footman's duty and would ride inside, but the look in Anne's eye gave him a sudden craving for fresh air.

It was only a few hours to London, but the uneven road made it seem longer. Valentine sat rather closer to Marche than was considered proper and did what he could to cushion the injured man from the jolts and jounces. Anne kept a modest silence for a few miles, but before long her forthcoming nature asserted itself and she spoke as she was accustomed to in the privacy of the Blythestone kitchen.

"Pardon my saying so once again, young master Valentine, but I cannot become used to seeing you in those flounces and ribbons. You look so much like Valeria that it gives me a turn whenever you speak."

"I find Sir Valentine's voice very pleasant, Mistress Kermartin," Marche said.

"As do I, your lordship. It is only the shock of it, you see. Valeria… the other Valeria, you understand"—Anne gave Marche a significant look—"has a voice like birdsong when she can remember not to shout like a hostler. You've a lovely, manly voice, my lord."

"Do you truly like it? I have had it for some years now."

"You see?" Valentine said Anne. "He is incapable of being serious for more than three minutes together. It is most frustrating."

"I'd not trust a man without a good sense of humor," Anne answered. "Nor one that does not take a drop on occasion."

"If only his sense of humor *were* good, but indeed it is most wicked."

Marche made an indelicate snorting noise.

"Do you need a handkerchief?" Valentine asked.

"No, thank you, and if I may say it, there is no harm in a bit of gentle bawdy humor between spouses. I think you would agree with that, would you not, Mistress Kermartin?"

"Aye, sir," Anne said, thawing by the second in the warmth of Marche's applied charm.

"Anne!" Valentine exclaimed. "You are not to take his side in this! You agreed with me that he was far too reckless."

"True, but he *is* a man, sir, and a fine figure of one, if it's permitted for me to say. Men have their moods, and, if they are balked, their health suffers."

"Nonsense!" Valentine said. "I am a man and I can control myself."

"Aye, sir, I should have said *most* men."

Marche chuckled, wincing a bit as sore muscles flexed.

"I am as much a man as the duke is," Valentine said, shooting Marche a look of reproach.

"I do not doubt it," Annie replied. "But you were given over to the brothers for rearing and were not exposed to the wickedness of this world. I can hardly compare you to a rake like Lord Marche or one of those chevaliers who are escorting us."

"No, I suppose not." Valentine laced his tapered fingers, and it occurred to him how soft they were, how smooth and white. At the monastery, he was not allowed to help with any manual labor beyond copying texts, and he was abruptly seized with a great desire to see his hands scarred and grimed, or at least a little callused. If only he could sit a horse like Darby and his friends, dashing along the road with swords at their hips, daring and bold. With increasingly greater anticipation, he looked forward to the day when he could resume his true form.

"What troubles your brow, poppet?" Anne asked as though Valentine were a small child.

"It is naught." Valentine smiled for her. "For a moment, I allowed trouble to weigh too heavily on me, but despair is one sin I am not guilty of. We will persevere through these present difficulties and resolve them."

"I wish we could resolve my shoulder," Marche said.

"I wish I could stand for you until you are well enough to stand for yourself," Valentine said.

Marche gave the young man a long look. "Thank you," he said at last. "I think that is quite the most wonderful thing anyone has ever said to me."

"If I doubted the two of you were in love, I do not any longer," Anne said. "I should disapprove, but in truth, my heart is glad for you."

"And I do not care if I am consigned to the fires of Hades for loving where I will," Marche said. "I believe it is a greater evil to marry where there is no love."

"I cannot fault you there, sir, but I do not know what my lady will make of all this hugger-mugger."

"I am praying Valeria will be with child by the time we must tell my mother the story."

"Aye, that would draw her attention away from all else." Anne smiled. "What do you plan to do, young master, if I may ask?"

"Well," Valentine took a deep breath, "I suppose we must first see to Lady Bolbracken's final rest, and then Murdmont must be brought to justice."

Anne nodded. "To be sure, but I was speaking of your life with Lord Marche."

Valentine glanced at Marche. "I have hopes, of course, but what the reality might entail, I cannot say. Valeria and I did not consider all of the ramifications of this subterfuge."

Marche made the snorting noise again.

"Are you certain you do not need your handkerchief?" Valentine inquired sweetly.

"If I do, I am quite certain that you will inform me."

Anne turned a chuckle into a cough. "Well, Master Valentine, be sure that I will do whatever I may to be of help to you."

With but one stop to rest the horses and take some refreshment, the party reached London well before night. The coachman pulled through the gate of Bolwood, the London seat of the much-diminished Bolbracken-Woodbine dynasty. A page stationed on the portico bustled inside, and soon the butler emerged to direct a brace of footmen in the unloading of the luggage. Anne joined in, blithely pointing out the lady's bags and bidding the men be cautious with them. Leaving the field to the doughty housekeeper, the butler came to greet Sir Loel, now Duke of Marche and Bolbracken.

"Your Grace," the man said with a bow. "Welcome home. And welcome to you, lady."

"Thank you, Ambrose," Marche said as Valentine nodded his thanks for the greeting. "Where is… where are my aunt's remains?"

"Arrived safely and placed with reverence upon the catafalque in the family chapel, sir."

"My thanks once more."

"The lady will be missed, sir." The butler lifted his chin and resumed a brisk manner. "Where shall I bestow your baggage?"

"An excellent question. Have you a suggestion?"

Ambrose glanced briefly at Valentine. "You and your lady might be most comfortable in the Willow Room. It was extensively refurbished very recently."

"I shall rely upon your judgment. Please be so good as to see to the young gentlemen's comfort." Marche nodded at the Dandies. "I doubt they will lodge with us, but a cup of something wouldn't go amiss."

Ambrose made a slight bow. "As you wish, sir. When you and your lady are ready, the staff waits to greet you."

As the baggage was conveyed above stairs, the lord and lady reviewed the gathered staff of the grand home. Marche said a few words honoring the late duchess's memory and assured the servants that he would interfere as little as possible in the running of the household. Valentine thanked everyone for the welcome, doing his best to memorize as many names as possible. After requesting that a light repast be brought up, Marche escorted Valentine upstairs where Negus and Anne were already busy unpacking.

"DAMME!" Darby cursed as he paced the drawing room carpet of Bolwood House. "Murdmont could be in the Antilles by now!"

Marche cleared his throat, and Darby looked up from the pattern of the rug to see Valentine in the doorway. The young baronet bowed deeply and made an apology. "Pray forgive me, ma'am. I burst in like a Red Indian."

"Pardoned with all my heart, dear Strand," Valentine said. "You have done us such great service as my husband recuperates."

"A pleasure, ma'am." Darby bowed again. "However, we have been in town for two days, and our quarry grows ever farther from our grasp."

"We do not know that," Marche said. "He might be hiding under our very noses."

"I have scoured London for him, sir. There is not a whiff of the villain. Those who work in his accounting houses are going about their business, but you can see in their eyes that they are troubled. If I may be so bold, perhaps you might turn your attention thither."

"Whatever for? I am well-pleased to see the back of the scoundrel, and I grow weary of forbidding you to pursue the matter."

"Then set him loose," Valentine said softly.

"Yes!" Darby seconded. "Set me on Murdmont's trail. I will be tireless."

"I am too weak to resist. Very well, Strand. You have my leave to hunt my game, but with the condition that you send me reports of your progress."

"I will, sir, most faithfully!" Darby bowed with an extra flourish to both Marche and Valentine and swept from the room.

"Now you will have peace," Valentine said.

Wincing slightly, Marche sank into a well-padded chair. "Think you so?"

"Well, at least you will be free of Strand's importuning."

"Will you not miss his hourly visits?"

"Strand is very… animated. I suppose I will miss his lively spirit."

"Why do you not call him Darby, as you do when you and he are alone?"

A tiny frown creased Valentine's forehead. "That is an odd question, surely."

"I notice you do not answer. Here is another question then. Perhaps you would tell me why it is that your voice is sweet as honey when you speak to Strand?"

"I had not noticed that I spoke any differently to *Darby* than to any other." Valentine emphasized Lord Strand's Christian name.

"Well, you do."

"And it vexes you, to judge by the sour tone of *your* voice."

"And so it does. Why should it please me to see the soft looks and sweet words you bestow on that feather-pated wastrel?"

Valentine rose and came to stand in front of Marche's chair. "I could almost believe that I hear jealousy in your words."

"And if you did?"

"Loel, you are being foolish. I know it is difficult for you to sit idle, but you must heal, and it would be much more pleasant for those around you if you did not behave like a bear with the toothache. Come and let Negus help you out of all that black," Valentine coaxed as he tried to change the subject. "I think Lady Willamina must have been very gratified to look down from heaven today and see how many came to honor her."

"You are quick to change the subject," Marche said as he got slowly to his feet.

"What more do you wish to say?"

"Do you find Strand attractive?"

"What?"

"It is a simple enough question."

"No, it is not simple at all. What is in your mind? Has the laudanum affected your brain?"

"I am not imagining it. You flirt shamelessly with Strand."

"That is not true, Loel. I give him my attention, but only because he is a friend to us."

"He is besotted with you, you know."

"It would be hard to overlook, but he loves me as a poet loves his Muse. He has no lustful intentions toward me."

Marche laughed, but the sound held little humor. "You are still so very naïve. Of course, he has lustful intentions; he is a man."

"As am I."

"That is different." The duke waved a hand in a dismissive manner.

"How so?" There was no trace of anger in Valentine's calm face or measured tone, but the small hairs rose on the back of Marche's neck.

Choosing his words carefully, the duke spoke again. "Of course there is no difference except for the one you share with me."

"It is true that I have no experience of women in that way. If I had, perhaps I should behave as the other fine lords and collect maidenheads like birds' eggs." Valentine paused. "However, I do not believe I would. What I feel when you touch me convinces me that I am not meant to love a woman, or indeed, any other but you."

"And very glad I am of that. Please, do not be cross with my foolishness, Val."

"It is my continued wearing of feminine attire that is to blame."

"Now who is being foolish?"

"I feel foolish." Valentine held out the filmy skirts of his featherweight muslin day dress.

"You look delicious."

"Do you really prefer me so? In yards of ribbon with paint on my face?"

"I prefer you in nothing at all."

Valentine finally smiled. "No matter where it may wander, your mind always returns to this."

Marche put his hands on the other man's waist and pulled him closer. "How can it do otherwise with such provocation as this face and form?"

"Loel! We are not in our private rooms!"

"And when we *are* in our private rooms, you put me off using my wound as an excuse."

"You heard the physician as well as I did. I am as eager to resume my lessons as you are to teach me, but I will not risk maiming you for life."

Marche chuckled. "It would be worth it."

"I have been thinking," Valentine said as they started up the grand double staircase. "I was five when my father sent me away, and though I had a fine education at the monastery, it is incomplete. As a young gentleman, I am expected to have certain skills. I have learned to dance somewhat, but I still lack any knowledge of swordsmanship."

Marche swallowed the first words that rose to his tongue. Valentine was right; Marche had been treating his lover rather condescendingly. He only wished to protect what he held dear, but he could see that it would be the better part of wisdom to amend his high-handed manner if he wanted to keep Valentine's regard. For Marche did not doubt that the young man would leave him over a moral principle, even if it broke both their hearts. If Marche wanted to keep him, he would have to be more mindful. "I will teach you myself as soon as I am able."

"I would like that very much, but I would also like to learn a bit sooner than that."

"We would have to find a sword master that has never seen the Duchess of Marche, perhaps not so difficult, and then you would have to practice in secret until we leave London"—Marche's thoughts swerved back onto what had become a well-beaten path—"which cannot be soon enough. The constabulary have made no progress and the thought of Murdmont breathing free air gnaws at me."

Valentine took Marche's hand as they reached their quarters. "Your aunt will have justice. You will see to it; I've no doubt."

Marche squeezed Valentine's hand. "Thank you for your confidence in me. Ah, here is Negus."

"I shall leave you to his capable hands." Valentine retired to the next room where Anne waited to help him change.

"Negus, we have need of the services of a discreet tailor," Marche said as Valentine walked away.

"Beggin' Your Grace's pardon, but your tailor *is* discreet."

"I misspoke. We have need of a tailor who will not recognize us or ask questions unrelated to the creation of garments."

"How soon will you be needin' 'im?"

"Make it a priority, if you would. Blythestone is chafing in his frills."

"It is now the only thought in my mind, sir," Negus said as he helped Marche off with his jacket.

"I very much doubt that, but the sooner you find me a tailor the happier my duchess will be."

"Thus contributin' to Your Grace's happiness." Negus laid the formal jacket away and held ready a loose dinner jacket of quilted velvet.

"I'll not brook any lewd remarks concerning him," Marche warned sharply.

"Not to worry." Negus tied a cravat of rich burgundy around his master's neck, keeping his eyes on his work. "I can see that he is different, sir."

"Can you? Excellent. Be a good fellow, then, and forget that I spoke sharply, will you?"

"Of course, sir. Will you be coming down for dinner or will you take it here?"

"I would prefer to eat here, but we must consult the Earl of Blythestone as well."

Negus covered his start of surprise. "As you say, sir," he answered and went to get Valentine's opinion.

CHAPTER 13

"WELL, now, here is a change." The Duke of Marche entered the small withdrawing room and stopped to admire the Earl of Blythestone's new finery.

A dove gray frock coat hung open over a waistcoat of rich violet and a snowy linen shirt. Buckskin breeches hugged the sleek lines of Valentine's long legs and tall, brightly polished boots emphasized the curves of his calves. His dark bronze hair was gathered into a long tail that cascaded in shimmering ripples to the small of his back. "Do you really like it?" he asked.

Coming closer, Marche buttoned the narrow-waisted jacket, demonstrating to Valentine that he'd regained the use of both his hands. "You look a proper young gentleman in this rig," he said, fingers toying with the black silk cravat. "Devilish handsome as well."

"Only that?" Valentine looked up at Marche through the veil of his long lashes.

"I would have said something far different if I did not fear your censure."

"Would you indeed?"

Marche nodded solemnly. "However, I have no great wish to hear that I have no more restraint than a rutting boar, nor that I have the conscience of a tomcat or the recklessness of a stallion eager to mount."

"I would hear your honest opinion." Valentine spread his arms as though offering all that lay between them.

"I think you look perfect, and I would brave hellfire for one sight of you. However, in honesty, what is uppermost in my mind is an urgent need to strip that finery from your back and lay you down on something soft."

"So," Valentine paused. "You desire me thus?"

"How can you doubt it?" Marche dropped his eyes.

Valentine followed the other man's gaze, and he smiled at the prominent swell in Marche's trousers. "You seem much recovered to me."

"I think I am ready and able to stand duty again." Marche loosed Blythestone's hair ribbon and bent his head to kiss a silken tress.

"I think so as well. Will you go with me to our bedchamber?"

"If that is what you wish, I will fly there carrying you in my arms."

Valentine laughed a trifle giddily. "I do wish it with all my heart."

"Then have at you," Marche cried, lunging at the other man.

Valentine leapt back and entered into the spirit of the game. He ran and Marche pursued, through doors and rooms, down halls and up stairs, around and over all manner of furniture until they reached their big bed. Valentine turned unexpectedly and caught Marche in his arms. Throwing himself backward, he took the other man with him to the mattress. They bumped foreheads and noses, and then their lips met in a bruising kiss. Marche propped himself on his hand and the kiss became tender, deep, and passionate, each tasting the other and finding the flavor intoxicating.

"By all the Powers, you light such a fire in me," Marche said as he drew back to look into Valentine's eyes.

"You've the same effect on me. It is much too hot now for all this clothing."

Marche was not slow to take a hint. Rising from the bed, he began working on the fastenings of Valentine's suit. Valentine rose as well, tugging at the laces of Marche's trousers. Peeling the supple buckskin down Marche's muscular legs, Valentine stood back to watch as the other man removed his stockings.

"You are a masterpiece," he said.

"Have you had a long enough look?"

Valentine shook his head. "It is as though I have been given permission to gaze my fill on a fine Grecian sculpture. How I wish I had a physique like yours!"

Marche's chest expanded, but he made light of the compliment as he knelt to remove Valentine's breeches and stockings. "Can you imagine it? Two hulking brutes smashing up the furniture in the throes of passion."

"I am imagining it."

Marche glanced up from the tempting flesh just inches from his lips and grinned at the expression on Valentine's face. "Why, Blythestone, how very wicked of you."

Valentine drew breath to scold Marche, but he let it out in a moan as warm lips enveloped the tip of his arousal. His knees went weak when Marche sucked softly, and he sank down to sit on the bed. Marche moved between Valentine's thighs, bobbing his head on the stiff shaft as he palmed the young man's pointed nipples. Determined to do more than simply allow his lover to pleasure him, Valentine hauled Marche up to lie atop him and pulled his head down for a long, deep kiss. With some judicious wriggling, Marche re-aligned their bodies until their cocks could rub together each time they moved. Welded at mouth and crotch, they twisted and bucked against the linen, hard flesh sliding against hard flesh in a feverish wrestling match. At length, Marche pinned Valentine's wrists to the mattress, holding him there as he pulsed his hips, stroking his rod across the other man's arousal. Valentine lifted his pelvis, grinding his hardness against the duke's, blindly seeking greater pleasure, whimpering with disappointment when Marche stopped.

"I understand," Marche murmured as he sat up. "I am eager, too, but I will not spoil this for you with too much haste. Lie back and I will prepare you as well as I may so that this first time will be enjoyable for you. I will not deceive you; there is always a little pain, but it makes the pleasure all the sweeter for the sacrifice. Do you wish to continue?"

Valentine gave Marche an incredulous look. "Would you really leave me in such a state? A state to which you brought me, I am compelled to add. You have professed your urgent need to bed me countless times, in countless ways, on countless occasions. Why, now that I share your need, do you hesitate, sir?"

"You are a terribly persuasive speaker," Marche said as he rose and went to his dressing table. Choosing a bottle from among several small containers, he returned to the bed. Stretching out on his side next to Valentine, he leaned in for a wandering kiss. "Lie back and spread your legs, please," he said, pouring oil on his fingers as the young man complied. "Beautiful," he whispered as he covered Valentine's lips again. Valentine flinched when Marche ran a hand along his cleft, but he settled back and returned the kiss ardently. Marche cautiously circled Valentine's opening several times before prodding delicately with a fingertip. Valentine tensed as the nudges grew more insistent, but Marche's confident touch soothed him again. Reaching out blindly, he put his hand on Marche's cock and wrapped his fingers around the rosy column, holding tight. Marche's breathing was a bit labored when he spoke again. "I am going to put my finger all the way inside you," he warned. "I will do it slowly and the oil will help, but it is most important that you remain at ease."

"I shall do my best."

March smiled fondly. "I know you will."

He eased the tip of his finger into the reluctantly yielding port and then paused to suckle his lover's beckoning nipples. Despite the stimulation, Valentine found it impossible not to tense up as the slippery finger slid in and out, pushing a little deeper with each pass. The contrast of pleasure and pain blended into a third sensation that he had no name for; a sensation that filled him like the bubbles in champagne, with a fizzing tingle that made him squirm against the linen. Breathless and trembling in reaction to the intensity of the feelings that flooded him, Valentine felt as though he might literally burst when Marche's probing finger touched on a new area. Abruptly, all of Valentine's being was focused on this one spot. "What is that you are doing?" he groaned.

"I told you; I am preparing you."

"It feels… not terribly unpleasant, but I have the urge to… expel your finger."

"Not terribly unpleasant," Marche repeated, moving his finger in a small circle. "I am about to change your opinion. If you are ready for more?"

Valentine nodded weakly and Marche dragged his fingertip across the young man's prostate. Valentine gasped loudly as Marche pressed down on the spot at the front of his sheath. "What are you doing to me? I have never felt anything like it."

"I have already explained that I am preparing you. Can you not keep it in your head?" March moved his finger in a "come hither" gesture and pumped Valentine's shaft at the same time.

"Jesu!" Valentine cried out in a strangled voice. For a few moments, the room was silent save for his panting breath, and then he asked, "Will it feel thus with your manhood inside me?"

"After a time." On the next stroke, Marche pushed another finger in beside the first. Valentine could not help tensing again, but he relaxed when Marche resumed his stroking. "This will stretch you somewhat and hasten your pleasure in the act, but I will say again that you will feel quite uncomfortable at first."

Valentine nodded his understanding as his hand shuttled absently up and down Marche's cock to the pace set by Marche's lazily thrusting fingers. "I feel a bit dizzy. I can scarcely credit that I am on my back with my legs thrown open and another man's fingers inside me. I feel so—"

"Valentine," Marche interrupted as he withdrew his fingers. "I am honored by your trust and I will not fail it."

"I promise you the same." Valentine put his arms around Marche's neck and took his mouth in an ardent kiss before letting him go. "Continue, if you please, sir."

Marche moved between Valentine's thighs again and poured more oil on his fingers. "Draw your knees up a bit more. Here, let me," he said, raising one of Valentine's legs to rest on his shoulder. Spreading oil the length of his arousal, Marche rested his rod in the groove of Valentine's buttocks. "There are several ways to do this, but I hope you will like this one for I favor it above all."

"If it pleases you, I am certain it will please me."

Marche turned his head to nuzzle Valentine's knee where it rested on his shoulder. "You cannot imagine how greatly this pleases me. I desired you the moment I saw you, and my desire has not lessened one jot. It has grown vast and deep until I can scarce comprehend it."

Valentine found the hard cock pressed into his crack terribly distracting and oddly liberating. The passion Marche's touch inspired in him swept away all his fine manners and exposed him as a creature with the same needs as any other. There was no sin; there was only his fear. A swift little shiver ran the length of Valentine's frame, but he met Marche's eyes steadily and found his voice. "I lust after you as well."

Marche suppressed a fond chuckle that Valentine would be bound to misinterpret as ridicule. His young lover's earnest attempt at pillow talk called for encouragement. "Lust is a part of it, I grant you," he said, leaning forward until their faces were inches apart. "But lust is not all." Valentine moaned as Marche pulsed his hips, rocking subtly in the cradle of Valentine's thighs. The duke's oiled arousal glided over Valentine's opening to nudge gently at his sack. Dipping his head, Marche brushed his lips against Valentine's at each shallow stroke.

"Such sweet torment," Valentine breathed into his lover's mouth.

"I love you," Marche answered. "Tell me your bidding and I will do it."

"I would have you love me as you wish to, without let or restraint or much conversation."

A slow grin bared Marche's strong teeth, but he said not a word. Wrapping his arm around Valentine's thigh, he took hold of his cock with the other hand. As he pressed the tip of his shaft against the furled entrance, he raised his head to meet Valentine's gaze. Slowly, letting his weight carry him forward, Marche sank into the untried sheath with selfless patience. The tight heat that encased his aching cock was a pleasure that approached rapture, and he was on fire to repeat the action, submerging himself in hot, wet velvet until he exploded in ecstasy. However, he wanted to see wonder, not pain, bloom in Valentine's eyes as he entered him. He paused each time the young man's face tightened, caressing him until he relaxed again before going ahead. With Valentine's wordless encouragement, Marche eased forward until his balls rested between his lover's taut buttocks.

Valentine let his breath out in a long sigh and released his grip on the sheet. "My God, Loel," he said in a strained voice. "I feel as if I will burst like an overstuffed sausage."

"Shall I withdraw? Or shall I do this until you become accustomed to me?" Marche leaned in and covered Valentine's lips with his as he busied his hand at Valentine's crotch.

Valentine panted and moaned into March's mouth as the other man stroked him back to stiffness. At first, he lay motionless, but after a few moments of this provocative coaxing, he responded to the fondling and the passionate kisses. Ignoring the burning pressure in his lower half, he reached for his lover, pulling Marche in closer, running his hands over the Herculean muscles. The feeling of unbearable tension gradually eased to a feeling of fullness that Valentine thought he could learn to savor. The very notion that part of his beloved was inside him, connecting them, was surely the most rousing thing imaginable. "Oh my," he said softly, breaking the kiss.

Marche looked down into a gaze dewy with desire and unshed tears. He watched as Valentine's misty eyes filled with an unfolding mystery in the same way that the evening sky slowly filled with constellations. As gingerly as he'd entered, the duke began to withdraw, gazing in rapt fascination as changing expressions chased one another over his lover's transfigured face like cloud shadows across some fair land. When March reached the brink, he stopped short of disengaging completely and paused. "Now we may...." Marche's words trailed off in a deep groan as Valentine clamped down just behind the head of his cock. "Devil take me! That feels bloody marvelous!"

"Are you speaking of this?" Valentine squeezed Marche's arousal again.

"You will drive me to Bedlam. Who would credit it? Wicked Lord Marche vanquished by a callow lad and tamed to his hand."

Valentine laughed merrily as tears rolled down to dampen the hair at his temples. "When will you cease your dallying and prove to me that lovemaking is worth the fuss you make over it? Why, one would think you were not—"

Marche flexed his buttocks, sinking half a handspan into the narrow passage and stopping Valentine's speech in mid-sentence. Gently rocking his hips, he repeated the motion, thrusting shallowly at random angles. Valentine found the sensation breathtaking and clutched at the bedclothes as though he were in danger of flying off the mattress. Marche thrust a bit deeper and a thunderbolt of pleasure galvanized Valentine all the way to his curling toes. "Saints save me!" he gasped.

Carefully, Marche duplicated the action, smiling when Valentine cried out his approval. Again and again, the duke thrust, never more than a finger's length into the clenching channel. The blunt head of his shaft bumped and dragged against Valentine's prostate on each stroke, and the young man's pleasure spiraled up and up. Gripping his lover's cock firmly, Marche stroked it to the same steady beat. A fond smile lit Marche's face as Valentine lifted his pelvis in an instinctive attempt to thrust.

Arching his back, Valentine pushed his arousal farther into Marche's fist, forcing Marche's cock farther into his sheath. Writhing like a man in a fever dream, Valentine whimpered his need for release, heightening his lover's excitement. Marche flattened his hand against Valentine's inner thigh and pinned his leg back, holding him in place to give him what he needed. Hips stuttering, the big man thrust in staccato, rapidly pumping Valentine's pulsing rod. With a strangled cry, the young man crested, borne aloft by a rushing wave that carried him along and pitched him headlong into a warm sea, rocking gently on the tide.

Marche let go of Valentine's sated shaft and brought his hand to his mouth. Licking his lover's essence from his fingers, he thrust slowly and steadily, sinking ever deeper. Shuddering through the aftershocks of a powerful climax, Valentine moved restlessly against the tumbled linen, moaning mindlessly as the thick cock plumbed him. Marche leaned in, bending the young man double until he could look into his face. Valentine gazed up, blurry-eyed, lips parted as he gasped for breath. The erotic energy that crackled through Marche's system surged at the sight of his beloved dazed by bliss. His cock swelled along with his pride and gave up its load as pleasure suffused him like sunlight through a stained glass window. Valentine grasped a fistful of Marche's hair and pulled his head down, taking his mouth in a long, languid kiss that enhanced Marche's joy.

"I will crush you," the duke protested in a whisper. He reckoned without his lover's strength and found himself resting blissfully in the harbor of Valentine's arms and legs, reverberating with the echoes of an all-consuming climax. Marche returned the embrace, nuzzling happily at the young man's neck, bestowing damp kisses and small caresses.

"You are still hard," Valentine said Marche's ear.

Marche chuckled softly. "I had no notion what you would say after our first time together, but I would never have expected that."

"If we stay thus, will I feel you soften?"

"Not bloody likely." Marche shifted a bit and a small moan leaked from Valentine's lips. "Are you well? You cannot be comfortable with me atop you."

A slow smile curved the corners of Valentine's lips. "On the contrary, my lord; I find that being topped by you is a sublime sensation."

"You are not jesting with me?" Marche raised his head to look into Valentine's eyes.

The young man's gaze was drowsy but glowing with gentle humor. "Indeed not, my honored husband, I liked it so well that I cannot wait to enjoy your tender attentions again. I fear I shall become quite wanton, importuning you at all hours for this foretaste of heaven. I said you would ruin me, and I am proven a true prophet."

"Then here is to ruination," Marche toasted Valentine's left-handed tribute with a shallow thrust.

Valentine gave a short cry that trailed off in a purring groan as Marche took a sensitive nipple between his teeth. "Can we do this again so soon?"

"I assure you, it is possible, but if you must find out for yourself...." Marche flexed his buttocks, moving his arousal almost imperceptibly in Valentine's sheath.

"Surely, you do not expect me,"—Valentine gasped as Marche withdrew halfway and pushed back in—"to take the word of a debauched reprobate."

"Assuredly not, sir," Marche answered and offered him abundant proof.

CHAPTER 14

"MARCHE," Valentine said as he swirled a finger through the other man's chest hair. "I should like to go to Mrs. Dahlram's Tearoom."

A line appeared between the duke's golden brows. "Wherever did you hear of the place?"

"Darby and his friends were talking about it when they thought I could not hear them. It is a bawdyhouse from the sound of it."

"Why would *you* wish to go *there?*"

"Why did *you* frequent the establishment?"

Marche sat up. "You know my reputation."

"Aye, and I've heard that it is well-deserved."

"That was before I married," Marche raised Valentine's hand and kissed each knuckle.

"I should hope. However, it occurs to me that Mrs. Dahlram's is the sort of place where you and I might enjoy the freedom to behave as we wish in a somewhat public setting. It may seem a foolish request to you, but…."

"Not foolish at all, my own. That is why the tearooms exist: to provide a sanctuary for those like us."

"A sanctuary, is it?" Valentine said as he rose and began to dress. "Take me to this cloister."

Marche left the bed, the sheet sliding from his powerful naked form. "You are much more… bold in men's attire." He put his arms around Valentine. "Come back to bed for a while."

"I am hungry, Loel."

"I will have something brought to us."

Valentine stayed Marche's hand on the bell pull. "No, indeed you shall not. If you will not come with me, I shall go on my own and ask directions of the first likely person I see."

"You would stoop to coercion?"

"Who taught me the ways and worth of duplicity?"

"It is bad form to answer a question with a question."

"Oh, do get dressed, sir. I am devilish curious to see this tearoom."

"Then I suppose I had better take you."

"And after we have refreshed ourselves, we can seek a sword master."

"I was just going to suggest it." Marche stood unmoving as a fully dressed Valentine tied his cravat for him.

"Going out, are you, sirs?" Negus asked as they passed him in the front hall.

"Young Blythestone has a powerful thirst for a dish of tea."

"Shall I be gettin' my cap, then?"

"Not this time, Negus. We are simply going to enjoy a light repast and travel on."

"Of course, sir. I hope I wasn't in the way of implyin' anything different."

"Why would you?" Marche cocked his head at his valet.

"What are the two of you dancing about for?" Valentine joined the conversation. "I would appreciate the compliment of being treated like an adult."

"As would we all, sir," Negus said with heartfelt emotion.

"Rascal!" Marche took a swipe at his servant with his hat.

Negus grinned unrepentantly.

Marche fixed the fox-faced man with an assessing stare. "It occurs to me that with your master gone, you will be at large. I trust there will be no repetition of your last grand gamble."

"Indeed not, Your Grace! I may wander into a card game as it were, but I'll not put another farthing on a dithering nag. There's no predictin' their moods."

"I am glad to hear it," Marche said as Negus opened the door for him.

"Do not let it trouble your noble brow. Though I daresay, your purse these days might stretch 'cross the Channel herself."

"Enough of your cheek." Marche hid a smile. "Come, Blythestone. The delights of the tearoom await us."

Bolwood House sprawled adjacent to the Crescent where the genteel *nouveau riche* lived in the most modern circumstances. Everyone who was anyone made a point to be seen strolling the boulevard in front of the row. On their way to the lower city, Marche and Valentine walked briskly, avoiding those who hailed them until a woman stopped dead in their path.

"Upon my honor, the Duke of Marche," said Georgiana, the widowed Marchioness of Hapwood. "I trust you are not too incapacitated by your wound, Your Grace."

Marche bowed. "I am quite recovered as you may see. I confess myself astonished, ma'am, to see you without your widow's weeds."

Georgiana laughed as though Marche had told a joke, ignoring his implied rebuke of her scandalous appearance in public so soon after her husband's death. "I fear Hapwood threw a leg over the wrong horse. I trust you will not hold his lapse in judgment against me."

"I hold nothing against you or for you, ma'am."

"Then I suppose I must remain in bad odor for a time yet." Georgiana abandoned the campaign and changed the subject. "But who is your charming companion?"

"I have the honor to present Valentine Randwick, Earl of Blythestone, brother to my wife."

"A pleasure," she said, offering her hand. "The family resemblance is quite… remarkable."

Valentine bowed and kissed the air over her knuckles. "So I have often heard it said, ma'am."

"It really is uncanny. I asked Strand why all the gallant swains are under your sister's sway. Do you know what he told me? He said that she is an original; that her beauty is entirely her own and there is not another lady of the *ton* that can touch her. So it would seem that she conquers simply by being different. I would call that most unusual, but perhaps it will become the fashion to be... unusual." Georgiana laughed. "However, if I am to follow the Duchess of Marche's example, I will need several more inches and the innocence of a newborn. Where *is* the delightful girl, by the way? I had hoped to see you both at Lady Bolbracken's eulogy, but I was not in attendance, of course."

"I haven't the power to change public opinion, ma'am," Marche said.

"Hapwood had no choice, you know. Murdmont holds the paper to all of—" Georgiana abruptly stopped speaking and smiled sweetly at Marche and Valentine. "Do forgive me for subjecting you to private business which cannot possibly be of interest to you. Enjoy the air, gentlemen." She dropped a small curtsy and walked away, her path clearing as soon as she was recognized.

"I cannot fathom how you remained so calm, Loel," Valentine said.

"It is easy when one is speaking the truth."

"She seemed to accept that I am Valeria's brother."

"Well... I hesitate to point out the obvious, but you *are* her brother."

"You know what I am speaking of."

"Of course I do, but I adore it when you pout."

"I am not pouting. I never pout. Sulking is childish."

"Indeed it is. Let us be gone from here before we are forced to accept an invitation to dinner."

MRS. DAHLRAM'S TEAROOM was an unremarkable building on the outside; nothing distinguished it from its brick and timber neighbors in the cobbled back street. However, once inside the door, the ordinary was left far behind. From ceiling to floor, the walls were hung with great sweeping swathes of rich fabrics creating the illusion of being inside an enormous Bedouin tent. Soft carpets, large pillows and low tables furnished the rooms and light was provided by oil lamps of pierced brass that freighted the air with fragrant sandalwood.

"What do you think?" Marche asked as he and Valentine stopped in the foyer.

Valentine was looking around in astonishment. "It is hard to credit that one is still in London or even England for that matter."

Marche nodded in response to a turbaned servant's soft question, and then he and Valentine followed the colorfully garbed figure deeper into the gloom. They were shown into a private room appointed in the same opulent style, but before they could enter, someone called Marche's name from down the hall. "Valentine," the duke said. "Would you think me terribly rude if I had a word with that gentleman?"

"As long as it is only a word."

"You may depend upon it, my own." Marche boldly caressed the young man's cheek right there in the corridor. "You will find the room most comfortable, and I will return soon."

Valentine entered the sumptuous chamber and found a table set with an elaborate tea. In addition to the tea itself, there were platters of delicacies and miniature pastries. Suddenly ravenous, he sat on a low divan and served himself. He was popping a third *petit four* into his mouth when someone rapped softly at the door. Unsure what to do, he hesitated, and the discreet knock was repeated.

"Are you in there or not, my large meringue?" The door opened a crack and a young man peered inside. "You're not the duke!"

"Indeed, I am not," Valentine said stiffly as he got to his feet. "What have you to do with him?"

"May I enter?"

Valentine gestured and the stranger came into the room. With a growing feeling of dismay, he noted the brightly dressed newcomer's handsome face and profusion of flaxen curls. What business did this pretty popinjay have with Marche?

"Mercy! You look at me as though I ascended from the Inferno!"

"I… I beg your pardon, but you have me at a disadvantage."

"I might say the same. I was told that the Duke of Marche was visiting, but I see that someone is playing a trick on me."

"The duke is indeed here; I may vouch for his presence, as I accompanied him. He is speaking with an acquaintance, but I expect him to return at any time."

"The Behemoth brought you here? That is bringing coal to Newcastle, I must say."

"I do not take your meaning, sir."

The blonde Ganymede laughed. "You are a very bright green indeed. Nay, do not sulk, pretty; I meant no insult. Look here, I will tell you my name, and you may give me yours, and we will begin again."

"Very well; I am Valentine Randwick, Earl of Blythestone."

"Ah, so you are a lord. For a few moments, I imagined a most lurid history for you and the large duke. You can call me Aurelio if you like, but my name is Tobias Fleet."

"Aurelio suits your golden hair, but I will call you Mr. Fleet until we are better acquainted." Valentine's tone left no doubt that he considered that eventuality unlikely at best.

"If that is your pleasure. Aurelio is merely a professional name; my friends call me Toby."

"And what is your profession?" Valentine asked, imagining Toby to be a performer of some sort.

"I am a merchant of joy." Toby smiled at Valentine's bewildered expression. "I minister to gentlemen in need of relief and bring sweet surcease of tension." When Lord Blythestone still appeared baffled, Toby spoke more plainly. "I work in the brothel."

"You are a-a-" Valentine stuttered. "You sell yourself?"

"I have an agent to handle the actual exchange of money, but I do trade my favors for income."

"Please excuse me." Valentine rose immediately and started for the door.

"Oh dear! You are not frightened to be in the same room with me, are you?"

"No, not frightened."

"Do you think you will be tainted by my mere presence?"

"I do not know. I have never met a whore before."

"By your tone, there can be no greater sin."

"So I was taught."

"Look at me, Lord Blythestone. Do I appear diseased or degenerate? Does it seem that I am enslaved and forced to lay with strangers by a cruel master?"

"No, but you cannot deny that it is a sin to fornicate outside of marriage."

"I do deny it, and I defy it several times a day. The priests would have us believe that sex is merely for the getting of children, but how can this be true?"

Valentine snuffed his righteous retort. He had spoken similar words to Marche quite recently. If he no longer believed that love between two men was wrong, then he could not subscribe to the notion that sex was for procreation only. The two beliefs could not stand together for no progeny could result from the union of two males. "I spoke in haste," he said as he took his seat again.

Toby tilted his head, regarding Valentine with shrewd green eyes. "You are not like most of the other fine gentlemen who dally here."

"How so?"

"You can admit that you are mistaken. That alone would set you apart."

Valentine smiled. "You are the first courtesan I have ever spoken with, and my ignorance of your profession is profound."

Toby smiled at his promotion from whore to courtesan. "Shall I sit with you a while and expand your education?"

"I would appreciate the company until Marche returns."

"I can see what he likes about you. There's more to you than your obvious beauty."

"It is kind of you to say so."

"Now we are friends." Toby's bright smile appeared again. "What would you like to know?"

Valentine asked the question uppermost in his mind. "How are you acquainted with Marche?"

"Do you wish me to be scrupulously honest?"

"It would please me greatly if you would."

"For some years now, it has been my honor to receive the duke in chambers."

"Is that what you term honesty?"

"I try to be candid without being crude; however, I will happily provide all the details you could wish."

"Perhaps not, on second thought." Valentine sat in silence a moment absorbing the fact that he was sitting across from one who had bedded Marche many times. He knew that Loel was far from abstinent before meeting him, but the reality of his lover's past was now in front of him, unabashed and alluring. "Forgive me. I am feeling… unwell of a sudden."

"You love him," Toby stated.

Valentine nodded, unable to deny it.

"Let me tell you something that may ease the sting. Always before, when the duke visited, his valet called upon the management to arrange my time in advance. Today, he did not even bother to inquire after me."

"The decision to visit was quite unplanned."

"You are not listening. The duke did not ask for me, because he obviously no longer has need of me."

"I do hope you are right. I do not think I could bear it if—" Valentine stopped speaking abruptly. Though he was in a private room and talking to someone who knew the subject well, he could not bring himself to speak of his love for Marche.

"It hurts you to think he has known joy with others," Toby guessed.

Valentine nodded again, relieved that he did not have to say it aloud.

"Don't let yourself be troubled by a past you are not part of. If you dwell on it, you risk ruining your future. And if my large meringue has found a true companion in you, I hope you are together until the last trumps blow."

"Has he inspired such affection in you that you can speak so generously?"

"Lord Marche comes here—" Toby caught himself and began again. "Lord Marche *came* here in order that he might relax his guard, a bit of a break in the battle of keeping up appearances. I would not give you a moldy fig for the toffee-nosed character he cuts in society, but when he is here, he is… well, I do not have to explain to you, do I?"

Valentine shook his head.

"There are not enough men like him," Toby said.

"So it was not all business between you, then."

Toby looked into Valentine's eyes. "That is the past, Sir Valentine," he said firmly.

"You are careful of my feelings, but to judge by you, he would prefer someone fairer."

Toby chuckled. "Marche would not care if I were bald-pated, I think. He did not choose me for my looks. In fact, he did not choose me at all. Mrs. Dahlram sent me to his private box at the opera to entice him as a patron. He was amused by my boldness, and though he sampled the charms of a few others, I was his usual diversion."

"There is so much I would ask you if propriety did not forbid."

"None but we will ever know what passes here."

"That is not the first time you have uttered those words."

"Ah, so you *can* jest. I was beginning to wonder if you were so terribly earnest all of the time. Ask me what you will."

"I would hear you speak of him."

Toby had expected a timid question regarding some sexual technique, but he smoothly covered his surprise. "Well, I have just told you how we met. Before he started coming to the tearoom, he satisfied his longings at private orgies held at country estates. He had to be discreet, of course, but at least he did not have to fear that his partners would expose him for they would naturally suffer the same disgrace."

"Did he never…." Valentine's words trailed off.

"You are wondering if he was ever in love? He told me of someone once, his first lover. The memory was painful for him, but when I asked, he spoke of an older man with dark eyes. He would not say how they parted, but I could see that his heart had been broken." Toby leaned across the low table. "Truly, I did not think he would ever love again. In the years I have known him, he has always kept a distance from other people."

"Even in bed?" Valentine could not help asking.

"Aye, even in the most intimate of moments, I never felt I had his full attention."

Valentine blushed at the memory of having the heat and intensity of Marche's full attention focused on him, like lying naked under a sun of deepest summer. To cover his embarrassment, he took another pastry. As he bit into the dainty tart, the door opened and Marche stalked in. The duke opened his mouth to speak but closed it again when he saw Tobias Fleet.

"Good afternoon, Your Grace," Toby said as he got to his feet. "Welcome back."

"Why, thank you, Toby," Marche said, his gaze flickering between Valentine and the courtesan.

"We have been speaking of you, Loel." Valentine reached for the teapot. "Would you care for some tea?"

"I would sooner hear what you have been saying."

"Are you quite certain of that?" Valentine poured and handed Marche a cup and saucer.

Marche accepted the tea, but his eyes were fixed on Toby. "I do hope young Tobias has not been indiscreet in his speech."

"I merely wished to know how better to please you," Valentine said soberly. "Mr. Fleet has been good enough to give me instruction. It is astounding the number of pleasures one may enjoy without removing a stitch of clothing."

It wasn't until Toby burst into laughter that Marche realized he'd been cozened. His expression of shock softened to a wry smile. "And so I am hoist by my own petard, very amusing. Toby, I wonder if you would not give us the privacy of the room."

"Of course, sir." The young man bowed fluidly, smoothing back a raft of pale blonde ringlets. "Would it be too bold of me to offer my congratulations?"

"Probably, but I would welcome your good wishes."

"You have them, with all my heart." Toby left the room, closing the door softly behind him.

"You look nervous, Loel," Valentine observed.

"May I know what you spoke of?"

"I told you the subject of our conversation. I can scarcely credit that Mr. Fleet is a catamite. There was no lewdness in his manner, though he spoke quite frankly to me."

"How frankly?"

"Really, Loel, do not be tedious. I can accept that we as men have needs, and Mr. Fleet is certainly appealing, as well as being quite pleasant to look upon."

"You found him appealing, did you?" Marche's warm baritone roughened.

"I am speaking objectively, of course, and now that you are married, you will not need the consolation of someone like Mr. Fleet, will you?"

A smile spread slowly over Marche's face. "My friendship with Aurelio, while pleasant, was but a stopgap measure. Now that you are mine, I have all the companionship that I need."

Valentine rose and crossed the short distance that separated him from the other man. "I love you so. I could not bear it if I were not enough for you."

Marche wrapped his arms around Valentine in a fierce embrace. "You are too much for me," he whispered into the young man's hair. "You are more than I deserve."

Valentine took Marche's face between his hands and kissed him firmly. The duke responded instantly to this provocation, tightening his arms around Valentine's back and pulling him closer. Valentine pressed his length against his lover's, savoring the slide of hard muscles under fine cloth. Tangling his fingers in Marche's tawny hair, he loosed it from its ribbon. Marche slid his tongue between

Valentine's lips in a blatant invitation to sin, and Valentine moaned loudly at the strength of his reaction.

"I want you," Marche breathed into the young man's mouth.

"Y-yes," Valentine stammered. "I-I want you too."

Marche's lips covered Valentine's again in a kiss that gave preview of what his cock would do in a lower opening. Sultry heat rose from Valentine's center at the memory of their recent lovemaking, melting his bones and setting his blood afire. Eagerly, he returned the kiss as Marche slid a hand under the back of his shirt. Marche flattened his palm between Valentine's shoulder blades and rested his other hand on Valentine's chest. As the kiss deepened, Marche took a nipple between his thumb and forefinger, tweaking it through the fabric. Valentine moaned into Marche's mouth as a bolt of dulcet lightning shot from his pinched nipple to the tip of his cock. All along the pathway of the thunderbolt, wildfires spread, setting his entire body alight. Impatiently, Marche yanked the shirt up and took the stiff brown nub between his teeth. Flicking his tongue over the tip of the sensitive bud, he drew another moan from Valentine. Sucking and nibbling at each nipple in turn, Marche worked his hand under the waistband of the young man's trousers. Valentine gave a short, sharp cry as Marche's fingers closed on his hard length and squeezed gently. Slowly stroking the hot, silken flesh, Marche claimed Valentine's mouth again. Valentine whimpered helplessly, feeling as though he were losing control over his body. Marche felt his lover's surrender and gave free rein to his desire. Valentine felt cool air on his thighs and realized that Marche had somehow managed to push his breeches down almost to his knees. The duke was palming Valentine's sack as he rubbed the ball of his thumb against the underside of Valentine's cock. Even as the young earl regained some of his wits, Marche stroked his cleft, lightly dragging a fingernail over his furled rosette. Valentine's groin melted in a liquid pulse that rendered him breathless.

"Have mercy, Loel; I feel as though I might swoon," he gasped. "Leave off and give me the chance to turn your brains to mush."

"Such sweet words," Marche said as he nudged the flexing port. "Let me get my fill of you before I lose my senses."

Valentine groaned at the exquisite caress and pressed closer, offering his lips. Marche did not linger long on the threshold. Hungrily, he pillaged the wet velvet chamber of Valentine's mouth, and a thrill ran through him when his partner reciprocated ardently. He eased the pliant young man a few steps to the chaise and with gentle pressure against Valentine's sternum, encouraged his lover to lie back on his elbows. Gazing trustingly up into Marche's eyes, Valentine relaxed as his trousers were pulled farther down. The duke put a knee on the cushions and leaned in, sipping once more at the sweetest lips he'd ever tasted. Valentine strained upward, acting as his instinct bade him. Opening Marche's shirt, he ran his hands over the broad chest as he returned the kiss with equal passion. Judging the moment ripe, Marche eased a fingertip into the hole he'd been circling and found lingering traces of oil. Valentine groaned against Marche's lips as he was entered, his hips lifting wantonly in welcome. The big nobleman's finger slid into the tight passage to the second knuckle, pulsing subtly against the front wall of Valentine's sheath. Each small stroke set off a rush of pleasure so intense that Valentine was well nigh overwhelmed. The young man was afraid that if his cock swelled any further, it would explode, and yet, every pass of the teasing digit wound the tension up another notch. "Wait," he said in a choked little voice.

Marche raised his eyebrows as he traced a tingling path down the length of Valentine's arousal with his forefinger. "I am paying for this room by the hour," he said drily.

A laugh rose in Valentine's throat, changing from nervous to merry in mid-stream. "By my faith, you have well and truly ruined me," he said amid his chuckles.

Marche's topaz eyes smoldered like those of a falcon tracking prey as he leaned in to take Valentine's mouth again. Still smiling, the young man put a hand on the back of Loel's head and pulled him closer, extending the kiss. When their lips finally parted, Marche searched among the items on the table until he found what he wanted. Taking up a small crystal flagon, he covered his fingers with oil. Easing his fore and middle fingers into the tight passage, he found the young man's pleasure center. As he circled the small mound, he trailed his fingers up the underside of the leaking shaft. Valentine whined and wiggled against the couch as Marche stimulated him again to an almost unbearable peak of excitement.

"I know it is fickle and selfish, but I have changed my mind. I want you to put your cock in me now," Valentine said breathlessly.

"Yes, my lord." Marche grinned. Freeing his hard length, he grasped it near the base and anointed it with the rest of the oil. He gave his stiff shaft a few strokes to ensure it was well greased before he seated it.

"Wait, please," Valentine said again as he felt the hot hardness press against his opening.

"Does this hurt?"

"No. It is only that when we first did this I could not...." Valentine's voice trailed off.

"You may speak your mind to me. Surely you must know that by now."

Valentine blushed. "I wish to see what it looks like. When you... enter me."

"Let me help you to sit up a bit," Marche said swiftly.

When Valentine was settled, propped on his elbows, he watched in fascination as Marche eased a finger into him. Grasping his arousal, Marche ran the head of his shaft up the crack of Valentine's ass and over the velvet balls to rest against Valentine's yearning arousal. The young man groaned as his husband took both cocks in one big hand and pumped them together while pressing insistently against his sweet spot.

"Loel, stop! I cannot hold back if you continue."

"Let it fly, my own."

"Have a care for your— oh! Oh my God!" Valentine's words broke apart into small cries of pleasure until a sharp gasp signaled his release. A thick stream of pale fluid jetted from the tip of his handsome cock to spatter against Marche's maroon waistcoat.

Releasing Valentine's shaft, Marche let his arousal slide down to the beckoning entrance. Gripping the base of his rod firmly, he pushed the swollen head through the tight ring of muscle. Valentine's breath hissed in through his gritted teeth, but he watched avidly, instinctively bearing down as the big cock forged ahead. Marche groaned as the contracting sheath hugged his length, and he began to thrust before he was halfway in.

Valentine soon found that his pleasure had not ended with the spilling of his seed. Marche continued to fondle him, nuzzling his neck, gently tweaking his tingling nipples, and tenderly stroking his contented cock. Under his lover's skillful hand, Valentine began to stiffen again. A pleased smile lit Marche's face as the sated shaft rose from its nest of sable curls, pushing against his palm like a hound begging for sweets. Slowly, steadily, Marche rocked his hardness in the snug passage, dragging haphazardly against Valentine's sweet spot in a most tantalizing manner. Marche leaned in to suck at the peaked nipples and grasped the young man's arousal firmly. In time with his thrusts, he shuttled his fist up and down the hard rod. Valentine's hips churned in response, pumping in truncated strokes, meeting Marche halfway.

"I thought we had reached the height of pleasure this morning," Valentine said breathlessly. "But we have surpassed it."

"I am sorry," Marche said in a strained voice, "but I won't last as long this time."

"Please yourself, my love. I am content."

Marche pushed Valentine's thigh back with his free hand and sheathed himself to the hilt. Valentine came with a surprised grunt, tossing his head from side to side, his hair trailing across the brocade as ripples of pleasure washed through him. Marche released the young man's shaft and pushed his knees wide apart to delve more deeply. He held his lover's long legs open, his thumbs rubbing circles on the soft inner thighs as he withdrew to the brink before sliding back in to the root. Valentine bore down hard, squeezing the pumping rod along its entire length as Marche groaned his pleasure. The duke's fingers sank into smooth skin as the exquisite sensation overwhelmed him and his shaft abruptly gave up its seed. He thrust twice more, but his climax was already rolling through him like the booming of battle drums. His knees failed him, and he settled his weight against Valentine's chest with a long sigh of utter fulfillment.

Valentine wrapped his arms around Marche and kissed the top of his head. "I love what we do together," he sighed. "And I love the way we fit together afterward." He shuddered deliciously as Marche's tongue circled his nipple and the shaft in his sheath twitched. Marche moved his hips subtly, and Valentine clutched at his shoulders. "Stop, please. If you rouse me again, I will surely expire. Three times in one day is ample, I assure you."

"Forgive me," Marche murmured, soothing his husband with light touches and kisses. "And in the interests of accuracy, I must point out that it was four times that you... found joy."

"Stop," Valentine said, moving restlessly. "No more. I beg you."

"I am not doing anything," Marche said.

"Liar. I can feel your cock wanting to plow me again."

"Then what shall we do about this situation?"

"I should like a few moments to catch my breath, if you please."

"Forgive me." Marche twisted his hips. "But if I do not disengage, I shall surely rise again."

Valentine shivered at the sudden feeling of emptiness, and then Marche pressed close again, seeking his mouth for a long kiss that banished the chill. "I fear I shall become spoiled," Valentine said when their lips parted. "You take such tender care of me."

"Enjoy it while you may, novice. As soon as you are educated in the ways of the flesh, I shall have no mercy on you."

"You are incorrigible."

"Excellent. If I am hopeless, then you may stop trying to save me and use your time for better pursuits."

"And what might those be?"

"Pleasing your husband would top the list, surely. You show admirable initiative in asking the advice of Mr. Fleet, but that is only a start."

"I think it is a point of pride with you to *always* be wicked. I will pray that you are not asked to pay for all your sins at once."

"Amen," Marche said with feeling.

CHAPTER 15

SWORD MASTER DOMENICO ANGELO left the group he was instructing to cross the sawdust-sprinkled floor. Angelo's man of business bowed to Marche and Valentine and stood aside in deference to his employer. After Angelo had a few whispered words with his agent, he addressed Marche.

"I am devastated that Your Grace was made to wait. You are a preferred client, and I will, of course, make an exception for you."

"No indeed, *signore*." Marche returned the famous swordsman's bow. "I would not dream of presuming on your good nature."

"I insist. I will take your young gentleman in hand and give him proper instruction. You will pay me when your difficulties are sorted out."

"Ah now, you have hit upon the stumbling block, sir. I must first discover the nature of my difficulties. I was not aware of any financial straits until your man informed me that my credit was no good."

"A mistake for which he will immediately apologize."

"I believe he acted in good faith and out of loyalty to you," Marche replied. "Do not trouble yourself, *signore*. I am sorry to have disturbed an artist with mundane matters. We will return when this is resolved."

"You were a wonderful pupil, Your Grace," Angelo said, "and I would be delighted to instruct your companion whenever you are ready."

Valentine bowed to the Italian master as Marche spoke again. "Thank you, an honor to have your good opinion. Come, Blythestone; I am afraid your fencing lessons must wait for a bit." The duke pivoted on his heel and walked swiftly away.

"May I know where we are going?" Valentine tried not to let exasperation enter his voice, but Marche was bowling along like a runaway phaeton and had seemingly gone deaf.

"My accounting house," Marche said over his shoulder. "As I should have done as soon as we returned to Town. I had planned on stopping there after the teahouse, but I was somewhat distracted by that time."

"I am sorry to have delayed an errand of such urgency with my whims."

Marche stopped, discommoding several pedestrians who were forced to step off the footpath. "It is my own arrogance that is to blame. Lord Kirkcap took me aside to tell me of a rumor he'd heard, and I did not give it enough weight. Sir Anthony is as flighty as an actress, but I do not excuse myself on that account. The moment I heard the gossip from Strand that several fortunes had gone missing along with Murdmont, I should have looked into it."

"Then do not tarry here." Valentine began walking.

Marche caught up in two long strides. "Don't you wish to gloat a bit?"

"Whatever for?"

"You've told me many times that I should take things more seriously, and I made sport of you for it. Now, it seems I shall suffer the consequences of taking my affairs too lightly."

"You cannot be sure until you speak with your banker."

Marche gave Valentine a sidelong look. "Actually, I think this was Murdmont's intention all along. I think he planned this coup for some time, but I will have to explain later." Marche stopped in front of a dark brick building with marble facing. "Will you wait outside?"

"I may not come with you?"

"It is a request, not an order." Marche sighed. "It has nothing to do with you or—"

"You needn't explain now," Valentine interrupted. "Go attend your business, and I will wait in the coffeehouse across the way."

"My thanks." Marche lowered his voice. "It is just my foolish pride, my own."

"I know." Valentine gave the duke a heartening smile as he turned away.

"I DO not understand," Valentine said, ignoring the stack of invitations on the foyer table as he walked briskly after Marche. Marche hadn't spoken since exiting the accounting house of Jonas, Moer, and McMurtrey, and nothing Valentine said seemed to penetrate his black mood. "Loel, please stop and talk to me."

"I want a drink," Marche called from the small drawing room. "Come and take one with me."

"Very well." Valentine accepted the glass of amber liquid Marche handed him. "But for mercy's sake, give me some small word."

The duke tossed back his cognac and set down his glass. "I am ruined," he said.

"No," Valentine corrected him without pause. "*We* are ruined."

Marche took the young man's hand and drew him close. "I hoped you would stand by me," he said, kissing Valentine's forehead. "But I did not wish to presume."

"Whether the world honors it or not, I feel myself wedded to you. What sort of husband would I be if I deserted you in a dark hour?"

"Dark indeed. I should have heeded my suspicions about Murdmont right away. Are you certain you do not wish to chide me a little?"

"You were somewhat distracted, to be fair. You endured the death of your beloved aunt, a bullet wound, and my constant company. Now tell me what has happened."

"Murdmont had my aunt's signature on several documents that allowed him a free hand for some time now. He holds the paper to all combined properties, and the family vault at Barclay's is empty. Murdmont had a plan in place for some time, and your advent was the catalyst that set it in motion."

"Has he some grievance against your family?"

Marche drank down another measure of spirits before he answered obliquely. "Others were fleeced as well: the Travertons, the Sudvilles, old Sir Jabez Wallwhit, and the Worrel-Shepards. Cleaned out, pockets to let."

"Can your fortunes not be recovered?"

"If it can be proven that Murdmont is a swindler, we will regain the property, but it will take time. Meanwhile, Murdmont has all our gold and is no doubt laughing up his sleeve on the Continent. Foremost in my mind is the wish to wipe the smirk from his face so my aunt may enjoy her afterlife in peace."

"I quite understand. Our baggage could be ready in somewhat less than an hour, and we may take ship to join Strand."

"You would not oppose the idea of pursuing Murdmont?"

"Not so long as I may come with you."

Marche put his palm to Valentine's cheek. "No better soul exists this side of heaven," he said.

"Then you must try harder to live up to me," Valentine teased gently as he rose on his toes to kiss Marche.

Marche chuckled. "Minx, where is the bookish prig who stole my heart?"

"Still here, my lord," Valentine moved toward the stairs. "Still awaiting his fencing lessons."

Marche caught up with the other man and slipped an arm around his waist. "When we reach our chambers, I will happily practice thrusting with you again."

"It has scarcely been three hours since last we dueled in that manner."

"Forgive me; I did not realize it had been so long." Marche squeezed Valentine's butt cheek as they entered their private quarters.

"You did not realize what was so long, sir?" Anne asked. Setting a stack of fresh linen on the trunk at the end of Marche's big bed, the housekeeper lifted her eyebrows at the nobleman.

"Your patience, Mistress Kermartin," Marche said smoothly, bowing over Anne's hand as he removed his from Valentine's backside.

"Have I need to be patient with Your Grace?"

"I daresay you have, ma'am, and I thank you for your forbearance and your good care of my dear friend Blythestone."

"Has there been any word from the shore?" Valentine broke in.

Anne's bright blue eyes twinkled. "There has indeed. Your mother received a note from your sister, informing her of the marriage. My lady decided to fetch her back, and Mr. Harston arranged for a carriage. They are on their way to Scotland."

"Why do you look so pleased?"

"Well, sir," Anne smiled at Valentine. "I believe the lady was hinting in her letter that she and Mr. Harston might follow your sister's example."

"Oh my."

"Surely that is happy news," Marche said at the blank look on his lover's face.

"Yes, of course, but the idea that one's mother...." Valentine pulled himself together. "Anne, His Grace and I are leaving straightaway for—" The housekeeper looked expectantly at the young man as his words ended abruptly. Valentine turned to Marche.

"Strand's last letter put Murdmont in Amsterdam, you will recall," Marche supplied. "Where the villain no doubt cached as much gold as the Dutch vaults could hold."

"Then we sail for the Netherlands," Valentine said thoughtfully. "Loel, what will become of the people who take care of you?"

"You shame me. I had not thought of them."

"I have given it a little thought, as it occurred to me that Anne will not be able to accompany us. Was Lamberglyn Park among the properties that Lord Murdmont embezzled?"

Marche paused before he spoke. "Damme, I think you've hit upon it. My aunt deeded the property to you outright. Murdmont could not touch it. I propose that the staff will move to Lamberglyn until our return. If you will oversee our baggage, I will meet with Ambrose. As he was butler to my aunt for many years, I am confident that I can leave arrangements in his hands. As soon as Murdmont is brought to justice, everyone may go back to his place."

"I could almost pity Murdmont when you find him," Valentine said.

"Don't waste your sympathy on the likes of him," Anne advised. "Go on, Your Grace, and tend to your affairs. We will manage the packing of the household without you."

Since they were in their bedchamber, Marche saw no reason not to kiss Valentine as he left. The door closed behind him, and Valentine turned to Anne, flushed with the rush of heat that his lover could ignite with a mere glance. Anne observed her young master's rosy cheeks and flustered manner and easily guessed the reason.

"You will never love a woman, will you, sir?" she asked gently.

Valentine went red to his hairline. "Do you disapprove terribly?"

"A bit, I suppose. When you didn't become a priest, I thought I might help raise your sons and daughters one day, but I see I shall have to rely on Lady Valeria."

"Did you never consider having children of your own?"

"I never found the right father, my dear."

"Anne, I am very grateful to you for all your help."

"*I* am very glad to see *you* in proper attire." The housekeeper looked up from a press full of shirts. "I should frown on your friendship with the duke, but if you love one another, it is not my place to tell you that you may not. And I am very glad that you have found someone who loves you as much as His Grace does."

"I love him too."

"I thought you must, else you wouldn't let him be so free with your person."

"If it offends you…." Valentine let the words hang.

"It should." Anne laid aside a pair of woolen stockings. "But I find that it does not. It embarrasses me, sure enough, but it does not seem to me unnatural, as the clergy say it is."

Valentine crossed the room to hug the housekeeper. "Thank you, dear Anne," he said. "You cannot know what your good opinion means to me."

"Go on now," Anne said, pushing him gently as she wiped away a few tears. "I need trunks to put all of these clothes in. You are going aboard ship and will need to wrap up well."

"MAY the angels watch over my darlings," Anne murmured as the carriage bearing Blythestone and Marche drove out the gates bound for the harbor.

"I feel certain the young master has the good will of heaven," Negus remarked.

Anne dabbed at her eyes before tucking her handkerchief into a pocket. "You don't seem like a man who's on close acquaintance with angels," she sniffed.

"Contrariwise, ma'am. I've the pleasure of serving the Earl of Blythestone as well as the Duke of Marche."

"Buffoon," she said, hiding a smile as she went back inside the house. "I'll thank you to hold your sacrilegious tongue."

"I meant no offense." Negus hurried after the housekeeper. "And I'm worried about my master as well, what with him going off to foreign lands without me. Who will he find among the French to tie a proper cravat?"

"I am a Breton woman." Anne came to stop in the middle of the hall, her hands on her hips.

"I'll not hold it against you."

"Imp! Begone and let me do my work."

"I've not many duties with the duke gone. Maybe I could be of some use to you."

"You surprise me." Anne looked Negus in the eyes. "If you're sincere, I could use a bit of help packing up for the journey. I don't like to ask the footmen."

Negus grinned as he nodded. "It's the livery. Makes 'em all look grand as dukes."

Anne smiled back. "The way they strut about with their noses in the air puts me in mind of a bunch of ganders in a barnyard."

"Never been in a barnyard; I'm city born and bred."

"I'll not hold it against you," Anne said as she began walking again. "And I wonder what you'll make of our new home. The place hasn't been lived in for years upon years."

"I've no doubt you'll put it to rights soon enough, mistress."

"Enough of your nonsense. We've no choice but to move the household, but while we wait for their lordships to return, we can make Lamberglyn ready for them."

"Aye, we shall, and don't you worry about the footmen or any other of the staff. They know that I speak for the duke when he's away."

Anne turned at the bottom of the stair. "Then I would be glad if you could set them to loading as much bedding and crockery as the carts and carriages can bear."

Negus touched a finger to his forehead. "I'll get 'em stirrin', never fear. See to your packin', and I'll see that the trunks find their way to a wagon. Suppose I'd best send someone to the livery to hire what wagons they have on hand."

"A good notion. Now, let us bustle."

The smile stayed on Negus's face as he went about his business. It wasn't pleasant to lose everything, but he had come from nothing and reckoned he could work his way up to something again. And Mistress Kermartin was here to make life interesting as well as comfortable until the duke sorted things out. He only hoped his master was finding the chase diverting.

CHAPTER 16

"WHAT the bloody hell was that?" Marche said into the darkness of the tiny cabin.

Valentine shifted where he'd fallen asleep atop the other man. "What is that infernal racket?" he mumbled. "Make it stop, please."

Marche shifted Valentine aside and slid to the floor. The deck abruptly pitched and Valentine was flung from the narrow bunk. As Marche caught him, another rattling boom shivered the wood under their feet. "Our ship would appear to be under attack," Marche said, hurriedly doing up his breeches.

Valentine pulled his jacket on as the door of the cabin burst inward. Marche put up his fists, but the press of intruders pinned him to the wall with Valentine sandwiched between. In moments, the only two passengers on the merchant ship *Clarissa* were prisoners of French corsairs. With hands tied behind them, the struggling captives were harried up on deck with the other spoils. As crates and barrels were transferred to the freebooters' ship, the pirate captain inspected the survivors of the attack.

"Who are you, sir?" Marche asked sharply.

"I am Roi des Corsaires, captain of the *Revenant*." The man bowed sweepingly. "You may address me as Roi."

"King of the Pirates!" Marche translated. "You do not rate yourself too highly, do you?"

"I salute your bravery, sir. Your clothing is plain, but you have the manner of a great lord. I think you will fetch a handsome price in ransom."

Marche laughed. "You may have every ounce of gold I possess."

"Merci," Roi thanked him absently in his native tongue as his gaze lingered on Valentine's long, glossy locks. "And who is your charming companion?"

"Mr. Randwick is my secretary."

"*Mister* Randwick, is it? And *he* is a secretary? How very convenient. My pen has sorely been missing an inkpot. Achille!" The corsair called to one of his men. "Take this young *man* to my cabin and see that he stays there." Marche struggled furiously as the pirate took hold of Valentine's upper arm and three men leaped to restrain him. "Interesting," Roi said. "Is it possible that this *secretary* has more intimate duties than sharpening quills and adding up accounts?"

"How dare you!" Valentine said. "If you insist on speaking of me, sir, have the courtesy to speak to my face."

"I shall. Take this one away now, Achille."

Marche was held fast by four men as Valentine was dragged away. "If you harm him, I will kill you," the duke said.

"Ah, so it is as I thought. You have tender feelings for your aide. Tell me, does *he* feel love for you, as well, or is this merely a… job?"

Marche glared but didn't deign to answer.

"I will inquire of him myself, then," Roi said before he ordered Marche taken below deck and put in irons. After putting his quartermaster in charge of the booty, he went to his cabin. "You may remove the ropes," Roi told the man guarding Valentine. "Well, *Mister* Randwick, are you ready to write a letter?"

"That would depend, sir, on the nature of the correspondence."

"You will write to your employer's family and inform them of the amount of his ransom."

"No, sir, I will not."

Roi leaned over the seated prisoner. "Has it escaped your notice that you are at my mercy?"

"That would hardly be possible." Valentine rubbed the reddened skin of his wrists.

"You will do as I say or you will suffer the consequences of your disobedience."

"I do not care."

"Then your companion will suffer."

"If you harm Loel, I shall find a way to punish you."

"Loel, eh? Tell me, *cheri*, he is a nobleman, is he not?"

"I will tell you nothing, and I will thank you not to call me that."

"Why not, *ma belle*?"

"It is inappropriate."

"Inappropriate? You have the nerve to scold me? I will have a forfeit of you."

Before Valentine could react, the corsair took hold of his jaw and kissed him soundly. "How dare you!" Valentine said as he pushed the other man away and rose to his feet.

"I will dare much more," Roi said, dismissing the guard. "Come, *cheri*. You are strong, but you will yield to me."

"Never."

"Not even to save the life of your patron?"

"He would not wish to live at such a price, and I would not betray him so."

"I do believe you mean that." The captain cocked his head at Valentine. "Keep your honor, *ma belle*. Your Loel is a fortunate man to have such a brave and loyal mistress."

"I think you have misunderstood the English word mistress, and you mustn't call me *belle*."

"Please forgive any offense."

"It is not so much offensive as incorrect."

Without warning, Roi grasped the front of Valentine's shirt and tore it open. "*Mon dieu!*" he chuckled. "*L'absurdité!* I thought you were a woman in disguise."

"How dare you!" Valentine exclaimed for the third time in under an hour.

"I beg your pardon once more, monsieur. I thought you were a wealthy man's mistress traveling in disguise for safety's sake."

"Why would you imagine that?"

"I did not look too closely, it would seem."

Slightly mollified, Valentine folded his arms over the remnants of his shirt. "Not closely enough, that is certain."

"I can see quite clearly now that you are not a woman, but you are very comely. My wife—"

"Your wife?" Valentine interrupted. "For shame, sir! You are a married man, and you intended to dally with me!"

The corsair pursed his lips at the young man's scandalized tone. "You are still my prisoner," he reminded him.

"That will not stop me from pointing out bad form when I see it, sir."

"So the kitten is a lion's cub, eh? And how you roar at me! On my own ship!"

"I don't mean to be unseemly, but neither do I see how I owe respect to a pirate."

"I could have you killed with a word."

"I daresay you could, but it would not make me respect you one jot more."

"Why would a *pirate* want *your* good opinion?"

"You did not... force yourself on me, thus I surmise that you have a code of honor."

"I have underestimated you, Monsieur Randwick." Roi inclined his head. "Your youth and your beauty are strong arguments against wisdom, but you have outwitted me."

"You do not sound angry."

The captain smiled. "I am quite good at playing the fierce freebooter, eh? In truth, I am a French officer with a letter of marque from the king. Under the guise of privateer, I accost British merchant ships and use the plunder to benefit France."

"Upon my honor! Is it truly so?"

"You will forgive me if I do not give you my real name, but I hold high rank in private life as well as in the military. You already hold my reputation in your hands should you escape."

"Why would you reveal such things to me?"

"Perhaps I wish to have your good opinion." Roi's smile grew broader.

"Then release Marche at once and set us down on a friendly shore."

"You called him Loel before."

"Most men have at least two names, sir."

"So they do." The captain held up his hands in a gesture of surrender. "We are close to the coast of Brittany. Will that do?"

"It will do admirably. I was reared there."

"Were you now? I find that interesting as you haven't a trace of an accent."

"I was educated at the Franciscan monastery in Cancale near Saint-Malo. I suppose you might say that my accent is more clerical than provincial."

Roi nodded his understanding. "I know Cancale well," he said. "I was taught by the Jesuits at the monastery on the other side of the river."

"The devil you say!" Valentine used one of Marche's favorite expressions of surprise. "Our *abbé* always accused the Jesuits of filching our apples as soon as they were ripe."

Roi chuckled. "Our *abbé* said the same thing of the Franciscans and our asparagus. Myself, I care nothing for asparagus; give me a steaming platter of oysters from the estuary."

"Please, sir, not another word. I have not had my breakfast, and you will set my stomach to grumbling with your talk. I could not bear the embarrassment."

"As I am the cause of missing *le petit déjeuner*, allow me to provide one."

"What of my companion and the members of the *Clarissa*'s crew?"

"The men of the crew are eating below deck and will be treated with all the courtesy of prisoners of war. I will have your friend brought here. Will that content you?"

"I am always happy when a wrong is righted."

"Do you not fear me at all?"

"I did at first."

"Yet you did not let it show."

"I had to be brave for my companion's sake."

"Ah, so it is like that with you. I do not understand the love of one man for another, not of that kind, but if it is your love that gives you courage, then I will not scorn it."

"I could wish that all men were of your character, sir."

"How kind of you to say so. I find your company most diverting, Monsieur Randwick. Give me but a moment and food will be brought, as well as your companion."

The food arrived somewhat sooner than Marche. He was escorted into the captain's cabin by two burly sailors as Valentine was popping the last bite of a fried pie into his mouth.

"I gave orders to remove his bonds," Roi said. The captain set down his coffee cup as Valentine jumped to his feet and went to Marche.

"Yes, captain," one of the guards replied in Breton, "but he kept fighting us."

"Did you explain to him that he was free?" Valentine asked in the same tongue.

The sailor looked at the young man in surprise. "We tried, m'sieur."

"Loel," Valentine said, removing the gag from his husband's mouth, "these men mean us no harm now."

"You make friends very quickly," Marche said as soon as he could speak.

"This is not the time for baseless jealousy or wounded pride," Valentine said softly. "You should know me a little by now."

The glower melted from Marche's face. "Forgive me. While I was alone, I imagined all manner of horrible things, and then to find you breaking bread with—"

"Then I shall take care not leave you alone again," Valentine interrupted.

Marche looked over Valentine's shoulder and made eye contact with the captain. "I am Loel Woodbine, monsieur."

The privateer bowed. "I am afraid I may not introduce myself. Do me the favor to call me Roi."

"Do I assume you have abandoned your plan to ransom me?"

"I was persuaded otherwise. You have a most loyal friend in Mr. Randwick. Not even to save your life would he yield his honor to me."

Marche's topaz eyes fastened on the Breton. "I hope I misunderstand your English."

"The misunderstanding was mine. Let us say that Mr. Randwick passed a test and speak no more of it."

"Do stop glaring at the captain, Marche," Valentine said. "Sit and have some breakfast."

"A few weeks ago, you blanched at vulgar language; now you are having tea with pirates."

"Well, I am *very* hungry."

Marche smiled at last. "There is not another like you," he said as he sat.

"WATCH your footwork," Marche called out as he lounged at the taffrail.

Valentine glanced toward his lover, and his momentary lapse was enough to doom him. Roi's saber penetrated the young man's guard, summarily ending the match. Valentine made a rueful face at the captain over the gleaming steel at his throat. Instead of withdrawing the blade, the corsair sent the flashing point ghosting across Valentine's cheek with a supple turn of his wrist. Valentine felt a sting and when he raised his hand to his face, it came away bloody.

"A small reminder," Roi said. "If you wish for skill with a weapon, you must always remember its purpose. You are not learning the steps of a pretty dance; you are wielding an instrument designed to kill. If you bear a weapon, you must accept that one day you may be called upon to use it. When that time comes, you cannot hesitate. Do you understand?" The corsair finished his speech and waited for the young man's reaction.

"I should not have let myself be distracted," Valentine said.

"*Bon!*" Roi took Valentine's jaw in his left hand. "Very good, Monsieur Randwick. You will have a small, a very small, scar to remind you, but more importantly, you kept your temper."

"Shall we clean that up?" Marche asked as casually as he could. The sight of Valentine's blood had a powerful effect on him, but he too held his temper.

"I would rather practice a bit more," Valentine said quickly.

"I think you will master the sword," Roi told him. "You have the necessary physical gifts, you learn so fast you make me dizzy, and you are able to master yourself. Now, *en garde*! We have just enough time for one more lesson."

When they said farewell at the port of Saint-Malo, Roi des Corsaires presented Valentine with the saber he'd used in practice. Though thrilled with the sword, the young man put it away in his baggage until he acquired enough skill to carry it. Roi approved of the cautious measure and offered some further aid before the English gentlemen debarked. "I know a man who knows a man," he said, giving them the name of a local merchant.

"Much appreciated." Marche bowed.

"I sincerely hope you will find the scoundrel you seek and trounce him," Roi said.

"My thanks, sir. Though our nations are at war, I cannot count you as an enemy."

Roi bowed in turn. "You have spoken what is in my heart, monsieur, or should I say monsieur *le duc*?"

"I am simply Mr. Woodbine for the time being."

"*Bon chance* to you, M'sieur Woodbine, and to you M'sieur Randwick."

"Thank you, Captain," Valentine said. "Though I deplore the circumstance, I am glad to have made your acquaintance. You shall be in my prayers."

"Merci. I am sure your words go directly from your lips to the ears of the angels. Bon voyage."

CHAPTER 17

MARCHE and Valentine had little trouble finding the establishment of the corsair's friend in Saint-Malo. Monsieur Fantod read Roi's note of introduction and welcomed the Englishmen warmly. A scant two hours later, the visitors had dined well and donned new apparel provided by their host. They also received the name of a tavern with a livery that would suit their needs. Thanking the merchant, they bid him *adieu* and walked to the inn near the docks.

The tavern was bustling at midday with all manner of laborers sitting at their luncheon. The working men at the trestle tables didn't look up from their trenchers, but they watched the strangers suspiciously from the corners of their eyes. Recognizing Breton fishermen, stevedores, and boat wrights by their clothing, Valentine smiled amiably as he crossed the floor, but Marche was glad enough to quit the common room for quarters more genteel. The landlord himself greeted them as they moved into the area reserved for guests with fatter purses. "Gentlemen," he said in Breton. "Be welcome. How may I serve you today?"

Marche deferred to Valentine, who answered the man in the same tongue. "We would like a bottle of your best local wine and some information on your livery."

"That would be a great pleasure, m'sieur. I will send in the wine and join you as soon as I have attended to a few details. Would you care to sit here?"

As the innkeeper gestured to a table near the only window, someone called from the corner. "Strike me! I cannot believe my eyes!"

Marche and Valentine turned to see Darby St. Denis sitting on a bench with his right leg propped on a cushion. Lord Strand wore a dressing gown and slippers and a thunderstruck expression. "Marche, what the devil are you…" his voice trailed off as he spotted Valentine. "My goddess!" he gasped.

"Good sir," Valentine said to the landlord, "we have happened upon a friend. If you would be so good as to send in the wine, I think our questions for you might wait for another time."

"I will see that you have privacy," the innkeeper said. He left the room, standing aside as Lords Tarmegent and Snowhurst entered.

"Stop that immediately," Neville said sharply as Darby attempted to stand. "Or do you enjoy the pain? Help me, Snow."

Snowhurst, his right arm in a sling, was staring at Marche and Valentine. "Tarmy," he said, "we have company."

"Damn your eyes, give me a hand with Strand."

"Allow me," Marche said, putting a hand on Darby's shoulder and forcing him back down. "Please be so good as to remain seated, Strand."

"And calm," Tarmegent said, adjusting the bandage on his forehead.

"Calm?" Darby turned his wide-eyed gaze on Neville. "How can I remain calm? Do you not see what I see? I am quite undone by the sight of the Duchess of Marche in breeches."

Snowhurst guffawed. "What are you on about, Strand? That is not the duchess."

"Of course, it is," Strand insisted. "I would know those purple eyes in the dark. I could draw the curves of those lips blindfolded."

"I grant you, he looks devilish like Marche's duchess, but he is *plainly* no lady. Are you certain you are *not* blindfolded?"

"Snow is right, for once," Neville said. "What lady would have occasion to acquire a wound such as this gallant sports on his downy cheek? That's a sword bite, or I'm a chimney sweep."

"Gentlemen," Marche broke in. "Allow me to unravel this riddle. I have the honor to introduce Valentine Edward Albion Randwick, Earl of Blythestone, and brother to my lady."

"Sir Valentine," Neville said as he made a short bow. "Neville Jameson Stokes, Viscount Tarmegent, at your service."

"Crispin Cornwallis Ludstall, Baron Snowhurst, your service, sir." Snowhurst inclined his head to Valentine.

Darby tried again to rise, but Neville kept him in his seat. "Forgive me for not standing. I've a trifling wound, but my friends prefer to think me at death's door. Darby Llewellyn St. Denis, Baronet of Strand, at your service, sir."

"I am pleasantly overwhelmed by the warmth of your greeting, my lords," Valentine answered.

"The Duchess of Marche is a paragon of womanhood," Darby said. "I hold her in the highest regard." The young nobleman peered suspiciously at Valentine as he spoke. "You are enough like her to be her twin, you know."

"I believe that is the first thing I said to you," Marche turned to Valentine.

"Indeed it was," Valentine said gratefully.

"Ah, of course," Darby exclaimed. "This is your home, Blythestone, is it not?"

Valentine nodded. "Valeria and I grew up very near here, though some distance apart."

"It sounds as though there might be a story in that," Crispin said. "And here's Annicka with a bottle. Good lass, but we'll need one or two more."

"It is no great tale," Valentine said as he took a seat. "As a young man with a temper, my father made enemies and chose self-exile in Brittany. He entrusted his English affairs to a man recommended by an old friend. Once my family left England, this agent set about selling all our property before disappearing with a fortune. I was an infant and so did not feel the loss of wealth as my parents did. My father sadly did not recover from the blow. By my mother's account, shame hounded him into an early grave."

"I think it's a rather affecting tale," Neville said. "But tell us why you grew up apart from your family."

"My father feared that his enemies would strike at him through me. He hid me away in a monastery, and I had no contact with my family for a long time."

"Raised by monks, by God!" Crispin exclaimed. "When did you escape?"

"I was there until a few months ago. I was devastated to miss Valeria's wedding."

"Then you must keep company with us; we have much to teach you."

"Not everyone is inclined to a wastrel's life, Snowhurst," Marche said softly.

"Eh?" Crispin turned to Marche and whatever he saw in the other man's eyes sobered him. Reaching for the bottle, he splashed more wine into his cup.

"Thank you for your kind invitation," Valentine said. "I am certain we will find occasion to dine together at least."

"I am not sure Snowhurst takes solid food," Marche said.

"Very good, Marche." Darby laughed. "We shall dine together, and I will tell you of our chase. As you may have guessed, Murdmont is not in our custody. The villain remains at large, but we know where he is going."

"The blackguard has set up shop in Nantes, passing himself off as a recluse called Monsieur Maurice D'Arc and working through local agents," Neville said. "Never have I crossed paths with a slipperier fish."

"Does he know he is being followed?" Marche asked.

Darby shook his head. "Not to my knowledge, sir."

"He is setting up his own bank," Neville said. "Can you imagine the gall?"

"We already know that he has no character," Valentine said. "What would he stop at? Is he not the cause of the bandages you wear?"

The three Dandies looked at one another with sheepish expressions before Darby spoke. "I wish I could say that our wounds were sustained in a pitched battle with Murdmont and his lackeys, but in truth we have not come face-to-face with him."

"In truth, we are victims of our zeal," Neville spoke up. "When we learned that Sir Malcolm had decamped Amsterdam in the dead of night, as is his habit, we were afire to take the road after him. In our haste, we commandeered a carriage from the inn yard."

"You are too kind, Tarmy," Crispin said. "I stole the carriage, which was—unbeknownst to me—waiting for repairs. There was quite a to-do, I can tell you, when the wheel came off. It is quite all right to laugh, Marche. The sight of me flying from the driver's seat like a pinwheel poppet was right comical, I'm sure, to those who witnessed the event. I've a broken wing to show for it, but hale otherwise."

"I came off lightly," Neville said. "A bump to the noggin, no harm done. Poor Strand was not so lucky."

"Oh, do stop nattering," Darby said. "It is nothing to speak of, nothing at all."

"Strand is a trifle sensitive about his injury," Crispin said, pouring more wine.

"It is a sensitive area," Darby snapped. "May we cease discussing it incessantly?"

"Oh dear." Marche affected a jaded drawl. "Has your oldfellow been in the wars, Strand?"

"His sword is indeed bent, though not into a plowshare," Snowhurst quipped.

Tarmegent could not forbear to join in. "It is a sad truth that his rod was not spared."

"Do stop tormenting the poor man," Valentine said, taking a seat next to the red-faced rake. "Can you not see how terribly this wounds him?"

Strand settled back as young Blythestone came to his defense, fussing over him and shielding him from the jibes of the others. "I can see that they rear a more refined sort of gentleman in the abbeys of Brittany," he said pointedly. "Tell me, dear, gentle Sir Valentine, what brings you here in the company of Marche?"

"When Marche informed me of this man Murdmont's crimes, I naturally offered my services to him as a sort of guide while he is in Brittany."

"Of course." Darby nodded his thanks as Valentine tucked another cushion behind him. "How could you do less for your sister's husband? What a foolish question. I think my wits must be quite scrambled." He looked up. "Not a word, Snow! And you, Marche, how pleasant for you to have a companion who speaks the local lingo."

"Indeed, I am very fortunate to be able to rely on my brother-in law, especially now that Murdmont has stolen all my wealth as well as my aunt's life. If it were not for my new family, I would be reduced to begging in the streets."

"Hardly that," Valentine protested as the other three men erupted with questions.

"Murdmont's a thief, you say?" Neville said.

"Devil take the rotter!" Snow exclaimed.

"Not before I find him, I hope," Marche said. "I'd not like to wrestle Old Nick for the pleasure of dispatching Murdmont. And now that I say it, perhaps we should not tarry. I think it might be best if we hire fast horses and leave for Nantes immediately."

"Surely not without a morsel or two to sustain you on the road," Darby said. "Sit, sir, and satisfy our curiosity about the latest skulduggery while Tarmy arranges mounts for you."

"Yes, allow me," Neville said as he got to his feet. "I've an eye for the nags."

"That is not necessary," Marche said.

"However, the kindness is much appreciated," Valentine added. "My thanks to you and to Strand for the suggestion."

"Not at all." Darby smiled at Valentine. "I find that my fond admiration of your sister extends to you as well."

"I am most flattered, sir."

"Who would not be?" Marche remarked. "If we are quite finished polishing one another's buttons, may we see to the ordering of supplies for our journey?"

"Allow me," Crispin said as he set down his cup of wine. "I won't be a moment."

"I hope you have not dined," Darby said as Lord Snowhurst left the room. "I am sure Annicka will be here soon with the first of several platters. If I may strain your belief, I must say that this tavern serves quite the finest food I have ever tasted."

Valentine's smile grew broader. "If you are fond of shellfish, you now find yourself in heaven."

Marche found himself left out as the conversation turned to a lively discussion of the local delicacies. A frown stole over his handsome features as he struggled to tamp down his irritation at this exclusion. He tried to ignore how it made him feel when Valentine laughed at Strand's vapid jests or touched the other young nobleman's hand in sympathy. Subjectively, he knew that nothing untoward was transpiring under his nose, but his heart was scalded each time his beloved's eyes rested upon the other man. It was a deuced painful business, being in love, and he was not sure he was equal to the challenge. He was actually relieved when Snowhurst returned and began a long-winded account of his adventures in the inn's kitchen.

The meal arrived, and, shortly after, Tarmegent returned from the livery. Over luncheon, Marche gave the Dandies an accounting of how Murdmont had gulled several clients of their fortunes.

"Surely, since Murdmont's actions are clearly criminal, you will regain your properties," Neville said.

Marche nodded. "I may hope it is clear to all, particularly the magistrates, and that it is only a matter of time. However, I wish Murdmont returned to England to face his victims and reap the shame he has earned. Then, it is my fondest hope that he will be convicted of my aunt's murder and hanged as quickly as possible."

"Really, Marche!" Valentine reproved. "It is wrong to wish the death of anyone, no matter how despicable."

"I am not so good a person as you," Marche replied. "I suppose it is because I hadn't the benefit of a religious education."

"If the dastard killed Lady Bolbracken, surely he deserves death in return," Darby said.

"I do not believe that I have any more right to take a life than Murdmont had," Valentine asserted.

"And there you have it, gentlemen," Marche remarked loftily. "Young Blythestone is quite out of our orbit when speaking of moral integrity." Valentine fixed Marche with a puzzled gaze as the other man shrugged and rose from the table. "If you will all forgive me," he said, "I am going to the livery to look over Tarmegent's choice."

"Pray excuse me as well," Valentine said as he hurried after Marche. "Please wait," he called as soon as they were out of doors.

Marche stopped in the shadow of the stables. "It is not necessary for you to accompany me. Please go back inside and enjoy the rest of your supper."

"Why are you behaving so oddly?"

"It is nothing I wish to discuss at the moment."

"Surely you are not feeling jealous of Darby again? He prefers females, as it happens."

"If I am jealous, at least I have the courtesy and good taste not to speak of it."

Valentine's eyes widened as though he'd been slapped. "Perhaps you find my ill-mannered company tiresome and wish to be rid of me."

"I wish you would go back inside and keep company with those closer to you in age."

"So I am immature as well as coarse?"

"You would know that better than I."

"I do not understand why you are being so unpleasant to me."

"Men have moods."

"That is all you have to say?"

"I could say a great deal more, but I would rather that you left me alone." Unable to bear the look on Valentine's face, Marche walked away. He would explain later and apologize sincerely, but just now, he needed to expend his anger in some fashion that did no harm to anyone. A quick gallop to test the mettle of the hired horses would do the trick. After a bit of exercise and time to think, he could rid himself of his foolish suspicions. He glanced once over his shoulder as he entered the livery, but Valentine was gone.

"Ah, well met sir," someone called out as Marche approached the stalls.

The duke recognized Monsieur Fantod, the Breton merchant who had been so helpful. "Good day again, sir."

"I have been looking for you." The merchant showed his teeth in a wide grin. "And as I sent you here, I assumed that this is where I would find you. Am I not clever?"

"And what may I do for you?" Marche said impatiently.

"You can die."

Something struck Marche in the back of the head and drove him to his knees. Another blow put him on his face, and then darkness claimed him.

CHAPTER 18

"BLYTHESTONE!" Darby called as Valentine returned to the inn. "Is all well?"

"Marche insists on seeing to the horses himself," Valentine replied. "I am fond of the man, but I could wish he were a bit more trusting."

Snowhurst and Tarmegent exchanged a glance.

"Why do you look so hangdog, sirs?" Valentine asked.

Darby cleared his throat. "I assume your acquaintanceship with Marche is very recent and of short duration," he said carefully.

"How could it be otherwise? You know my history, but pray do go on."

"I will only say that in London, Marche is not known for his sweet temper or his sufferance of those he deems beneath his regard."

Valentine lifted his chin. "And yet Valeria writes to me that she finds him very pleasant."

"That does not surprise me," Darby replied. "The lady's divine influence would make a poet out of a pig. However, Marche has little time for anyone outside his own set."

"I might have heard rumor that he is a bit of a rake," Valentine ventured.

The three Dandies exchanged another glance. "I am not sure how much I should say," Darby began hesitantly. "These are not things one speaks of to acquaintances, if at all, and Marche is part of your family now."

"You may speak plainly, sir," Valentine said. "We are all men, are we not? And gentlemen at that. Never fear that I shall betray a confidence."

"It would never cross my mind that you would do anything of the sort. I am not part of Marche's crowd, naturally, but of course, one hears rumors. I say this not as warning, but merely so that you may better understand your brother-in-law. I have it on somewhat good authority that he prefers the company of his own sex."

"In the bedchamber," Crispin clarified in a stage whisper.

"I confess myself shocked," Valentine said, biting the inside of his cheek to keep from laughing. "I would never have guessed. He seems so very... manly."

"You have my agreement on that, sir," Tarmegent said.

"Makes me feel like I'm still in swaddling," Snowhurst chimed in.

"He is only the size of a small mountain," Darby continued. "It is difficult not to feel somewhat... unsettled when you are standing in his shadow."

Valentine nodded sagely. "I have felt the effect myself."

"Please do not give too much weight to my words. I do not mean to imply that Marche is not a gentleman—"

"Only that he is a homosexual and deserving of scorn," Valentine finished for him.

"That is not what I was going to say. I hope you did not hear either ridicule or contempt in my words when I spoke of Marche."

"No, I did not. Then may I assume that you approve of Marche's... penchant?"

Darby was in a quandary. Should he do the correct thing and denounce all those who practiced the Greek vice? Or did he tell the truth and risk losing Blythestone's regard?

"Pish!" Crispin took the decision out of Darby's hands. "Strand don't give a fig what a man does for his fun, so long as he's given the same leave."

"How very liberal of you," Valentine said to Darby. "I am always glad to meet a man with tolerance for others."

"I try not to prejudge a man on the basis of anything other than his wardrobe."

"Are you being witty or honest?"

"You surely cannot consider my remark clever, so it must be honest."

Valentine smiled. "I do hope we shall become good friends, Strand."

"You have an open invitation to be my guest whenever you are in England."

"It seems we are forgotten," Crispin remarked to Neville.

"Indeed, it does," Neville replied.

"Perhaps you have grown dull," Darby suggested.

"Oh dear, can we not be pleasant?" Valentine said.

"Where the devil is Marche?" Neville adroitly changed the subject.

The serving girl came in to light the lamps, and Valentine noticed how deep the gloom had grown. It did not seem as though much time had passed as he sat talking with the other young men, but out the window he could see the sun balanced on the line between sky and sea. Surely, Marche should have returned by now.

"Steady there," Crispin said as Valentine jumped to his feet, making the goblets rattle.

"I beg your pardons," Valentine said. "I will see what is delaying Marche. Pray keep your seats." He gave them no opportunity to reply as he moved swiftly across the room and out the door. As he walked the short distance to the livery, he marveled again that most of a day had been spent in nothing more than conversation. At the abbey, talking was actively discouraged unless the words were in praise of God and idle time was almost unknown. Valentine was surprised at how much he'd enjoyed simply sitting down with pleasant company for food, drink, and plain talk. It was neither elevating nor productive in any tangible way, but it had left him with an undeniable sense of well-being, as his soul was uplifted by an inspiring sermon. When he found Marche, he would keep his temper, and if His Grace was still in bad humor, he would gentle him out of the black mood.

"Pardon me," Valentine called out in the local *patois*. "Are you employed by the livery?"

The sandy-haired man filling the water trough didn't look up as he answered. He'd been told not to speak to any Englishmen today, but this fellow was clearly from the province. "Aye, m'sieur. How can I serve you?"

"A Mr. Woodbine came here to hire horses. Do you know where he has gone?"

The hostler shrugged. "If he's wealthy, it's odds he's down at the docks with my master."

"I do not understand. I can see that you have much work to do, but might I impose again on your kindness to ask why Mr. Woodbine would go to the docks?"

Another shrug. "I keep to my own business."

"Is there nothing more you can tell me?"

"It is my guess that your gentleman went away with my master and M'sieur Fantod. It's certain he wasn't here after they left."

"Fantod the merchant?"

"You know him, then."

"Thank you," Valentine said as he dug a coin from his waistcoat pocket. "For your trouble."

The groom took his attention from his task long enough to catch the money. "Thank you, sir!" he said when he saw the size and color of the coin. "Good luck to you."

"Good health to you and yours," Valentine replied automatically as he hurried away. He could not imagine why Marche had gone down to the harbor, but given the man's mood, he would not attempt to predict his actions. It never occurred to Valentine that Marche might be engaged in some activity that would make company unwelcome. His only thought was to find his lover. As his search led him out onto the wharfs, but he spotted a familiar figure supervising the loading of a small ship.

"M'sieur Fantod! May I have a moment of your time, sir?"

The merchant focused on Valentine, and his ruddy face lost some color. He called to the pair of burly men about to ascend the gangplank, and they set down the crate they were carrying. "How very convenient," Fantod said. "I thought we would have to come collect you, which would have caused a great deal of bother, but you have solved all of my difficulties."

"Collect me, sir?" A slight frown narrowed Valentine's gaze. "If you are issuing an invitation, you might have chosen your words with more care."

"And you should take more care than to come to the docks alone."

"What an ominous thing to say! Do you imply that I am in some danger, sir?"

The merchant chuckled. "Forgive my untimely humor, but I can see why Murdmont hates you so. I shall take great delight in mocking him with it when I see him again."

"Do you speak of Sir Malcolm Murdmont?"

"That expression on your face is terribly charming—just like a startled doe. You've no notion of yourself at all, have you? How that must bedevil Murdmont!"

"How would that be possible when I have never met the man?"

"Brazen it out, if you wish. You did not fool him, my *lady*."

"Your speech grows confusing. What have either of us to do with Lord Murdmont?"

"In simplest terms, he owns me. He owns my shipping business. He owns this ship," Fantod gestured. "What I do, I do at his bidding."

"I do not know what you are doing," Valentine was goaded into saying. "However, if Murdmont ordered it, it can only be wickedness. If you know where he is, I demand that you tell me."

"*Mon dieu!* Such innocent self-righteousness! Have you any idea how fetching you are with your eyes afire? No, I think not. If you were aware of your effect, Murdmont would not despise you with such ardor.

It's plain you know him and oh, how your mere existence must gall him."

"You speak in riddles. I wish only to know if you have seen my companion since we left you."

"Indeed I have. Would you like me to take you to him?" The merchant gestured and the pair of dockworkers approached Valentine.

"What is your intention, sir?" Valentine asked.

"Really, your naïveté is so sweet it is near cloying. Be sweet a while longer, and these fellows will reunite you with your… friend."

Valentine backed away, ran into an obstacle, and spun about.

"Beg pardon, Lord Blythestone. I thought that were you, and it seems I've arrived in good time."

Valentine stared at Tobias Fleet. "What are you—?" His words ended abruptly as Toby drew a sword.

"Take this," Toby said.

Valentine wrapped his hand around the hilt of the rapier. "What of you?"

"I've no need of it." Toby drew a long knife from under his shirt. "I prefer to be a bit more personal."

"Take them both," the merchant shouted, and his men attacked.

As soon as one of the brutes was in range, Toby kicked him squarely in the crotch. The man went down, clutching his privates, and Toby kicked him in the jaw, knocking him unconscious. He whirled around to see Valentine keeping the other attacker at bay with the sword as the merchant worked at moving the crate. Stymied, Valentine's opponent pulled out a knife and threw it. The young man knocked the blade aside and lunged as Roi had taught him. The point of the sword entered the dockworker's shoulder, and the man recoiled in pain. When Toby came to Valentine's side, the wounded man took to his heels.

"Neat work." Toby jerked his chin in the direction of the ship. "Is yonder fellow of interest to you?"

Valentine's gaze followed Toby's gesture, and he saw Fantod shoving the crate up the plank. "As it happens, yes, he is. I have lost Marche, and I am certain that man knows where he is."

"Then after him!"

Fantod saw them coming, abandoned the box, and dashed aboard the ship. Toby ran onto the deck after him, but a thump from the crate stopped Valentine in his tracks. He knocked with his fist and received a muffled answer. "Marche?" Another shout confirmed Valentine's guess.

Frantically, he looked around for something to open the box. When nothing better presented itself, he began prying the lid up with blade of the sword. With one corner loosened, he could hear Marche's voice clearly. "I will have you out in a moment," he promised. Working his fingers under the edge, Valentine pulled on the lid with all his strength. Nails popped in the raw wood as Marche pushed upward. In a blink, the big man emerged like a jack-in-the-box as the lid went flying.

"My thanks," he said. "Where is Fantod?"

Valentine saw murder in Marche's eyes, but before he could answer, Toby reappeared with a mob of sailors in hot pursuit. Marche's eyes widened in surprise, but he didn't stop to make inquiries. Shoving Valentine ahead of him, he ran for the gangway. As soon as Toby set foot on the dock, Marche used his prodigious strength to push the plank into the water. Fantod shouted curses as the three men disappeared into the crowd.

"It will not take him long to find us again," Valentine said as they reached the inn.

"We will be gone before he arrives." Marche turned his gaze on Toby. "And how is it that we have the pleasure of your company?"

"I came with a message for you, but how is it that I arrived so closely behind you?"

"We were waylaid by pirates," Marche said casually.

"Pirates!" Toby exclaimed, shooting Valentine a look of reproach. "You never mentioned."

"I hardly had time," Valentine replied.

"To be frank, we were more in the way of guests than prisoners," Marche added. "Blythestone here has quite an affinity for scoundrels, it seems."

"Mr. Fleet knows that," Valentine said. "It is self-evident in my friendship with Your Grace."

"A touch!" Toby gave Valentine a fencer's salute as they entered the private dining room.

"Upon my honor!" Crispin exclaimed. "You look as though you've had an adventure!"

"You are not wrong, Snowhurst," Marche said. "We find ourselves in haste, so pray do not interrupt me. Our local benefactor is revealed as one of Murdmont's lackeys. As soon as we left him, he sent a message informing the scoundrel of our presence here, and then he abducted me to await Murdmont's pleasure. When Blythestone happened upon us, I was sealed in a crate, ready to be stowed away."

Toby's voice rose above the exclamations of disbelief. "That is why I am here, my lord. Mrs. Dahlram sent me with a message for you that concerns Lord Murdmont."

"The devil you say!"

"Shall I speak it, sir, or do you wish for more privacy?"

Marche looked around the room. "These are my friends," he said at last. "You may speak in front of them."

"I don't know if you're aware, sir, that Lord Murdmont is a patron of the tearoom, or rather of a similar establishment that Mrs. D manages."

"Are you speaking of the Brass Cage?"

Toby nodded. "As Your Grace surely knows, the Brass serves those gentlemen who prefer their pleasure mixed with a little pain, and—" The young man paused. "Lord Murdmont visits often, I hear, and he makes a point of informing Mrs. D when he returns to Town."

"Murdmont has returned to London?"

"Not yet, sir, but he is on his way. Mrs. D thought you would want to know."

"Why would she think that, Toby?"

"I may have told her somewhat of your recent troubles, my lord, as related by Lord Kirkcap." Toby's golden head lowered until he was looking at the floor. "I hope I haven't done wrong."

"I am not pleased that you gossip about me, but I cannot deny that you have done me a great service."

"Two, at the least," Valentine put in.

"Thank you for the reminder," Marche said. "I have not thanked either you or Toby for saving my life."

"What is all that commotion?" Crispin exclaimed at the sound of shouting beyond the door.

"M'sieur Fantod is not giving up easily, I would guess," Marche said. "I believe it is time to depart."

"Go," Darby said, struggling to his feet. "We will see that you are not followed."

"Count on us," Neville seconded his comrade.

Marche didn't go through the formality of protesting the offer. "You have my gratitude," he said simply. "Blythestone, Mr. Fleet, if you are quite ready?"

"Please do nothing rash," Valentine implored the Dandies. "You are already injured, and I would be devastated if you came to more harm on our behalf."

"An honor," Darby said dismissively. "Make haste now."

Marche, Valentine and Toby kept out of the light of the torches as they left the inn by the kitchen door. "I don't think it would be a good idea to return to the livery," Marche said.

"If I may, sir," Toby spoke up. "The ship that brought me here will take us back to England for the right price."

"You think the captain would be willing to leave tonight?"

"He will sail at your word."

"Will he take my word as coin?"

"He will have Mrs. Dahlram's security on it," Toby assured Marche.

"Why would Mrs. Dahlram be so accommodating?"

Toby grinned. "You've no notion how many friends you've made among my sort."

"Your sort?" Valentine said. "I assume you are speaking of the kind and loyal folk of this world."

"You should put your brand on this one, sir," Toby cheekily told Marche. "He's a tempting armful and no mistake, and he's got pluck to the backbone. He's the top, my lord."

"Yes, I had noticed," Marche said. "Devil take this moonless night! Where is the ship?"

"There, sir, that tidy miss with the blue glass lantern at her stern. If I may make so bold, perhaps Your Grace would allow me to make arrangements?"

"I would take it as a great favor."

Marche and Valentine stood to the side as Toby hailed the ship and spoke briefly with a sentry. They were passed on board and sent belowdecks where they would be out of sight. Soon after, they felt the small vessel begin to move, and Toby stuck his head in to tell them he'd be helping the captain for a while.

"So it seems our great adventure in Europe is over before it could begin," Marche remarked.

"Do you think so? Being kidnapped would be quite enough adventure for me."

"It was but a few hours' inconvenience, thanks to you. And Toby, of course."

"Inconvenience?" Valentine stared at Marche through the gloom of the hold. "How can you refer to your abduction and captivity as a mere inconvenience?"

"I am free and unharmed, am I not?"

"True enough, but if I had not happened upon you, you might have ended up in Murdmont's power. It is a wonder to me that his minion did not do away with you when he had the chance. Why spare your life when your death could only benefit them?"

"I assume that Murdmont wishes some sort of personal revenge. However, it is in the past, and I see no need to speak of it other than to offer you my thanks for foiling the plot."

Valentine could keep his composure no longer. "Does it mean nothing to you that my heart nearly died at the thought of living the rest of my life without you?"

"It means everything to me, but… you know I do not deal easily with large emotions."

"May I at least embrace you?"

"I am a fool," Marche said as he swept Valentine into his arms. "I am sorry, my own. If our places had been reversed…."

Valentine's breath was driven from his lungs by the fierceness of his lover's embrace. "I was so worried when I did not find you at the livery," he gasped.

"But you found me, my sweet sleuth, and you saved me." Marche kissed Valentine on the forehead.

"Am I forgiven, then?"

"What do you need forgiveness for?"

"Whatever it was that I did that sent you off in such a black mood, a mood that distracted you and rendered you easy prey for your enemies."

"You did nothing to cause my mood. It is my temper that is to blame." Marche paused. "You are right about my jealousy. I can hardly bear it when you look kindly on others."

"That saddens me." Valentine pulled away. "It makes me think that you do not trust me."

"It is not you that I do not trust."

"Do you fear that I shall be taken advantage of? I assure you that I can defend myself should it become necessary."

"You are right."

Valentine froze in the act of sitting on a crate. "I beg your pardon?"

"I said that you are right."

"Forgive my shock at your speedy capitulation. Do go on, sir."

Marche smiled gently. "You faced down a pair of ruffians and rescued me. How can I doubt your readiness to do violence?" Valentine's gasp was loud in the silence, closely followed by Marche's chuckle. "I cannot seem to forbear teasing you, even at such a moment. Can you forgive me this, as well as much else?"

"With all my heart."

"You have not heard *all* yet. This series of catastrophes is my fault entirely."

"How is that possible?"

Marche was quiet for several moments before he answered. "I have never spoken of this to anyone. Not even Negus knows this chapter of my wretched history."

"You may speak to me of anything, Loel."

"I fear you will feel differently about me if you know how pathetic I truly am."

"I love you, you great silly man, with all your pride, your temper, and your stubbornness, as you love me despite my self-righteousness and my prudery."

"We make quite a pair."

"I'll not dispute it. Now, as we have time to pass, tell me your tale." Valentine extended a hand and Marche came to sit beside him.

"Did you know Murdmont was intended for the priesthood?"

Valentine shook his head but didn't betray his surprise at Marche's words.

"I had his story from his own lips at a time when he had no ill will toward me. He was schooled in a monastery, much as you were, and left it just as unexpectedly. His father died in debt, and there was no more money for things such as an education. He took a position as a tutor in order to feed his mother and himself." Marche took Valentine's hand between his and looked him in the eyes. "It is difficult to speak of what happened."

"Perhaps you might start by telling me how you met the man."

"My great-aunt had the raising of me from my fourth year, as you will know. When I was fourteen, she decided that my tutor was deficient and sent me to an academy that was very much in vogue at the time, very modern. In my second year, Mr. Malcolm Jonas was my arithmetic instructor, though he taught me a great deal more."

Valentine squeezed Marche's hand. "Do you mean to say…?"

"That he seduced me? He did, indeed, but it was no great feat. I worshiped him, you see."

"He must have been a very different man then."

"He was quite… pure, I suppose you would say, absolutely dedicated to the science of numbers and absolutely uncompromising in his standards. I was proud to be counted among his inner circle of acolytes and would have done anything for a word of praise."

"And he betrayed your trust by seducing you."

Marche shook his head. "I thought him the handsomest, most admirable man in all of Creation, and I wanted him with all my heart. I reveled in the new world of physical pleasure that he introduced me to. I did not feel there was anything wrong in what we did together, no matter what society taught me."

"What happened?"

"We were found out, of course. The affair was kept quiet, but Murdmont was dismissed from his post in disgrace, and I was sent home."

"I cannot imagine that you accepted this resolution, even as a child."

"I was outraged at the interference in my private life and even angrier that I had to hide my reactions. As soon as I had opportunity, I sought to reunite with Malcolm and got a bigger shock. He wished to have nothing to do with me. He blamed me for his disgrace and railed at me for dragging him down from the pure faith of mathematics to rut in the mire."

"Absurd! He was an adult and you a child."

"I was sixteen by then and counted a man by most."

"Absurd," Valentine repeated. "Surely you cannot believe that Murdmont planned his revenge from that day?"

"It is possible."

"But hardly probable." Valentine sighed. "At least, it explains the antipathy you hold for one another. What a pity you never informed Lady Willamina of the incident."

"I told no one. I was mortified by Malcolm's accusation that I had ruined him and his rejection destroyed me. I became what he named me. For years, I sought love with one bastard after another, until I became the bastard. If you knew the number of young men I have ruined…."

"No!"

"Yes. Until you came into my life, I behaved as badly as the one who broke my heart. I became what I despised, though I did not know it until I saw myself through your eyes."

"You will make me weep if you go on in this manner."

"That I would never wish to do. It breaks my heart to see tears in your eyes."

"The thought of you in pain is unbearable to me, yet..." Valentine took hold of Marche's hands. "Promise me that you will never exclude me again. I wish to share your tribulations as well as your joys. I do not want you to face trouble alone."

Marche pulled Valentine closer. "You have my word on it."

Valentine dropped his eyes, a warm color rising in his cheeks. "Now, I truly feel as though we are wed," he said softly.

Marche was nearly incapacitated by the wave of emotion that suffused every fiber of his being. Pulling Valentine into his arms, he held him tightly. "I love you more than I can say."

Valentine drew Marche's head down to rest on his shoulder, stroking the other man's hair as he murmured of his feelings. Marche let himself relax into the embrace as Valentine leaned back against the hull. As the trim ship clove the waves, they held one another until Toby came to wake them.

CHAPTER 19

"GOOD day to you, gentlemen!" Mrs. Dahlram hove into the room, her voluminous skirts billowing as she sat. "I trust that Tobias and Samuel have seen to your comfort?"

"Indeed, ma'am," Marche said, rising to his feet along with Valentine.

Mrs. Dahlram waved them back to their seats. "If you wish, we may now get down to brass tacks, if you will excuse a work-a-day term."

"You know very well that I will excuse the words and much else besides." Marche smiled fondly at the woman as he settled back on the sofa. "Mistress Lydia Dahlram, I have the honor to present Sir Valentine Randwick, whom I hold in the highest regard."

Valentine bowed before he resumed his seat. "Ma'am, please accept my gratitude for your great kindness to us."

"I am very happy to be in a position to do His Grace a kindness. He may wish it otherwise, but I am well aware that he has helped many an unfortunate young man out of the gutters."

"A small loan here and there hardly bears mentioning, nor does it balance the ledger when set against the ill I have done," Marche said. "I hope we may let the matter rest and speak of one more urgent."

Mrs. Dahlram nodded. "I am afraid I have been indiscreet and pried into your business. In speaking with several of my clients, I learned some shocking facts, the first being the theft of your fortune, among others, by Lord Murdmont. I have a rather clever young man in my employ to keep my accounts, and I sent him 'round to Murdmont's place of business to speak with a clerk he's friendly with."

"Your expression portends bad news, ma'am," Marche said.

"Nothing you cannot handle, Goliath," was Mrs. Dahlram's opinion.

"As I recall, Goliath was outmatched by a flung stone."

"Perhaps that was not the best example, but I've no doubt you'll settle matters and recover your property. However, it might take some little time as Murdmont has signed papers that give him leave to do as he sees fit with the holdings of several families."

"I am afraid that that is no news to me."

"And surely that will not matter once Murdmont is convicted of murder," Valentine spoke up.

"There is the point around which all must turn," Marche said. "Our first priority must be the bringing of Murdmont to justice for my aunt's death. His other transgressions may wait upon this resolution."

"I wish I might have made the lady's acquaintance," Mrs. Dahlram said. "From all I have heard, she was quite the original."

Marche bowed his head, and Valentine put a comforting hand on his shoulder. Mrs. Dahlram noted the tenderness in the kind gesture and ceased her wondering on the nature of the gentlemen's friendship. Though she was unhappy to lose a patron like the duke, she was glad to see that the bluff nobleman had chosen a companion that truly cared for him—for chosen he had or she was no judge of hearts. If she needed any more proof of his thawing, she need only observe the moisture that flowed down his cheeks.

"Forgive me for causing you pain by reminding you of your grief," Mrs. Dahlram said softly. "Shall we return to business?"

"Of your mercy," Marche said in a voice squeezed small by sorrow.

"We must decide," Valentine said. "Do we go to Lamberglyn Park, or do we find quarters in Town? Once we have settled that question, we may begin to discuss our course of action."

"If I may not be of help in any other way, you are most welcome to private quarters here," Mrs. Dahlram said. "If that would suit."

"As all of our current belongings are at Lamberglyn, I think we must make at least one visit. We might send a message and have Negus deliver what we need, but I shall leave that decision to you." Marche turned to look at Valentine.

"It would take the same amount of time for us to travel there and back," Valentine mused. "And I would dearly like to speak with Mistress Kermartin to see if there is any news of my mother or sister."

"Then it is settled," Marche said. "If we may impose, ma'am, would you arrange a carriage for us?"

"You shall have mine if you wish." Mrs. Dahlram smiled. "Though I wonder what you will make of the cherubim painted on the doors. The little dears are rather fond of one another, you see, and the artist took some license, which—"

Marche interrupted. "A plain coach from the nearest livery will do famously."

In half an hour's time, Marche and Valentine were ensconced in a spidery curricle drawn by a pair of glossy-coated chestnut geldings. Toby had come out to wish them well and brushed off their thanks for his help.

"I was just a messenger," the young man said as he gave one of the horses a pat on the haunch. "Anyone would have done as much."

"Well, you have my gratitude whether you wish it or not," Marche replied.

Toby smiled at the brusque tone as he bowed his head. "Aye, Your Grace."

"And when I've resolved my difficulties, you'll find my gratitude is worth more than words."

"I did not offer my help with any thought of reward in mind."

Marche returned Toby's smile. "I know." Taking up the reins, he steered the light two-seater away from the curb.

"Good luck to you," Toby called out.

Valentine turned to wave, and then the curricle was around the corner and they were in traffic. Marche adroitly maneuvered the carriage around larger vehicles until they were out of London. Once on the open road, he urged the horses to a faster pace, and they were soon racing along, hair flying in the wind of their passage. At the mid-point of their journey, they drove into the fields to enjoy the luncheon Toby had packed for them.

"I feel much refreshed," Valentine said as he rose from the grass to brush at his clothing. "If I could now rid myself of the dust, I would be most content."

Marche waved a hand at the river. "Contentment lies yonder."

"And ride the rest of the way in sodden garments? No, thank you, sir."

"If you first remove your garments, they will not become sodden."

"Do you mean to suggest that I swim... uncovered?"

"Did you never do so as a lad?" Marche paused. "But I am forgetting your upbringing again."

"We were never naked at the monastery. Bathing was done in basins, swiping with a soapy rag under your cassock. All I ever saw of the Brothers were grim faces and busy hands."

"Well, I am going in the water," Marche said, changing the subject. "It's no doubt cold, but the sun is very warm today. Come bathe with me."

"I could not. What if someone happened along?"

Marche looked pointedly at the screen of trees that surrounded them. "I purposely chose this spot for its remoteness. Come, my own. Favor me with a glimpse of what I most desire."

"You will still be making me blush when I have a white beard," Valentine predicted.

"May it be so," Marche murmured fervently as he leaned close for a gentle kiss.

Valentine's gaze slid to the water. "It is bound to be freezing," he objected.

"Not for long," Marche promised. "Come, my little monk. Shed your dignity for an hour and your clothing as well. Is it possible that you can face down a brace of ruffians but fear to be seen in your linen?"

"It would seem so." Valentine sighed before a smile brightened his face. "However, I am certain that the effect of your proximity will one day rid me of all restraint."

"Not all restraint, surely," Marche said quickly. "Your charms are for me alone, I hope."

"Mooncalf." Valentine laughed softly as he put a hand to Marche's cheek. "Of course they are."

"Then show them to me." Marche tugged at Valentine's cravat.

"If you will do the same," Valentine said daringly.

The last word still hung in the air when Marche's shirt joined his coat on the grass. With a boyish grin, he doffed his boots and peeled his breeches down. Valentine's breath caught as always at the sight of his lover's powerful body unveiled. Surely, there was no other anatomy so perfect in form, no other hair that precise shade of antique gold, no other eyes as warm as amber, glowing with roguish humor.

"Are you going to join me?" Marche prompted, jarring Valentine from his rapt contemplation.

With the duke's hindering help, Valentine divested himself of clothing and stood naked in the open for the first time. His nervousness intensified each sensation. The breeze against his body was the stroking of silken fingers. The sunshine lay on his skin like the heat of a banked fire. When Marche loosed Valentine's hair from its ribbon, the young man gasped at the sensuous feel of the heavy tresses sliding down his bare back. "I feel quite strange," he said. "Anxious, but exhilarated."

"You look like a faun strayed from an ancient forest on the first morning of the world."

"It is past noon."

"Minx! I offer you poetry and you scoff?"

"Was that poetry? I thought perhaps a calf had strayed from an ancient field to bawl for its mother."

"You shall pay dearly for that," Marche promised.

Valentine didn't have time to cry out before Marche's shove tumbled him into the river. He surfaced sputtering and flailing, gasping for breath and Marche's grin changed to a look of horror. Diving in, the big man caught hold of his lover and bore him up. "Are you all right?" he asked. "I had forgotten that you do not swim."

Valentine put his hands on the other man's shoulders and pushed downward. Marche's head disappeared under the water, his eyes wide with surprise. He lost his hold on Valentine as the young man found the bottom with his feet.

"I was only larking about," Marche said reproachfully when he caught his breath.

"Turnabout is fair play."

"I thought you were drowning."

"You *thought* you had drowned me," Valentine corrected.

"Will I never get the better of you again now that you're back in breeches?"

"You shall have my best, always." Valentine moved close and his arms went around Marche's neck. "Never doubt it, Loel."

Marche's arms tightened around Valentine's ribcage, pulling him even closer, the warmth between them contrasting sharply with the chill of the water. He tilted his face, inviting a kiss, and Valentine obliged. Covering Marche's mouth with his, the young man parted his lips and ran his tongue along the tender seam. Marche moaned softly, and Valentine swore he felt his heart melt and run down his veins to his cock. The feel of hot flesh sliding together in the cold river was almost unbearably sensual, and Valentine found he was eager... more than eager to indulge in this play.

"Enter me," he whispered, and then made his request again in language that could not be misinterpreted. "I want your cock inside me."

Marche swallowed audibly. "I am willing, but—"

"Can you not feel how much I want you?" Valentine pressed his hardness against Marche's belly. "I know you do not wish to hurt me, but I believe the water is cold enough to numb—"

"Very well then," Marche interrupted his lover's practical speech. "If you are sure, then I will not be so churlish as to deny you. Truthfully, I am so excited at the thought of making love to you here that you will not have to bear the intrusion for long."

Valentine laughed and quickly covered his mouth, looking about nervously.

"Do not be shy with me," Marche implored. "Do you know how happy it makes me to see you take such obvious pleasure in what we do together?"

"Then if you will suit action to words, I will make you positively giddy."

Marche grinned. "You are a wonder and my heart's delight. Give me but a few moments to…." His words trailed off as he reached below the water and found Valentine's opening. Looking up into Valentine's eyes, he eased a finger into him in small thrusts. When the young man's eyelids fluttered and drifted down, the duke settled into a rhythm, licking at Valentine's nipples as he stroked him.

"Now," Valentine panted.

The passionate syllable spurred Marche to instant action. Holding Valentine open with two fingers, he gripped the base of his arousal and seated it. Valentine kissed Marche and then leaned back, spreading his arms. Anchored by his legs around his lover's waist, he floated upon the surface looking up at the cloudless sky. The heat of Marche's cock against his opening was like a brand, and he savored the sensation as it forged ahead. Marche took hold of Valentine's hips and leaned in, entering in increments, watching intently for cues. Valentine met Marche's eyes, silently urging him on until he was sheathed.

"Upon my honor," Marche breathed, "I have never felt the like."

"Say it again, my love."

"Would you hear that you are the finest I have ever joined with? I admit it freely."

"It is only that—" Valentine's words ended in a gasp as Marche shifted footing. "You have so much more experience than I. I am sure that Tobias Fleet is ever so much better at—"

"I am not in love with Tobias, and that is all the difference in the world, my own."

Valentine's eyes sparkled with sudden moisture. "You truly do not mind that I am so… inept?"

Marche smiled. "Quite the contrary. You cannot imagine what it means to me to be the one who instructs you."

"Are you ready to continue my lessons, or are you content to lecture?"

"If you continue to give me cheek, you will suffer the consequences."

"And what might those be?" Valentine asked as the strain in his lower half eased.

"Such sauce! When did you grow so bold?"

"When I grew so hard."

Marche's smile broadened and he took hold of Valentine's arousal. "Do you speak of this? I think it will grow harder yet."

"Impossible." Valentine gasped again as Marche stroked him. "That is most marvelous. I can scarcely credit how stimulating it is to be doing this in the chill of the river."

"Nor I. The sensation of your warmth around my cock is like to make me spurt untimely."

"Do I truly rouse you so much?"

"You are greedy for compliments today." Marche paused. "Nay, do not frown or turn your face away. I was jesting, and I am heartily sorry that I do not compliment you often enough."

"It is not that I wish for praise…. That is a lie. I do crave it, but only from your lips."

"I have caught you in a lie! I did not know you were capable of it. This day will live in my memories forever."

"Foolish man." Valentine smiled. "And once again you have soothed my baseless fears and brought me gently back to a good humor."

Marche squeezed Valentine's hard length and began shuttling his hand up and down. "And this? What does this do for your humor?"

"I feel as light as a cloud. My heart is buoyant as chaff borne on a mill race."

"Naught more?" Marche shifted balance again, easing his shaft in and out.

"I am a prayer on wings of desire flying straight to heaven."

Marche's throat tightened suddenly, and he found it quite beyond him to form words. With one hand splayed at the small of Valentine's back and the other on the young man's cock, the big nobleman shunted his length at an ever-increasing pace.

Valentine was grateful for the support as his wet hair dragged at his head and the gentlest of thrusts had a most disproportionate effect. Nearly weightless on the current, he found it a very sensuous experience to be handled so easily. It was plain that his lover was enjoying the new position as much as he was, and it added immeasurably to his pleasure. "I am going to spill," he said in wonder.

"So quickly? Ah, to be young again," Marche said breathlessly.

"Mock me at your will, but I pray you, do not stop what you are doing."

"Not for all the tea in Cathay." Marche rolled his hips several times, stirring the tight channel that hugged his length so jealously.

"Jesu!" Valentine cried as his shaft gave up its seed. "Sweet Jesu!" The evidence of his release dissipated instantly in the running water, but the aftereffects lingered as Marche continued to move rhythmically. "Ah, God, Loel, that is so sweet."

This declaration proved too much for Marche and his joy fell upon him like an avalanche. Gripping Valentine's lean flanks, he buried his spurting rod in the young man's velvet sheath. A long groan purled from his lips as his essence poured forth deep within his beloved. Shuddering with the intensity of his orgasm, he slipped his arms around Valentine and lifted him from the water. Valentine cradled Marche's head to his chest, murmuring nonsense into his hair. Reluctant to disengage, Marche held Valentine up as he relished the feeling of the narrow egress contracting around the base of his shaft.

"Thank you," he said, his lips moving against Valentine's left nipple.

Valentine moaned softly, shivering at the intimate touch. "You are most welcome," he said, between pauses for breath, "but I assure you, it was my pleasure, as well."

"So you have told me, but… I wish I could be sure that you are not merely indulging my baser nature."

"Please do not say such things, Loel. If I thought that my prudery had destroyed your enjoyment of this sacred act, I could not—"

Valentine's words ended abruptly as Marche withdrew and let him drop until their faces were level. Taking Valentine's mouth with fierce tenderness, Marche kissed him deeply, thoroughly, with all the love he'd kept pent up for so long. When their lips parted, Valentine leaned back to look into the other man's eyes.

"Are you weeping?" he asked in surprise.

"Am I? I have forgotten what tears feel like."

"What is the matter?"

"Not a thing that I can think of. Against all odds or expectation, I find myself overcome with joy and gratitude. To think that you feel the same as I is… I cannot express it in paltry words."

"You do not have to, my love. I do feel the same and words are unnecessary."

Marche dropped his eyes, blinking several times before raising them again. "I do not know what I have done to deserve such an angel, but I will strive to be worthy of you."

"So you consider me a blessing rather than a tribulation?"

"Now I must thank you again for saving me from the embarrassment of becoming overly sentimental."

"I would never complain," Valentine said as he kissed Marche lightly on the tip of his nose, his chin, and either side of his mouth.

"Now I have caught you in another falsehood and I will claim a forfeit of you."

"All that you see is yours already." Valentine spread his arms.

"Then your penalty is to remain forever at my side."

"Done! Though I would sooner be in front of you."

With an impish grin, Valentine pushed away from Marche and waded as fast as possible for the bank. Marche used his long legs to advantage and caught up with Valentine before he could reach his clothing. Pulling his lover into an embrace, Marche kissed him soundly before releasing him.

"No matter how fast or how far you may flee, you will never escape me," he vowed.

"I would never wish to."

Satisfied in body and soul, the two men donned their garments and resumed their journey.

CHAPTER 20

"MISTER VALENTINE!" Anne cried as the two men came through the kitchen door. "And the duke! You've knocked my poor heart into a cocked hat surprising me like this!"

"Forgive me," Valentine said, embracing the housekeeper warmly. "Our errand to Brittany was of no consequence after all."

"I was abducted," Marche said mildly.

Anne's mouth fell open. "No! What villains would dare?"

"Some large colleagues of our dear friend Lord Murdmont," Marche said.

"I do not know how you can be so light-hearted." Anne shook her head. "Tell me what happened, if you've time."

"It was but a brief inconvenience, as I tried to tell young Blythestone. Some brave soul hit me from behind." Marche rubbed the back of his head. "I've still a fair-sized goose egg. Nay, be still, Mistress. I need no remedies, and my staunch friend here rescued me in good time."

"Say you so!" Anne looked at Valentine in wonder. "You are more like your sire every day, by my reckoning. But why do I stand here nattering when you are likely starving. Sit. Sit. I will bring plates."

"Is Negus about?" Marche asked.

"I am astounded that I am not tripping over the rascal, as usual. Begging Your Grace's pardon."

"No need for apologies; I quite understand the man's nature. Please excuse me. I will return soon. Please stay seated, Blythestone. I am certain you must have an appetite after our arduous journey." Marche smiled at the young man's pink cheeks as he left the room.

"Have you had any word of my mother or sister?" Valentine asked as Anne set a platter in front of him.

"Oh, aye. Lady Amandine's letter arrived just after you left with the duke, and the innkeeper was clever enough to send it on to me before we left London. The duke's man read it to me; would you ever believe that strutting banty rooster was so learned?" Anne continued before Valentine could frame an answer. "I hope you won't mind that I took the liberty of sending a reply. I wanted to set her mind at ease about her *continued neglectful absence*, as she writes. She and Mr. Harston are touring the western coast, you see."

"Blessed Saints, what a state of affairs this is. I've scarcely seen my mother in three years, and yet I spent the past few months hoping we would not meet. Now that I may face her as myself, she has no mind to come home."

"Be fair, sir. The lady has no notion you are here at Lamberglyn."

"You are right, of course. Thank you for putting my mind at ease as well."

"Eat what's on your plate. That will do you a sight more good than any words of mine." Anne laid her hand briefly over Valentine's as he reached for his knife. "I am so very glad that you are home, sir."

"Anne, do you think you could call me Valentine?"

"I can try, sir," Anne said as she went to pour him something to drink. "Would you care for ale, water, or wine?"

"Water will suit, thank you."

"And His Grace, does he still suit, if I may ask?"

"I'd not have believed it on our first meeting, but he has proven himself a very good man. He deserves no scorn of me, and I wonder now that I ever thought myself superior to him. I was a blind, intolerant prig."

"And how have you changed, pray tell?" Marche asked as he returned.

"My vision has cleared somewhat," Valentine said without pause. "Many things that appeared monstrous to me were revealed as harmless, nay, pleasing even."

"I can see that the talk will soon grow too deep for a simple woman," Anne said as she untied her apron. "Did you find the jackanapes you sought, Your Grace?"

"I spoke with Negus briefly but succinctly, ma'am."

"I believe that is the same thing, Marche," Valentine said.

"I bow to your greater knowledge. What should I have said?"

"I've no idea. What did you mean to say?"

Marche sighed. "Honestly, what good is it to point out fault if you cannot correct it?"

"I can. Simply tell me what you meant, and I will tell you how to say it."

"I've no doubt, professor, but if I could tell you what I meant, I would not need your assistance."

Anne's chuckle took both men by surprise. "Look at the two of you," she said. "You fit together like a dove-tail joint. As much as I might wish that Valentine would marry and have little ones, I can see that he is well matched already. Now, if you will tell me where that ne'er-do-well valet of yours is hiding, I will take my leave."

"I left him in the laundry, oddly enough. I've never known Negus to do washing before."

"It's sure he's got no skill at it, but practice is what makes us perfect, eh, sir?"

"You will get no argument from me, ma'am." Marche bowed before sitting next to Valentine on the bench. "I think someone else might be well matched," he said when Anne was out of hearing. "Would that not be a fine jest?"

"That your valet is courting my housekeeper? Why should that be humorous?"

Marche took up his fork and applied himself to his plate. With his mouth full, he was less likely to say something objectionable.

"I think it would be lovely if Negus and Anne found they had feelings for one another," Valentine continued. "Both are alone and that is no way to go through life."

Marche swallowed. "Again, I must bow to your wisdom. Would you be so good as to pass me the saltcellar?"

Valentine and Marche passed a very pleasant night at Lamberglyn, and by the time they broke their fast the next morning, a coach loaded with selected belongings was on its way to Town. As they said farewell, they thanked Anne again for making the manor house habitable. After Marche had a last word with Negus, he took up the curricle's reins and called to the horses. They made best speed to London, and as they entered the cobblestoned warren, the graceful, wooded expanses of Lamberglyn Park began to seem like an idyll, a dream they'd dreamed together.

"WELCOME back, sirs," Toby said as he showed Marche and Valentine into a private salon at Mrs. Dahlram's Tearoom. "Please sit and I'll return in a twinkling."

"There you are, Marche." Harmon Sudville, Lord Donshear stood as the duke entered. "I believe you are the last of our benighted company to arrive."

"Donshear." Marche bowed. "And Tarncott. Allow me to present my brother-in-law, Valentine Randwick, Earl of Blythestone."

"Do not overlook me, I pray you. My milliner would be quite devastated," Lady Georgiana said as Merrold Worrel-Shephard, Lord Tarncott returned Marche's bow.

"Ma'am." Marche bowed again, and Valentine followed his lead. "What of Sir Jabez? I understood that Wallwhit was fleeced as well."

"He sent word that he's kept away by his faithful bedfellow, the gout," Donshear said.

Before anyone could say more, Toby returned with a slight, silver-haired man. "My lords and lady," the young man said. "I present Sir Anthony Wedhight, Baronet Kirkcap."

"I wish I could say it was a pleasure, Kirkcap," Marche said.

"I, too, am sorry that this meeting is necessary," Anthony said. "I appreciate your confidence in calling upon me to represent you."

"I can hardly call upon my regular solicitor," Marche replied, provoking a round of bitter laughter. "Has Murdmont been seen, by the way?"

Toby glanced at Kirkcap for permission before he spoke. "Sir Malcolm has returned to London, but he is keeping low to the ground. You will not find him at his Town house or at his places of business— of which there are many more than some might imagine. If you can credit it, he was holding the book on half the wagering in London."

"I told you he was no gentleman," Donshear said.

"Devil take the scoundrel," Tarncott exclaimed.

"I am sure that we all wish the wretch to Van Diemen's Land," the Marchioness of Hapwood spoke up. "But, gentlemen, let us hear what news Sir Anthony has for us before we transport the blackguard."

Kirkcap inclined his head to Georgiana. "I have arranged for a hearing in the private chambers of a magistrate. All that remains is to see that Murdmont is present."

"Never you worry, sir," Toby said. "Arrangements are being made."

"I've no doubt you have things well in hand," Marche said. "However, I would caution you that Murdmont is a slippery weasel."

"No disrespect intended, my lord, but it is possible that Mrs. Dahlram knows a deal more about the man than any else in this room."

Marche's gaze rested on Toby for a long moment. "I shall take your word, and I do hope you have not misled me in the past concerning your involvement with—"

"I've never lied to you, sir. I've never had need." Toby paused. "Nor have I ever accommodated Sir Malcolm at the Brass... or anywhere else."

"Please forgive my coarse insinuations."

"I am not offended, Your Grace," Lady Hapwood said.

"I was speaking to Mr. Fleet," Marche said.

Anthony cleared his throat. "If we are all satisfied, we may meet again tomorrow morning at ten of the clock in the chambers of Lord Berinbroke. I am happy to send a coach for any who wishes it."

"I would be most grateful for the favor," Georgiana said.

"Of course, ma'am. You are also permitted the company of your maid."

Georgiana gave him a charming little grimace. "Until Murdmont is compelled to return that which he has stolen, I must do without the small comforts that make life so pleasant. I am afraid that conveniences such as carriages and maids are quite beyond my resources just now."

Some of those gathered looked away at the frank talk of poverty, and the meeting soon broke up. When the room was nearly empty, Valentine stopped Georgiana with a soft word.

"Lady," he said, bowing slightly from the waist. "It grieves me to see any woman in difficulty. Is there anything I might do to relieve your distress?"

Georgiana gazed on Valentine's earnest face for several moments before she answered. "I am amazed and... shamed by your generosity. Have you forgotten that it was my late husband who tried to kill your brother-in-law?"

"I have not, but you have never done me any harm, ma'am."

"Have I not?" she murmured as she dropped her eyes.

"What do you mean?" Marche broke in.

"It must be obvious to you that Murdmont could not have accomplished his grand scheme without the aid of a spy. He had an agent who could mingle freely with those he marked as targets, an agent born to the manner who would be accepted as he never could be."

"I assumed the late marquess of Hapwood was Murdmont's cat's-paw in this despicable plot."

"Gilbert?" Georgiana raised her eyebrows. "He was a handsome man and displayed to advantage but not terribly long in wit. Murdmont easily cozened him out of the paper on his real estate holdings. By the time I tumbled to it, we were virtual paupers. When Murdmont needed a stalking horse, I saw an opportunity to recoup some of our wealth."

"*You* were his spy?" Marche's disbelief was patent in his tone.

Georgiana nodded. "He insisted that I keep him informed of your bride's smallest doings. I gave her glove to him so he might implicate her in a scandal and cast doubts on her character. He hated your sister, sir," Georgiana glanced at Valentine. "I was astounded to see the depths of his malice toward a young woman he'd never met before."

"You must be mistaken," Marche said. "My duchess's advent presented Murdmont with a perfect scapegoat, that is all."

"That is not reasonable, if you think it through. Murdmont originally planned to blame Lady Bolbracken's death on a servant. It would have been much easier for him to send some poor chambermaid to prison than to accuse a woman of the nobility. Furthermore, as a lovely young bride, Lady Valeria would have the sympathy of any jury. No, sir, I have made no mistake. The instant Murdmont saw her, he vowed to destroy her."

"He will find that difficult." Marche's voice grated out from between clenched teeth.

"I daresay," Georgiana said wryly. "Since no one seems to be able to locate Her Grace."

"My wife is a gentle and retiring young woman. She prefers the country life."

"And which country might that be?"

"My sister is at our manor of Lamberglyn," Valentine said.

"A pity." Georgiana shrugged elegant shoulders. "I do hope to see the two of you together one day so that I might study your resemblance more closely. You could not possibly look as much alike as it appears."

"I hope I shall see her soon as well. I miss her very much."

"Though you are her brother, you could not possibly miss her as much as I," Marche said.

Valentine bowed to the other man. "You have my sympathy, sir. Since your wedding, you have had precious little time alone with your bride."

"Each moment away from her side is torment, I assure you."

"I am quite certain that your duchess feels the same longing."

"Does she indeed?" Marche locked his gaze on Valentine's eyes. "I must find time to visit her very soon then."

"I know that she desires that above any other thing, sir."

Georgiana glanced from one man to the other. "You have an enviably close friendship with your sister, it would seem."

"Breton families tend to be close-knit, ma'am," Valentine said.

"Upon my honor, the duchess is a very lucky girl to have two such men doting on her!" Georgiana pulled on her gloves. "I find the conversation fascinating, but I have an appointment elsewhere, and my dressmaker becomes quite cross when I am late."

Valentine moved to hold the door for the lady, inclining his head to her as she passed. Georgiana leaned close, her lily of the valley perfume filling the young man's nostrils as she whispered a few words. With a rustle of taffeta, she was gone, leaving Valentine gaping.

"Well?" Marche touched his husband's elbow. "What did she say to you?"

"That I am a very lucky girl, indeed."

"What an odd thing to say."

"Do not make light of this. She knows."

"It is quite possible. The lady has the wisdom of a serpent as well as the tongue."

"Must you be so harsh?"

"Must you be so charitable?"

"That is… different," Valentine's voice trailed off. "But of course, we are very different, are we not? I am sorry I upbraided you for following your nature."

Marche put a hand on the young man's shoulder. "I would have you remind me when I lapse, my little monk. I need your help to improve my nature."

"If you will do the same for me."

"You need no refinements."

"You are too fond."

Marche cocked an eyebrow at Valentine. "I concede, and now how shall we pass the time until tomorrow's hearing?"

"Marche, did you hear me? Lady Hapwood knows that I am—"

"She cannot know anything for certain unless she was in your dressing room. She may suspect, but she has no proof. Now may we cease speaking of it?"

"First, I wish to hear how we will end this charade."

"It is ended." Marche indicated Valentine's attire. "You are yourself."

"And is your duchess to retire permanently to the country?"

"Will that not serve?"

"You shall gain a reputation as a Bluebeard."

"Do you really think so? It would be certainly be preferable to my current image as a dissipated sleeve-hanging rake."

"I am sure no one thinks of you in those terms, but I think you are right about the lady. She has her suspicions, and there is naught I may do about that. I propose that our best course is a quiet dinner in our rooms and a good night's sleep."

"You truly do not mind staying here?" Marche asked as he led the way to quarters set aside for them.

Valentine shook his head. "I do not like the necessity of secrecy, but I agree that it would be better if Murdmont did not know of our presence just yet."

"Surely his creature Fantod will have sent him a message that I slipped their trap."

"Not if Strand and his friends prevailed."

Marche's expression clearly conveyed his lack of confidence in the trio of Dandies. "At the least, Strand will have delayed our enemies for a time."

"And we shall have to trust to Mrs. Dahlram's staff to deliver Lord Murdmont to the hearing," Valentine said as he entered their quarters.

"I would rather go to the Brass Cage right now and drag the bloody coward out into the street for damned good thrashing."

"As satisfying as that might be, we must let the authorities punish him."

"He threatened to destroy you, my own."

"You will not let that happen." Valentine smiled. "So you see, I am quite safe."

Marche pulled Valentine into his arms. "I could not bear it if I lost you."

Valentine returned the embrace warmly. "I apprehend now why Mr. Fleet named you his Large Meringue," he murmured.

"Minx."

"Hungry minx," Valentine amended.

Marche kissed the top of Valentine's head. "Wait but a few moments, and I shall return with a bill of fare."

When Marche had gone, Valentine removed his jacket and settled into a chair. He was wishing for a book when someone knocked on the door.

"It's Toby, sir."

"Come in," Valentine called. He got to his feet as the door opened, admitting a large man in a constable's uniform. Another uniformed officer had a firm grip on Toby's biceps.

"Sorry, sir," the young man said.

"Quiet, you." The man that held Toby cuffed his ear and drew back his fist for another blow.

"Do not dare!" Valentine cried out. "What sort of man strikes a helpless prisoner?"

"Aurelio is far from helpless," the other officer said. "Are you Lord Blythestone?"

"I am."

"Then I arrest you, sir, for the murder of the Duchess of Marche, and I'll ask you to come along with me."

The blood dropped from Valentine's face into a cold leaden pool in his belly. "I beg your pardon," he said numbly.

The policeman produced a piece of paper from his tunic. "I have here a warrant for your arrest, sir, all legal like, as you can see."

Valentine stared at the document without seeing it. "I would like to wait for the Duke of Marche," he said.

"You are required to come with us, my lord, and come with us you will. No one's above the law, sir."

"No, though it seems that some are decidedly beneath it," Valentine said sharply as he donned his coat. "If you are quite finished mauling Mr. Fleet, may he be dismissed?"

"Ordinarily, an informant would get a pass. However, this one was most uncooperative. He'll be getting some time in the hole to think about the error of his ways."

"A taste of correction is just what the likes of him needs." The second constable glared at Toby. "I'll not spare the rod once I have him in irons."

"I must protest these threats," Valentine said as he was urged toward the doorway.

"You may protest anything you like at the station." The officer pinched Toby's earlobe. "Look sharp, boy. I'm sure you can show us the back entrance."

Valentine dragged his steps, looking about for anyone that he could pass a message to, but they exited unseen into the alley behind the tearoom. The constables hustled Valentine and Toby into a coach with shuttered windows and drove away. As the two young men were taken from the carriage at the police station, Toby broke away and ducked under the horses' bellies. One of the officers gave chase, calling for help as Toby leaped atop another coach and thence to the wall around the yard. The shrill sound of whistles split the air and the gates were hastily re-opened, as the escapee threw himself over the wall.

"Smile while you may," said the constable in charge of Valentine. "He may be gone, but you are still here."

CHAPTER 21

JUGGLING an armload of packages, Marche managed to turn the handle and push the door open. "I could not find Toby and so ventured forth myself. I have brought you the finest delicacies to be had up and down the entire street. There are so many people selling hot food from carts that the footpath is impassible. I had no idea of the variety of...." Marche's voice trailed off as he realized the sitting room was empty. Depositing his burdens on the nearest table, he called loudly for Valentine. When he received no answer, he crossed the room in three strides and yanked open the bedchamber door to find it empty as well. Becoming alarmed, he hurried back into the hall. It occurred to him then how quiet it was. Even as his anxiety ratcheted up a few notches, he mentally promised young Blythestone a verbal thrashing if this should prove to be a prank. It also occurred to Marche that this was how Valentine must have felt when he went missing in Brittany. Vowing to have more consideration for the feelings of others, the nobleman all but ran to the entrance.

"What is amiss, Your Grace," asked the young man at the door.

"Samuel, have you seen Lord Blythestone tonight?"

"Aye, sir, he came in with you and Tobias not two hours gone."

"Yes, of course," Marche said, keeping a tight rein on his impatience. "Have you seen him since I went out?"

"No, sir, that I haven't."

"Have you seen anything that struck you as out of the ordinary?"

"There's been a deal of traffic at the back entry." Samuel paused and smiled as he realized what he'd said. "But that's not out of the ordinary here, as Your Grace has cause to know."

"I am not in the mood for cheek just now. Do you mean to say that people have entered and left this establishment without being remarked?"

"Well, not all gentlemen can match your style or your courage, sir. You're one of the few that uses the front door."

"Is Mr. Fleet about the place?"

"A moment, sir, and I'll send for him." Samuel rang a bell and sent the boy that answered in search of Toby.

"And Mrs. Dahlram? Is she still here?"

"Nay, sir, she's gone home to her dinner."

Marche paced the foyer until the boy returned and reported that Aurelio was not on the premises. "I'm sorry, Your Grace," Samuel said. "Shall I have a few of the lads look for Lord Blythestone? It wouldn't be no trouble at all."

"Perhaps I am being hasty," Marche said. "But my stomach tells me that my companion did not feel the sudden urge for fresh air. If you would be so good as to organize a search, I will go out the back and see if I might learn anything that will help."

"No need to stir yourself. Rest easy, sir, and I will inform you the moment there is any clue."

"I could not possibly remain idle," Marche answered as he turned away. "If Blythestone returns, for mercy's sake, keep him here by any means necessary."

"Aye, my lord," Samuel called after the departing nobleman. As the door attendant gave orders to the runner, Marche had already reached the end of the hall.

The alleyway behind the row of buildings was well kept by local standards, but the stench rising from the gutter was still enough to make Marche grimace as he stepped outside. He saw nothing remarkable on the narrow lane; to the left and right, for the length of the block were muddy puddles, dilapidated sheds, and a few tiny herb gardens. He could have chosen either direction, but instinct drew him toward the less traveled left-hand side. Within a dozen steps, his eye was caught by light glinting off some small object at the foot of a rotting fence. He bent and plucked the piece of polished metal from the muck, knowing what it was before he opened his fingers. He had given Valentine this gold cuff link and its mate when the young man had admired them. Two pair of domed ovals connected by chains and deeply incised with the Woodbine ivy emblem, the jewelry had been in Marche's family since 1685. It was inconceivable that one such as Valentine would be careless with an heirloom. Either he'd dropped it on purpose or it had been wrested from him in a struggle.

"Murdmont," Marche hissed. It seemed plain to him that Murdmont had sent ruffians to take Valentine. He did not stop to wonder why the villain would do something so reckless, for it was also plain to Marche that Murdmont existed solely to torment him in a foretaste of hell. It was a wonder to him that he could have ever believed himself in love with the man. Youth did not excuse him; he should have perceived Murdmont's malevolent nature, but perhaps his own wickedness had blinded him to the evil of the other man.

Marche pushed aside thoughts of the past. That did not matter now. If Murdmont harmed Valentine, his days of making mischief would end tonight.

"HERE you are, m'lord." The hansom driver tipped his hat as Marche pressed some coins into his gloved hand. "Are you sure this is the place you want? You look like a gentleman of quality, if you don't mind me sayin', and perhaps you've been misinformed as to…." The driver's voice trailed off as the big man disappeared through the door of the Brass Cage. "I tried to warn you, mate," he said as he drove away.

"Good evening, sir," said the woman who opened the door for Marche. "Does sir have an appointment, or…." She let the words hang in the air.

For all the notice Marche took, the woman's beautiful face and stunning figure might have been carved from wood. "I am not here for entertainment, ma'am. Either you can tell me where Lord Murdmont is, or I can walk the halls shouting for him."

"Those are my choices, are they, Samson?"

"Lord Marche, Your Grace, or simply sir will do."

The woman in skin-tight red satin straightened from her insouciant slouch. "Forgive my familiarity, Your Grace; I am not yet acquainted with all of my mistress's preferred clients. May I ask your business with Lord Murdmont?" When Marche simply stared at her, she spoke again. "Even if you are a duke, the owner will not take it kindly if you cause the sort of bother that attracts constabulary attention."

"I have no plans to involve the officials."

"I should not do this," she said. "Mrs. D will give me the heave-ho for certain."

"I will trouble myself to be sure that she does not, and if she does, I will find employment for you myself."

"Handsomely said, but promises come easily to a man in his passion."

Marche pulled out his watch and detached the heavy gold chain. "Take it," he said.

Snatching the chain, she answered swiftly. "You will find what you seek at the end of that hall in the last room but one."

Marche left her pouring the glittering gold from one hand to the other. From behind a closed door came a faint cry of distress. Without hesitation, he grasped the knob and turned it hard. It was locked, as he expected, but the mechanism was no match for the force he brought to bear. Wrenching the door from its hinges, he left it hanging askew as he plunged into the room. The candlelit tableau in the center of the chamber froze him in his tracks, his heart pounding so hard that his ears were ringing.

Malcolm Jonas held a riding crop poised to strike the naked youth bound face down on a table of rough planking. Strands of long dark hair wet with sweat clung to pale skin already striped with bright red welts. A length of black silk was tied around the young man's eyes and another was employed as a gag. Though Marche struggled to avert his gaze, the long, lean-muscled limbs in their bindings of black drew the eye like a well-executed painting. It was easy to admire the graceful lines and the contrast of pale flesh and dark silk. Then the captive whimpered around his gag and Marche's vision cleared. This was not Valentine; this was some poor lad from the streets in a wig. "Malcolm," Marche said softly as Murdmont whirled to face the intruder. "Where is Lord Blythestone?"

"What the devil are you talking about? Leave here at once."

"I am certain you would prefer that, but I do not care about your preferences. I will not leave until you tell me where Blythestone is."

"How would I bloody know the whereabouts of your paramour?"

"You took him."

"You're mad. Why would I do such a thing when I can prosecute him for murder?"

"I believe Prince George has already settled the question of—" Marche stopped abruptly, aware that he'd nearly stepped into a trap. "Be clearer, sir. Do you tell me that having accused my wife of murdering my aunt, you will now accuse her brother?"

Murdmont smirked. "Oh, do go on, sir. It amuses me to watch you create. This is one lie that is going to ruin you, my fine deceiver."

"I will see you in your grave first if you have inconvenienced Blythestone in the slightest." Marche paused. "I did not intentionally deceive you, whatever you may think."

"Ah, but you never bothered to correct me, did you? You let me assume you were of age, and you were such a large lad that I believed you."

"You could have asked anyone at the academy. The truth is that you knew I was too young, but you did not wish to cease the affair. Your own obsessive desire brought you down."

"You were a greedy and willful child, and you have not changed a whit. I have your money and your property, and soon I will take away the last thing you value. Your precious Sir Valentine will be found guilty of murder and he will dangle, count upon it." Murdmont raised the crop as Marche took a step closer to him. "If you lay a hand on me, I will have you up on charges as well. There are laws to protect citizens from those who believe that might makes right."

"You were always a coward, and you have not changed either." Marche turned from Murdmont and walked to the table. Gently, he removed the gag from the young man's mouth. "Are you here of your own will?" Marche asked.

Too frightened to answer, the lad shook his head. Immediately, Marche began untying the cords that bound the young man to the table.

"What do you think you are doing?" Murdmont demanded to know. "I paid well for that guttersnipe's time, and he's not given me satisfaction yet."

"I have no quarrel with what pleases a man so long as his pleasure is not coerced from another. You frankly sicken me."

"That is rich coming from you, Your Grace." Murdmont made a curse of the honorific.

"I have never forced anyone."

"You believe your bedmates accommodate you for the sheer pleasure of it? You are surely not so thick as that."

"I assumed it was the color of my coin they found attractive."

"You are a duke; you have power. What common wagtail would dare say no to you?"

"I will not debate this point with you. If you know where Lord Blythestone is, you would be wise to tell me at once."

"I have already told you, were you but clever enough to apprehend. Your leman has been taken into custody to await trial."

Marche crossed the room in a blink to wrap a hand around Murdmont's throat. "You craven worm! What does it profit you to send that gentle lad to such a loathsome place as jail?"

"The pain in your voice is worth more than chests of gold to me," Murdmont managed to say. "I have already warned you of the consequences of threatening me, but if you wish him to suffer more, by all means continue."

Marche released his grip, and Murdmont staggered back, rubbing at his neck. "Where is he being held?"

"I would suggest you ask a member of the constabulary." Murdmont flinched as Marche took a step toward him. "If you touch me again, I will have you arrested as well."

"I see no members of the constabulary present. If I were to choke the life from you and do away with your body, who would be the wiser?"

Murdmont glanced at his shivering victim who hadn't moved since he was released. "There is a witness," he said.

"Lad," Marche called out. "What would you do if I killed this man?"

"I would thank you, sir," the young man said hoarsely.

"You are quite alone," Marche told Murdmont. "There are none of your poor minions here, none of those you have brought under your sway by underhanded means."

All the blood dropped from Murdmont's face. "You would not dare. You would never get away with it. There are too many people in this establishment. Someone would be sure to see you and inform the police."

"I think it is more likely that any who saw me would offer the same thanks as this misused lad."

"Aye, sir." The youth's voice was stronger with each word. "If you wish for help in digging a hole, I know where you might find a spade."

"Ungrateful cur!" Murdmont's color returned in a rush. "I took you from the gutter and offered you more coin than your miserable hide is worth and you repay me with rank treachery?"

The young man shrank back as Murdmont threw the crop at him. Marche's fist crashed into Murdmont's jaw and knocked him to the floor. Holding out a hand to the lad, the duke gestured for him to follow as he left the room.

"Have you clothing, boy?"

"I ain't a boy, begging your lordship's pardon; I am twenty and one. My clothes were taken from me when I was brought here."

Marche unfastened his cloak and slung the heavy garment around the young man's shoulders. "Do you have a name then?"

"Aye, sir. Folk call me Long Tom."

"Do they? And why is that? You are not particularly tall." Tom looked down and Marche's brows rose at the length of the lad's endowment. "Ah, I see, very apt indeed. Come with me and I'll see you set up in a place that's a deal more comfortable than this one."

"Do you mean another brothel, sir? I make no claims to quality, but I'm a good lad."

"I've no doubt, but you do understand that Lord Murdmont will not take your defection with good grace. He is a spiteful sort that will seek you out, no matter the cost."

"The city ain't no place for the likes of me, but I can't go back home. The farm's too poor to feed so many mouths."

"Then will you not accept my offer of help?"

Tom shook his head. "I will take a berth on a ship, sir. Always wanted to see a bit of the world and ain't afraid of work."

Marche took some money from his purse and pressed it into Tom's hand. "I would do more for you, but I am in haste and Murdmont will not sleep forever."

"Are you going to kill him?" There was no hint of judgment in Tom's voice.

"I cannot. Once, perhaps, I might have been able to justify murder, but no longer."

"And why is that, sir?"

"I met someone who convinced me that all life is precious and that it is not my right to end it."

"A priest?"

"Not precisely. Angel would be closer to the mark."

"Then I will make bold to tell you that you are a lucky man."

"Does it seem so to you? Just now I do not feel lucky at all."

"Well, if your angel has run afoul of the authorities, you should go and ask them where he is."

"I will do that. Be sure and have the wounds on your back seen to, and I hope you have a safe journey. If you should encounter more difficulties, you may call upon me. Go to Mrs. Dahlram's Tearoom and ask for Aurelio; he will know how to find me. Away with you now."

Tom bowed his head to the large nobleman and hurried away. Marche returned to the front entrance and asked the first person he saw for directions to the local police station.

"I AM sorry, Your Grace," said the sergeant on duty. "I can appreciate your concern for a comrade and the fact that you are a duke, but I cannot allow you to see any of the prisoners."

"Will you at least tell me if Blythestone is here?" Marche said in carefully controlled tones.

"You are not a barrister by any chance?"

"What has that to do with anything? Lord Blythestone is a member of my family."

"It is past the hour when—"

"I do not care about the time of day! I wish to see Blythestone immediately!"

"I know that, sir. It is not possible."

"Make it possible." Marche leaned over the desk.

"Intimidating me will bring you no closer to your goal."

"Then pray tell me what will move you."

The sergeant finally looked down at the book in front of him. "I can find no one of that name here. I think you must look elsewhere for your—"

"My what?"

"Sir?"

"I am almost certain I heard censure in your voice."

"You are mistaken."

"I think it more likely that you are in Murdmont's pocket and that he has told you certain things about myself and Lord Blythestone. I warn you that if he is harmed in the slightest, those responsible will not go unpunished."

"I am afraid that I must ask you to leave now, sir."

"You may ask anything you like. I will not budge until I have seen Lord Blythestone."

"Then I will have no choice but to place you under arrest."

Marche's fury flared so fiercely that it paralyzed him for several moments in which he could not speak or scarcely draw breath. The need to destroy the one who stood in his way was so strong that it shocked him, and then he pictured Valentine's reaction at coming upon him crouched over a bloodied and broken body. Slowly, the rage drained from him and his fists uncurled as the fire in his eyes was banked for now. "You must forgive me," he said. "I allowed my concern for my comrade to get the better of me."

The sergeant looked suspicious, but was inclined to let the matter drop. "I see it all the time, sir. Folks get wrought up when they come in here."

"If I were to return with a lawyer, would I be allowed to see my brother-in-law?"

"Possibly. The lawyer at least would have a legal reason to see his client."

"Then Blythestone is here."

The policeman sighed. "Very clever, sir."

"I bear you no ill will for doing your duty, but if I find that my suspicions are true and this is a plot of Murdmont's, your involvement would compel me to—"

"No more threats, please, sir," the sergeant interrupted.

"I ask your pardon again." Marche lowered his voice. "I would not be surprised nor would I disapprove if certain establishments in the area made regular donations in gratitude for the exemplary service you provide. If a favored client of one of these businesses were to ask a favor of you, I would never fault you for accommodating him."

"Are you saying you would like to make a donation, sir?"

Marche quickly took stock of his portable wealth and pulled the ring from his right forefinger. "How would this suit?" he asked as he placed it on the high desk.

The sergeant scooped the ring into a drawer. "You have the gratitude of the widows and orphans of slain constables, sir," he said.

"They are most welcome. Now, may I see Lord Blythestone?"

"No, sir, you may not. Remain calm," the other man said as Marche scowled. "I truly cannot authorize a visit from anyone other than a lawyer. By my orders, I cannot even confirm for you that the gentleman is being held here. However, I can send a message for you."

Marche did not comment on the absurdity of offering to pass a message to a man who wasn't there. "No more than that?"

"I'll not risk my job for you, Your Grace. Not when I've a wife and seven little ones at home."

Marche nodded, his temper back in check; it was becoming easier the more he practiced. "I appreciate your position. Have you something I may write with?"

"Of course, sir."

"YOU had better have a bloody good reason for waking me, Marche." Sir Anthony Wedhight, Baronet Kirkcap, drew his dressing gown closer around him as he dismissed his sleepy-eyed servant.

"Blythestone's been arrested."

"The devil you say!"

"I am not larking about, Kirkcap. I need you to go to the jail and free him."

Anthony sank down onto a chair. "Calm yourself. Sit and tell me what has happened." The lawyer listened attentively while Marche told all that he knew. "I see. I am sorry to disappoint you, but the sergeant was quite right. There is nothing we can do at this hour. If Murdmont is behind this despicable act, he is using his knowledge of the law to his benefit."

"There must be something we can do."

"Yes, of course. We cannot let Blythestone suffer alone. Allow me a few moments to dress, and we will go to the station. I am certain I can persuade the authorities to allow me to talk with the young man. At the least, I may reassure him that his friends know of his plight."

"And you may see if he is in need of a physician."

"Yes, of course," Anthony repeated. "Though I abhor it, the bullying of prisoners is not unknown."

Marche shook his head. "The constables would be following Murdmont's orders. I have the word of one of his minions that he despises Blythestone for his own mad reasons."

"I would not take such words at their face value, but I can see you are concerned, and I will make haste, sir, never fear."

When Marche and Kirkcap arrived at the station, a new officer was on duty at the front desk. He claimed to have been there since midnight and refused to give any information on any prisoners, except to say that the Earl of Blythestone was not among them. Kirkcap made enough of a fuss that he was at last allowed to verify the sergeant's words with his own eyes. Valentine was not in any of the cells.

"Murdmont must have followed me and had Blythestone moved as soon as I came to find you," Marche said as he and Kirkcap left the building.

"I can have no opinion on that without more facts. It will be dawn soon, and I must have some rest before the hearing. You should get some rest as well."

"I will not sleep tonight."

Anthony patted the duke on the shoulder as they entered his carriage. "You are very fond of him, I know, but you will be no good to him if you are exhausted."

"I beg your pardon for any embarrassment I may have caused you."

"Please do not mention it, sir. We both know what we are even if we never speak of it. I will not judge you for your affection for Blythestone and your reactions are perfectly natural."

"It's good of you to say it."

Anthony glanced at the other man's profile in the dimness of the coach. "You have changed somewhat, Marche. Your manner is less... abrupt nowadays. Withal, I find your company has become quite agreeable."

"That is Blythestone's influence on me. Tell me what I must do to free him."

"It is imperative that you attend the hearing tomorrow if you wish the return of your property. Justice Berinbroke has scant tolerance for those who flout the dignity of the law as embodied by him."

"What do I care about wealth if I should lose Valentine?"

Anthony sat back. "You love him," he stated.

Marche covered his face with his hands as he nodded.

"Then take the advice of your counsel. There is nothing that you may do to help Blythestone tonight, short of springing him from his cell, which I do not recommend. Take a bed in my home for the few hours left before the hearing. I will dispatch a colleague to ascertain where Blythestone is being held and see what may be done to release him."

"That is not good enough."

"I know." Anthony patted March's shoulder again. "But it will have to do for now."

CHAPTER 22

"GOOD heavens." Lord Justice Berinbroke stopped in the doorway and observed the group waiting in his chamber. He knew Sir Anthony Wedhight, of course, and recognized most of the others. The Duke of Marche was conspicuous by his size alone, but today His Grace was also remarkable for the state of his dress and grooming. The big man looked as though he hadn't slept in days and his appearance was decidedly rumpled. Berinbroke's habitual frown deepened as he cleared his throat.

"Your Worship," Anthony said, breaking off his conversation with Georgiana. "Good of you to agree to see us on such short notice."

The magistrate waited for his clerk to pull out his chair and sat. "I warn you, Kirkcap," he said without preamble or amenity, "I am in a foul temper this morning so tread lightly."

Anthony bowed. "I will do my utmost to see that Your Worship's time is not wasted. Today, I bring before you Georgiana, Marchioness Hapwood, His Grace, the Duke of Marche, Baronet Tarncott and Lord Donshear, all of whom have suffered the loss of their fortunes due to the embezzling of Lord Murdmont. As Your Worship knows, we wish to establish certain facts that will show cause for Murdmont's immediate incarceration."

"And is Lord Murdmont also present?"

"Regrettably, I do not know his whereabouts at the moment, however…."

Anthony was interrupted by a knock. Berinbroke's clerk went to the door and admitted a pair of constables. Between them walked Valentine with Murdmont bringing up the rear.

"Pray forgive the intrusion," Murdmont said in his resonant voice. "However, I have reason to believe that my presence here is greatly desired."

Anthony's hand on Marche's shoulder kept the duke in his seat as Valentine was marched to a straight-backed chair beside the magistrate's desk. The two policeman took up stations behind the chair and clasped their hands behind their backs. Valentine was pale and disheveled, but hardly cowed. He sat upright, his gaze fixed on Marche, sending a silent message of reassurance. Marche was heartened to see that his beloved was unharmed and unmanacled and that his eyes were clear and determined.

"Explain yourself, sir," Berinbroke growled.

"I am Sir Malcolm Jonas, Esquire, accused by these fine nobles of malfeasance. I will be indelicate and state that they wish to blame their misfortunes upon me when all I have done is try to stem the flood of their wrong-headed and willful misspending."

"I will decide who is wrong-headed or willful in my chambers," Berinbroke replied before waving a hand at Valentine. "Who is this gentleman, sir?"

Before Murdmont could speak, Valentine answered. "I am the Earl of Blythestone, Your Honor, and I have been wrongfully taken up and held against my will at that man's behest." Valentine pointed at Murdmont.

Anthony kept his hand on Marche's shoulder, and he could feel the duke's muscles vibrate under his palm. He squeezed hard in warning as he left Marche's side to move closer to the bench. "What have you to say to that, sir?" he addressed Murdmont.

"I will conduct the questioning, if you please, sir." Berinbroke glared at Anthony and then transferred his baleful gaze to Murdmont. "I am not pleased at this summary commandeering of my court. Never mind that we are not in court now, as your smirk would seem to imply."

"I meant no disrespect, Your Worship," Murdmont said. "I present myself here—no doubt to the consternation of my accusers—to lay more serious charges where they belong."

"More serious charges, sir?" Anthony said, before he caught himself. "Begging your pardon, Your Honor."

"I am curious also," the magistrate said. "I am willing to forgive this irregularity so long as all involved remain within the bounds of dignified behavior and can show good cause for these rather extraordinary circumstances."

"Your Worship." Murdmont bowed. "Seated there you see the Duke of Marche, recently wed to the Honorable Miss Valeria Randwick. All this pother over lost assets is but his attempt to draw attention away from the greater crime that has been committed."

"Do not be coy, sir," Berinbroke warned. "Say what you came here to say."

"Very well. I charge the duke's paramour with the murder of the duke's wife. I cannot be plainer than that, Your Worship."

"You can if you will name this mysterious… demimondaine."

"I am speaking of the Earl of Blythestone."

The magistrate had to raise his voice to be heard above the shocked outcry from the small assemblage. "You shock me, sir. Not only by your words, but also by the fact that you utter them at all in such company. If you have anything more to say in that vein, I will thank you to put it in writing or speak to me alone. Ma'am," he nodded to Georgiana, "I hope you are not too incommoded by such frank language."

"Nothing Lord Murdmont said would shock me, Your Worship," she replied. "The man is quite without character, if you will forgive *my* frankness. I wonder if we will soon return to the matter that compelled my presence here, though I am loath to occupy the same room as yonder serpent posing as a man."

Murdmont gave the lady but a passing glance. "I submit that my accusation takes precedence. His Grace is now a duke twice over thanks to the murder of his great-aunt, a crime that has yet to be answered for. Now he appears in London without his bride, cheek by jowl with the girl's brother, who appears to be scant years out of the nursery."

"Let me see if I have this correctly," Berinbroke said. "You are accusing the duke of murdering his wife *and* his aunt with the help of this gentleman."

"I am, Your Worship."

Marche kept his eyes on Valentine and was able to keep his temper under control. He could see that blustering and breaking furniture would avail him little and certainly cause him to be ejected from the room, possibly in irons. Though it was hard to sit and listen to Murdmont's lies, Marche would do his best to avoid any action that might prejudice the magistrate.

"If I may, Your Worship," Anthony spoke up. "I have the word of the Duchess of Bolbracken's physician that the lady was indeed killed by poisoning. Dr. Sawyer also states that Lord Murdmont at that time accused the Duchess of Marche. The duke challenged Lord Murdmont, as you may imagine; however, Sir Malcolm was absent from the field at the appointed time."

"Is this true, sir?" Berinbroke turned a cold eye on Murdmont. "For if so, you have no honor and your word must perforce be suspect."

"I could not allow Marche to kill me and so silence the truth, Your Worship."

The door of the chamber opened drawing everyone's eyes. "I could not help but overhear, and I must remark that you would not know the truth, sir, even if it offered its card."

"How dare you interrupt these proceedings!" the magistrate barked. "You there! Constable! Have this man removed at... Darby...?" Berinbroke cleared his throat. "Baronet Strand! What the devil are you doing here?"

Darby St. Denis strode to the bench, his dignified bearing unmarred by a slight limp. "I do crave Your Honor's pardon, but when I heard of the travesty being engineered by this... this... I can find no words adequate to the depths of Murdmont's perfidy."

"It is the first time I can recall you being at a loss for words since you learned to speak," the judge said. "What have you to do with these folk?"

"Some of them are my friends, sir, and I stand with them in their dark hour."

"I pray you; keep the poetry from your speech, if it is possible. I assume you think you have a valid reason for disrupting this hearing."

"I am here to speak for my dear companion, the Earl of Blythestone."

"And why do you imagine that I would allow it?"

"I have some training in the law, sir."

"Ah, but you did not finish your studies, did you?"

"Not as yet, but I find in myself a rekindled interest."

"Then I will not snuff it. If Kirkcap and Murdmont have no objection, you may have your say."

"Your Worship," Murdmont began before a scowl from Berinbroke shut him up.

"Thank you for your indulgence," Darby said with a sweeping bow. "I have but recently, very recently indeed, returned to London after a brief trip to the Continent, where I made the acquaintance of the Earl of Blythestone. I find him to be an altogether admirable fellow who has had a very salutary effect on me in the short time I have had the extreme privilege to know him. Like his angelic sister, he is a paragon of...."

"Your Worship," Murdmont protested.

"Lord Strand," Berinbroke said. "It is not necessary to catalogue the gentleman's qualities."

"My apologies. I only mention Blythestone's character so that you will appreciate my shock when Mr. Fleet, a mutual acquaintance, called upon me with the news that my friend had been taken up by the police. Naturally, I tried to discover why Blythestone was arrested and to have him released, but he had vanished most mysteriously. If you wish corroboration of this, you may inquire of Sir Anthony or His Grace or certain constables whose names I am prepared to supply. Furthermore, as nearly as I can determine, the gentleman was taken to jail on no more than a word, and perhaps a few coins, from Sir Malcolm Jonas, a man who fled a duel of honor at the same time as several fortunes went missing as well."

"How did you come by this information?"

"I questioned everyone involved and came to certain conclusions."

"Did you really?" Berinbroke's tone softened a trifle. "And in so few hours? You must have bustled, sir."

"I will sleep when my comrade is free and his good name cleared of these absurd charges."

"Well spoken. However, you have yet to justify your presence here."

Georgiana stood. "If the Baronet's word is not good enough, perhaps you will take my testimony. I did not speak before now, because to accuse Murdmont is to reveal my part in the sordid business. Now I wish to confess my treachery. I betrayed those who believed me to be a friend. I learned their secrets, and Murdmont used the knowledge to ensnare them. They thought he had the most amazing intuition and that he would use it to enrich them. The truth is that he—"

"You are ruining yourself with every word, lady," Murdmont pronounced.

"The truth is," she went on as though he hadn't spoken, "that he uses all sorts of slippery tricks to part people from their money. I suppose that should not be surprising in a man who made his first fortune collecting debts owed by wagerers. His mob of hired bullies was rumored to be the most vicious in the city."

"You've no idea what you are speaking of."

Georgiana gave Murdmont a cool stare. "Do you imagine that I would not have studied your history after I realized how you had duped poor Gilbert? Of course, I never imagined that I would end up under your claw as well. What a proud fool I was."

"Please sit down, lady, you have—" Valentine said, half-rising before a constable pushed him back into his seat.

Marche was on his feet without thinking. He took a step forward, and then Georgiana's hand settled on his forearm.

"You are very gallant, Your Grace," she murmured. "How did you know I was feeling faint?"

"Not at all, ma'am." Marche helped her to a seat. "I think Blythestone meant to say that you have been brave enough for now."

"Indeed, ma'am," Berinbroke turned to Murdmont. "I will hear your answer to the lady's speech now."

"I can only suppose it is her poor attempt to implicate me in this patently ludicrous fantasy of dark machinations. It is obvious that the lady wrongly holds me responsible for the death of her husband, and there you have her motive in blackening my reputation."

"Reputation!" Darby stared at Murdmont. "How easily you say the word, sir, as if you had such a thing about you. When will you apprehend that you have no reputation any longer?"

"The opinion of a piddling puppy does not signify," Murdmont returned.

"You will be mindful of the dignity of this hearing," the judge told him.

"Am I not allowed to answer a personal attack, Your Worship?"

"Do you perhaps wish to challenge me, sir?" Darby said softly.

"You must wait in line, Strand," Marche could not forbear to say. "Murdmont and I have unsettled business that takes a prior claim."

Darby bowed to the duke before returning his attention to Murdmont. "I await your answer, sir."

"This is not an appropriate setting for such a matter," Murdmont said. "I will give my answer at a later time."

"No doubt from a remote location," Darby replied.

"I must ask you to cease discussion of this personal matter and return to the issue that concerns all in attendance," Berinbroke said.

"Your pardon, Your Honor," Darby said with another sweeping bow. "I submit that it is Lord Murdmont's unreasoning antipathy toward the Duke of Marche and nothing else that caused His Grace's friend, the Earl of Blythestone to be confined against his will in a foul cell among the very dregs of society. For that, if nothing else may be proven, I would demand that Lord Murdmont be charged and punished as severely as the law allows."

"Very well, so charged, contingent, of course, upon the testimony of the constables who witnessed the crime.

"They are waiting in the hall, sir."

For the first time since Murdmont had entered the room, he looked ill at ease. However, there was no trace of hesitancy in his mellow voice when he spoke. "I am happy to refute any such charges at the proper time. Just now, we have the issue of two murders before us."

"Blast you!" Marche burst out. "My wife is not dead."

"Then I assume you could produce the lady if necessary, Your Grace?"

Valentine's heart dropped into his stomach as he watched Marche search for an answer. "May I speak, Your Worship?" he asked, distracting attention to himself.

"What would you say, sir?"

"I would say that it is absurd to think that the duke could harm either his aunt or his wife. I have known him but a short time, but it is clear to me how much he loved Lady Willamina and how much he loves his wife. I know it is indecorous of me to discuss things of such a private nature, but the seriousness of the accusations made by Lord Murdmont compel me to speak. I know that evil and goodness are not immediately apparent in a man's face or his bearing, but his actions will reveal his nature, and I have no doubt that the duke is a good man, the best, in fact, that it has been my pleasure to know."

Berinbroke looked somewhat nonplussed, but Marche's eyes glowed like amber in the sun as they met Valentine's gaze. "I return your regard tenfold, sir," the duke managed to say before the magistrate overrode him.

"Your mutual regard notwithstanding," Berinbroke said. "I am afraid that the Earl's good opinion is not enough remove suspicion. Perhaps the answer to a simple question will go some ways to unraveling this knot. Has anyone present seen the Duchess of Marche recently?"

There was a long moment of silence before Marche spoke. "My wife prefers the serenity of our country home to the commotion of the city."

"I commend her good taste, but that is not precisely the question before us. Is there anyone here who may vouch for the duchess's good health?"

Marche saw the struggle on Valentine's face. "Let me state that I wish no one to lie on my behalf. I could not bear to think I had led such gentle folk to stain their honor."

"Well said, Your Grace." Berinbroke cast his eye over the others. "Has anyone else anything to say? Kirkcap?"

The lawyer coughed. "I have never had the pleasure of making the lady's acquaintance."

"I have had the privilege to stand in her light and receive the blessing of her sweet words of praise," Darby said. "Any man that could harm such a flower is a very monster."

Murdmont's lip curled as he responded. "So it would seem. I propose that the lady be summoned so that we may all assure ourselves that she yet graces this world."

"I will fetch her, if it pleases Your Worship," Valentine said.

"Indeed, I believe you are the only one who could produce the lady," Murdmont sneered. "However, I will ask that you be required to return with her."

"And are we expected to cool our heels until the duchess arrives?" Georgiana asked. "Forgive my impatience, but it will take several hours to send a message to Wandeleigh and many more before the lady may be ready to travel. I speak from experience, sir."

"Perhaps it will be sooner than you may imagine." Darby smiled as a disturbance in the hallway became audible. Going to the door, he opened it despite the magistrate's protests.

"If it pleases the court," a young woman called out in a ringing voice. All heads turned as she came forward, leaving wondering murmurs in her wake. "I am here to answer anyone who would impugn my name or my honor, which are in truth the same thing to me."

"Welcome, Your Grace." Darby St. Denis bowed as she passed him on her way to the judge's bench.

Murdmont's face was frozen in shock. "That is not possible."

"Will you deny my existence to my face?" Valeria tilted her chin at a pugnacious angle.

"I would not advise it, sir," Valentine said.

Murdmont's gaze went to Valentine and then returned to the young woman before him. He knew in that instant that he was beaten. The truth did not matter here; it only mattered what his peers were willing to believe. He had scant chance of convincing these people that Marche had married a lad in a dress and escaped detection for months. This jury would never accept that they had been so taken in. "I… I feared you had come to some harm. I can see that my sources were happily in error." He rallied. "However, there is still the matter of Lady Bolbracken's death."

"Your Worship," Darby said, gesturing to the doorway. "May I call upon Baron Snowhurst? He stands ready to give testimony that Lord Murdmont was the last person to see the late duchess alive. It should also be clear that as the lady's attorney, Murdmont had much to gain by her demise once he had altered certain papers, deeds of land, in fact. I have come to suspect that he has had a hand in several other deaths, each of which added to his ill-gotten fortune, beginning with the Earl of Blythestone's father."

"Ill-gotten!" Murdmont said. "You preening ne'er-do-well, I worked hard for every penny."

"Perhaps, but it was not precisely *honest* work, was it, sir?" Darby replied.

"It is unconscionable that I be subjected to the yappings of this overweening whelp. I have a degree in law and a license to practice."

"Yes, I was coming to that," Darby said. "My old professor was not best pleased to entertain me at the hour of four in the morning, but as he was already out of bed, he indulged me. It may interest you to know that you are acquainted with him. In fact, he remembers you quite well. In particular, he remembers that you did not finish your schooling."

Murdmont's features were locked in a sneer. "The answer is as simple as you yourself. I received my degree in France."

"Clever of you not to name a university in England, but tell me, sir; how is it you were granted a license to practice law on English soil?"

"What do you mean?"

The magistrate leaned forward. "I will answer that. There exists no law prohibiting a Frenchman or any man educated in France from holding a license in England, however... due to certain prejudices arising from the conflict between the two nations, I would find it odd indeed that any patriotic person would employ you if they knew of your matriculation."

"That is...." Murdmont faltered. "That is reprehensible."

"Heavens," Georgiana exclaimed, "not only is the man a complete fraud, he's a French sympathizer."

Murdmont shot her a look of pure venom. "Preposterous!"

"That will be for a court to decide," Berinbroke said as he gestured to the constables. "Place Lord Murdmont under arrest."

Before the officers could react, Murdmont sprang forward and took hold of Darby. Wrapping an arm around the young man's throat, he stepped backward, dragging the struggling young noble with him. "Stay back," Murdmont warned. "It would be easy enough to break his neck."

Valentine launched himself from his chair. He crashed into Murdmont and Darby and all three went to the floor. Murdmont got to his feet first and found he was facing a small mob. With the speed and desperation of a cornered rat, he spun and threw open a window. Marche's long reach caught the fleeing man by the collar, but Murdmont slid out of his coat to drop into the alleyway. The duke dropped the garment, his hands flying to his ears as a constable's whistle shrilled at close range.

"Clear the window, sir!"

Marche moved quickly aside and the young constable was over the sill and off after Murdmont in a trice. The other officer's running footsteps could be heard receding down the hall. The duke started to follow when he saw that Valentine was still on the floor. The young man's head rested in his sister's lap, while Darby fanned him with a sheaf of legal documents. The Duchess of Hapwood and the Lords

Donshear and Tarncott watched the uproar in the corridor from the doorway. Lord Kirkcap stood beside the magistrate's clerk and Berinbroke himself was gazing into the middle distance with a dazed expression.

"Your Worship?" the clerk said diffidently.

"Yes, Clemp, what is it?" Berinbroke's eyes fell on the supine Earl. "Has anyone sent for a physician? If not, do so at once."

"At once, sir!" the clerk said.

"No doctors, I implore you," Valentine said as he tried to rise.

Marche's hand covered Valeria's as both settled on Valentine's chest to keep him down. "Your pardon, ma'am," the duke said.

"Freely given, Your Grace," Valeria replied. A hint of a smile dimpled her right cheek—the mirror image of the one in Valentine's left cheek—as she met Marche's eyes. "We are kin of a sort, after all."

"I daresay a husband has a right to touch his wife even in these chambers," Berinbroke said as he came from behind his high desk.

Marche covered his guilty start at his faux pas by looking up at Darby. "Strand, you astound."

Darby bowed. "You flatter me, Your Grace."

"Hardly empty flattery," the magistrate said. "The duke is expressing my sentiments as well."

Darby's jaw dropped. "Th-thank you, s-sir," he managed to say, stuttering for the first time since he left the nursery.

Berinbroke had already turned his attention elsewhere. "Are you quite well, Blythestone?"

"I am, sir," Valentine said. "If I had room, I believe I could stand."

"My sweet brother," Valeria said as she rose from the floor. "What have I done to you?"

"None of this is any fault of yours." Valentine looked a bit bemused as Darby, Marche and Valeria all offered an arm to assist him.

Valeria's winged eyebrows rose toward her hairline. "You have learned to lie quite well since last I saw you."

Valentine looked up from dusting his coat to meet her eyes. "The world outside the abbey has given me much cause to practice the art."

"There is sad truth in your words," Berinbroke said. "Are you certain you are not injured? You have quite a goose egg coming up on your pate."

"Indeed you do," Valeria said. She touched a lace-gloved forefinger to a lump on Valentine's forehead. When he winced away, she shook her head. "That is going to hurt like the dickens and turn as black as the devil's heart," she predicted.

"It is merely a bump. Pray do not fuss over me."

"Though it may chafe, I recommend that you bow to your sister's will in this," Marche said.

"You are in league against me," Valentine complained. "It is not fair. How am I to stand against the both of you? I will surrender myself to your care."

The judge cleared his throat. "I suppose I might adjourn this hearing, seeing as how one of the principals has departed precipitously."

"He'll not get far," Darby said. "I left Tarmegent and Snowhurst on sentry at either end of the street. With their guidance, the constables will have the villain in hand in no time."

"I hope you are right, Strand," Marche said. "Murdmont is greasier than goose tallow."

Berinbroke cleared his throat once more. "Kirkcap, it is patent that Malcolm Jonas is guilty of at least some of the charges your clients have brought against him. Of course, you understand that until an official ruling is made, I cannot simply return the fortunes and land that he stole."

Anthony bowed. "Of course, Your Worship. I am overjoyed to know that you look kindly upon our suit."

"Between gentlemen, I will say that it is plain to me that Murdmont is a blackguard and that your clients may be assured of the return of their property. I will also say that if you are in need of a partner, you could do worse than young Strand here, assuming he completes his studies."

"I could not agree more. I shall make his better acquaintance; you may be sure, sir."

"I am wanted elsewhere," Berinbroke said. "So I will bid you all good day."

"I must be going as well," Georgiana said. "I do hope I can manage to find a hansom."

"May I offer you the security of my carriage, ma'am?" the magistrate said.

"I could not impose upon Your Worship."

"Nonsense, ma'am. It would be an honor."

"Then I will accept with gratitude, sir." The Duchess Hapwood dropped a graceful curtsy. "Sir Anthony, may I depend upon you for reports?"

"Of course, ma'am. I will convey any pertinent news to yourself and these gentlemen immediately."

"I do not mean to tell you your office, sir, but you know what cause I have to wish a swift conclusion to this affair. And if the courts should find me culpable...."

"I will not hear of it," Berinbroke said. "You shall be a witness for the Crown, my dear, and I will see to it personally that you receive full immunity from prosecution."

"You set my mind greatly at ease, Your Worship. If only my monetary woes could be so easily dissipated."

After a brief glance at Kirkcap, the magistrate spoke again. "I think some form remuneration might be arranged to compensate the lady for time she will spend in the Crown's service."

"Do you really think so?" Georgiana gave Berinbroke a look of sweet gratitude.

"I am sure of it, my dear. Now come, I insist that you dine with me for luncheon." Berinbroke tore his gaze from Georgiana's pretty face. "And you gentlemen are welcome, of course."

"That sounds splendid," Donshear said. "Are you coming, Tarncott?"

As the small group left the room, the magistrate turned to speak once more. "This matter is far from settled, but there is no reason you may not go about your normal lives until Murdmont is brought to trial." He waited for the murmurs of thanks to end before addressing Darby. "Strand, you may feel free to call upon me for advice at any time."

Darby stood like a man blasted by lightning as Georgiana leaned toward Valeria. "Forgive me for seeming to snub you. I am happy to meet you again."

"The pleasure is entirely mine, I assure you," Valeria replied without hesitation.

"I told your brother once that I longed to see you side by side so that I might compare your resemblance in the flesh, as it were. I could not believe that Nature could produce two such beauties in one century, but here you are. You cannot imagine my astonishment."

"My imagination is quite vast," Valeria said.

It seemed Georgiana had no answer for that and took her leave on Berinbroke's arm. As she swept past Darby, his paralysis broke.

"Thank you, father," he said to the magistrate's back. If Berinbroke heard, he did not acknowledge the young man's words but continued down the hall.

CHAPTER 23

"FATHER?" Marche gave Strand a measuring look.

"Did you not know?" Anthony spoke up. "His Worship is Daniel St. Denis, the marquess of Berinbroke. Strand is his only child."

"Once again, it seems," Darby said. "I have been disowned for some few years."

"Not legally," Anthony clarified. "And for what it is worth, I think you have been reinstated. I will go farther and submit that you have impressed the old lion."

"He has certainly impressed me," Valentine said. "Thank you, dear Strand, for coming to my defense. I do not know how I can repay you."

"What I did, I did for love and because it was right." Darby's eyes slid to Valeria. "It is my fate to love too well but unwisely, if I may quote the Bard."

"You may quote whomever you like," Marche said. "I would like to hear an accounting of how all of this came to be. I do not mind confessing, sir, that when I came here today, I had no idea how this hearing would end. In my worst imaginings, Blythestone had vanished—victim to Murdmont's malice—never to be seen again. Instead, my friend and I are vindicated by the presence of my bride, a serendipity that would seem to be of your doing."

"I would like to hear this tale myself," Anthony said. "However, I have obligations elsewhere just now. Please call upon me at your earliest convenience."

"Indeed we will," Marche assured him. "Thank you for all you have done."

"I serve the law, sir," Anthony said. "However, it gladdens my heart when I may help a friend." He leaned close to speak in Marche's ear before he left. "The best of luck to you in the matter of which we spoke last night."

"Now, sir," Marche said to Darby. "I propose we find a congenial spot where you may apprise us of the doings that led to Murdmont's rout."

"At once, Your Grace," Darby said. "If you will wait here but a moment, I will call for my carriage." The young man bowed and turned to go.

"A moment, if you please, sir," Valeria said. "If it would not trouble you, I will accompany you. I feel a powerful urge for a breath of air."

"That would be my very great pleasure, ma'am," Darby said delightedly.

Valeria looked over her shoulder and gave Valentine a wink as she walked away with Darby. "The bold hoyden!" Valentine exclaimed when the door closed, leaving him alone with Marche.

"A very minx," Marche agreed. "She puts me in mind of someone, but I cannot quite recall...."

"Oh, do give over, Loel. You cannot possibly be as calm as you seem. Did not the events of the past hour cause your heart to pound?"

"I'll not deny it." Marche took Valentine's hands in his. "When you entered the room, it was all I could do not to run to you and embrace you."

"That would have been most welcome but likely not well-received by His Honor."

"I can scarcely credit what I am about to say, but it is not fair at all that I may not show my love for you as freely as any man in love with a woman."

"And that is hardly free."

"More than anything, I wish to hold you now."

"Oh Loel, would you, please?"

The two men reached for one another and embraced, each thankful to be free and in the arms of the one he loved. They could not get close enough and found it impossible to let go until footsteps stopped in front of the door. Breaking apart as the door opened, they composed themselves as well as they were able.

"Oh dear, look at your faces!" Valeria said. "You have cream on your whiskers, the both of you. I suppose I will have to sit between you in the coach."

Valentine smiled at Marche's expression. "I did warn you about her tongue," he said.

"Do not be tiresome," Valeria said. "I know when to hold my tongue. We are quite alone just now, and I am so pleased to see you happy that I cannot resist teasing you a bit."

"I have no idea what you can be implying."

Valeria tucked her chin and gave her brother a stern look from under her brows. "I hope you do not think that you may fool me as easily as you have fooled half the nobility in England. I am a Breton woman, as you know, and I am not so easily hoodwinked. Why, if I had entered this room a few moments earlier, heaven knows what manner of indecorous behavior I might have witnessed. Do not bother to deny it; it is writ upon your face. You are head over heels in love with this Hercules."

"And you deduce this from a look at my face?"

"You have a most expressive visage, dear brother." Valeria smiled. "And dear Anne was good enough to tell me everything."

"I beg your pardons," Darby said from the doorway. "The coach is ready."

"Isn't Lord Strand kind not to point out that I was sent to fetch you?" Valeria asked. "Do forgive me, sir, for my absentmindedness. It is only that I have not seen my brother for quite some time, and I am so very fond of him."

"Not at all, ma'am. I only came on account of the coachman doesn't like to keep the horses standing in front of the courthouse."

"Where are we off to, then?" Marche asked.

"I thought we could all use some refreshment, and so I took the liberty of sending your man ahead to Beale House to bespeak a room."

"That will do very nicely, Strand." Marche's warm tone of admiration belied the lightness of his words. "My dear?" he offered his arm to Valeria.

Valentine felt an odd twinge as he watched Marche and Valeria link arms and move away. He was not jealous, but he felt again the cold injustice that denied him the right to walk at Marche's side. It simply was not fair, and Valentine was torn between anger and sorrow.

"Blythestone?"

Valentine shook off the dark thoughts. "I am with you, Strand. A bit of a delicate stomach is all that is troubling me, nothing more dire. Lead on."

"With pleasure," Darby said as he gestured to the door. "I do hope you will take up residence here, sir. I know we would be fast friends."

"I cannot say what the future will hold," Valentine said as they walked to the entrance. "However, I hope that I will spend a great part of my time visiting the Marches."

"Another aim we share, sir." Darby led the way onto the street. "And here is my coach."

Valeria was already inside the handsome brougham, but Marche still stood on the footpath looking up at the box. The redheaded man sitting next to the driver ceased his speech when he saw Valentine and cried out to the Earl.

"Thank all the saints! Your lordship is well and all of a piece."

"You made no such to-do over me, Negus," Marche said with exaggerated affront.

"Pish! I knew Your Grace could fend for yourself," the valet answered. "But I was feared for my hide did I go back to that trucklesome Frenchwoman without good news of the earl."

"Do not tell me Mistress Kermartin is here," Marche said.

"Nay, sir. She'd no fancy to suffer a fast coach ride to Town, and any road, the Duchess Blythestone is returned from Scotland as Mistress Harston."

"I can see we have much to speak of," Valentine said. "If the duke is quite finished blocking the footpath, perhaps we may be on our way."

"My very thought, brother," Valeria said, putting her head out of the window. "He looms like the Colossus at Rhodes. You had best stay out of his shadow for you know that nothing grows in shade."

"Negus, a smirk is a most unbecoming expression on the face of a servant," Marche commented as he climbed into the carriage.

Valentine and Darby got into the brougham, and the valet signaled to the driver. Having traveled from Lamberglyn to London with Mistress Valeria Cleary, Negus could well imagine his master squirming under her seemingly innocent remarks. The smirk was still on his face when the coach stopped in the yard at Beale House.

"I CANNOT imagine a more pleasant setting," Valeria said when she and her companions had been shown to a private salon and refreshments were provided. "I should like to visit again."

"If your husband is unavailable as escort, I will be happy to accompany you," Valentine said as he settled next to his sister.

"Forgive my discourtesy," Marche said as he sat. "Before you plan a future, I would be very glad to hear an accounting of the recent past. Strand," the duke looked over his shoulder, "join us and illuminate us please."

"At once, Your Grace. I was just seeing to some small details."

"Good man, now sit."

Darby sat, his gaze bouncing from Valeria to Valentine and back several times before he spoke. "I still can scarcely credit the resemblance." His guileless face bore an expression of vague puzzlement, as though he were trying to remember a portion of a dream. "I hope you will all pardon me if I make some observations, but it seems to me that the lady's manner is somewhat changed since first we met. The retiring air is entirely dispelled."

"Perhaps some credit for that might be placed at my feet," Marched drawled.

"To be sure, sir." Darby looked a bit affronted by the duke's insinuation. "A woman must perforce gain a measure of confidence when she becomes a wife, however...." The young man's eyes strayed to Valentine and Valeria again. "Damme, I cannot be rid of the most extraordinary notion that the two of you have changed personalities."

Valeria's laugh rang out. "When first I came to England, I was quite overwhelmed by the scale of things, but I have grown quite easy with the grandeur and the customs. Now, my natural and, according to my mother, regrettable vivacity has asserted itself."

Darby smiled. "I did see glimpses of it before, most notably when you pelted Marche with snowballs the day after your wedding."

"A notable occurrence indeed," Marche said. "I still profess myself curious as to how you came to be our savior today, Strand."

"Ah, well, there is not so much to tell. Tobias Fleet was arrested with Blythestone but managed to escape. Upon fleeing the constables, Fleet sought me out, remembering me kindly from the tavern in Brittany and rightly deducing that I had no reason to betray him and might, in fact, be of some help. He did not know who had informed Murdmont that you and Blythestone were at the tearoom." Darby cleared his throat. "He suggested I inquire at Kirkcap's home before going 'round to the station, and I learned that Kirkcap was already attempting to have the earl released. Upon hearing that Blythestone was charged with his sister's murder, I thought the best thing would be to bring the lady to London. Therefore, I dispatched Fleet in my phaeton to Lamberglyn Park. Between your duchess and your valet, sir, they contrived the rest of the happy outcome."

"You are much too modest, sir," Valeria said. "I know that you were awake through the night garnering the ill will of several gentlemen in your efforts on behalf of my brother and... my husband. I am sure they were not best pleased to be routed from bed and questioned."

"Your words, as ever, have the clear sweet ring of truth, however, once I had apprised these gentlemen of Murdmont's duplicity, they were eager to provide whatever information they possessed."

"But surely the constables you questioned were not so forthcoming without some persuasion," Marche said. "Those I spoke with were most uncooperative."

"Constables?"

"The men you brought with you to testify to Murdmont's bribing of police officers," Valentine said helpfully. "You said they were waiting in the hall."

"I must confess that I made them up out of whole cloth. Mr. Fleet was a font of information on the less savory practices of a number of constables at the station nearest the tearoom. From his accounts, I was able to paint a picture of corruption that I thought might unsettle Sir Malcolm and cause him to lose a step."

"Well, sir," Marche said, slouching in his chair. "I do believe your sire is right. You do bid fair to become a proper lawyer."

"Strand," Valentine said, "do you know where Mr. Fleet might be now? We owe him another great debt of gratitude."

"Indeed, we do," Marche agreed. "I believe I shall look into setting him up in a business of some sort. What do you say to that, Blythestone?"

"You have my whole-hearted support in the scheme, Your Grace."

The puzzled look returned to Darby's face. "Do you know, Blythestone, that I have seen the duchess gaze at Marche in exactly the same way as you are doing now?"

"Is that so?" Valeria cocked an eyebrow. "There must be something about my husband that inspires instant and deep affection."

"I never knew that to be true before, ma'am," Darby said without thinking. "Begging your pardon, Marche."

"I am not offended. I quite agree that I was a most unlovely fellow, but it is my hope to grow more and more genial."

"And I was speaking of the past, of course." Darby managed to bow while seated. "At least, I hope I have managed to satisfy your curiosity, Your Grace."

"You have clarified several points for me, and I assume I may look to my wife to provide more detail should I wish it."

"I will describe my part during the long dull journey back to Lamberglyn," Valeria said.

"Dull?" Marche mused. "Do you find it so? For myself, I take a particular pleasure in it."

"Then when I have finished my tale, you shall regale me with the delights to found on the road to Lamberglyn Park."

Darby leaned close to Valentine. "Does it not warm your heart to see the obvious affection between them? Though my heart also breaks at the sight, I am comforted by the knowledge that she is beloved and happy."

"You are a truly noble man, Strand. Had you been of lesser character, you might have let Marche and myself go to prison and wooed my sister in her husband's absence."

"Do you know that I never thought of that? What an opportunity missed!"

Valentine chuckled, drawing the attention of Marche and Valeria. "Has young Strand said something amusing?" the duke asked.

"No, no, you know I make no pretensions to cleverness. I am content to display my genius in my wardrobe. In fact, Blythestone and I were mightily entertained by the pair of you."

"How pleasant to know that I amuse you," Valeria said.

"My words were meant to be complimentary," Darby assured her. "You are a delight, as the prince regent has more than once remarked, and Marche is a lucky hound. However, I would add that you are a fortunate lady as well to have a husband so well matched to you."

Valeria tilted her head to the side in a mannerism that her real husband found irresistible. "What a lovely thing to say! Since you and my brother are comrades, I hope that you will come often to Lamberglyn. Your company would be most welcome. Indeed, I feel quite sure that my mother will adore you."

"Honored, ma'am," Darby said. He would have said more, but he was interrupted by a knock.

"Pardon me," Negus said when he stuck his head in the door. "You did ask me to call for you in an hour, sirs."

"Thank you," Marche said and turned to Valeria. "Are you ready, my dear?"

"Blythestone," Darby said. "Why don't we allow the Marches some time to themselves? I invite you to stay with me tonight, and we will journey to Lamberglyn in the morning."

"Oh no," Valeria broke in. "I have not seen my dear brother in eons. I must insist on keeping him to myself for a bit."

"I am feeling a bit unwell," Valentine said. "My head began to ache before our luncheon, and it has grown worse rather than better."

"Perhaps you should lie down for a bit," Marche said.

"I may do that in the coach," Valentine answered. "Come, I cannot wait to hear mother introduce her new husband."

"Do not be wicked!" Valeria's tone was stern, but her eyes sparkled with humor. "Bid Sir Darby a good evening and join us in the carriage."

"Do you mean Strand's brougham or some conveyance I've not yet seen this day?"

Valeria flinched slightly at Valentine's tone, and Darby hastened to speak. "Of course, my coach is yours to use as long as you have need."

"Thank you," Valentine said, his peevishness vanishing as quickly as it had appeared. "Forgive me for speaking so sharply. I hope you will charitably blame my headache."

"Poor thing," Valeria said, putting her arm around her brother's back. "Come with me and lie down. You will feel better."

"I am hardly incapacitated. I do feel a trifle queasy, but I ate a terrible lot of rich food after several hours fasting."

"You'll be right as a trivet after a few hours sleep," Valeria said.

"Good day, Strand," Marche said, bowing to the young man. "You may never know what a service you have done me, but I wish you to know that you may call upon me at need."

"I am honored, Your Grace." Darby returned the bow. "You will encounter me again and that right soon, I promise you."

Marche walked away feeling as though things had fallen out as well as they possibly could have considering the odds against them. He waved to Negus—doing duty as driver—and climbed into the coach to sit next to Valeria. Opposite them, Valentine was stretched out upon the velvet-covered seat. In Negus's hands, the large carriage moved easily through the late afternoon traffic and soon reached the outskirts of London. By the time they were out of the city, Valentine was fast asleep.

"How soft your face is when you gaze on him," Valeria murmured.

Marche turned to look at her. "You know the nature of my love for him?"

She nodded. "Anne was... not specific, but she managed to convey her meaning when she spoke of your friendship with Valentine."

"And may I ask your opinion on our friendship?"

"You will get it whether you ask or not. You might suppose that Valentine and I are not close because we grew up apart, but you would be wrong. I longed for him with such intensity that I spoke to him as though he were always beside me. For a time, I think my poor mother feared I might be simple, but Anne told her that many children invent playmates. I imagined how he might change, as we grew older, and I never fell out of the habit of discussing my daily doings with him. He has been my dearest friend for all of my life, and I would not look kindly on any who meant him harm. You would never hurt him, would you, Your Grace?"

"I would throttle any who tried."

"I thought that might be your temper. Nay, do not frown; I approve. When you know me better, you will find that I have more of a taste for blood than my gentle brother."

"Then I will keep to your leeward side, lady."

Valeria laughed. "And I will do the same. Tell me, have you given thought to how you will explain the decampment of your duchess?"

"Must you go? I was rather hoping you might stay at Lamberglyn and make the occasional appearance with me in Town. Now that I am married to such a respectable young woman, I may even be accepted at Almack's. Surely, you would not want to miss the grand balls of the Season. Such a beautiful lass would shine down every other female present."

"You tempt me, sir, but naturally, I can make no decision without consulting Mr. Cleary. He is a Breton, you see, and anxious to return to his farm."

"We have farms in England. Why not take a portion of Lamberglyn and cultivate it?"

"I will certainly put your argument to him. I love Brittany with all my heart, but I love my family more, and it appears that they are destined to live in England."

"It is only a small Channel." Marche smiled. "And having more than one residence is not unheard of among the gentry."

"You make very good points, and I would not be averse to holding country court as the Duchess of Marche, but I fear Randall will take a deal of convincing. If I am to pose as your wife, the role of paramour must fall upon him."

"I am speaking half in jest, but truly, you would only need to be in London for a few weeks out of the year during high season."

"Or you might become a recluse," she countered.

"A stunningly simple plan and a very attractive one. If Blythestone is amenable, it would solve the better part of my problems."

"Marche," Valeria said, placing her hand over his. "You must feel free to call him Valentine when we are alone."

"That is a sweet freedom, lady."

"Well, we are family now." She held his hand through the rest of the journey as she spoke of growing up in Brittany and related bits of family history. They were surprised at how quickly the time had passed when the carriage pulled up in the drive. "Wake up," Valeria said, giving Valentine's shoulder a shake as Marche stepped down from the coach. "Come, sleepyhead!" She gave him another poke that produced no response. "Marche!" she called out.

The duke put his head in the coach door. "What is it?"

"I cannot wake Valentine."

CHAPTER 24

WHEN Marche could not awaken Valentine, he lifted the young man in his arms and carried him into the house. Those waiting to greet the travelers found their high spirits quelled by the sight of the pale and motionless earl.

"What is wrong with him?" cried Amandine as she hurried forward.

"Do not get into a state, my dear," said the gray-whiskered fellow at her side. "Let's put the poor lad on the sofa, and I'll have a look at him."

"And who might you be?" Marche asked as the man went to one knee on the carpet and bent over Valentine.

"Pray forgive the discourtesy, Your Grace," Valeria spoke up. "When time shall serve, I will formally introduce you to my mother and her husband. For now, suffice it that Mr. Harston is a physician, albeit retired. You may put your mind at rest on that score."

Marche bowed briefly but was unable to keep his gaze from the young man on the brocade-covered sofa. "Forgive my distraction, but you know of my fondness for the earl." Though he fidgeted, he stayed put, watching intently as Mr. Harston examined the unexpected patient.

Valeria hovered until a dark-eyed young man entered to stand by her side. Like a boat that has dropped anchor, she steadied immediately. "Do let me know, Mr. Harston, if I may fetch anything at all for you," she offered.

Anne appeared at the drawing room door as Valeria finished speaking. "If aught needs fetching, I will get it for you, but what are you all doing in here? Your dinner is on the table and cooling and... Sweet Virgin! What has happened to the young master?"

"Eh?" Mr. Harston looked up. "Ah, there you are, Anne. The very person I need. The earl has taken a blow to the pate and languishes in the sort of swoon that often follows. He will require a quiet place in which to rest, and cold compresses for his forehead would not go amiss."

"Thank you," Marche said. "How long will he sleep?"

Harston got to his feet. "I am afraid that no one may predict his waking with any accuracy. This is the sort of injury called a concussion, and it heals itself... or it does not. All we can do is wait and make sure that he is comfortable."

"Nothing more?" Marche said sharply.

"Your Grace," the physician said, "I know it is difficult to sit idle, but truly there is nothing more to be done for him."

"But you are certain that he will wake."

Harston's eyes went to his wife. "I wish I did not have to inform you, but it does happen at times that the patient never wakes. Instead, the poor soul slips from sleep into death."

"From such a small bump?" Amandine asked, her eyes pleading for reassurance.

"Sometimes there is not even a sign of injury," Harston said. "The brain is a prodigious yet fragile organ about which we know grievously little. Were I a young man, I would make it my only study and devote my life to it." The doctor put a comforting arm around his wife. "Now, I think it would be best if the earl were gently carried to a bed where he might rest peacefully."

Carefully, Marche gathered Valentine in his arms again and awaited instruction. The doctor and the lady preceded him up the stairs while Valeria and her husband accompanied Anne to the kitchen. Amandine waited in the hall until Marche and Harston got Valentine out of his clothing and into a bed. By that time, Valeria had joined her with a silver bowl of linen cloths soaked in cool water. Harston pulled a chair close to the bed for his wife and Valeria put the bowl in her mother's lap. Amandine dabbed at Valentine's forehead with one of the soft cloths, but the young man gave no sign that he felt the soothing touch. Tears welled in the lady's eyes and trickled down her cheeks.

"Do not weep, my dear," Harston said. "Your son is young and healthy and will likely wake at any moment and demand his supper."

"Do you really think so?"

"I do, and furthermore, I shall pray that it is so."

"I saw so little of him when he was a child. I do not want to lose him before I have the opportunity to know him as a man." Amandine made a visible effort to compose herself, straightening her back and raising her chin before she spoke again. "And now I should like to meet my son's chosen companion. Valeria, I think you might do the honors."

"Of course, dear mother. I have the honor to present His Grace, the Duke of Marche. Your Grace, I present Mrs. Frederick Harston, the Countess of Blythestone. I also present Mr. Harston, Doctor of Medicine retired."

"I am honored," Marche said, bowing low.

"If I may be excused," Harston said. "I will see what sort of aromatic herbs Anne may have on hand in the kitchen. Breathing in a refreshing air might help recall the earl the sooner."

"Your Grace," the countess said after her husband had gone. "I wonder if we might not speak plainly for a moment."

"I am at your service, ma'am," Marche said, taking the chair she indicated.

"I would not usually be so familiar on such short acquaintance," Amandine said. "However, my emotions have outstripped my manners just now."

"I find myself in the same condition of disruption."

"Disruption," Amandine repeated. "The very word I wanted. I can see that you are an educated gentleman as well as a most imposing figure of a man."

"I hope both those qualities find favor with you, ma'am."

"Charming, as well." Amandine's gaze went to Valeria. "It would seem that Anne is correct on all counts, daughter."

"I am most taken with the duke myself." Valeria smiled. "I may yet regret my scheme to avoid marriage with you, sir."

"Oh, you *will* regret your mad undertaking, my dear," Amandine said. "I love you, but I will not easily forget that you deceived me."

"I know it was wrong, mother, but now that you are so very happy with Mr. Harston, I feel sure you will find some softness in your heart for my trickery."

"No doubt," the countess said wryly. "I trust you have asked the duke's pardon as well."

"Ma'am, I do not ask for apologies from anyone. To have gained the earl's friendship is all the recompense I need for any damage that may have been done."

"My housekeeper has related what she observed of you, and I am glad that my son has such a mentor. His monastic upbringing did not fit him for life outside cloistered walls. Trust is a fine thing, but it can render one easy prey to the less principled among us. I understand that you have been a guide through the traps that society sets for the unwary and that you have stood with him steadfastly, even though you met him as a circumstance of his foolery."

"My foolery, mother," Valeria said.

"I make the count at four conspirators at least, miss, but leave that for now. I am trying to make my feelings clear to His Grace, though heaven knows they are hardly clear to me. They are in a terrible muddle, and so I am afraid I must speak more plainly yet."

Valeria drew breath to speak but let the words die unvoiced. Moving nearer the bed, she took a cloth from the bowl and replaced the compress on Valentine's forehead.

"Now, sir," Amandine said. "I hope you do not fear some scolding speech as your expression seems to say. My daughter and my trusted servant are both of the opinion that you are a fine companion for my son. They are also distressingly certain that both of you are likely to be bachelors for life. I do not know if Valentine has chosen this path because of his upbringing at the abbey, nor can I know what led Your Grace to eschew marriage, however…." She paused before continuing in a stronger voice. "I have come to believe that it is wrong to force one's children into a mold of one's own liking. My daughter has managed, quite on her own, to find a man admirably suited to her nature—for all he is a commoner—and I see that my son has chosen, as well." The lady reached out to stroke Valentine's hand and fetched a deep sigh. "When my late husband decided that Valentine would only be safe in a cloister, I had to resign myself to the fact that my son might never marry, but I still had hopes. When Anne told me that Valentine had formed an attachment to you, I confess I was aghast at first, but as she spoke on, my mood was changed. Now I look into your eyes and though you try to hide it, I see how much you care for my son. Once, I would have been scandalized, but I am a wiser woman now, and I am content if my children are healthy and happy."

"There is a bright side," Valeria said softly, when several moments had passed in silence. "You always hated the idea of being called a Dowager, and if Valentine never marries, you shall always be Countess Blythestone."

"Don't speak nonsense, girl. Ah, good, here is dear Harston with the infusion. That smells heavenly. Do set it down here."

Unable to trust his voice, Marche got to his feet and took his leave with a short bow, while the others were distracted. He let his eyes rest on Valentine's still form for several long moments before closing the door gently behind him. Once he was out of sight of the others, he let his shoulders slump and proceeded with dragging steps down to the front hall. The duke's legs failed him when it struck him that Valentine's eyes might never open again. His vision blurred by tears, he staggered through the first open door and found he was in the chapel. The duke went to his knees, bowing his head to hide the tears that streamed down his face.

"Please do not take him from me," Marche murmured. "I know that I am a sinner and that I corrupted one of your finest creations, but it is only because I love him so much. None but You could have set that pure, sweet fire in my heart, and I know that I am a better man for loving him. I am not practiced at bargaining, and You cannot be bargained with anyway. However… if You are listening, and it does suit Your plan, please let me keep him so that I may continue to improve… and for my own selfish reasons as well. I have not spoken with You since I was a lad, and I hope you will judge me more for my friends than for my reputation." He stopped, unable to think of words that might sway a deity, and ended by repeating his plea. "Do not take him from me, please."

Negus stopped in the chapel doorway, rendered immobile by the unprecedented sight of his master kneeling humbly in prayer. "Your Grace," he said softly. "The earl is awake." Marche leapt to his feet, and Negus was astounded to see tears in the duke's eyes. "He is asking for you, sir." The slight valet stood wisely aside and so avoided being bowled over as Marche reacted to the message. Smiling at the way the duke took the stairs two and three at a time, Negus followed at a more prudent speed.

Randall Cleary was waiting in the hall to open the door for Marche and the duke nodded distracted thanks as he entered the bedchamber. Around the bed, Valentine's family raised faces wet with tears of gratitude to smile at Marche and invite him to share their joy. The duke had eyes for no one but the young man propped upon a raft of pillows. Without thought or regard for anyone might think, Marche knelt beside the bed and took Valentine's hands. "Thank all the Powers that you are all right," he said in a choked voice. "I was so afraid—"

"My Behemoth frightened?" Valentine squeezed Marche's hand. "Then I am glad that I slept through any calamity so dire that it put the wind up the fearsome Duke of Marche."

Marche looked up. "Now I know that you are well if you have the strength to make jest of me."

Valentine smiled. "You make such an irresistible target."

"It is as though you were never ill." Marche gazed in wonder into Valentine's bright eyes.

"If the sleep lasts a short time, it is often so that the patient wakes refreshed," Dr. Harston said. "Of course, if the coma lasts for weeks, or even months, there is a loss of...."

"Perhaps we may wait to hear the particulars," Amandine interrupted her husband.

"What would please you most just now, dearest brother?" Valeria asked as she smoothed the tumbled hair from Valentine's brow.

"I have wakened to find myself well-loved and safely in the arms of my family and friends. I cannot think what more I might need."

Valentine paused, squeezing Marche's hand again. "On further thought, there is something I crave."

"Name it and it shall be yours," Amandine said, cupping her son's cheek in her hand.

"If I may be indelicate, I am fair famished."

"Of course you are, lamb!" Anne exclaimed. "Look at me, standing about when I should be bringing you a tray. Give me just a few moments."

"I'll lend a hand," Negus said, following the housekeeper from the room.

"I am grateful, Anne," Valentine called. "However, it will not be necessary to fetch anything. Give me a few moments to dress, and I will join you all at the table."

"Darling, are you certain you should...." Amandine's voice trailed off as she gazed on her son. "Though I daresay you look in the pink. And you were so sickly looking when you came in."

"It is a curious condition—" Harston began before he was cut off.

"It sounds utterly fascinating," Valeria said as she took the doctor's arm and drew him toward the door. "You must tell me all about it over supper."

"Yes indeed, high time we were all at table," Amandine agreed.

Marche rose but stayed when Valentine called his name. "Your Grace, would you do me the favor of helping me into my clothes?"

"At your service, sir," the duke replied. When everyone but Marche and Valentine had left the room, Randall Cleary pulled the door closed and walked away.

Valentine swung his legs over the side of the bed and opened his arms. In an instant, Marche swept him into an embrace so powerful that it overcame them both. Valentine dropped back to the mattress, taking the duke with him as he sought the other man's mouth. Marche covered the questing lips with his own, silently but eloquently expressing his joy, his relief, and his gratitude that Valentine was alive. Valentine returned the kiss with equal ardor, bending his knees to hold Marche in the cradle of his body.

"I was so afraid that you might sleep forever," Marche said as he broke the kiss.

"While it would be pleasant to spend eternity in bed with you, I do not think I would wish to spend it in sleep."

"I am shocked by your forwardness."

"But you will forgive me, will you not?"

"As you are so recently recovered, I will give you some license." Marche leaned his forehead against Valentine's and sighed. "Do you know how much I love you?"

"It cannot be as much as I love you."

"Ah, but I loved you first."

"Then I shall have to love you best."

Their lips met again in a kiss of surpassing sweetness. "I prayed, if you can credit it," Marche said, his breath warm on Valentine's cheek.

Valentine's eyes went round with surprise. "You prayed for me?"

"Well… I suppose it was more for myself, but I got upon my knees and begged the Almighty to spare you. I am not contemplating taking vows just yet, but this God of yours seems fond of you, and henceforth I will be respectful when I speak of Him."

"Then yes, I believe I have an idea how much you love me." Valentine drew Marche into another kiss that seemed likely to never end, and then the young man's stomach growled. Their mouths parted on a laugh, and they rose to make Valentine presentable for supper. Their hands strayed more than once during the process, but at last the earl was dressed, and they went down to the dining room.

Marche felt somewhat apprehensive about his reception now that the crisis had passed, but he was welcomed warmly. He was astounded by the ease with which Valentine's family accepted their union. Though he was thankful, he was also wary as he took his place at the table. As much as he wished for a family such as this, the habits of a lifetime were hard to break and so he remained a little on guard. Speaking seldom, he let the conversations flow around him as he listened and learned what he could about the people who were dear to his beloved. It was late when the meal was over and everyone sought his or her bed after fond good nights were said. Marche went to the room set aside for him, but he did not stay there.

"COME," Valentine whispered, shielding his candle with his hand. "Follow me."

Marche was still dressed except for his jacket, and Valentine gestured to him to leave it. Trusting his friend, Marche followed the earl out of the bedchamber and down the hall. They did not stop at Valentine's room but took the stairs to the third floor. Passing swiftly down the corridors of the empty servants' quarters, they entered a narrow stairwell. At the top, Valentine led the way through a small door, and they stepped onto the roof near the north corner tower. Another set of stairs, fashioned of wrought iron, spiraled around the turret to a walkway at the crown. Valentine leaned upon the rail and looked over his shoulder at Marche.

"Is it not beautiful?" he asked.

"More beautiful than anything I have ever imagined," Marche answered, kissing his lover's brow. "And the view is charming as well. However did you find it?"

"Cleary told me about it. He does not say much, but when he chooses to speak, he usually has something of worth to say."

"A most unusual fellow, but I am certain that his wife will make up for his lack of words." Marche put his arms loosely around Valentine's waist and leaned against his back. "Devil take me!" he said as the full moon sailed from behind the clouds gracing everything with silver radiance. "It *is* beautiful!"

"I have never lived here, and yet, I know that this is my home."

"Then it is mine as well. Wherever you are, my heart is there with you, and so I must always be at your side, or be heartless."

"That would never do." Valentine turned in the circle of Marche's arms and placed a hand on the other man's chest. "I will give you my heart to keep so you will always have one."

"That seems fair to me." Marche leaned back a trifle. "Why, look here, sir! You are in your shirtsleeves and your collar is hanging open."

Valentine let his eyelids drift down, gazing up at Marche through the fringe of his lashes. "Does that surprise you in one as wanton as I? It would take little provocation to induce me to shed more clothing."

"Here in the open? You shock me again."

"It will not be the first time, sir, nor, I trust, the last that I have taken my pleasure out of doors."

Marche dipped his head to nuzzle at the base of Valentine's throat. "I can assure you that it will not be the last," he said, his lips moving against tender flesh.

Valentine ran his hands down Marche's back to grasp his shirt and pull it free of the waistband. His fingers roamed over bare skin, one hand heading upward and the other down, cupping the contours of hard muscles, digging into the dips and hollows, stroking and squeezing as Marche lavished kisses on him. His pulse quickened and his arousal grew so hard it ached almost unbearably. "Your effect has not lessened with time or custom," he breathed.

Marche made an indeterminate noise as he nipped at Valentine's earlobe while opening the front of his shirt.

"One kiss from you and I am ready to spurt in my linen," Valentine elaborated.

Marche paused in his efforts and met his lover's eyes. "Am I meant to complain of it?"

"I was only remarking…." Valentine's words trailed off in a groan when Marche pinched his nipple.

"I am happy you are so easily roused by me. And you are young, so you will recover swiftly between bouts. I should be able to enjoy you several times each day."

"You are the most—" Valentine gasped as strong teeth closed on his other nipple. "Contrary and…." A low moaned unraveled from his throat as Marche's tongue flickered over the sensitive tip. "The most contrary, irreverent, and oh God, Marche, that feels marvelous." Valentine pushed his hips forward, pressing his crotch to the other man's hardness.

"Had you finished listing my qualities?"

"Except to add that you are magnificent." Valentine's hand slid under Marche's waistband to grasp a handful of muscle and pull him even closer. "Can you feel how much I desire you?"

"Indisputably." Marched jumped as Valentine ran a finger down his crack.

"What is your pleasure, Your Grace? Shall we disport ourselves here or retire to a place with softer corners?"

Marche worked a hand between their bodies to squeeze Valentine's arousal. "I like all of your soft corners," he said huskily. "And I will make love to you wherever it takes your fancy."

"I am the happiest man under the moon." Valentine tilted his head back to smile up at the argent disk. "I do not care what tomorrow brings, for tonight I am in your arms."

"Let us go to bed, then, for tomorrow brings the Baronet of Strand."

Valentine took Marche to his bed, but Strand did not arrive the next morning or indeed for several more days.

CHAPTER 25

"WELL, Mr. Cleary, what do you say to that?" Marche sat back in his chair to give the young man time to think.

"I say you should start calling me Randall, or Cleary if you prefer, but the mister must go."

Valeria took Randall's hand. "I believe my husband is attempting to say that he agrees and that he considers you part of his family."

Randall nodded, shaggy dark bangs falling over his eyes. "She's right, as ever. I am best suited to conversing with draft horses."

"Then you should get on famously with the duke," Valentine said.

"You wound me, sir," Marche replied.

"I think my brother meant to say that you have a way with beasts," Valeria said sweetly. "Thus explaining your affinity for him."

Valentine's mouth dropped open at his sister's betrayal.

"You deserved that, darling," Valeria told him.

"Truly?"

She nodded. "Recently, you have become quite… oh dear, what is the word I want? Randall?"

"Cocky?" Randall suggested.

Valeria tapped her husband's shoulder with her fan. "Precisely. Do you not think my brother has become very full of himself recently?"

"I have become full of something, that is sure," Valentine answered.

"Shush, here comes Mama!"

The countess came down the lawn to where the group of four sat under an ancient oak. She took a seat and paused to catch her breath before she spoke. "Upon my honor, you could not have chosen a spot farther from the house."

"At least I can give you good tidings for your trouble. It appears that Lamberglyn Park shall be our main residence after all," Valeria said.

"Oh, thank Heaven," the countess sighed. "I did not like to foist myself on your discussion, but I could not wait a moment longer to hear your decision."

"Your arrival was most well timed, lady," Marche said.

"So I should hope. Anne and I have been watching you from the kitchen window for ever so long. She said she could tell from the way the duke settled in his chair that the matter had been settled as well."

"It has, ma'am," Randall spoke up. "I shall miss Brittany, but the land here is good for farming, and my wife promises me that we will visit the old place from time to time."

"Every winter while the fields lie fallow," Valeria said.

"Perhaps we should have our family Christmas in Brittany," Amandine said.

"That is a lovely notion, Mama." Valeria turned to her brother. "You will be there, won't you? And you, Your Grace?"

"Of course," Valentine said. "I might even take a gift to the abbey. I think they would appreciate a few bottles of decent wine. God knows they could use them."

"Do you think the monks would even recognize you now?" Valeria asked.

"You are both impertinent children," Amandine said. "However, you are not dull, so I suppose I should count my blessings."

"Ma'am," Marche said as he leaned toward the countess. "I vow to you that when young Blythestone is out of your influence, he shall be under mine."

"Thank you, sir. That is a great comfort to me. A young man needs a mentor."

"Some more than others," Valeria put in and received another betrayed glance from Valentine.

"To be sure, darling," Amandine said. "I am not certain it needs saying, but I hope you know that I will fall in with your masquerade. If any should inquire of me, they will hear how happy my daughter is in her marriage to the duke. Mr. Harston, bless him, has a scientific mind and finds it difficult to credit that my son took my daughter's place without any being the wiser. He has chosen to believe that it is a family jest, so you need not fear he will give the game away."

"Thank you, ma'am," Marche said, inclining his head to the lady. "As I stand to gain the most by this continued pretense, my gratitude should be the greatest. At risk of embarrassing some of those present, I declare that I consider myself wedded to Valentine in truth as well as fiction. All that is mine is his. As you are his family, it is yours as well." The duke smiled. "If Doctor Harston wishes to open an institute for the study of the brain, he need look no farther for funding. It is crass of me, I know, but I have little to offer other than money… of course, I do have rather a lot of that."

"I find your crassness refreshing," Valeria said. "Why can we not say what we mean to one another without dressing it up fit for a ball?"

"To keep murder to a minimum, I would guess," Marche answered.

"You are a rogue, sir," Amandine said, but the words didn't sound like a reprimand.

"Pardon me, but I believe Negus is trying to get my attention." Marche glanced toward the back of the house. "What in thunderation could he be so bothered about?"

"Sir," Negus called when he was still several feet away. "Lord Strand has—" The valet's next words were trampled under the sound of hooves. Strand rode around the side of the house flanked by Snowhurst and Tarmegent. The three men stopped a few yards away dismounted with a flourish. Negus trotted over to take the reins, and the visitors marched to the seated group.

"Sweet ladies and gentle men," Darby said, making a sweeping bow. "I come with news from Town. I hope there is still a welcome here for me and my companions."

"Welcome indeed." Valentine stood when it occurred to him that he was the host. "Please consider my home as your own. Why don't we go inside so you can wash the dust from your throats and give us the news."

"THE devil you say!" Marche banged a fist on the table.

"I am afraid it is true," Darby said. "Murdmont has escaped. His trail ends at the coast where he cozened a fisherman out his boat. There was a terrible storm that night, and I entertain fantasies wherein he capsized and was eaten slowly by large fish with sharp teeth."

"To fish with large teeth!" Snowhurst held his goblet aloft.

"Yes, thank you, Snow," Darby said. "To continue, the sitting magistrate in this case has personally taken on the overseeing of the restoration of property stolen by Murdmont. I have the honor to be assisting him in this matter."

"Congratulations," Valentine said. "For your smile tells me that congratulations are in order."

"Dash it all! Who would have thought?" Darby said. "I find the legal life agrees with me and working with Pater is not the ordeal I'd feared."

"Perhaps because you are not being forced into it?" Neville observed.

"No doubt you are right, Tarmy. However, we are not here to discuss my history. I have the happy duty to inform Marche that all of his property is released to him."

"Ah, good, now I may fulfill my promise to the Randwicks," Marche said. "Thank you for coming all this way to give me the news."

"I confess I may have had other motives as well."

"Strand is still besotted with your wife, sir," Snowhurst said in a stage whisper.

"If she must be afflicted with an unwanted suitor, she could do much worse," the duke drawled.

"Scandalous!" Amandine stood and her husband stood with her, along with all of the other men.

"If you will pardon us," Harston said. "My wife and I are wont to retire early."

The gentlemen bowed to the countess and the doctor as the couple left the dining room. Mr. Cleary was the next to leave and, soon after, Valeria made her apologies. Snowhurst pulled out his watch and shook it a few times.

"What is the trouble, Snow?" Darby asked.

"Damme, the bloody thing's slow again."

"Let me see." Darby compared Crispin's timepiece to his. "It's right as rain, bacon-brain."

"Do folk truly go to bed at seven in the evening?"

"Country folk do, it would appear," Neville said. "Blythestone, I hope we are not keeping you from your bed."

Valentine smiled a trifle smugly. "I believe the delights of the bedchamber will wait upon me. We have just heard wonderful news and that occasions a celebration of some sort."

"I had one already planned," Marche murmured.

"Then you must tell us, sir," sharp-eared Darby said. "For now that your duchess has gone, some of the sparkle has left the atmosphere."

"Well, it will not be I who brings it back," the duke said. "I am more easily entertained than entertaining."

"I could differ with you on that point, sir," Valentine said.

Crispin giggled. "That sounds like a bit of a challenge to me."

"I've no doubt it would be a challenge to you." Marche winked. "Come, gentlemen. Let us retire to the drawing room where we will imbibe Blythestone's finest spirits and make merry."

"I say! I do like the run of your thought," Crispin said as he rose from the table. "My glass is empty anyway."

"We must remedy that immediately," Valentine said, gesturing to the others to follow him. In the smaller withdrawing room, he poured drinks and handed them round. When everyone had a glass, he raised his in toast. "Good health to my friends, both present and absent." After the glasses were drained and he'd poured another round, he invited the three gallants to stay the night, or for as long as they wished. His invitation was warmly accepted and the dandies settled in to drink.

"Tell us the rest of the news from Town," Marche invited. "Surely, the lawsuit is not the biggest gossip in London."

"Murdmont's duplicity takes that honor, sir," Darby said. "His is currently the blackest name in Society. Even uttering the syllables of it will get you ousted from most respectable places."

"Good, but is there no gossip that does not concern this affair?"

"Snowhurst is getting hitched."

Crispin bowed as he stood to refill his glass. "Lovely girl," he slurred. "Cannot wait to meet her, by the way."

"Congratulations," Valentine said.

Crispin flapped a hand at him. "My thanks, sir. Should be quite an affair; I'll see you're on the guest list."

"Did I say that Kirkcap sends his regards?" Darby changed the subject. "His clerk will be sending along an invitation for some excursion involving tea. He seemed to think that you and Blythestone would be keen on it."

"His business must be doing well," Marche remarked. "He has an assistant *and* a clerk?"

"As Your Grace has divined, I accepted a position in his law practice. When I saw the state of his papers, I suggested that a secretary might be useful. Fortunately, I had the name of a bright young man in need of employment. I believe you know Mr. Fleet."

"I have had business dealings with him in the past."

"Have you indeed?" Darby cocked an eyebrow. "Fleet tells me that you paid for his schooling and never asked for a penny in return."

"I may have done him a small kindness or two. As you say, he's a bright fellow and deserves a chance at betterment."

"To be sure." Darby nodded sagely. "And in the end, all of society benefits."

"I had not thought of it in quite those terms. Perhaps I am a visionary."

Darby laughed and set the others to laughing as well. "Yes, you are the very soul of altruism, Behemoth."

"A patron saint of social reform," Valentine added. "I think we should all follow Marche and Strand's example."

"What d'you mean?" Crispin asked. "Sponsor some urchin, or such like?"

"Something of that nature. Surely, we all know of some good we may do with our wealth. Perhaps in the name of the late duchess?"

"We might endow some sort of educational endeavor," Neville said.

"With free tuition for bright young people without means," Darby added.

"Done," Marche said. "The yearly revenues from Brackenmourse should go a ways to paying for instructors and books and such."

"A handsome donation," Darby said. "Brackenmourse is your largest estate."

Marche shrugged. "I have at least three others, by my count, and my greatest attachment is to Wandeleigh. I think my late aunt would be pleased with the decision."

"I believe so too," Valentine said. "Of course, I never met the lady, but you speak of her so often that I feel I know her a little. I think she would be very proud of you, Marche."

"Hear, hear!" Crispin went 'round filling glasses and fell into Valentine's lap.

"And that is the signal for the end of another evening of debauchery," Darby said. "Snow, do get off Blythestone before you cause a scandal."

Marche stood and helped the tipsy young man to his feet. Valentine got up also, brushing at the brandy spilled down the front of his waistcoat. Apologies ensued and were waved off, and then Crispin's companions escorted him up the stairs. Marche watched their progress with a quizzical expression.

"What are you thinking, my large love?" Valentine asked.

"Are you certain you wish to know my wicked thoughts?"

As no one was watching, Valentine felt emboldened to put his arms around Marche's waist. "Quite certain," he said, looking up into the other man's eyes.

"My first thought was that Strand has a rather fetching rear view."

"A passing thought?"

"Very fleeting, and you must know that I would never entertain those sorts of thoughts about a puppy like Strand."

"He is older than I."

"In years, perhaps." Marche tucked a loose strand of hair behind Valentine's ear. His hand lingered to trace the delicate whorls as he spoke. "I was also thinking that Strand and company are very fortunate, because they are friends. Should one of them stumble, the others are there to steady him. I never thought I needed someone like that; Negus's company was enough for me, and I used the barrier of servant and master to keep him at a distance. I thought I was content with my sojourns in the tearoom, and perhaps I was, after a fashion." The duke paused to kiss away the small line that appeared between Valentine's eyebrows. "I could very well have continued thus, but it was not really a life, merely a way of passing time. Now that I know what it is to share that time with someone, I see how empty I was."

"My darling Loel," Valentine murmured, rising on his toes to kiss Marche's cheek. "My heart aches for the boy you were." He kissed the other cheek. "I promise you that I will devote my time to making your life a very full one indeed." He put a hand on the back of Marche's neck and pulled his head down. "I am your friend, and I love you to distraction." He touched his lips to the duke's in a melting kiss that mingled sweet surrender with brazen hunger.

"I love you too," Marche said when the need for air became too great and their lips parted. "You are neither one thing nor the other, but somewhat of each, and you fascinate me."

"I beg your pardon?"

Marche chuckled as he untied Valentine's hair ribbon. "You are sweet, yet fiery. You prize peace, but are a very devil with a sword in your hand. Chaste, yet shameless in the act."

"I see. That will be quite enough, I think, for me to discern the direction of your speech."

"Ah good, then I may save my breath for better things."

"And I think it is time we stopped making love in the hall and went up to our bed."

"Gladly." Marche took Valentine's hand at the foot of the staircase and started up. "When I heard about my engagement, I never imagined that I would be happy about it one day."

"Really? Why, when Valeria first told me of her mad plan, I immediately envisioned myself living happily for the rest of my life with you."

"She has quite an effect on you, and you on her. Both of you are more… yourselves when you are together."

"Are we terribly vexing?"

"Not to me. I love you best when you are brash."

"You have no regrets then?"

"Only one. I wish that Murdmont might be brought to justice for my aunt's murder."

Valentine opened the door to their private quarters and gave Marche a beckoning look over his shoulder. "Come, sir, and I will endeavor to clear your mind of unpleasant thoughts."

"Have at you, wanton!" Marche lunged, kicking the door closed behind him.

Valentine grasped the front of the duke's shirt and dragged him to the bed. They undressed one another with undiminished delight in the process of revealing the veiled marvels. Each took selfish pleasure in the fact that these wonders were theirs alone, a private preserve where no other would ever frolic. With touches tender, playful and greedy, they drew one another up to the peak of arousal. Bonded, skin to skin, heart to heart, and soul to soul, they danced the oldest dance to the wild music of their groans, cries, and whispers of vulgar encouragement. First one leading and then the other, they reached the crest together, wrapped in fierce embrace. They drifted into sleep that way for the first night of the long life they would spend together in their new home.

EPILOGUE

THE tiny fishing boat was awash and in imminent danger of capsizing, or the privateer would never have stopped for her. The captain reluctantly ordered his crew to take on any survivors and then waited crossly in his cabin for a report.

"Pardon, captain. Mister D'Anton sent me."

"Just give me Achille's message."

"There was one man on the boat. Mister D'Anton said he was mad to try the Channel in such a tub. I agree, sir."

"Go on." The captain waved a hand at his new cabin boy. "*Mon Dieu*, why do you English insist on giving an opinion whether it is called for or not?"

"I beg your pardon, sir. The fellow kicked up something awful, cursing everything French, begging your pardon again, so Mister D'Anton gagged him and put him in irons."

The relish with which the young sailor uttered these words made the captain curious. "Is this troublesome Englishman perhaps known to you, Tom?"

"Aye, that he is. He gave me some stripes once in a bawdy house."

"*Vraiment?* Is this true?"

"Aye, sir. He bound me and took a whip to me for no other reason than it gave him pleasure."

The privateer came out of his cabin to look down at the prisoner on the deck below. Malcolm Jonas, Lord Murdmont glared up at the captain with a defiant sneer. The corsair gave him a pleasant smile before turning back to Tom. "It seems the boot is on the other foot, now, eh Tom? If you inquire of M'sieur D'Anton, I am certain he will provide you with a whip, which you may use as you see fit."

Tom stepped from behind the captain and had the satisfaction of seeing Murdmont's face go pale. He did his best to gloat, but it just wasn't in him. "I haven't the stomach for it," he said. "But if I may be so bold, maybe you know some slavers."

Le Roi des Corsairs pursed his lips in thought and then nodded. "I know a man who knows a man," he said.

PERSEPHONE ARTEMIS ROTH lives in Savannah, Georgia, with two beagles, three foundling cats, and one husband, who works in public transportation. An avid rider, she wishes some day to live on a farm and breed horses, but for now, she's a city girl. She got her name from her father, a keen student of mythology, and her love of books from her librarian mother. Persephone is a lifelong admirer of Georgette Heyer and romance in general. She also loves Thai cuisine, glass painting, and walking at night.

Other historicals from DREAMSPINNER PRESS

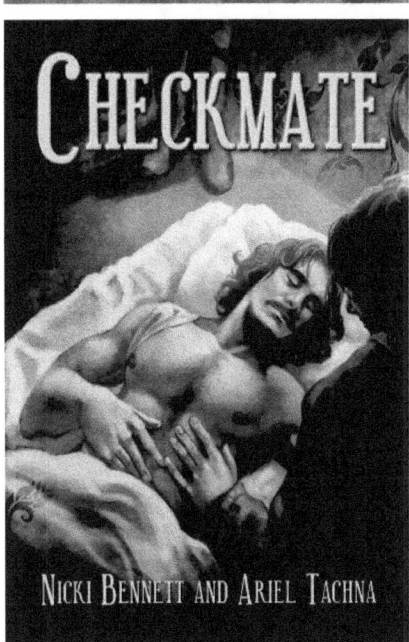

http://www.dreamspinnerpress.com

www.ingramcontent.com/pod-product-compliance
Lightning Source LLC
Chambersburg PA
CBHW070058030726
47506CB00002B/512